Anything Rae Touches

Anything Rae Touches

GOLDEN BAY BEACH
Book One

HOLLY CASTE

For those who were taken too soon and never had a chance at a happily ever after.

Foreword

Dear Reader,

Hey! Thanks for picking up my book! Before you dive in, please check out the trigger warnings:

Explicit language, detailed sex scenes (praise/degradation, dom/sub dynamics, exhibitionism), addiction, grief, death scene*

*This scene might be triggering for some. I purposefully did not add the details to savor a major plot point. However, if you're unsure and would like more info, please go to the last page of this book under "More Trigger Info," where you can get more details of the scene depicted (Don't worry—I won't kill off Rae or Miles ☺)

As with my other books, this story isn't for everyone. The characters are flawed, and the journey is raw. Even though the ride might be emotional at times, I promise there's a happily ever after!

Anything Rae Touches

CHAPTER ONE

TEN YEARS AGO

SOMETIMES, I feel like I wasn't meant for this world. As if some heavenly entity accidentally ordered the knockoff version of my sister and then realized their mistake. I don't quite belong anywhere. I don't fit in with any friend groups and stick out like a sore thumb everywhere I go. I'm different.

Unique, as my family kindly uses to describe me. But I know they're just being nice.

Oddly enough, the only place I feel a sense of belonging *is* with my sister. I guess sharing a womb with someone has its perks.

We're polar opposites. Where I'm smart-mouthed and crabby most of the time, Cara is warm and welcoming to any living creature—including me. We don't even look the same, no one would know we were twins if Cara didn't tell every person she interacts with.

"Wake up!" Cara obnoxiously bounces on my bed with a wide grin on her face.

Groaning, I try to use my legs to kick her off. "Too. Early."

She dodges me and somehow scoots closer, ripping the blanket away from my face. "It's almost time to leave for school."

I peer at the clock on my nightstand. "Cara, we have a fucking hour before we have to leave! Let me sleep!"

"Nope! I'm too excited!"

She pushes off my bed, and I can see that she's already in her cobalt-blue-and-pearly-white cheer-leading uniform. Her platinum, naturally wavy hair is up in a ponytail.

Early mornings like this make me regret not taking up Mom and Dad on their offer for us to have separate rooms when they did the extension on the house. But who am I kidding? Even though I could punch her for being a morning person—I wouldn't have it any other way, and neither would she. We wouldn't survive if we lived in separate rooms. We tried it once when she was in cheer camp last summer, and we ended up Face-Timing every single night.

"Did you finish the signs?" Cara asks as she flutters around. I point to the stack of colored poster boards on my desk. Gasping with excitement, she runs over to examine them. "They're so awesome, Rae! Thank you!"

"No prob." Normally, I wouldn't make cheer signs for the squad, but since Cara wanted them to look *extra special*, she recruited my help.

Most schools put all their energy into the football team, but our golden sport is baseball, so the cheer squad puts all their effort into doing cheers for them. Spring training officially ended, and today's the first game of the season, which means our school's going all out. Banners, a balloon arch—all the works. We're even supposed to wear blue and white. So, obviously I'm going to wear anything *but* those colors.

"Oh my god—this one is my absolute favorite." Cara holds up a light-blue poster board that reads *Go, Miles* in black and silver paint marker.

"Yeah, I figured it would be."

Pivoting away from the posters, Cara goes to our full-length mirror and toys with her uniform. Even though I'm not one for cheerleading, I will admit she's incredibly talented. She secured her spot on the varsity team, earning her some petty shit talking from some of our classmates because how dare a freshman skip right over junior varsity. They were quick to shut up once I began defending her, which, in turn, just made me more of an outcast. But whatever, I'd rather my sister enjoy her time in high school because she belongs in that type of environment. Not me.

I suck at school, with barely passing grades. It's not for lack of trying, it's just that my brain doesn't work that way. I don't think in numbers and logic. I think in colors and emotion. Which is why the only class I'm thriving in is art.

Cara reaches for her blue ribbon and begins to tie it into a bow around the elastic of her ponytail. "This is going to be the day it happens, Rae, I can feel it," she states.

I roll my eyes. "Whatever you say." I've been up for three minutes, and she's already obsessing over Miles Kingston. She's been drooling over the star baseball player since she spotted him in the hall on the very first day of school. However, she hasn't said boo to him, considering he's a senior and we're mere freshmen.

"I don't want to hear any of your negativity, missy." Cara smiles at me through the mirror.

I push up onto my elbows so I can see her better as I speak. "Cara, you've been saying you were going to talk to him since we first entered Northview High School. It's *April*. No offense, but I have little faith that after all these months, *today* is going to be the day you tell him you're madly in love with him."

She spins on her heels to face me. "Can you not be an epic bitch first thing in the morning?"

"If you would've let me sleep in, I would've been a moderate bitch."

We bicker back and forth as we do, because although we're attached at the hip and love the hell out of each other, we also drive one another crazy.

"What I was going to say before you got all snarky with me," Cara says, "was that I have a plan for today."

"A plan?" I ask, sitting cross-legged on my bed. I'm wide awake now, whether I want to be or not.

"Yes. The cheerleaders are having a little rally before the game, and we're going to be on the field with the guys, and I'm thinking of doing something to get Miles's attention, like smile at him or something—"

I fake gasp and bring my hands up to my cheeks. "A smile? How scandalous."

"Shut up!" Cara laughs and runs over to her bed, grabbing her pillow and smacking me with it across the head.

"Ow!"

"*Anyway*, as I was saying—I'm going to do a little nonverbal flirting and then at the after-game party tonight, I'm going to accidentally spill a drink on him and be forced to talk to him."

I purse my lips together. "Cara, I say this because I love you, that is the stupidest plan I've ever heard."

"Well, I can't think of anything better! I'd have you accidentally spill something on him if you were coming to the party—"

"Oh god, not this again."

"Why won't you come?" Cara whines.

"Because those parties aren't my thing." I don't fit in there. Cara tries to involve me in every single conversation she has, but I don't feel like I belong. Cara has no problem speaking to any person—minus Miles. He's the only person I've ever seen her clam up around, and it's actually kind of endearing to watch how much he turns her brain into mush, even if he doesn't know she exists and she just stares at him from a distance.

"I swear you'll have fun at this party. It's at Drew's house—he's not one of the best on the team compared to the others, but I heard his house is ginormous," she states as if everyone in Northview has tiny homes. We live in a well-off community, and no one hides their latest luxuries. Cara continues, her wheels spinning as she tries to think of something else that'll get me to the party. "I can even try to hook you up with Ben."

I snort. "I don't want to hook up with Ben."

"Oh, I thought you had a thing for him. I saw you guys talking in the hall a bunch of times last week."

My stomach twists. "No, he was just helping me with math." Breaking eye contact, I move off my bed. I don't like lying to her. I'd never lied to her before this year.

I hate that I've had to, but she won't approve of why

I'm talking to Ben. She's too straitlaced. I think I might legitimately give her a heart attack if she found out I was buying drugs from him. I've only gotten high a handful of times. Weed was the majority of it, but last week I tried these pills he had and I liked it. I *really* liked it.

However, once I was sober, I swore to myself I wouldn't touch any type of drug again. The high isn't good enough to make this icky feeling of lying to my sister worth it. So, yes, the last time I spoke to Ben about *math* was last week. And I don't plan on talking to him again.

I slip into a pair of ratty jeans with holes and paint stains on them and toss on a black T-shirt. Walking over to my dresser, I grab my brush and run it through the messy knots in my hair, yanking out strands. My hair is blonde, but not like Cara's. It's yellowy and straw-like and lacks any waves or volume.

Glancing over at my sister, I watch as she puts mascara on her long lashes.

She's perfect.

I don't envy her for it. If anything, it makes me love her more. She's like an angel. As if the heavens opened up the sky and sent her down here just to make the world a better place. At the very least, she makes *my* world a better place.

I don't know what I'd do without her.

A loud thud comes from the other side of our door, making the both of us jump.

"Mom wants to know what you want for breakfast," our ten-year-old brother, Grayson, asks from the other side.

"Yogurt and strawberries, please," Cara states.

"Not hungry," I answer.

"Okay." Grayson shuffles away from our door, and we continue getting ready.

"You look gorgeous," Cara says as I finish applying dark eyeliner around my eyes. "But I think you need an accessory."

"I hate wearing jewelry. You know this."

"You hate wearing *my* jewelry, but what if you wore something that was a little more...Rae-inspired?" Her lips curl upward.

"What do you mean?"

She moves across the room and goes to her drawer, pulling out a small shopping bag. "I picked this up for you yesterday when I went to the mall. It's a thank-you for making all the signs for me and the squad."

My brows furrow. I don't need a thank-you. We do shit for each other all the time, it's no big deal. Hesitantly, I put my hand in the plastic bag and pull out a thick black choker.

"Let me put it on!" Cara says before I can get a word out. She moves my hair to the side and takes the choker from my hand and places it around my neck.

Once it's clasped, she tussles my hair and spins me to look in the mirror.

Oh. This doesn't look half-bad.

"So cute!" Cara beams.

I start to grin. "You're right."

She claps her hands, bouncing on her toes. "Ah! I even got your grumpy ass to smile!" She grabs me and gives me an obnoxious hug. As I try to wiggle free, the both of us begin to laugh. "I'm your favorite sister!" she claims.

"You're my only sister."

"Therefore, your favorite."

"And also my least favorite," I say, finally escaping her embrace. I turn to the mirror to admire the necklace once more. Placing my fingertips along it, I drop the act of being annoyed by her as sincerity laces my insides. "You're gold, Cara," I say as a way of thanking her and she gives me a knowing grin.

I've been calling her gold ever since we had to read *The Outsiders* a few years back. The character Ponyboy automatically reminded me of her, smart yet naive and, of course, resilient. And if Cara was Ponyboy, then that meant I was his best friend, Johnny. The last line Johnny said was, "Stay gold, Ponyboy. Stay gold," which somehow carried over into our world and is now a way I show my love for my sister. Cara *is* gold; radiant, joyful, pure. I don't want anything to ever steal that away from her.

There's another knock on our door.

"Mom has breakfast," Grayson says.

"Come on," I say to Cara. "Let's head downstairs and come up with an actual plan on how to start your love affair with Miles."

"You're the best." Cara lights up. "I can feel it in my bones—today's going to be the day everything changes!"

CHAPTER TWO

PRESENT

THEY SAY the third time's a charm—but I met death in the face three times, and I'm still here.

The first was my entry into the world, and if *that* isn't some sick precursor to how my life would unfold, then I don't know what is. Cara came out of the womb like the shining angel she's always been. I, on the other hand, was getting strangled by the umbilical cord, my oxygen supply was getting cut off, I had fluid in my lungs, and I almost passed away before I fully began living. I brought out all the work in order to come out of Mom's body, only to be screaming and crying to be shoved back in.

The second was an event that happened in high school, which inevitably led me down a path that forced me to have my third encounter with death—my OD.

I wasn't purposefully overdoing it in order to kill myself. I had three weeks clean, but my veins thirsted for that sweet nectar to a point where I couldn't ignore it any longer. I took some oxy, but that didn't cut it. Scrambling for my phone to hit up my dealer, I was riding my heroin high within thirty minutes.

Apparently, extra oxy plus my usual amount of heroin equals an overdose.

The next thing I knew, I was waking up in a hospital room to a blinding white light. They told me my younger brother, Grayson, had found me. The weight of my guilt crushed me, knowing that his sensitive heart had to bear witness to my impending death. So, when my parents entered the hospital room pleading with me to go to rehab, I agreed.

Three hours away is the fanciest fucking rehab within the state. Hope's Garden, North Carolina's bougie facility where all the celebrities hide when they don't want to be found at one of the rehabs in California.

My parents paid for the whole thing. A big fat check in order to save their little girl's broken spirit.

Ninety days later, I completed the program.

So here I am, seated in the back seat of a taxi, twirling the green sobriety chip between my fingers, grazing over the raised nine, then over to the zero. I would say I'm proud of myself, but that's still a term I've yet to feel comfortable uttering—even if only inside my head.

"What brings you to Golden Bay Beach?" the driver asks me in a desperate attempt to start a conversation for the fourth time.

I roll my eyes, not even caring that I'm making it known that I'd like this discussion to be over before it even starts.

"A new life," I answer, pressing my head against the

leather seat. I keep playing with the coin as I stare out the window.

It's a typical beach town, and in a few weeks, tourists will be trickling in from every nearby state to spend their summer here. My family and I used to vacation here when I was a kid—but it's nothing like it used to be when I was in elementary school. Now, it's built up with rows of shops and restaurants.

We drive past the boardwalk and the pier with Adventureland—an amusement park that now has countless roller coasters and a gigantic Ferris wheel that overlooks the ocean. I shudder at the thought of being that high up on a flimsy ride.

Drugs don't scare me, but heights sure as hell do.

"Here we are," the taxi driver states as he pulls into a parking lot several minutes away from the amusement park. The building we park in front of is seven stories tall and attached to the quieter side of the extensive boardwalk.

The driver hops out of the car and grabs my bags from the trunk. Getting out of the car, the breeze of the salty air whirls around me, and I take a deep inhale, letting it settle into my lungs.

"Good luck with the new life." The driver hands me my belongings.

"Thanks." Grabbing my bags from him, I hike up the steps of the building and enter the lobby of SeaScape Condos. I internally cringe at the cliché nautical theme, which takes over the entirety of the space. Anchors and seashells pop up around the aqua-and-cream-colored room, and just as I'm about to give in to the urge to back out of this building and catch another cab somewhere else, I hear a squeaky "Hi!" coming from the opposite end of the lobby.

Turning, I see a perky redhead standing behind the front desk. She has a smile so wide her teeth are blinding me. "I'm Emma!" she states. "You must be Rachel Hansley."

My brows draw in as I take a step backward, alarmed that this stranger knows who I am.

"Your parents told me you'd be coming in today. I was told to be on the lookout for someone with a lot of tattoos and most likely wearing a choker."

"Oh," I say, adjusting the black fabric around my neck. Feeling less freaked out by Emma's presence, I tiptoe closer to the desk.

"They moved some of your stuff in and set up your condo yesterday," Emma explains.

Of course they did. It's not enough for them to be paying for my fresh start, but they had to buy furniture to go along with it. I'm grateful they're willing to help me, but that doesn't take away from the guilt that's weighing down my bones.

And the added pressure of not fucking this up for them.

"I just need to see your ID, Rachel, and I can give you a key to your new place!" Emma sparkles with excitement. I swear if I did ten lines of coke, I still wouldn't be as peppy as her.

"It's Rae. Not Rachel," I state, giving her my ID and whatever other information she needs.

The elevator down the hall dings, and three guys step out, being obnoxiously loud. They're around my age, maybe slightly younger, all wearing sleeveless jerseys.

"Sup, Emma," one of them says, winking at her.

Her cheeks automatically turn beet red. "Hi, Travis," she responds, suddenly forgetting my key while the three boys saunter over to her.

"Who's your friend?" one of the other guys asks Emma, referring to me as he gives me a quick once-over.

"This is Rae. She's moving in today."

"Nice," he says, wetting his lips. "I'm Evan, and this is Travis and Brad." Evan points to the other two. "We live here too. If you ever need anything, we're happy to be of service."

"I'll keep that in mind and make sure to call literally anyone else before you," I deadpan.

The three of them laugh off my comment and continue bullshitting with Emma. With my patience wearing thin and the need to get away from a conversation I have zero interest in, I rudely clear my throat. "My key?"

"Oh my god! I'm so sorry," Emma apologizes. "I'll talk to you later," she says to Travis before going back to typing my info into her computer.

"No problem," Travis states. "We gotta head out anyway. See you ladies later."

The three of them say their goodbyes, and I catch Emma watching them walk out of the building. "They're so hot," she says, but I'm pretty sure that thought wasn't supposed to be said aloud, judging by the immediate look of embarrassment on her face.

I shrug. "They're all right."

"I have the biggest crush on Travis, and he has no idea. I'm in a business class with him, and I'm pretty sure I'm flunking because all I do is stare at the back of his head for the entire lecture."

I glance around, checking if there's someone else she's admitting this to because I have no idea why the hell she's choosing to bare her soul to me, of all people.

Noticing that the lobby is completely empty, I scramble for something to say to her. "Oh...I'm sure you'll pass?" I say as a question because she could quite possibly suck ass in school, seeing as I met her about five minutes ago and know nothing about her. "Weird that college kids can afford this nice place." I try to move her along.

"They had a fire at their apartment, so they're living here in the meantime. The university didn't have any dorms to offer them." Emma tilts her head, focusing her attention back on me. "Are you in school?"

"No."

She glances down at my ID. "That's right. You're twenty-four, so you must've graduated already."

"No."

"Oh." An awkward silence falls over us. Awkward for her, I'm assuming, because I don't care that I never went to college and never intend on going in the future. People can make an impact on the world without a piece of paper that they paid over fifty grand for.

I don't know what exactly *my* impact will be, but I know it's possible for other people to succeed without a degree.

"Well..." Emma breaks the quiet. "Here's your key." She slides it across the off-white marbled desk. "Condo 214 is your new home! If you need anything, just give a holler!"

"Thanks." I grab the key and head up to the elevator to the second floor.

My new home.

I guess that doesn't sound terrible, considering the amount of trouble I found myself in at my "old home." My parents wanted me far enough away from the chaos but close enough to still keep tabs on me. So, we settled on this place.

Pushing open the door of my new residence, relief settles around me when I realize my parents didn't try to overdo it by decorating. Just simple gray couches and a wooden coffee table in the living room, two barstools for the kitchen island, and a few appliances on the granite countertops. My bathroom—which, of course, is aqua—was left alone, and my bedroom has a queen-size bed and two nightstands, that's it.

Any lingering tension I was carrying in my muscles releases now that I know they went as minimal as possible. I already feel indebted to them with medical bills and rehab. I didn't want another giant bill added to that. Not that they would make me pay a cent of it.

They're wonderful parents who want the best for me. While I am their asshole daughter, who spiraled so hard that I made their lives awful for years as they tried to reach down and drag me up from the depths of hell so many times.

An envelope rests on my mattress, and even though I'm hesitant to open it, I do.

Hi Honey,

We knew you'd want to add your own personal touch to your place, so we left the walls alone. Check your closet, there are a few things in there that might help you make your home more "Rae." Call us after you settle in.

We love you,
Mom & Dad

Heading over to the walk-in closet, I pull the white doors open and find it filled with art supplies. Paint, canvases, brushes, easels, ribbon, oil pastels, tarps, colored pencils, sketchbooks—you name it. If you can find it in an art store, you can currently find it in my closet.

My eyes sting as they begin to well up, but I choke back the emotions that are making their way to the surface.

If there's anything that's kept me alive for so long, it's art.

It's the only way I've been able to process the dark inner demons that have been ripping me apart for nearly a decade.

Art is my lifeline.

It's inked all over my body, sketched inside my brain, and splattered across my soul.

In the back of the closet, there are several of my portfolio bags of both my past artwork and my most recent ones, which my parents picked up from rehab the other day.

Reaching for the different-sized bags, I toss them on the bed and open them up, staring at my drawings from over the years. The anger, fear, and trauma are splashed on every inch of the various-sized papers and canvases. Blood, monsters, skulls, dismembered bodies—shit you'd only think to see in your nightmares. All the artwork looks different, except for the one image that I draw over and over again whenever the thoughts become too much and I desperately search for a sense of calm.

The image of him.

Miles Kingston.

Usually, the majority of him is shaded over, a shadow casting over that teen heartthrob face that so many girls in high school fell in love with. It's rare that his entire face is shown in my pictures. Usually they focus on the one thing that seems to comfort me. His lips. The plump bottom one and the slightly thinner upper one, which has a small scar on the left side. Rumor has it he was involved in a fight on the baseball field the year before I started high school, and that's how he got the gash in his lip.

Cara thought he was such a badass for that, and it instantly made him hotter in her eyes.

They never did talk, though, she was too daunted by his popular senior status. Still, that didn't stop Cara from fantasizing that they'd get married one day.

I never thought anything of Miles. Was he cute? Yeah. But Cara called dibs, so my mind drifted elsewhere.

Miles was nothing out of the ordinary to me until, one day, everything changed. He saved my life, and I don't know whether to thank him or curse his existence because my life has taken a radical, hellish turn ever since.

My fingers run over a sketch of just his lips, the pencil shavings faintly dusting my skin. I hate myself for using his lips as comfort.

Especially since I never saw him again after that. It was one fleeting life-and-death moment. It was a kiss goodbye.

It wasn't supposed to stick with me for ten years. It wasn't supposed to ease my jitters late at night when I was woken up by horrifying images. It wasn't supposed to be a distraction from the drugs.

But it was. Is.

Shaking my head to get out of the memory of Miles, I drop the image as if it's suddenly on fire, blazing my hands.

An itch crawls over my body, and an immediate thirst for relief hits my bloodstream. A beastly craving nipping at my nerve endings, tantalizing me to kill the memories—if only for a little while.

Fuck. I hate this feeling.

In a desperate attempt to not give in to temptation, I search my belongings for my pack of cigarettes. At the bottom of my tote bag, I find the heaven-sent tobacco package and my black Bic lighter.

Heading to the door so I can go downstairs and smoke numerous cigarettes until this feeling dissipates, my attention is grabbed by long, sheer curtains at the end of the living room. I walk over, pushing the fabric aside, pleasantly surprised to find a glass door leading out to a private balcony.

Stepping outside, I notice two Adirondack chairs and a side table—from my parents, no doubt. I plant myself on one of them, reclining back as I light up my smoke.

Taking a long inhale, I let the toxins swirl around my lungs and accept that this is my latest cure for my urges.

Thank God I'm only on the second floor because if my condo was any higher, I'd spend most of my days panicking and not going by any windows.

As I relax into the chair, I check out my surroundings. The bordering condos are big enough so that our balconies don't touch, and they all overlook the beach.

I stare out to where the ocean kisses the sky, merging the two vast existences together.

I stay here chain-smoking and gazing until stars begin to emerge in the darkness. A chill hits the air, but I don't bother moving.

I choose to stay here and welcome my third chance at living.

CHAPTER THREE

Rae

BLACK PAINT COVERS the tips of my fingers and streaks my arms in random places. I stayed up until one in the morning sketching, then got bored with that and moved on to painting a mural on my living room wall, thanks to the stepping stool and endless paint my parents left for me.

By the time four a.m. hit, I had a dark-blue wall as the background and a giant skull with dead black roses coming out of its crevices plastered on my wall. Its hollowed-out eyes are crying tears of blood, which drip down the length of the skull's jawline and spill onto the dark background. Part of the top of its head is smashed in, and leeches crawl out of it. Or inside of it, I can't really tell.

I passed out on the gray couch, which I ended up staining with the paint that was caked on my skin.

Rubbing my fists over my eyes, I groan at the sunlight pouring in through my balcony door.

"Too fucking bright," I say to no one.

Forcing myself to get up, I push up off the couch

and head to the kitchen, starting my day with much-needed coffee.

I raid my pantry and cabinets, only to end up empty-handed. My parents stocked me with all the other basic necessities except for the most important one, coffee.

A cranky whine comes from the back of my throat the second I realize I'm going to have to venture out of my home and interact with people before I have any coffee in my system.

After rinsing the paint off of my hands and arms to the best of my ability, I throw on a pair of black jeans with holes in them. I'm wearing an oversized, once-white T-shirt, which is stained with different-colored paint, but I don't bother changing it.

Throwing my bleached white-blonde hair up into a messy bun, I note my natural, straw-colored blonde starting to surface at my roots. I adjust my choker, then head for the elevator.

"Afternoon, Rae!" Emma chimes as I walk past her and into the lobby.

"Fuck, is it afternoon already?" I didn't bother checking my phone. I deleted all my contacts, minus my parents and Grayson, and considering I spoke to the three of them last night, I knew they'd give me my space and not blow up my phone first thing in the morning.

Emma giggles. "It's one thirty."

"Great. Listen, I'm in need of some caffeine. What's the best place for some coffee around here?"

"Sam's Dinette. It's about a five-minute walk on the boardwalk. You'll pass a few other places—but trust me, this coffee is the best. Plus, the food's incredible. It's the only original diner still standing around here, everything else has been upgraded."

"Sounds good. Thanks." I dart out the door before she continues chewing my ear off about shit I don't really care about.

The boardwalk isn't crowded since it's early April and school's still in session. However, there's an occasional family or person on a bike that smiles at me as I speed past them. Ignoring their friendly gesture, I keep my eyes focused on the shops and restaurants, remaining focused on my one goal.

I almost stroll right past the little diner, but the small red-and-white awning with the name Sam's Dinette catches my attention just in time.

There's a chime over the door when I push it open, and even though there are only a few people in there, I can sense their eyes on me. I assume they're used to out-of-towners, but maybe not ones that look like me and certainly not before tourist season hits.

The smell of crispy bacon and maple syrup battle it out for the overpowering scent in the restaurant.

It's got an old-timey feel, with newspapers and a few vintage signs hanging up on the walls. The booths are lined with seafoam-colored vinyl, and all the tables seem like they've been through some shit, with a weathered look on the wooden tops. There's a long counter where a few people drink and read on backless stools.

"Table or booth?" an older man with gray hair and wrinkled skin asks from behind the register at the counter.

"Doesn't matter," I respond.

"Take your pick." He gestures to the entire restaurant with several options available.

I nod, deciding on a table by the window so I can look out onto the boardwalk and not be faced with having to converse with anyone.

The wooden table in front of me has a paper placemat with a basic menu printed on it. And in bold black letters on the top, it reads "$10 credit card minimum."

Fucking hell.

I don't have any cash on me. I have a credit card that my parents supplied me, assuring me that they'll be checking my statements on a weekly basis. I'm not allowed to have cash for the time being because it's easier to get my hands on drugs that way—or so they assume.

I have to rely on my parents for everything until I'm able to find a job, but they don't even want me rushing into that. They want me to take my time and adjust to sober living. Sounds lovely and wonderful to an outsider, but to me, it sounds pathetic. My whole existence is pathetic.

"Can I start you off with anything?" The old man from before stands in front of me with a pad and pen.

"Uh, just coffee for right now. Black." I'm not hungry at all. Maybe if I order enough coffee, it'll amount to ten dollars. Or close enough to it so I don't have to buy an entire meal, maybe just a piece of burned toast.

In a matter of seconds, my drink is placed in front of me in a maroon ceramic mug. I sip on it, letting it bring some life back into me as I stare out the window. The bells above the front door chime a few times, signaling people coming and going, but I don't pay them any mind. There's more chatter nearby, but I tune it out, only focused on gazing out the window, lost in my own world.

I grow aware of someone getting closer to me. A man clears his throat, getting ready to speak, and I assume it's the person from before, ready to hear my nonexistent lunch order. Or, technically, breakfast order.

"Hey," the person says, and my attention swings from the window to the man standing in front of me. First to his green-blue eyes, then down to the beard framing his face, then hyperfocusing on his lips.

The scar.

An anchor drops in my gut.

He freezes as if he's just seen a ghost, but I nearly burst out of my skin, slamming my coffee mug down, spilling it everywhere. "Shit."

Bile jumps to my throat. My hands shake, grabbing whatever napkins are on the tiny table.

Miles fucking Kingston is here. In front of me.

My eyes prick with tears, and it burns to hold them in. I furiously wipe the table, and after he stays still for a few seconds, he helps me clean the mess. Or at least I think he is. I think he's saying something to me.

I think the old man is, too.

More napkins appear, but I don't bother wiping myself up. Instead, I dart out of the diner and run as fast as I can away from there. Away from Miles and away from all the memories that are surfacing in my head.

My body moves faster the more the floodgates in my mind open. I try to outrun the past as fast as possible before being fully pulled under, drowning in pain.

Panting, I make it back to my condo, bypassing Emma.

I pace my living room, trying to calm myself down.

Back and forth, back and forth.

I didn't think I'd ever see him again. In my mind, he became my place of refuge. But seeing him in front of me after ten years on day fucking two of my new life—this is some sick joke from the universe.

How am I supposed to have a future when my past keeps haunting me?

CHAPTER FOUR
Miles

THERE MUST BE something in the air today because my phone has been ringing nonstop. Everyone needs something. Not that I mind, I just don't have the time to fit everyone in my schedule in one day.

As I'm finishing up fixing Mrs. Tedeschi's fence that her dog keeps digging a hole under, my phone rings for the third time this afternoon. "Sam" pops up, and my lips immediately draw upward. The old man has been calling me for assistance whenever he needs it for the past few years, ever since I moved here.

"Can't get enough of me, huh?" I answer the phone.

"Keep that big ego to yourself," Sam replies. "I have a leak in the kitchen ceiling—"

"Your place or the diner?"

"Diner."

"All right, I'll see if my big ego and I can make it there today to fix it for you."

"Gee, thanks," he jokes before giving me the details of what's going on and what I should expect.

Once we hang up, I knock on Mrs. Tedeschi's front door to let her know the job's done.

"Thank you so much, Miles," the petite middle-aged woman says to me. "How much do I owe you this time?"

"Don't worry about it."

"I have to give you something."

"How about you bake me some of those delicious chocolate chip cookies, and we'll call it even?" I give her a wink, which makes her blush.

"Are you sure?"

"Positive. Just keep an eye on Ernie and make sure he doesn't dig any more holes."

She thanks me again, and I give her a charming goodbye as I drive off to my next job, Sam's Dinette.

I live about ten minutes away from the boardwalk, and I've befriended all the neighbors and beach regulars to the point that I've unofficially become the town's handyman. I enjoy it. It gives me purpose and makes me feel like I belong somewhere—something that I've struggled with for many years. But I've finally gotten into a good groove and genuinely appreciate where I am in life.

Pulling my car into a parking spot behind the boardwalk, I grab my toolbox from my back seat and head inside to see Sam.

The familiar bells chime overhead when I open the door, and my stomach automatically growls when I get a whiff of syrup. Sam greets me and waves me over to the counter. He's quick to pour me a coffee before he has me get to work, so I place my toolbox on the ground and shoot the shit with him for a bit.

Sitting down on the backless stool, I twist it back

and forth slightly as he goes on to tell me about his wife, Gloria's latest project. Gloria is Sam's second wife, and he always talks about how grateful he is that she entered his life since he was pretty messed up after his first wife and never thought he'd meet anyone else.

Sam and Gloria have become like family to me, treating me as one of their own and helping me back on my feet when I was at my lowest point.

As Sam continues to tell me about Gloria wanting to expand her garden, my eyes drift around the room. I give a nod to the people I know who are eating lunch and a smile to an older lady reading the paper.

Then, my attention fixates on a person by the window, lost in thought.

Her hair is dyed a whitish-blonde color and sits like a bird's nest on top of her head. She wears a thick black choker wrapped around her neck and a white shirt stained with paint. From what I can tell, both of her arms look like she has a full sleeve of tattoos. Zeroing in on the descriptive and detailed artwork drawn all over her skin, I get the sudden urge to find out where else on her body she's covered in tattoos. Her dark lashes flutter a couple of times as she zones out the window. Her eyes are blue—but not warm and inviting, they're cold and icy.

There's something familiar about her, but I can't pinpoint what it is.

For a brief second, I rack my brain to see if I might've fucked her when I went to the University of Florida, but I would've remembered if I was banging *her*.

She looks slightly intimidating but incredibly stunning.

My pulse picks up the more I stare at her, and I can sense my heart flip-flopping in my chest.

She's wearing a scowl on her face, looking annoyed as all hell.

So, naturally, I take the challenge and decide to warm her up with my award-winning grin. If anything, she looks like she'd be wild in bed. This could be a one-time deal, and I'm more than ready to break down her walls just enough for us to have a fun time—even if it's only for the night.

Approaching her, she still doesn't snap out of her daze, so I clear my throat, hoping that'll get her attention.

Still nothing.

"Hey," I say, and the second I speak, my eyes drop down to the tattoo on her wrist. The one that reads *Cara* in cursive lettering.

My attention snaps up, and the moment our gazes lock, I know *exactly* who she is.

All the blood drains from my head. I stand there like a deer in headlights as she spills coffee all over herself and the table. My stomach sinks to the floor, and after a couple of seconds of witnessing her panic in front of me, I get my ass back into gear.

"Let me help," I say, grabbing a few napkins from the table next to me while Sam comes over with more. Before I can utter another word or assist in cleaning, she's dashing out the door.

I'm frozen as I watch her run away.

A dreaded silence blankets the diner.

"Girl from your past?" Sam asks.

I nod, still fixated on the boardwalk, even though I can no longer see her. "You could say that."

"Things ended badly, I presume?"

"No. It was nothing like that," I answer. "I don't even know her name."

I know absolutely nothing about her.

But I still remember her as if it were yesterday.

Probably because I've thought about her every day since. It's been a decade since the event that scarred us forever, but the nameless girl from my past crosses my brain at least once a day. Sometimes it's just a passing thought, and sometimes I get stuck on her, wondering if she's okay now. Wondering if she's had a difficult time, too. My brain used to get caught in an endless loop of that awful day, but now I'm able to pull myself out of it whenever that starts to happen.

A loud crash of breaking plates instantly brings me back into the moment. I race over to the kitchen, where the noise came from. "Everything okay?"

One of the cooks, Joe, gives me a strange look but then smiles. "Yeah, man, just dropped a dish. No need to come in here and save the day."

My shoulders ease, and I wipe away droplets of sweat that formed on my forehead just from thinking about the one and only interaction with the girl from before.

I knew nothing about her then, and I know nothing about her now.

But now that she landed right in front of my face ten years later, I'm going to find out everything I can about her.

CHAPTER FIVE

THE CRIMSON red bleeds into the white canvas, each stroke of my brush tainting the pure surface, destroying whatever clean area there is.

Swipe, swipe, swipe.

Back and forth.

Harder and harsher each time.

The paint dirties my fingers and inevitably marks my hands and wrists.

I become soaked in the red liquid and continue getting lost in the gory, ugly world that's coming to life on my easel.

It's a blunt contrast to the scenery in front of me, tranquil and soothing as the waves slowly roll into one another. The beach is quiet, with a few people meandering down below on the boardwalk, but for the most part, the only sound is the ocean and the seagulls croaking in the distance.

And I've decided to ruin this picture-perfect image by sitting on my balcony and creating an abstract rendition of a bloody memory that, unfortunately, takes up residency in my brain.

My heart races as if I've been running for hours. Adrenaline courses through my veins, and I sense myself starting to get trapped in the canvas. It's bordering on no longer cathartic and inching its way to dangerous.

I know I need to stop.

Exhaustion cloaks me as I stare at the painting for a beat too long. Defeated, I toss my brush into a glass jar with water in it. I shimmy the small table with the easel on it off to the side and relax into my chair, forcing myself to enjoy the view of the ocean and not the image on the canvas. Plucking my pack of cigarettes and lighter up off the floor, I light up and lean back.

Staring out at the water, I get lost in the colors. The greens work their way into the blues, melding together to create the white foam that kisses the shoreline. It's a tie-dye of cool shades, endlessly blending into one. The emerald, the sapphire, the opal. It's mesmerizing.

"Oh shit—are you bleeding?" a guy calls out.

Startled, I jump in my seat to see who the fuck is bleeding. My head twists to see one of the college boys I met when I first moved in two balconies down. His eyes are bulging out of his head as he stares at my hands.

That's when I realize... "No, just paint," I respond and take another drag.

"Who you talking to?" one of the other guys asks as he steps out onto the balcony, joining his friend. He follows his line of sight and lands on me, his face lighting up. "Hey, Rae!"

I give a small wave. I don't remember any of their names.

"I didn't know you lived this close to us," boy number two continues, resting his forearms on the railing in an attempt to get closer to me.

Luckily, the condos are wide enough that there's space between the balconies, and none of them connect. There's mine, an empty one, then the college boys—which still feels too close.

The third boy makes an appearance, and all three try to flirt their way into my coming over to their place.

"Wanna chill and have a beer?" one of them asks me.

"No."

"You want some vodka instead?"

"Also no."

"A joint?"

My hand freezes in front of my mouth just before I can put my cigarette between my lips. Weed normally doesn't do it for me compared to all the other shit I was hooked on, but it sounds like a tempting option right now.

My pulse picks up ever so slightly, and I can sense moisture on my palms.

It's weed, it's not even a real drug.

Saliva coats my tongue.

Do my sober days still count if I take a hit?

My insides rip at the seams as I struggle with what I want to do instead of what I *should* do.

I know the fucking answer to my own question. I talked about it time and time again with my addiction counselor in rehab. Still, I would love nothing more than to destroy the images in my head, even if it's only temporary.

The boy who offered the joint takes it out of his

pocket and lights up. The pungent smell drifts over to where I'm sitting, and I'm instantly pissed off. More with myself than with them. I'm not even at the point where I can be around fucking weed without feeling the yearning in my veins. The deep-seated craving in every fracture of my body with the hunger to get high and get the hell out of my head.

The need to be numb to it all.

Annoyed, I smash my cigarette into the nearby ashtray and wipe any of the paint that hasn't dried onto my hands on my bare legs. My stomach churns when I realize it looks like I have blood on my legs.

Taking a deep breath, I calm my thoughts.

It's only paint, Rae. You know this, you just spent an hour using red paint.

After covering the Dali-inspired deformed human tattoo on my thigh with smears of red, I stand up to go back inside.

I sense their eyes on me as I stroll back into my home wearing only my oversized T-shirt that I usually paint in. I'm sure they can get a glimpse of my ass as I turn around, but I don't give a shit.

Standing in my bathroom, ready to wash off this feeling—and the paint—I go to turn on the shower, only to be met with a few drips trickling out of the showerhead.

Wonderful.

Grinding my teeth together, tension rising in my shoulders, I search for the maintenance number for this place.

The longer I look for this number, the more my blood begins to heat up with anger.

"All I want to do is take a goddamn shower and distract myself from getting high—is that too fucking much to ask!?" I yell out to the universe.

With patience completely wiped from my essence, I call down to the lobby.

"Hello, this is Emma at SeaScape—" she says through the phone.

"My shower isn't working." I pace.

"Rae?"

"Yeah. My shower isn't working."

"Oh my gosh, I'm so sorry!" Emma apologizes as if she were the one who fucked up the plumbing. "Our maintenance man is at our other location right now, he should be done in a few hours—"

"A few hours!?" I shout.

She pauses, probably scared of me snapping at her. It's not her fault I'm a bitch—that's just how I can be sometimes. "I, um," Emma stammers. "There's another guy I can call to see if he can get here sooner. He sometimes helps us out—"

"That's fine." I sigh, trying to calm myself. "Thanks." Before she can respond, I click the end call button.

Walking into my kitchen, I grab leftover Chinese food to eat for dinner. I've only been ordering in and cooking pasta since I haven't left my home in three days. Not since seeing my past forced in front of my face.

I've kept myself hidden within these walls, not ready to face the possibility of me running into Miles again. Quite honestly, I'm perfectly content with never stepping foot outside ever again if it comes to that.

About ten minutes after calling Emma and shoving an unhealthy amount of lo mein down my throat, there's a knock on my door.

"One sec," I say, putting the container of food down on my countertop. Still unbothered by my appearance, I open the door.

My heart comes to a screeching halt when I see the person staring back at me.

He looks just as surprised but is quick to mask it. "Uh, I was told the shower wasn't working?" Miles tilts his head to the side, and a small smile glides across his face as if he's amused that he's here for me.

I blink a few times and clam up. "Yeah," I say, stepping out of his way so he can enter.

My stomach coils with an unfamiliar feeling as he makes his way inside. A fluttering feeling erupts in my chest, and I try to brush it off as if it's nothing. Just a body doing bodily things. No reason to read into anything.

He's here to fix my shower. Quick in and out. Then we can go back to never seeing each other again.

Before Miles takes more than four steps, he freezes, shocked by my skull mural in the living room. "Whoa," he says, his eyes widening, taking in the abrasive image. I stand tall, my feet firmly planted in place, waiting for him to make a passive-aggressive comment about how scary or creepy it looks, like people usually do. "That's intense," Miles states.

My spine becomes rigid, automatically going on defense. "Excuse me?"

"You painted that?" He looks back and forth between me and the mural, and I nod. "No fucking way."

"Yes, fucking way—I'm an artist, asshole."

His brows rise, tickled by my response. "You're also a little snarky," he teases, grinning.

"Shower's that way." I dismiss him, pointing toward the bathroom. Taking the hint, he starts to make his way down the hall.

What a dickhead—who comes into someone's house and calls them snarky? Miles might've unwelcomingly saved my life back then, but our encounter with death didn't seem to humble him at all.

I mean, yeah, he's hot, but that doesn't give him the right to be a jerk. I hate people like that—men, in particular, thinking they can use a glowing smile and drop some smooth lines to get what they want. Manipulative fucks.

A clanking of metal comes from the bathroom, and after several moments, there's silence.

I pad back to the Chinese container, picking at the lukewarm noodles even though my appetite has vanished.

"So, what've you been up to?" Miles's voice calls out from the bathroom.

My eyebrows draw in. "What?"

"You know...in life, what've you been up to?"

"Are you trying to have a conversation right now?" I call back to him.

"Trying is the operative word. It'd be a lot easier if you came in here so I could talk to you."

I toss my fork down and march into the hallway, crossing my arms in front of my chest. "You can't insult me and then try to comb it over with some surface conversation," I say, walking into the hallway. "We don't know each other, so there's no point in acting like we do."

Miles pokes his head out of the bathroom, and his eyes zero in on mine. "What if I want to know you?" His voice is warm, causing a strange buzzing sensation under my skin.

I think I hate it.

"Your artwork is incredible," Miles says, gesturing behind me to the mural. "I'm sorry if I insulted you when I said it was intense—I just wasn't expecting to walk in and see that. But, truly, it's phenomenal work." We hold each other's gaze for a moment longer as I try to decipher if he's being genuine. "And," he continues, "I'm sorry I called you snarky. Can we call it a truce and start over?" He extends his hand out for me to shake.

I stare at it for a beat, debating if I actually want to start over with Miles or if I should end this talk where it is and keep the memory of him closed in a box, locked in the dark recesses of my mind.

My focus instinctively drags up from his hand to his lips, and a wave of calmness washes over me. Almost immediately, I want more of that feeling. I need it—crave it.

Tiptoeing closer to my bathroom door, which he's standing outside of, I round my shoulders, giving no inkling of being fazed by his presence as my hand connects with his.

His large, rough palm zaps a shot of adrenaline straight to my heart. Vibrant colors swirl around my insides, coloring every shadowy gap with new emotions.

This I definitely hate.

I don't feel numb.

I feel *alive*.

Snapping my hand back, I bring my attention to why he's here. "Do you know what's up with my shower?"

He shifts his stance to look into my bathroom and puts his hands on his hips. "Well, it definitely doesn't work."

"No shit, Sherlock."

Miles chuckles and glances down at me. For the first time, I notice how tall he is. He was tall in high school, but he must've had at least two more growth spurts since I last saw him. He's massive—muscular, lean, and towering. His dark-hickory-brown hair is shorter on the sides and a little poofy on top to give him an added inch to his height.

He's still staring at me, smiling.

My mouth dries up as I struggle to figure out what to say next. I sense my cheeks heat up. What the actual fuck. I'm flustered—a guy has *never* gotten me flustered before.

"What?" I bite out, hoping he'll stop looking at me.

"I take back what I said," Miles states, walking into the bathroom and sitting down on the ledge of the tub. "I'm not sorry I called you snarky. I kinda like that you are." That small little comment is enough to make my heart do a somersault.

"Okay...good, I guess?"

Miles still riffles through his shit as he talks. "I don't mean to come across like more of an asshole, but what's your name?"

"Rae."

He lifts his head up. "Nice to officially meet you, Rae. I'm Miles."

"I know."

"You know?"

"Yeah, you were the star baseball player at Northview High, and everyone knew who Miles Kingston was."

"Oh. Well, if you knew who I was, why didn't you ever say hi?"

"I'm sure that would've gone over well, the no-name freshman approaching the popular senior athlete in the middle of the high school cafeteria," I sarcastically reply.

He shrugs. "I wouldn't have cared."

"Whatever, jocks were never really my thing."

"Shame. Snarky artists have always been mine." Miles has a playful look on his face as his eyes lock with mine.

His words tumble through my body, making me feel lighter.

This isn't happening, his sorry attempt at flirting isn't actually working. It's just been way too long since I got laid.

"Real professional," I say, once again pretending I'm unaffected by him.

"Hey, I've been here this entire time ignoring the fact that you're not wearing any pants and forcing myself to only look at your face—I think that's professional as fuck."

Amusement swells in my chest, and I feel my lips curling upward.

Miles points at me. "Holy shit—are you about to smile?"

"Oh, shut up." I grow irritated, quickly wiping my face of the evidence.

Spinning to exit the bathroom, I catch a glimpse of Miles's reflection in the mirror. His gaze lands on the back of my thighs, and a sudden surge of pride and desire flows through me.

I decide to let it be and let him enjoy the view as I walk out of the room.

You're welcome, Miles.

CHAPTER SIX
Miles

THINGS JUST GOT a whole lot more interesting.

When I got a maintenance call, I didn't think I'd end up at Rae's door.

Rae.

Now I can finally put a name to the face.

I watch her walk out of her bathroom, the back of her T-shirt riding up her legs, giving me the smallest peek of the bottom of her ass cheeks. From what I can tell, she's tattooed there too, and her legs are just as covered as her arms. Bold and candid images—similar to her personality, mark her skin, leaving few spots empty. I wasn't able to study them to see what they are, because I meant what I said before—I really *was* forcing myself to only look at her face.

Although, when I first saw her standing in her doorway, I was quick to notice her hands. They were splattered bright red, and for a split second, I thought it was something else, but quickly realized it was paint. I have no clue why she got defensive when I was in shock that she painted the mural—but hey, it somehow moved us to this point.

After a few minutes of tinkering with the shower and getting it to work, I begin putting my tools away. "All fixed," I shout to her.

Not a moment later, she's standing outside the bathroom, looking at me. "It works?" she asks.

"Yep, now you're all set to"—my eyes drift around her body, from her bare thighs to her messy T-shirt, which I'm betting she's not wearing a bra under, up to her unwelcoming eyes—"you know, shower and stuff."

"And stuff?" she snaps, crossing her arms over her chest.

"I don't know what you do in there—you could make murals on the tiles out of soap bubbles for all I know," I joke, and I watch her shoulders soften just a tad.

Nice fucking save.

We stand there for a beat too long, staring at each other. I can practically feel the invisible walls she has up all around her. Made of steel, no doubt. Cold, abrasive, impermeable. But they don't ward me off like she intends.

It's impossible for her walls to cage me out completely because once you have lived one of the most traumatic events in your life with a person, there's an unspoken connection. A moment of complete surrender on both of our parts.

I've already seen her with her armor down.

Rae blinks and shifts her stance back and forth as if she doesn't know what to say. So, I move the moment along.

"Mrs. Tedeschi usually gives me some baked goods as a tip." I smirk.

"Well, good for whoever the fuck Mrs. Tedeschi is," Rae responds.

"And good for my stomach. You didn't, by any chance, happen to make an apple pie before you realized your shower wasn't working, did you?"

She glares at me, and there's a tingling feeling in my chest. She has a cute little scowl on her face when she gets annoyed.

"Nope," she says, popping the *P*. "All I have is cold, leftover Chinese."

"That'll work." I rub my hand over my abdomen.

"That wasn't an offer. You can't just invite yourself over."

"I didn't, technically you did when you called for a handyman." I wink.

Rae rolls her eyes, unimpressed by my charisma, and stomps her way into the kitchen. I follow, like a hungry dog begging for food. As I walk behind her, I try to look anywhere else aside from her hips that sway from side to side.

I'm not really hungry, but I'll use food as an excuse to spend any time I can get with her.

Without giving me a glance, she reaches into the fridge and grabs a Chinese container, plopping it down on the counter, then slides me a fork. I pry the white box open to find half-eaten pork fried rice.

Rae sits down on her stool, digging into whatever she has in container, uninterested in my presence.

I tense up, conflicted about if I should stay or not, but that sensation in my chest still lingers, telling me I should ride this situation out a bit longer. That, plus, I haven't been able to get her out of my mind for the past ten years. The memory is stuck in my brain. It stays there, biting at my insides.

And I've been wondering if it's eating her alive, too.

"You care if I use the microwave?" I ask.

She shakes her head before taking a forkful.

Popping the food in the microwave, my ears focus on the humming since that's the only sound existing in this room. Just the droning of the microwave and the awkward silence expanding between us.

Maybe this wasn't the best idea on my part. I clearly overstayed my welcome, so once I shove this food in my mouth, I'll get out of here.

With only a few seconds left to heat up my food, I decide to occupy myself by whistling a tune that's stuck in my head.

A clamoring sound comes from Rae's direction as she drops her fork down on the countertop. "What are you doing?" she asks, obviously peeved.

"Whistling..."

"Why?"

"Because there's nothing else happening..."

She lets out a long sigh and stares at her food. I watch her icy-blue eyes build with conflicting emotions, the crease between her eyebrows deepening as she becomes lost in thought.

Beep. Beep. Beep.

The microwave pulls my attention away from her, but only for a brief moment.

"Why do you want to get to know me?" she asks, still looking away from me.

Her question stumps me. Why *do* I want to get to know her?

We met once, a decade ago, on the worst day of our lives.

After everything, wouldn't it be better to leave it all in the past?

"I'm not sure," I tell her, and she nods knowingly as if she expected that response.

She finally lifts her line of sight to meet mine. "I don't like getting close to people," she declares.

"Me neither."

Rae squints, assessing me before she speaks. "If you get to know me, then I get to know you, too."

"Sounds like a fair deal."

"I know it does. That's why I said it."

A chuckle rumbles in my throat, but I try to mask it with a cough. It doesn't work, though, because she glares at me, and now I'm full on laughing.

"What's so funny?" she snaps.

"Your attitude," I state, sitting on the stool next to her with my food.

"It's not my attitude, it's my personality. You don't like it, then there's the door."

"Oh, I didn't say I didn't like it." My cheeks rise as I get a closer look at her. The drumming in my rib cage ramps up as I study her heart-shaped face and pouty lips.

She's not just sexy—she's gorgeous. It's so easy to get lost in her energy whirling around me, I'm not sure how many seconds have passed.

"Well?" She wakes me up. "What do you want to know me?"

I smirk. "This isn't an interview, Rae. I'm not going to sit here and ask you specific questions and then leave."

"You sure as hell aren't going to ask me specific questions and then *stay*."

"That's not what I meant. Let's just hang out and talk." I take a bite of the days-old rice. "Where'd you end up going to college?"

"I didn't."

"Oh, okay."

"I graduated high school by the skin of my teeth. I could barely tolerate sitting in a classroom for more than ten seconds at a time."

"I feel you there."

We chew on our food and unspoken words. After a few moments, Rae speaks, "Did you?" I cock my head to the side, unsure of what she's asking. "Go to college," she clarifies.

"Oh. Yeah, but I didn't finish—I dropped out at the end of sophomore year."

She doesn't press on and try to get more information or ask why I would choose to drop out when I was already halfway through the program. But that's because she probably gets it.

And maybe that's why I'm here, seeking someone who gets it.

"I always wanted to see what college was like," Rae admits. "Not the education part—I don't give a fuck about that. But the environment. Dorm life, parties... you know, all the stuff you see in the movies."

"It's not all that it's made out to be," I assure her.

"What did you do in college?"

I suck in a breath as my mind flashes to that period of my life. "Ate a lot of pussy." I make a joke right before bursting into laughter at the sight of her face.

"Gross!" Rae acts as if she's about to get sick to her stomach.

"At least college taught me something." I turn my palms up.

"Well, thank God I missed it then. I'd hate to be anywhere near guys like you."

"We're not all that bad, I swear."

She scoffs. "Yeah, okay."

"We're not. I promise I was never one of the ones you would've wanted to do a hex on."

"I don't do hexes. And even if I did—I find that hard to believe."

"Oh, come on." I push the container away from me. "Let me show you that I'm nothing like whatever story you have made up in your head."

She mirrors my action and also moves her food away from her. "And how are you planning on doing that, Miles?" She flutters her lashes in a sarcastic manner, but the sound of my name floating from her lips to my ears brews excitement around my veins.

"Let me take you out to lunch tomorrow."

"No."

"Dinner?"

"Hell no."

"Coffee." There's a slight pause, and that's when I know I got her. "Aha! You want coffee!"

"Only because the coffee maker I ordered online isn't here yet."

"It's settled then, coffee tomorrow. How does ten sound?" I ask, and her eyebrows rise. "Eleven?"

"Eleven thirty," Rae states.

"Works for me."

I quickly eat the rest of my food before I *really* over-stay my welcome.

Rinsing off my utensil, my eyes scan the kitchen. There's a little figure of a head that looks like it was carved out of soap sitting next to the sink and a pile of dirty paintbrushes on a mat, waiting to be cleaned.

"I wasn't bullshitting you before," I tell her. "You really are an amazing artist."

She scoffs. "Thanks."

Her back is turned to me, and I study her from behind. My mind races, wanting to see every curve that hides behind her oversized shirt. But this stirring in my bones has me wanting to know what else is hidden behind those icy-blue eyes and standoffish manner.

I need to know if anything she keeps hidden looks a lot like what I hide as well.

CHAPTER SEVEN
Rae

I'M ABOUT to get coffee with Miles fucking Kingston.

How the hell did this happen? How did accidentally bumping into him turn into him fixing my shower and then get to here—me staring at myself in the bathroom mirror as I get ready to go out with him?

It's not a date, but still...it's something. I don't know if I want something with anyone. Especially not Miles.

Cara would kill me if she found out I was going out with him. Or maybe she'd be thrilled. Who knows? It was forever ago that she was head over heels for him.

I hope she's okay with this.

I apply thick, winged eyeliner on one eyelid and then the other, fix my signature choker necklace and run a brush through my hair. I'm already running late because who the hell decides to meet up for coffee this early on a motherfucking Saturday? Maniacs, that's who. Miles must be a freaking maniac, doing this to me, making me get up early and taking me to coffee because he wants to *get to know me*.

My thoughts begin to spiral, thinking about what he could possibly want from me. This has to be some sick joke. What does he want to know about me? That I'm fucked up? I can confirm that in one simple word, yes.

Instantly growing more annoyed, I grind my teeth together as I begrudgingly get my jeans on. My fitted dark-red T-shirt is next as I lethargically move into the kitchen. My movements are too slow, though, because before I can get there, there's a knock at my door.

Sighing, I unlock and open the door.

"Morning, sunshine!" Miles chimes with a big dopey smile on his face.

I wince at his chipper attitude. "Dear God, you have a lot of energy for someone who hasn't had coffee yet."

"Not a morning person, I see."

"Not an any-time-of-day person." I grab my small tote bag and sling it over my shoulder. "Come on, let's get this over with."

"All right." He claps his hands and rubs them together. "Starting this day off as a challenge, I like it."

I glare, pushing past him, although I can hear his annoying chuckle coming from behind. The sound irks me as I step into the elevator. I have a split-second thought of pushing the close button so it shuts on his face, but he steps in before I can make the choice.

"I like your hair down," Miles states.

I whip my head to look at him. "What?"

"Your hair, I've only ever seen it up. It looks nice when it's down, too."

A bubbling of emotions I can't put my finger on begins to rise in my stomach. "Oh."

His ocean green-blue eyes soften as he continues to

look at me, so I quickly turn my gaze to the metal elevator door as it makes its way to the lobby.

The quietness isn't uncomfortable.

However, it's the unspoken words that make me want to claw out of my skin. That, and the fear of them possibly being said during our time together, has me thinking of running straight into the sea and letting it swallow me whole.

"Ladies first," Miles says, gesturing with his hand as the elevator opens.

Stepping out, Emma immediately spots me. "Morning, Rae! How are—" She stops herself as she sees Miles appear by my side. "Oh." Her eyes widen with excitement, letting me know she'll be waiting for me to spill the tea once I come back, as if she were my best friend.

She's dead wrong.

There is zero gossip to be had. And even if there was, she's not my best friend. That's only Cara's title, and I tell her everything.

"See you later, Emma." Miles gives her a wave as we exit and move onto the boardwalk.

The sun is blinding, and being by the beach makes it even brighter. Squinting, I pull my sunglasses out of my bag in hopes of blocking out this irritating light. "Where are you taking me, anyway?" I ask.

"Sam's," Miles states.

I stop short, startling him. "No way," I say. "I can't go back there. I dined and dashed. Or rather, spilled and dashed."

"It was a cup of coffee, Rae, that hardly qualifies as dine and dash."

"Can't you take me to a Starbucks like a normal person?"

"No can do, princess." The pet name is enough for me to bite his fucking head off, but then he smiles and my focus goes to his lips. Even with the scar, they're perfect. Enough to melt the panties off of any girl.

My heart flutters, and I hate it. I hate that my mind just envisioned him in a compromising position. And I hate it even more that *I* was involved in that image and he was calling me princess but in a completely different way.

Cigarette.

I need a fucking cigarette.

Digging in my bag, I pull one out and light it up, continuing to walk. If I'm going to Sam's Dinette with Miles, I'm going to need to smoke as much as I can beforehand.

Miles struts next to me, proud that he won this round.

We move forward, strolling past people. All of them give Miles a wave, say hello to him by name, or ask him how he is.

"What are you, the mayor of this place?" I sarcastically ask, blowing out the gray toxins.

"Unofficially," he says.

I tilt my head to the side, taking a moment to assess him. "How'd you end up here anyway?"

"That's a conversation for another time." Miles guides me to the front of Sam's and opens the door for me.

Automatically, I put my hands on my hips, glaring at him through my glasses. "You don't get to do that."

"Do what?" Confused, his eyes dart to the open door as if I'm referring to him holding it open for me.

"You don't get to force me to get coffee with you so

you can *get to know me* and then not give me any information about you—that's some fucking bullshit." I spin back around, prepared to march straight back to my condo.

Before I can get too far, a gentle touch on my upper arm stops me. The feel of his calloused hand on my bare skin sends a spark through my bloodstream. I'm quick to brush the feeling, and him, off.

"Don't go." Miles's voice becomes soft, and I turn to face him. "I'll give you whatever information you want. I just didn't think now was the time to dive headfirst into the heavy shit."

"Isn't that what this is?"

"Not initially, no. I want to...I don't know...become acquaintances first and get to know who you are without talking about *that day*."

There's a painful tightness in my throat.

I take a long drag of my cigarette, blow it out, then do it again, trying to put the pieces together in my head. "This is weird," I state.

"Really weird. But I also don't want to pass this up. After all this time, we've been brought back together, doesn't that strike you as important?"

"You mean, is our meeting again fate?"

"Sort of, I guess?"

Shaking my head, I answer, "No. I don't buy into all that. I'm not an 'everything happens for a reason' type of person."

"I'm not either, but I believe *some* things happen for a reason. One of those is us being brought back together."

Staring at him, the war inside me intensifies. Do I believe our connecting again is destiny? Hell no. But there's something about the way he's looking at me that's making me want to believe in it, even if for a brief moment.

I see the boy from that day standing in front of me. But I also see the man he's turned into, carrying that boy with him. The baggage that we get to carry around for the rest of our lives.

The longer he stares at me, the more I feel myself giving in. Letting out a sigh, I say, "Fine. You get ten questions."

"Can I get twenty questions? Like the game?" Miles asks.

Jeez, this guy is like a damn puppy needing to play a game in order to keep him entertained. "Sure," I say with little to no enthusiasm. "I ask you one, and then you ask me one until we hit twenty. Then it's over."

"I think we need to set some parameters, though."

"Meaning?"

"For instance, if I'm in your condo again and I need a bar of soap for the shower, does the question 'Rae, where do you keep the soap' count?"

I flick my cigarette on the ground and smash it with the bottom of my shoe. "And why the fuck would you be showering over at my place?"

"You never know." Miles's mouth twitches as he holds back a smile.

"If this is your plan to get into my pants, it's not working."

"Noted." He rocks back on his heels. "So, would that type of question count toward the twenty?"

"No. Only questions of substance."

"Who gets to decide what qualifies as substance?

Because I feel like if it's you, I'm going to get the short end of the stick in this arrangement."

"Oh my god, can you just shut up and agree?"

His cheeks rise as his gaze sweeps over me. "Fine. You have yourself a deal, Rae."

Before we start walking back to the diner, Miles bends down and picks up my cigarette. "Bad for the environment," he says.

Great, now I feel like the biggest asshole in the world as I watch him walk to a nearby garbage can and toss it.

"Shall we?" Miles asks, getting closer to me and pointing to Sam's. I nod, allowing myself to enter with him. "For reference—that didn't count as one of the questions."

"Shut. Up."

The bell chimes above us as we enter. "Ah! If it isn't Spill and Run Girl!" the old man from last time states from behind the counter.

"Fucking kill me," I mutter under my breath.

Miles loops his arm around my shoulder and tugs me closer to him. "This is Rae," he beams.

"Nice to meet you, Rae. I'm Sam," the man states.

"I'll pay you back for the coffee," I tell Sam.

"Don't worry about it," he says. "Take your pick of any table." He gestures toward the window, where there are a few open spots.

We sat at the same small wooden table I was at a few days ago.

"Two coffees," Miles calls out to Sam, and he gives him a nod in response.

My fingers play with the end of the paper placemat, unsure of where to start this conversation. Clearly, asking how Miles ended up here seems like it's going to be a long story. Possibly a painful one, like mine.

"Here you are." Sam brings us over two mugs. "Listen, Rae, if this guy gives you any trouble—you come to me, and I'll take care of it." He smiles and clamps his palm down on Miles's shoulder.

"You know me, the biggest troublemaker this town has ever seen," Miles says back to Sam, and the two of them chuckle. "How's that patch in the ceiling holding up?"

"Just fine. I knew you'd get the job done. That's why I called you."

"Oh, I always get the job done." Miles looks directly at me when he speaks. His eyebrow quirks the slightest amount, amused with himself.

Did he seriously just drop an innuendo in front of this old man like it's nothing?

I assumed Sam wouldn't catch on, but judging by his laughter—I'm wrong.

"Have fun, you two. And like I said, Rae." Sam points to me. "Any trouble with this one—"

"I'll come find you," I state.

Sam gives me a grin and then walks off, going to help other customers.

"Sugar?" Miles asks.

"Are you just trying to fuck me?"

Miles blinks. "I was asking if you wanted sugar for your coffee." He holds up the sugar packets that are on the table. "I wasn't calling you *sugar*."

"I know that, asshole." I swat the packets out of his hand. "I'm asking you if you're taking me out so you can get laid."

His ocean eyes spark with pleasure. He rests his

forearms on the table, leaning over so he can get closer to me. His entire body acts like a magnet, drawing me in. "Rae. If all I wanted was to fuck you, it would've happened by now."

The way his voice drops in pitch sends sparks into my core, shooting throughout my body and dancing underneath my skin. Tightening my thighs together, I toss my hair over my shoulder. "Awfully sure of yourself."

"There are only two things I'm good at: my job and sex."

"And baseball," I remind him.

Miles scoffs. "I haven't played baseball in years."

"How come?"

"Stopped playing when I dropped out of college."

"Which college did you go to?"

He shakes his head. "You're not playing by the rules. You ask a question and then I go."

Rolling my eyes, I sit back in my chair. I watch as he silently grabs the sugar packets—as many as he possibly can in his large hand—and tears them open, dumping an obscene amount into his coffee.

"That's disgusting." I wince.

Miles shrugs. "We all have our bad habits." His spoon clatters against the mug as he stirs his grossly sweet drink. He takes a sip before asking, "If you take your choker off, does your head fall off?"

"What kind of random question is that?"

"I read a children's book where that happened to the main character."

"What the fuck?"

He nods. "Stayed with me after all these years. You

know, you kind of look like the girl in the book. Are you sure it's not based on you?"

"Yeah, I'm pretty sure about that one." I lift my mug to my lips before drinking. "I should count that as a real question."

"But you won't because you secretly like talking to me."

"You think very highly of yourself. I'm just here for the coffee."

"Says the girl who didn't want to come in here not even five minutes ago."

I put my mug back down on the table. "All right, let's go then—first real question."

"How long have you been an artist?" Miles asks.

"Since I was old enough to pick up a paintbrush. I was always creating something; my artwork just became morbid since high school, which turns people off."

"Then it sounds like you're doing something right."

"What do you mean?"

"Doesn't the saying go, 'Art should comfort the disturbed and disturb the comfortable'?"

My brow arches as I study him. Out of all the responses he could come up with—that's the last thing I expected him to say. I can't deny the lightness in my chest that's directly caused by him noting the importance of my art.

"Can I see some more of your art one day?" he asks.

"My turn to ask a question," I remind him. Miles sits back with a look of slight disappointment flashing across that stellar face of his. Enjoying that I get to be the one with the upper hand, I perk up. "How long have you lived in Golden Bay?"

"Since I was twenty-five."

"And now you're..." I try to do simple math in my head, but he speaks before the numbers add up.

"Twenty-eight."

Duh. He's four years older than me—when I was a freshman, he was a senior.

Miles drums his fingers on the table, playfulness flickering in his expression. "Can I see more of your art?" he repeats.

The realization that he's being genuine when asking the question makes my body tense, as another invisible wall shuts me off from him. "Why are you so obsessed with my art?" I snap.

He puts his index finger to his lips as a signal for me to shut up because it's not my turn to ask the question, it's my turn to answer it. Damn me and my stupid rules.

"So...can I?" he asks.

Images bounce around my mind—particularly the morbid ones that I usually sketch so they're not eating me alive. Whenever I show them to other people, the most horrified looks they can conjure up appear, and they assume I'm some twisted fuck they should stay away from. They're not wrong, but for some reason, I don't think Miles will have that same reaction. And I definitely don't think my art will make him run. If anything, I have the stirring feeling in my gut telling me it'll make him want to get closer.

Which, I can't decide if I want or not, so I choose to say, "Maybe. Not today, though, I have somewhere to be later."

"Another charming gentleman dragging you out for coffee?"

"No. NA."

He pauses. "NA?"

"Narcotics Anonymous—"

"Yeah, I know what NA stands for, I just didn't know that..." Miles trails off, not finishing his thought.

"Yep." I outstretch my arms to show him the track mark scars by my elbow creases, although most of them are faded or hidden under ink. "Yours truly is a junkie."

His features contort as if he's offended on my behalf. It's the first time his cocky smile doesn't pop back on his face in a matter of seconds, and honestly, I'm not sure if I like the expression he's wearing right now. It's much more...personal.

Miles clears his throat, then begins to speak softer. "You're not a junkie, Rae. You're in recovery."

The way his low tone vibrates against my skin makes a whizzing sensation around my chest. The urge to melt into his words causes instant panic. My heart speeds up so much the thrum of my pulse begins hammering against the thin flesh of my neck.

This is too much.

I push my mug away from me. "I think this is enough for the day," I say, sliding my fingernails up and down my arms as they grow itchy.

"I'm sorry, I didn't mean to upset—"

"You didn't." I avert my eyes. "I think this is just a lot for me to process." A frigidness wraps around my bones even though my heart pumps harder.

"Rae." Miles tries to get my attention, but it's lost, zoning out on the paper menu on the table. The words blur and the colors mesh together. Black, white, and red.

So much red.

"Rae." Miles's voice becomes stern and louder until suddenly, it's commanding, "Rae. Look at me."

My eyes flash up to meet his, my breath now stuttering for other reasons. My focus drops down to his lips, and a sense of ease washes over me. My shoulders soften as I force myself to bring my attention back to the greenish-blue eyes staring back at me.

"It's too much. I get it," he states.

I nod because even though I don't know him, I know he gets it—as confusing as that might seem. "I think we'll have to finish the rest of the questions another time," I say.

There it is, that sexy smile back on his face. Confident, alluring, and charming, all wrapped into one mouth. So fucking unfair.

I'm starting to see what drew Cara to him.

"Can I get your number so we can finish this game?"

My arms fold over my chest. "No. But you can give me yours."

"Fair enough."

I have him type his number into my phone, but I don't text him because I'm not sure if I want him to have my number—or if I ever want to meet up with him again, for that matter. Miles might be nice to look at, but he brings back too much pain that I'm trying to move on from.

Scooting my chair back, it makes a screeching noise against the linoleum flooring as I stand up and say a quick goodbye. "Thanks for the coffee."

"Thanks for saying yes."

CHAPTER EIGHT

Rae

"HOW'S THE CONDO, HONEY?" Mom's voice flows through my speakerphone as I sit on the floor of my bedroom, painting Miles's mouth for the third time in the past four hours.

My mind has been cycloning nonstop and the urge to numb every thought and emotion that surfaces is on overdrive.

But I can't. I won't.

"Emotions aren't permanent. Work through it."

The phrases from rehab pop into my brain when I settle on the carpeted floor.

"Let the feelings flow" is what the hippie art therapist there would tell me.

It works though, because it's what I'm doing as I swirl my paintbrush around my canvas. Letting the paint flow, along with everything harboring inside me.

This picture is different from the rest. It's Miles's entire face, now that I know what it looks like up close and not in a dark setting like the one time we kissed in high school. And *god*, is he gorgeous to look at in the sunlight.

Drawing his lips over and over again has brought calmness to my jumpy nerves over the past ten years, but now that I have a mental image of his whole face as a grown man to work with, I get lost in all his features as I paint.

His olive skin tone, the dark, thick hairs of his close-shaved beard, and not to mention the kaleidoscope of cool tones spiraling around his irises.

"Rae? You there?"

The sound of Mom's voice has me jolting in place. I was so busy zoning out on Miles that I forgot she called.

"It's nice," I respond, short and to the point.

"Have you gone down to the amusement park yet and gone on any rides?"

"No."

"Oh. Why not?"

"Who am I gonna go with, Mom?" I snap, tossing my canvas and paintbrush to the side. Automatically, I wince for being a bitch to her. It's not her fault I have no friends. All my so-called friends back home only cared about one thing: getting high. We'd lie through our teeth, steal from our loved ones, and fuck whoever we needed to in order to get what we wanted. Then we'd sit in a state of numbness as the heroin coursed through our veins. And once we were sober, we'd start the cycle all over again.

We never had each other's backs. We only wanted one thing and didn't give a shit about whom we had to cheat or hurt in order to get it.

The strange thing is, we'd all hang out together. We knew we were the scum of the town and no one wanted to put up with us, so we sat in our gloom together, becoming leeches for the turmoil.

Misery loves company.

That's why I'm here and not back home. The farther away from the assholes, the less likely I am to fall back into the pattern of spending time with them.

"Well." Mom speaks again. "The young lady at the front desk seemed nice when we were moving you in."

I scoff. "Yeah, she's a little too peppy for me."

"You used to spend all your time with Cara, and she was peppier than—"

"Mom," I cut her off to silence her. My eyes screw shut, and I take a long inhale, sucking in as much oxygen as possible. I need to cool down before I flip out on her. She's helping me, even if it stings. I sigh out my breath, regaining my composure. "Thank you for the condo. I'm going to look for a job soon and start paying you and Dad."

"We don't want you to rush into anything, honey. Please, take this time to get back on your feet slowly." The sound of her voice isn't necessarily calm, it's begging. A desperate plea from her and my father for me to stay alive.

"Fine," I mutter.

"Have you gone to any meetings?"

"Going to one tonight."

"Good. You'll call us if you need anything?"

"Yeah."

"I love you, Rae," Mom states, shooting an arrow full of guilt straight to my heart.

"Love you, too."

We hang up, and I lean back against my bed.

Resting my head against the mattress, I glance up at the ceiling. It's white, bland, and lifeless.

I should paint it gold.

I twirl a frayed string from the small hole in my jeans around my finger over and over again. It's better than bouncing my leg up and down so hard it might cause this old building to collapse.

The NA meeting is held in the basement of the community center, a block off the boardwalk. It's humid and sticky down here, even though there are a few fans blowing in our direction.

We sit in a circle as people open up and share their stories. I know how this goes—it's not my first time at a meeting, and I'm well aware that it won't be my last.

There are seven people in attendance, all of whom seem to have some type of relationship with one another as they bullshit and laugh about everyday life.

I guess these people can be my friends?

"How about you?" The woman running the meeting looks at me, and in turn, everyone else does. "Would you like to share anything today?"

"No."

She smiles. "Okay, well, you're welcome to speak when the timing feels right. This is a no-judgment zone."

Bullshit. Everyone judges addicts—even fucking addicts judge addicts.

Instead of calling her out, I give her a curt nod, and she moves on to the next person. I only pay half attention as they share about their week while my eyes wander the room. It's so dull and boring. No drop of color aside from the fold-up table that has yellow napkins with some cookies and coffee.

Before I know it, the meeting is being wrapped up, and people begin to head over to the snack table. I stand and start to push my chair over to the side of the room, where there are two stacks of unused chairs.

"You don't have to do that," the woman who ran the meeting—whose name I can't remember—says to me.

"You don't want me to put it away?" I ask.

She shakes her head. "AA is starting in a few minutes."

"Closing the night out with the alcoholics. And here us junkies were thinking you were saving the best for last," I attempt to make a joke. It clearly doesn't land because she blankly stares at me.

On that fucking note, I'll be heading out and hoping she's not the only one who leads the meetings in this town.

Making a quick stop at the snack table, I avoid making eye contact with anyone as I pour coffee into a to-go cup. Grabbing a lid, I start to snap it on top when a voice makes me stop. "Not even a *little* bit of sugar in your coffee?"

Slowly, my gaze drags upward and lands on Miles. Annoyance stomps through my nerves. "Fucking seriously? I didn't want to give you my number, so you show up to my goddamn NA meeting, you dickhead?"

Miles chuckles. Amusement tickles every word as he says, "Relax, sweet pea, I came here for AA. Not for you." He grabs a handful of cookies. "To be fair, I also came here for these."

I remain frozen for a beat, and out of nowhere, Sam pops up next to Miles. "Grab three more chairs, will you?" he says to Miles.

"You come here, too?" I ask Sam.

"Yep. I run some of the meetings," he answers. "Thirty-one years sober and counting, young lady." He gives me a smile and walks away.

Miles begins to follow him, but I grab his attention. "You didn't tell me you go to AA."

His cheeks rise. "You didn't ask." And with that, he turns and trails away from me.

My jaw clenches in frustration at his smart-ass response. I half consider deleting his number and going on pretending like I don't know who the fuck he is. But something prickling beneath my rib cage is yearning to know more about him. Especially after finding him here, in the dreary basement with all the other addicts in town.

Maybe he's struggling, too.

Maybe that day still haunts him as well.

Maybe he's a lot like me.

CHAPTER NINE

Miles

AFTER DROPPING Sam off at his house following our AA meeting, I finally pull up to my driveway. It's been a long day of work and overthinking. My bones are heavy, my muscles are sore, and my feet are screaming at me. But despite all that, I know I'll have difficulty sleeping. My mind has been consumed by a girl with striking features and a chip on her shoulder all day and night.

Opening my front door, the smell of cedar welcomes me. Around three years ago, I started renting this small bungalow, which is several minutes from the beach. Sam owns it, and we have a nice rent-to-own deal going on, so I get to do whatever I want with the place. It needed a lot of extra love to get it to where it is today—and it *still* needs some renovations. Over the years, I put all my free time into this fixer-upper.

Flipping on the light switch, my latest project stares at me. New crown molding around the top of my living room walls.

Bypassing it, I go to my bedroom and let the quiet

consume me. It's the silence that always gets to me. My brain has this annoying habit of needing to fill the dead space with thoughts instead of just letting me enjoy the stillness.

I've been living alone for quite some time, I should be used to it by now. But a blanket of loneliness covers me each night when I crawl into bed alone. When I was younger, I tried to trade that feeling more times than I could count. It was either sex or booze that sparked my interest. Neither of which made the hole in my heart any less painful.

That ache was always there and still is.

I've tried to have girlfriends, but only a few weeks in, I was ready to break up with them. Not because I'm a commitment-phobe but because the emotional connection was never there. I never felt comfortable opening up to any of the women I dated. They couldn't fathom what I'd dealt with over the years. So, I stopped trying to find an emotional connection and settled for the physical one instead.

I like having fun. I usually take them out on a date, we fuck, and they're gone in the morning.

Simple. But lonely.

Lying down in bed, I turn my head toward the window and listen to the distant sound of the ocean waves. Looking up at the night sky, I become fixated on the stars. It fascinates me that they only shine through the darkness and sparkle brightest on the blackest of nights.

They intrigue me, much like Rae does. There's all this murkiness around her, but regardless, she shines through. Captivating, strong, and beautiful.

Before I can get too hung up on my thoughts about

her, I reach for my melatonin on my nightstand. Downing it with a glass of water, I pray I get a few hours of sleep in while I go back to resting my head on the pillow, wondering about Rae until my eyelids get heavy.

The piercing sound of my phone ringing wakes me up from my sleep. "Hello?" I groggily answer, blinking myself awake.

"You're still sleeping?" Sam asks. "Usually you're done with your morning run by now."

Moving the phone away from my ear, I check the time. Holy shit, it's ten o'clock. I don't remember the last time I slept this late. I've suffered from insomnia for a decade, and if I don't drink myself into a coma, then I don't sleep more than four hours tops. I'm usually up at the ass crack of dawn doing laps up and down the boardwalk.

"Yeah," I reply, sitting up. "Guess I needed the extra rest."

"Good. You worry me sometimes with how much you work."

"Can it, old man. You work just as much as me."

Sam chuckles, unable to deny it.

Getting out of bed, I stretch and put him on speakerphone to find out why he's calling.

"There's a storefront on the boardwalk, near Adventureland, that's gone up for sale. I want to check it out to see if it's a good space," he says.

My brows crinkle. "You're looking to rent a new

space? For what?" I can't imagine him owning another business, the diner already taking most of his time.

"I'm not looking to rent it. I'm looking to buy it and be the landlord to rent to others."

"Ah, okay." That makes a lot more sense, seeing that he rents out a few other bungalows around town. Renting out a storefront seems like a move he'd make. "Give me about an hour, and I'll meet you at the diner and we can walk down together."

"Sounds good. Thanks, Miles."

I smile. "No problem."

After hanging up, I manage to squeeze in a quick workout, shower, and breakfast. An hour on the dot, and I'm walking into the familiar restaurant, which has become my second home. The bells chime overhead, and I immediately spot Sam laughing with one of the regulars.

I do a quick scan to see if Rae happened to pop in, but unsurprisingly, she's not there. At least I have the chance to bump into her at the community center for meetings. Although, I probably pissed her off enough that she'll stubbornly pick a different time of day to go just to avoid seeing me.

"Ready when you are," Sam says, walking over to me.

"Lead the way." I hold the door open for him, and we both give a wave to the customers sitting at the back tables.

Ambling along the boardwalk, I breathe in the salt air. It's a beautiful day with the sun shining bright and the temperature rising. Days like these always lift my mood, energizing me even more.

"Hi Sam, hi Miles." Mrs. Welsh, one of the town residents, waves to us as she walks past.

Sam and I say a quick hello, then carry on walking.

Since moving to Golden Bay, Sam has taken me under his wing. When I stumbled into town three years ago, I dragged myself to AA, where I met him. He helped me get back on my feet and gave my name to all the local business owners so that they would call me for any handyman work. Since I no longer talk to my parents, Sam and Gloria have been my only semblance of a family after all these years.

I didn't have the lifelong career goal to become a handyman, it's just something I always enjoyed doing when I was younger. Fixing things. I tried fixing whatever I could whenever possible. I've expanded my skill set along the way and ended up here.

"Here it is." Sam points to a storefront with a huge "For Sale" sign hanging in one of the floor-to-ceiling windows.

Knocking on the door, we're greeted by a real estate agent as he goes on with his spiel about the prime location.

"Mind if I look around?" I ask the agent, wanting to search the place for any hidden flaws.

"Be my guest," he replies and continues speaking with Sam.

I walk around, surveying the space. It's a wide, open floor plan with a bathroom and storage room in the back. I check the outlets, plumbing, and heating and cooling system.

"How's it look?" Sam asks, wandering around the room.

"Everything seems good."

He grins. "Perfect, I'll talk to Gloria and put in an offer later."

"What kind of place are you hoping to rent out?" I ask, still checking out every nook and cranny.

"Not exactly sure yet," Sam says with a shrug. "But it's in a great location on the boardwalk. I'm sure I can make a pretty penny on it in no time."

"Or it could be pretty risky, and you lose a good chunk of money."

"I've got a good feeling about this space."

"Whatever you say."

Within minutes, he's shaking the agent's hand and telling him he'll be in touch by the end of the day. I don't know what he's envisioning for this space, but I hope it's not another T-shirt and souvenir shop. I lost count of how many of those take up space on the boardwalk.

"Make sure whoever rents from you does something cool with it," I tell Sam as we head back to his diner.

"Quit your whining," Sam teases. His pace begins to slow down, and the sun warms our backs as we gradually move forward. "Are you ever going to tell me what's going on with you and that girl?"

Heat trails up my neck. And not from the sun. "What girl?" I play dumb.

"The one with all the tattoos."

"Rae?"

He nods. "Rae."

"I'm not really sure. Might be nothing."

"I've never seen you interact with the same girl twice."

"Don't say it like that, it makes me sound like a douche."

"Am I wrong?"

I sigh. "No, but I have a rule—"

"Only be with the ones who are here on vacation, yes, I know," Sam says.

He's correct. That *is* my rule. I don't get involved with anyone from town because I'm not looking for anything serious, so when the itch strikes, I go for a tourist. They're gone in the morning and go back to wherever they traveled from. No harm, no foul.

"But," Sam continues, "I've seen you with Rae more than once, *and* I've caught wind that she lives here."

My pulse speeds up as he calls me out. "I know."

"Is she someone special?"

"Yeah." My tongue dries up as a mouthful of cotton forms between my cheeks, and I swallow a couple of times. My heart rate shoots off as I manage to push out the words, "She was there that day."

Sam freezes in place, and my steps stutter before I pause with him. His eyes widen in shock. He knows exactly which *day* I'm referring to. I've spoken to him about it in great detail only once.

"*She's* the girl?"

I nod. "She's the girl."

CHAPTER TEN
Miles

TEN YEARS AGO

THE SOUND of a light scratch against my wall from me marking a tiny X with a pencil is the only noise in my bedroom. I've been attempting to be as quiet as possible, so I don't wake up Mom and Dad while I hang up my new shelf. I tried going back to sleep for the past hour, but no matter how much I tossed and turned, I couldn't force myself to shut my eyes. I'm too excited for the first game of the season.

Adrenaline woke me up bright and early, pumped for my last year of baseball at Northview High.

I'm not the only one on the team who can't sleep. We're all in a group chat, and most of us have been up texting for the past forty minutes.

Restlessness hit my core, and I decided to work on my most recent project: adding a new trophy shelf to my wall. Granted, I'll be leaving for college depending on who gives me the best offer, but that won't be for another several months. So, in the meantime, I want to declutter the top of my dresser and add a big shelf where I can house all of my baseball awards. I'm planning on getting a shiny new one at the end of this year.

However, as much as I am proud of myself for my accomplishments, I can't rid myself of this feeling of resentment stewing inside me. I have a genuine love for baseball, plus I have the added bonus of being a kick-ass player, but my relationship with the sport is becoming a complicated one. Over the course of the past few years, it slowly morphed into more of an obligation. It's one of the ways my parents gain more accolades in town. Another win for me means another vote for Dad.

Brushing off the tug-of-war inside me, I concentrate on my measuring tape and add a second X where the other side of the shelf will end.

Before I can do anything else, my phone lights up with a series of texts.

Without even needing to read them, I know they're about the party tonight at Drew's house. I had wanted to host the party here, but my parents wouldn't go for it. Regardless, I was still able to swipe some bottles from their liquor cabinet.

Picking my phone up from my bed, I check the massive group text. Mostly about who they want to hook up with tonight, some messages are about how we're going to dominate this season, and the last message is for me.

Drew
You got enough shit for us tonight, Miles?

Glancing under my bed, I check that the alcohol is still in its hiding spot for the thousandth time. Ten bottles of different types of liquor are lying on their sides, stashed under dirty clothes. Having a fake ID helped me score some of them, but I have to be careful when and where I use it. I have to drive way out of town because if I use it in Northview and word gets to my parents, they'll have a heart attack and keel over. Not from the shock of my drinking but from my ruining their reputation. With Dad as the town councilman and Mom up his ass to run for a higher position, they have to keep their image squeaky clean.

If only the news knew what happened behind closed doors, I doubt anyone would vote for Dad or give Mom the time of day.

Of course, *I* can't fuck up, but the two of them can do whatever the hell they want as long as it's in secret.

My parents are bitter, toxic people who are only together so they can climb up the ladder. The little time they spend at home together is either in silence or arguing. Judging by their latest blowup, I'm pretty sure Dad found out Mom's screwing some random douchebag. Even though they're both unfaithful to each other, neither of them will divorce the other.

Mom comes from old money—a lot more than Dad does, and she funds his campaigns and whatever the fuck the two of them are scheming to do in the future. If she gets Dad to move his way up in the political world, then she becomes more famous. Political celebrity status—why she would ever want that kind of life is beyond me, but I guess it's the closest taste to the limelight she'll ever get. She's desperate for the American dream.

Dad's not much better, buying into every plan she lays out, getting off on the prospect of power. He'll never drop Mom for both the money and the fact that she adds to the wholesome family image.

Which leads them to me—an actor in their play.

Nothing more.

My phone vibrates in my hand.

> **Drew**
> yo, Miles, you there?

> **Me**
> yep. We're all set for tonight.

I smirk at the bottles of alcohol, excited to let loose tonight—I fucking need it. It's only been two weeks since my last party, but I'm already craving to get shit-faced and forget everything. Not to mention celebrating my win for today's first game.

Focusing back on the task at hand, I shove my phone into the pocket of my gym shorts and sift through my toolbox. I don't have everything I need here, but the more I do projects like this, the more I add to it.

Whistling, my fingers push through some nails and hooks until I connect with a drywall anchor.

Taking my drill from my desk, I start to make a hole where the small X is marked on my wall.

The grinding of the metal piercing into the wall only lasts about five seconds before Mom comes bursting into my room, swinging my door open. I let go of the trigger on the drill the moment I hear her enter.

"My god, Miles, what on earth are you doing?" she asks, clutching her hand over her heart as if I scared the life out of her.

"I'm just hanging a shelf," I reply, gesturing to the shelf I made in wood shop a few days ago.

"Do you have any idea what time it is? You should be sleeping!"

I open my mouth to answer but then note her appearance. She's not in any type of sleepwear, she's in gym clothes. "Well, if you can work out this early in the morning, then I should be able to make noise in my room."

She huffs. "I'm only up this early so I can squeeze in some time with Ethan before I leave." Ethan is her personal trainer, and if he didn't talk nonstop about his husband, I'd assume Mom was screwing Ethan, too. But Ethan's too good for Mom. "You, young man"—she points to me as she continues to reprimand me—"should be sleeping as much as you can before the season starts."

"I'll be fine at the game tonight," I assure her.

"We need you better than fine, Miles."

There it is, that feeling of resentment simmering in my gut.

"You know what I mean," I start to overexplain myself, but my brain catches up with what she just said prior. "Wait, leave where?"

"What?"

"You said you wanted to meet with Ethan before you leave. Where are you going?"

Exasperated, she throws her hands up and lets them slap against her thighs. "Oh my god, Miles—you and your father never pay attention to me!" Mom marches out of my room, and I place my tools to the side, trailing after her.

We wind down our long hallway, filled with posed, happy family pictures from over the years. Each and every one of them is as fake as our smiles.

Mom storms past our dining room, which has a crystal chandelier hanging over an extremely long table for a family of three, and into our massive kitchen. Furiously grabbing various fruits from the strategically placed fruit bowl, she begins prepping a smoothie for herself.

The knife slams down onto the cutting board in fast, angry slashes against an innocent mango. She refuses to look at me as her lips purse and her nostrils flare.

I continue to stare at her, confusion clouding me because I know for a fact that she never told me she was leaving the night of my first game. It's been our tradition to go out for dinner afterward before I part ways to hang out with my friends. Of course, last year, it seemed more like an opportunity for them to get more attention at a local restaurant than some loving family moment—but I was still counting on that for tonight.

"Where are you going?" I ask once more.

"I'm going to Miami for the week with Annette and Vanessa—I told you this," she snaps.

"No, you didn't—"

Mom slams the knife down onto the marble countertop and forces herself to look at me. "Miles, I'm sure I did. You're just too busy thinking about baseball to remember anything else." She goes back to chopping. "It's quite disgraceful how little you make an effort to be a good son, the least you could do is remember when I tell you I'm going out of the state."

My fists ball up at her comment at the same time my chest gets kicked in.

All I ever did was try to be a good son for her.

All I've ever wanted was for her and Dad to treat me like I mean something to them.

"What are you two doing up so early?" Dad struts into the kitchen, already in his business suit.

"I wanted to meet with Ethan before I leave," Mom states, plopping her fruits into the blender and letting the loud noise echo in the room.

When she finally releases the button, I begin to speak. "Dad, did you know Mom was leaving for Miami tonight?" I ask, waiting for a shocked response. He must not know, otherwise he would've told her to wait until at least tomorrow. My game is prime schmoozing time for them and a sliver of family time for me.

Dad nods as he heads toward the French press to make his coffee. "Yes, we're both headed to the airport later."

"You're going too?"

"No, I'm taking a quick flight to Charleston."

My mouth hangs open. I blink a few times, watching the two of them move around the kitchen, preparing for their day as if I were not standing a few feet away. Neither of them is fazed by my presence, it's as if I'm invisible.

"Why the fuck are you going to Charleston?"

Mom gasps as soon as she hears me cursing. "Do not use that type of language, Miles Kingston!"

Ignoring her, I glare down at Dad. He pours sugar into his mug and takes a sip before responding. "I have a meeting tomorrow morning. It's easier for me to fly there today than catch a red-eye."

Tomorrow's Saturday. And what type of meeting would he have out of state?

Watching the two of them continue about their

morning without acknowledging each other, my shoulders drop when the realization hits. They're both jetting off to hook up with other people. I doubt either of them spoke about their plans to the other, but once one of them caught wind, I'm sure the other made their own plans accordingly.

And I get to sit here like some stale leftover while they have this silent battle.

"So, neither of you is coming to my game today?" I ask, stunned they'd give up the opportunity for a photo op.

Both of them make a sharp snap of their head in my direction.

"Of course we'll be at your game," Mom says, appalled that I would dare to ask that question. "I don't leave for my flight until you win."

"Same with me," Dad confirms. "We'll each be there for press and then we part ways."

There it is.

How stupid of me to think they wouldn't be there for the news.

The muscles between my shoulder blades grow tense, turning into knots as my frustration builds. Instead of staying in the kitchen, waiting for them to magically turn into the parents I've always wished for, I leave and head back to my room.

My phone vibrates over and over again in my pocket as the group chat with my team continues to go off.

Forcing the feelings about my parents out of my head, my thoughts focus on other people.

I told Greg I'd help him with math during our study hall seventh period.

I have to drive Quincy to the train station this weekend.
Drew needs me to play wingman after the game.

Continuing to storm into my bedroom, I keep my mind on others.

My phone keeps buzzing against my thigh, and when I reach my room, I plop down on my rolling desk chair and check the messages.

They're all pretty much the same shit, hyping each other up for today. Needing to make myself feel better and get rid of the burn of rejection searing a hole in my chest, I decide to join in, hoping the cheeriness will actually feel real to me.

> **Me**
> you guys ready to be fucking champions for another year in a row?

> **Quincy**
> hell yeah we are!

> **Drew**
> fuckers aren't gonna know what hit them

The texts go on like that for a while, and the longer I stare at the screen, the more I sense my lips tip up.

We go on to talk about the party, and that's when my line of sight drifts over to under my mattress. Staring at where the alcohol is hidden, a spark of impulsivity goes off inside me.

> **Me**
> change of plans tonight. Party's at my house.

The chat blows up once again. Everyone knows I have the biggest house, and when I tell them my parents will be gone for the whole weekend, they get even more pumped.

> **Greg**
> does this mean we can invite more people?

There's a beat of hesitation before I type, wondering what would happen if my parents found out I threw a gigantic party with the entire school.

Fuck it. They don't think about me ahead of time, I won't think of them.

> **Me**
> invite everyone.

> **Drew**
> ohhhh shitttttt!!!!

Once again, everyone's excitement explodes, and I eventually feel it myself, forgetting the conversation with my parents earlier.

The texts with my team shift from drinking to girls in a matter of no time.

> **Greg**
> Miles, you gonna hook up with that freshman cheerleader?

My brows crinkle, unsure of who he's referring to.

> **Me**
> what freshman cheerleader?

Greg
idk her name, but rumor has it she
wants you

Drew
yeah, her and the entire female
population at our school wants Miles.

Drew
her twin sister's pretty hot though.

Greg
she has a twin!?

Drew
not identical, but still hot

Quincy
Miles, you gotta get on this

Chuckling, I respond back.

Me
invite them both. We'll see what
happens.

I don't care who I hook up with tonight. Twins or
no twins. All I need is some liquor and a pretty face to
keep me company.

My parents will probably flip out if they find out.

But hey, I'm only young for a short amount of time.

And I'll only live once.

CHAPTER ELEVEN

Rae

PRESENT

"RAE!" Emma squeals as she sees me enter the lobby.

My muscles immediately tense, and my body screams at me to turn around. But Mom's voice in the back of my head stops me from running. I need to make a real friend, no matter how much I'll hate it.

Grinding my teeth together, already cursing myself for doing this, I approach Emma. "Hey."

"How are you? I barely see you around, I was this close to sending someone up to your room to make sure you were still alive." She laughs, her red hair swishing back and forth.

I toy with my choker. "Still alive. Unfortunately."

She continues chuckling, assuming I'm making a joke.

I'm not.

Clearing my throat, I change the subject. "So, I was wondering if you want to, like, hang out or something...I guess." Christ, I feel like a thirteen-year-old boy trying to ask out his crush.

Emma's face lights up. "Girls' night?!"

"Um, sure."

"Oh my gosh, this is so exciting. What do you want to do?"

I shrug. "I don't know."

"Oh! Let's do karaoke!"

"No way."

"Let's get our nails done!"

"Let's not."

"You're not giving me a lot to work with here, Rae," she teases.

"Sorry." I scratch my forearm, working my way up to my elbow crease. "I don't really like to go out and do that type of stuff. But I'm trying to be more...social." I noticeably cringe.

Emma tilts her head to the side, assessing me. "Have you been to the pier yet—the one with the amusement park?"

"I went to Adventureland when I was little, but not since it's been built up and turned into a giant attraction."

"Perfect. That's where we'll go. I'm off in an hour, does that work?"

"Sure. It's not like I'm doing anything else with my life."

She smiles at me before I head upstairs to get ready. Although, there's nothing I need to do before going out.

I could use the time to clean up my messy condo and put away my paints and canvases, but I don't. Instead, I decide to work more on my painting of Miles, getting sucked into the color of his eyes as the sea green, teal, and navy paints inevitably coat my skin. I try to wipe it off to the best of my ability as I wait for the painting to dry. The hour isn't up yet, so on a whim, I decide to pull out my portfolios and look at my old artwork. I take out all my sketches of Miles and scatter them around my bedroom. There's got to be at least a hundred, if not more. However, since his lips are the one thing I've continuously drawn over the years, it's the only thing I can use to measure my progress as an artist.

I skim over them, noting how my shading and linework have steadily become more detailed with time. At least I'm making growth in some area of my life— even if it is just through my drawings.

By the time an hour has passed, I'm downstairs in the lobby once again, meeting up with Emma.

"All set?" she asks, grabbing her purse. Her cork wedges clink against the shiny hardwood floor.

"Ready when you are."

In the blink of an eye, I'm walking next to Emma on the boardwalk, and she rambles on about what it was like growing up here. Nerves jump around in my stomach because I don't remember the last time I spent time with someone just to hang out.

Cara and I used to waste our days away when we were younger. That seems like a lifetime ago when the world as we knew it was different.

Sadness drapes over my shoulders, and they begin to slump. I'm lost in thought about my early teenage days and what I'd trade to have them back when Emma puts a hand on my arm.

"Hey. Are you okay?" she asks, the space between her brows creasing.

"Yeah, just thinking about shit." I shove my hands in my jeans pockets. "So, this is it, huh?" I ask, gesturing my chin to the infamous pier filled with rides and games.

"Yeah, but we don't have to go if..."

"No, it's cool. We can walk around." My feet move before she has a chance to respond.

Everything is in bright, happy colors. Bursts of neon explode all over the rides, benches, and even the garbage cans. Obnoxious music-box tunes go off as we pass by the games. There are hardly any lines since it's not peak season yet, but there are still rides going off left and right. The loud metal clamoring sound of the roller coaster cars inching up the incline catches my attention, and within a matter of seconds, I'm watching it drop down, people screaming their heads off as they flip upside down and twist around the track.

Emma suggests we get a snack, and we stop at a concession stand, the scent of popcorn filling my nostrils. She noshes on a pretzel and root beer while I skip the food and order a Diet Pepsi.

"Okay, I've been keeping it cool for way too long," Emma announces. "Are you ever going to tell me what happened?"

My features draw in, confused. "What are you talking about?"

"With Miles! He's the town hottie, and you bagged him."

I snort. "I did *not* bag him."

"He took you out for coffee the other day."

"How do you know that?"

"He told me before he took the elevator up to your condo." Emma beams.

"God, he's a blabbermouth."

"So, are you two official? What's the deal?" she casually asks as if we've known each other for a while and are used to swapping stories about the men in our lives.

"I haven't seen his dick yet, if that's what you're asking."

She nearly chokes on her soda. "Oh my gosh, no, I didn't mean that at all." Her cheeks turn almost as red as her hair. Clearly, I've made her feel uncomfortable, but whatever—if we're going to have a decent friendship, then she needs to get used to me being uncensored. "I'm sorry if that came across as intrusive," she apologizes.

"It didn't. I don't care." I shrug. "And for the record, there's nothing going on with me and Miles." Although the mention of his name causes tingles down my limbs. And, yeah, maybe the image I generated in my head of what his dick looks like created a little too much heat in my body.

As we stroll, we pass by the enormous Ferris wheel, and just seeing the height of it close up sends a shiver down my spine.

"What do you know about him?" I ask Emma, unable to get my mind off Miles, despite the attention-seeking environment I'm in.

"Aside from the fact that he's Golden Bay Beach's celebrity crush?" Emma snorts. "Just the basics—he moved here a few years ago, he's good at his job, Sam has helped him out a lot, he's nice to everyone..." She trails off.

"So, he's a good guy?"

"Yep."

"That's what I figured." Which sucks because it makes it that much harder to dislike him when I know he's a genuinely good person.

The reminder of our unfinished twenty-questions game bombards my mind. As much as I try to push the thought of calling him out of my head, there's a strong desire in my core, tempting me to play with fate one more time.

My fingernails tap against my cool granite countertop over and over again. I've changed rhythms, but I've been standing in my kitchen doing this for a solid twelve minutes.

After Emma showed me around some more and made it clear that she'd like to hang out again, we parted ways. She went back to her home, and I came back to mine. I guess having her as a friend isn't too terrible. At the very least, she can fill me in on any of the Miles gossip.

My hand smacks down on the countertop, a loud slapping noise filling the silence.

For fuck's sake—*why* do I keep thinking about Miles! Why do I want to get to know him on a deeper level? Why can't I just leave him in the past and keep him a figment of my imagination?

Losing the battle with myself, I pick up my phone and impulsively decide to message him.

> **Me**
> my garbage disposal isn't working

Dropping my phone on my kitchen island, anger clogs my joints. *That* was the best I could come up with? That was fucking stupid, my garbage disposal is working fine.

Letting out a frustrated sigh, I stomp to my sink and stare at it. The only thing that's in it is a couple of dirty cups. I flip the garbage disposal switch, and it makes its normal loud, gurgling sound, signaling that it's doing its job.

My phone buzzes, and I go to grab it.

> **Miles**
> I'm sorry, I don't have this number saved, who is this?

Well, I might as well finish what I started.

> **Me**
> Rae.

There's a long pause before he responds. My heartbeat strums a bit faster, which makes me automatically annoyed. The skin on my palms becomes clammy as I wait for his response.

And wait.

And wait.

> **Miles**
> hmmm, I'm not sure I know which Rae this is. Send me a picture

Dickhead.

> **Me**
> you know who I am, asshole. Are you coming to fix my garbage disposal or not?

> **Miles**
> did you mean: "Miles, can you please come over and help me?"
>
> why certainly, Rae.

> **Me**
> you're annoying.

> **Miles**
> I'll take that as a thank you. See you in a few mins, sugar.

What I thought was a quick pulse before is nothing compared to the mild heart attack I'm having now. A jittery feeling flies under my skin, waking me up.

It's an exciting rush, like right before I'm about to get high. Only this time, my brain isn't looking for a cheap fix to escape. It's looking for an overcomplicated way to be present...with Miles.

My stomach does a strange fluttering thing, and I run my hand over myself, giving a gentle massage.

How the hell do I break a garbage disposal?

Staring at my sink again, I do the only thing I can think of—shove a fork down the drain and jam it in there.

A light tap on my door causes me to jump. Excitement snakes up and down my body as I open the door.

"How'd you get here so fast?" I ask, stepping aside for Miles to enter. He's in a worn T-shirt that clings to his muscles and broad shoulders.

"Just finished up at the building next to you," he replies. He's still for a moment, as if waiting for me to ask him more questions or have some type of conversation.

"You know where the kitchen is." I point directly behind me.

Fuck, I'm so bad at this.

Miles gives me a cheeky smirk and struts his way toward the sink. My heart pounds away in my chest as he approaches the drain. He flips the garbage disposal switch, and it makes an awful grating noise.

Wincing, I watch as his long, muscular arm reaches down and pulls out a fork.

He stares at it for a beat.

Then, as if in slow motion, he pivots his body to face me. Holding up the fork.

Miles stares at me, his eyebrow arching.

A wave of heat hits me as we have a silent conversation.

Finally, he speaks. "Is this a booty call?"

"What?" I snap.

"You know," he says, his voice low and smooth as he slowly stalks over to me. "It's when you make up some lame excuse for someone to come over just so you can fuck."

My body tenses as he gets closer. "That's not why I texted you."

"No?" Miles glances down at the utensil in his hand. "In the few conversations we've had, you seemed like an intelligent person. Intelligent enough to know to look down the drain if your garbage disposal wasn't working and pull out the one item that was jamming it." A sly smile slowly grows on his face, as if he's getting enjoyment out of calling me on my bullshit.

A fire lights inside me, pissed that he thinks I'd squirm away from the awkward position I'm in and back down. So, I do the opposite and stand my ground. "I texted you so we can finish the game, not so we can fuck—because, believe me when I say I doubt that you and I are into the same thing when it comes to sex. So, you can wipe that smile off your face."

Miles's smirk only grows wider. His eyes leisurely drift down my body, taking his time to drink in every curve. My brain can't keep up with the emotions circling my insides as the fire built from anger suddenly transforms into a burning feeling of desire.

"What are you into, Rae?" The tiny hairs on my arms stand up as his pitch drops.

My jaw tightens in frustration from what his presence is doing to me. "It doesn't matter since we won't be doing anything," I grit out.

"You said you called me here to play the game, yes?"

"Yeah."

"Well, I still have a bunch of questions left, and I'm using one of them on that question." He rests his forearms on the countertop, leveling with me. There's a spark in his eyes, and I can tell he's playing with me.

My fingers twitch. "I need a cigarette." Spinning away from him, I hear Miles bellow out a laugh while I search my condo for some fucking relief.

I should've never invited him over.

CHAPTER TWELVE

Miles

RAE SEARCHES the room for a pack of cigarettes as I stand here, watching her. Smitten as can be. She might not have texted me to have sex, but she *did* text me to talk, which is even better. It means that somewhere underneath her stone-cold walls, she wants to know me.

"Fucking hell," Rae mutters to herself as she rummages through her shit. Her home is messy, with clothes and art supplies scattered around, but it's nothing horrible.

As she searches between her couch cushions, I catch the dried specks of blue and green paint on her arms.

"Were you painting?" I ask.

Her head snaps so quickly to look at me, it almost falls right off. "What?"

"You've got paint on you." I point.

"Oh." She twists her arms to check, then picks at the colors. "That was from earlier in the day."

I move closer, going from the kitchen into the living room. "Working more on your mural?" My eyes shift to the wall on my left, which has a bloody skull on it.

"No, I was working on canvases."

"Can I see one of them?"

Her icy-blue eyes narrow, assessing me. "Why are you so obsessed with my art?"

"It's like getting to know you on a different level. I don't know if you're aware of this, but you're a little on the defensive side when we're talking."

Rae continues to study me in silence as if she's debating with herself on what to do. After a long beat, she says, "I sketched something on a piece of paper last night. It's behind you. On the floor." She points.

Cautiously, I follow where her finger is gesturing, and I bend down to look at the paper. At first glance, it appears to be a bunch of geometric shapes, but when I get a better look, I can see all the details. It's a girl's face, screaming. All the shapes hold their own images of distorted figures of horror.

A chill trails down my body. A stabbing pain hits my gut as if a knife has just seared through my flesh and twisted it over and over again.

I blink away the prickle of moisture forming behind my eyes.

It's a disturbing painting, but somehow, also...beautiful. She's incredibly talented—the evidence is clear in my reaction.

"This is remarkable," I say, still admiring the drawing.

"It's okay." Rae's voice comes from directly next to me. I didn't even know she was that close.

Standing up, our eyes lock. There's a magnetic pull between us, making me inch nearer. The second I do, I notice every muscle in her body tense up.

"I still need a cigarette," she says.

I smirk. "They're behind you. On top of your blanket." I point to the fluffy purple blanket that's in a ball on the floor.

"Why didn't you tell me they were there instead of watching me look like an idiot as I searched for them?" Rae huffs, going toward them.

"I just saw them when I walked over here. Besides, you didn't look like an idiot, you looked cute."

Rae scrunches her nose. "*Cute?*" The word comes out of her mouth as if it tastes like acid. "I'm far from *cute.*" She plucks a cigarette from the pack and sticks it in her mouth. Seeing something between her lips makes my insides stir with heat.

All right, maybe "cute" wasn't the best word to describe her.

"Come on," she says, then disappears behind floor-length curtains.

Following, I walk through the glass doors and spot Rae making herself comfortable on a chair on her balcony. I plop down on the other chair, resting my back against the large frame.

The sun has almost completely set, and the sky is getting darker, with a few stars popping through.

Rae lights up and inhales. "Why didn't you tell me you were in AA?"

"Are we playing the game?"

"Yes—and don't answer with some bullshit that I didn't ask you."

I chuckle. "Fair." My gaze drifts over to the amusement park in the distance and then to the ocean directly in front of us. "I wanted the conversation to be about you," I admit.

"How come?"

A billow of smoke clouds my view, and I turn to look at her. "Because you already know a little bit about me. I know nothing about you."

"Correction—I know about the old you. The high school Miles. Not the rugged man Miles."

My cheeks lift up. "You think I'm rugged, Rae?"

"Shut up."

"Rugged in like a 'loner lumberjack in the woods' kind of way, or a 'sexy, not afraid to get my hands dirty' kind of way?"

"Oh my god, forget I used the term 'rugged.'"

"Sorry, I'm never going to forget that a beautiful woman complimented me," I respond, and she immediately scoffs. "But I can pretend like it never happened."

"Good." Another cloud of smoke envelops us.

"I got into heavy drinking after high school," I share.

She nods, almost like she expected my answer. "Ever gone to rehab?"

"No. You."

"Yep. That's why I'm here." She takes a drag. "I OD'd and got sent to rehab. My parents didn't want me coming home and hanging out with the same people, so they bought me this condo so I can start fresh."

My eyebrows rise. "Damn."

Two near-death experiences for this girl. I have a hard time living with my one, I can't imagine how she's wrapping her head around two.

"How long have you been sober?" she inquires.

"Three years."

"So...since you moved here?"

"Yeah."

"Huh."

My head tilts to the side. "What was that for?"

Rae shrugs. "Just find it interesting, that's all."

I shift in my chair so that I'm leaning over, getting closer to her. "First you call me rugged, and now you admit that you find me interesting? Better be careful, Rae, or you might be going back on your word, and I might be finding out what you're into real soon." I wink.

The most appalled scowl appears on her face, and I can't help but burst into laughter. Her lips twitch, and I can't be positive, but I *think* I might've just seen a semblance of a smile. It's tough to see now that night has fallen and the only thing lighting her face is the moon.

"You're a dick," she states before inhaling.

"They allow you to smoke in rehab?"

She nods, blowing out. "Yep. Cigarettes are socially acceptable because they don't cause instant death or make me want to break into cars, looking for money to buy them."

"Breaking into cars was your MO?"

"I've done shadier shit to get high," she admits, unashamed. All of a sudden, there's a switch. "Hey, I'm supposed to be asking some questions, you can't monopolize all the question-asking."

"I think we messed up the rules of the game enough and are just hanging out at this point." I lean back, and the both of us silently agree to drop the facade of this being a game. "But go ahead, I'll be an open book."

Rae takes a second, then asks, "Who did you fight?"

My brows draw in. "I've never gotten into a fight."

"Yes, you did, in high school. That's how you got that scar," she says, gesturing to my upper lip.

More laughter falls from my mouth. "Where the fuck did you hear that?"

"That was the story going all around school—at least it was among the freshmen."

"I can assure you, I didn't get into a fight. I got knocked in the face by a foul ball during a game and was a bloody mess. Needed stitches and everything. But I guess a good fight story did wonders for my street cred for the underclassmen."

"It sure did. My twin sister was obsessed with you—not in a creepy way, but in a high school girl, hopeless romantic kind of way."

"I didn't know you had a twin."

Rae nods. "Yeah. She was convinced that if she could just get you to lock eyes, you two would fall head over heels and get married."

"What's her name?"

"Cara."

"Oh."

There's an instant coldness in my bones. I don't have to ask where Cara is now because I already know the answer.

Quietness takes over.

The rolling waves of the ocean are the only thing that keeps me in the present until Rae speaks again.

"You know, you were my first kiss," she says.

My heart stops, and my eyes nearly fall out of my head. "*What?*"

"Yep."

Stunned, I blow out a puff of air. A million emotions form a lump in my throat. Sorrow and sadness for her. Guilt, even though I'm not sure it belongs. Anger, for having that special moment taken away from her.

I swipe a hand over my face. "Fuck, Rae. I'm sorry."

"It's fine. At least I'll never forget my first kiss."

"That's like the worst rendition of seven minutes in heaven," I say, automatically wincing. It wasn't supposed to come out like a joke.

To my surprise, Rae starts chuckling. Her cheeks rise as the most innocent sound escapes her lips. "I think you mean seven minutes in hell," she states, continuing to laugh.

I join in the laughter, settling into this fucked-up moment with her.

The rest of the world would probably curse us for laughing or rush us to a psych ward to get our heads evaluated. But out of all the billions of humans on the planet, we're the only two that could possibly understand the memory we're referring to and have the twisted sense of humor to make light of it.

This is the first time I've experienced Rae as someone aside from a guarded outsider. I want to hold on to this lighter side of her for as long as I can. Not only for me to selfishly drink in but also for her sake. Because I get the feeling she doesn't allow herself to feel anything except misery.

"Let's go," I say, suddenly standing.

Confusion stifles her chuckling. "Go where?"

"You trust me?"

Even though it's dark, I know her gaze is piercing right into mine. My heart beats fast against my rib cage as excitement sparks through my bloodstream.

"I trust you," she declares, instantly bringing a smile to my face.

I put my hand out for her to hold. "Then, let's go."

CHAPTER THIRTEEN

Rae

"MILES! WHERE ARE WE GOING?" I ask as he rushes us down the boardwalk. He's moving so fast I can't even process the fact that my hand is in his. A rush of exhilaration runs through my veins, whirling around my heart.

The cool night air whips against our bodies as we pick up the pace, running toward the beach and eventually onto the sand.

The sand kicks up as we run, my leg muscles straining as I work against it. Miles pulls my arm to match his pace as I begin to slow down.

"Keep up, half pint."

I practically growl at him for the nickname, but it's true—compared to him, I seem small.

We keep racing forward, getting closer to the ocean. We're away from the lampposts and any lights from the shops on the boardwalk. It gets darker the farther we move; the moon is the only thing making Miles glow. That and his happiness.

He comes to a sudden stop.

"What are we doing?" I ask, heaving.

Miles starts taking off his shoes. "Going skinny dipping."

My eyes bulge. "What?"

"You scared?" The sound of his question taunts me like a dare. "No one's around, you'll be fine." He motions to the empty beach surrounding us.

"I'm definitely not scared of being naked outside," I bite back, pissed he thinks I'm intimidated by that.

His eyebrow quirks, and a look of amusement dances across his face.

I'm quick to shut it down. "I'm scared of dying of hypothermia."

"It won't be that bad." Miles unbuckles his belt. "Besides, you survived a lot worse—cold water isn't gonna be the thing that does you in."

My jaw springs open. "That was fucked up," I say, even though I start chuckling. "You're lucky I have a dark sense of humor, otherwise, I would've been offended."

"I knew I'd have to say something twisted to hear that pretty laugh of yours again."

My stomach does some weird fluttering shit, so I place a hand over it, rubbing back and forth to soothe myself. Why do I keep getting this feeling around him?

That's when it hits me. It's butterflies.

It's been *that* long since I've experienced the feeling that it's foreign to me. I can't remember the last time. Has to be before high school.

"I hate you."

"That's debatable." Miles has a wide grin plastered to his face as he drops his pants. His boxers stick to him, outlining his package, giving me a decent idea of how much he's working with...which seems to be a lot. He reaches over his head and tugs at his shirt, pulling it off him in one swift motion.

Heat shoots between my thighs when I see the muscles in his arms and abs flex as he drops his shirt on the sand. The moonlight hits his almost naked body, and he looks like he's been carved by Michelangelo. His muscles are perfectly crafted, the ideal image of strength and nobility standing right before me as if he were some Greek god.

"Eyes up here, sweetheart," Miles gloats.

My eyelids narrow. "Why do you keep calling me ridiculous pet names?"

"It's fun getting under your skin," he admits. Little does he know, he's been living in every crevice of my brain for the past ten years. "Now, are you coming in or what?"

"I don't know..."

"Do you trust me?" Miles asks for the second time this evening.

The answer is yes, more than anyone I've ever met —even if I don't know him that well. I trusted him then, and I trust him now.

Even though I don't want to trust him.

"Yeah," I begrudgingly answer.

"Good. So, lose the clothes," he demands with a smirk on his face. Glaring at him, I slowly kick off my shoes. He chuckles. "Don't worry, I'll be a perfect gentleman and turn around to give you privacy."

He does as he says, facing the ocean while I stand behind him.

Then, he drops his boxers, and I stare at his perfect bare ass in the moonlight.

Slipping out of my jeans, I then wiggle my thong down to the cool sand. Miles obnoxiously whistles an upbeat tune as I strip down to nothing—minus my choker necklace.

"I'm done," I state.

Keeping his word, his attention remains focused ahead when he holds out his hand for me. My heart beats a little faster as I walk up next to him and clasp my hand in his.

Tingles shoot up my spine. The rush of being next to him—touching him—builds and builds and builds until—

"You ready?" he asks in a husky voice.

"I guess?"

"Good."

The wind is almost knocked out of me as he rushes us forward—running to the water. We run as fast as we can, my pulse racing along with our feet.

Running, running, running until ice water hits my toes. I don't even have time to react as his strength on my hand tightens as we move deeper into the water. It feels like little icicles slicing up my skin, but holy fuck does it wake me up.

"Oh, shit, that's cold!" Miles screams over the sound of the waves.

"I told you!" I yell back. In one swift motion, I release Miles's hand and cup my other, pushing it against the current so that the water smacks him square in the face.

Miles is stunned, completely caught off guard.

He spits out some water. "Did you just splash me?" he asks, droplets of water dripping down from his hair.

I chuckle, liking the fact that my image of him being perfect was easily washed away by the sea. "Maybe."

"Oh, you're gonna be sorry for that!"

A blast of coldness is thrust in my face, and now I'm the one getting sucker punched by the water.

I go back at him, and we get in a full-blown splash fight as if we were in the seventh grade. The sound of my own shrieks and laughter vibrates against my bones —a strange but blissful feeling spiraling through me.

Miles suddenly stops. "That right there"—he points at me—"is the most beautiful sound I've ever heard."

If I rolled my eyes any harder, they'd be glued to the back of my head. "Oh god, stop with the lines."

"It's not a line, Rae, I mean it." He swims closer. "When's the last time you laughed that hard?"

As I tread water, I try to recall the last time I experienced more than just a light chuckle. My brows draw in as I begin to frown. "I don't know."

"Exactly. You needed this." He spreads his arms wide above the ocean, reaching out to the vast sea. I scoff at his comment but don't respond. "Admit it, you're having fun."

I shake my head no, but a smile threatens my lips.

Miles floats nearer, his face lighting up with joy when he realizes he *might* be right. "Yes, you are, Rae." Miles inches closer. My heart pounds faster. "Wanna know how I can tell?"

"How?"

He lifts his hand, and his long finger daintily brushes over my lips. The motion is gentle and leisurely, as if he's taking his time to memorize the outline.

Sparks go off in my chest.

A tornado of heat swirls around my insides at the same time chills dance across my skin.

My breath stutters against his finger.

"Because you're trying not to smile right now," Miles states, letting his arm drop away from me. I blink a few times, taking a second to process his comment. "Am I correct? Are you having fun with me?"

"I'm having...a not horrible time."

There's a rumble of chuckling in his throat. "I think that's the best I'll get, so I'll take it."

"Good." I lift my chin upward. "You don't have another choice."

In an effort to calm down my pulse, I create some space between us. Spinning away from him, I take a deep inhale, admiring the dark blue ocean. Hoping the chill of the water will cool down the fire that Miles lit inside me.

Drifting forward, the salty water leads me into the openness as I take some time for myself.

I let it wash over me again and again. Cleansing my body and spirit. I become lost in its vastness. The darkness of the sky and ocean meld together, becoming one.

Shutting my eyelids, I let the motion of the sea take control, offering me relief. The ache in my bones for years on end lessens as I let nature offer me new life.

For the first time since being in Golden Bay, I feel a sense of freshness pumping through my veins. Maybe this is the kind of life my parents hope for me. The one where all my worries can drift off to sea.

Running my hand over my hair to smooth it out, I open my eyes, glancing at Miles. He's watching me intently, with a look of adoration.

"You don't have to stare at me, you know," I tell him.

"I want to make sure you're safe," Miles says. His words flow through me like honey, settling around my core.

The idea of safety is foreign to me. Although, the last time I felt any semblance of it was in his arms.

Without realizing it, my body swam me over to him. And despite the invisible string yanking me closer, I say, "I don't need you to keep me safe."

He smirks, and my gaze fixates on his lips. My heart flutters in my chest. He has no idea that the image of this—*us*, standing face-to-face in the darkness—has been my form of comfort.

Our naked bodies naturally draw nearer. My foot brushes against his bare leg, an innocent act that makes my mind picture very impure images.

My shoulders rise and drop quickly as it gets harder to breathe the more Miles invades my space.

Miles tucks a stray strand of hair around my ear, then tenderly cups my face. "I *want* to keep you safe, Rae," he whispers.

A force of air leaves my lungs as I look into his eyes, illuminated by the moon. The butterflies take off once again.

Miles won't let go of my cheek, and I know what's going to happen next.

I want it to happen.

Guilt pokes its way into my brain, but my desire for his lips on mine quickly stifles any second-guessing.

Our bodies touch. Skin on skin.

I feel him—*every* part of him—and my thirst intensifies.

Placing my hand on his muscular chest, I can feel his heart race. It has to be pumping just as hard as mine.

Miles swallows. "If I kiss you, will you freak out?"

"Fifty-fifty chance."

"I'm willing to play with those odds."

Miles leans down, and the second his mouth touches mine, it's as if a bolt of lightning strikes me. I'm zapped with need and longing. Flooded with emotions that had been bottled up inside me.

His tongue tangles with mine, and my arms wrap around his neck, pulling him closer. Needing more of him. Needing him to consume me because this feeling right here is the greatest fucking high I've ever felt.

I don't ever want to come back down.

As if he's reading my mind, Miles scoops up my left thigh, wrapping my leg around his torso. I do the same with my other leg, and he holds me. His strong arms keep me steady, and I clasp my hands around his jaw, getting a deeper kiss.

Miles's fingers trail over my skin, caressing me. The small waves crash into us, the tide strengthening just like our hold on each other.

He snakes one of his hands up the back of my neck and into my wet hair. Grabbing a fistful, he breaks our kiss, pulling me slightly back.

Our chests are heaving as we stare into each other's eyes like a whole new world just opened up for the both of us. Our warm breaths land on one another's swollen lips.

"*This* is our first kiss. Understand?"

Eagerly, I nod and plant my mouth back on his. Our hands are everywhere as we touch and explore. His cock brushes up against me, and the heat between my legs intensifies.

Even though my legs are still looped around him, I

grind up against his waist, wanting friction. Wanting *him*.

Miles moves his lips down my jawline and onto my neck, sucking and licking around my choker. If I wasn't so turned on by him, I'd be feeling guilty right now. But that's the thing about being on a fantastic high—you don't feel all the awful shit until you come crashing down.

He bites at my skin, and I shudder around him as a soft moan escapes me.

"You're making it extremely difficult to have any type of self-control," Miles says, marking his way around my throat.

"You don't need to have any," I say, tilting back, allowing him more access.

He groans against me. "Fuck, Rae."

My hips move faster against his skin, and just as I'm about to move down and sink onto him, a giant wave comes crashing into us.

I'm thrust away from Miles, moving closer to the shoreline. The force of the water takes me under, and my mouth fills with saltwater.

Within seconds, I sense the soft sand between my toes, and I begin to bob my head up so I can catch my breath. There's a slight stinging in my eyes, so I keep them shut as I sense my way back to land.

Out of nowhere, a hand wraps around my waist, lifting me up.

I spit out the remainder of the water in my mouth. "I don't need you to carry me," I say, blinking my eyes open.

"Okay," Miles replies but doesn't put me back down. Instead, he walks us over to our clothes and then carefully places my feet on the ground. "You all right?" he asks.

"Yep. Let's go." I toss my shirt over my head.

"Go where?"

"My place."

"You sure?"

"More than sure." I'm not letting a goddamn wave interfere with Miles fucking me. Desire still pools around my insides, yearning to discover what it'll feel like when we do more than just kiss.

"Sounds good to me," he beams, shuffling into his pants. Our sandy clothing sticks to us like another layer of skin. "Fuck, I didn't think this through. This is uncomfortable."

I shrug. "Doesn't bother me." Before he can fasten his belt, I'm tugging him up the beach, and we both start running again.

Wet, half-clothed, and horny, we dash our way to the boardwalk in the blink of an eye.

Miles's laughter tickles my ears, and I allow my own laughter to flow through me as my cheeks rise with joy and excitement.

When we approach SeaScape Condos, we make a beeline for the elevator so we can go up to my place. The elevator door dings open, and the second we're inside, we're on top of each other.

Mouth-to-mouth. Hands gripping, touching, embracing. My pulse skyrockets as his fingers become tangled in my hair, tugging.

When the elevator opens to my floor, he lifts me up once again and kisses me all the way to my door.

"Keys," he says against my lips.

I somehow manage to shove my hand into my

pocket, reaching for my stray key that I luckily didn't lose on the beach.

Miles plucks it from me, shoving it into the door-knob. As soon as it unlocks, he races me to my bedroom. My mouth connects with his neck as I twirl his short hair between my fingers.

We get to my bedroom, and I can hear Miles slapping against the wall, searching for the light switch. Too busy making out with his neck, I don't bother letting him know it's on the left side.

When the light finally turns on, Miles's body instantly goes rigid.

"Whoa," he says.

I pull away from him. "What?"

His jaw is open, eyes wide with concern. Twisting around to see what's got him so freaked out, my stomach suddenly drops.

I left all my drawings and paintings of him out. They're everywhere. Scattered on my floor, covering my entire bed. Barely any space is untouched.

As if he's made of lava, I jump off him and immediately pace my room, stepping on the sketches. "Fuck," I mutter.

How the hell do I come back from this? It looks like I have a fucking shrine of him in my room.

I don't. That's the answer.

"What...um...what is this?" Miles's voice comes from behind me.

And just like that, I crash. My high is instantly gone. Shame, remorse, and self-hatred bite at my veins, injecting my body with the awful feelings I knew I'd experience after kissing him.

My eyes start to burn, but I push down the tears. "Just go, Miles."

"If I knew you were that fascinated with my mouth, I would've kissed you a lot sooner," he tries to make a joke as he forces a half-assed chuckle.

I make a sharp pivot to face him. "I'm not fascinated with your mouth."

"Well, then, can I know what the hell this is all about?" Miles gestures around my entire bedroom.

"You're not even supposed to be here right now!" I snap.

"You're the one who invited me over."

"No—I mean, you're not supposed to be in my life!" I barrel toward him. "Leave!" I push him, making him take steps backward to my front door.

"What the fuck is going on?"

"Nothing! Just go!"

"Seriously?" Miles pauses in front of the door.

"Yes, seriously. We shouldn't have even started something—whatever this is, it's over. Understand?"

His ocean eyes study me, his brows dipping down in confusion. But he doesn't say anything.

The silence between us spills over, and I sense the tears creeping back up.

"Go. Please," I whisper.

He nods, and without a word, he's gone.

CHAPTER FOURTEEN

Rae

TEN YEARS AGO

THE BELL for the beginning of second period goes off. Passing under the massive balloon arch, celebrating tonight's first baseball game of the season, I drift past several classrooms. I should be making an entrance into my math class, but instead, I scoot down the long hallway into Mr. Falcone's room.

It's my favorite place in the entire school, the art room.

Living in an affluent neighborhood means all the classrooms are up-to-date and treated nicely. The art room was renovated right before I began high school, and the moment I stepped foot inside, I became obsessed with it.

It's perfect. Large wooden tables that we can create on, a kiln for pottery, and a massive closet with endless art supplies.

I'd love it if my bedroom could be half as cool as

this. But I doubt Cara would want our bedroom covered in paints and clay.

Attempting to be quiet as I enter, I tiptoe over to the oil pastels.

"Cutting math again, Ms. Hansley?" Mr. Falcone looks up from his desk. The room's empty aside from him.

"I have no idea what you're talking about," I coyly respond, grabbing the pastels and paper.

Silently, I make my way to a table, beginning to sketch something out.

I'm not really sure what it is, but it popped into my head during first period, and now I need to get it out.

It starts out as a feather, blues and purples encompassing the bottom half, then it shifts into flames at the tip. Pink to transition. Then oranges and reds up top.

"That's beautiful." Mr. Falcone appears next to me.

I jolt in my seat, unaware he was this close, watching. "Oh. Thanks."

"You're easily the most talented student I've ever had."

"That's not saying a lot, considering you've only been teaching for a few years."

Mr. Falcone laughs. "Okay, how's this? You're a better artist than anyone I know."

"I don't know who you know, they could all be science nerds," I joke. It's not uncommon for us to have a little back and forth.

"You're something special, Rae." His voice softens as his fingertips dance over my hand. He inches closer, his breath hitting the side of my face.

My body freezes.

The entire school year, this place has been my one

spot of solace. My place of peace from all the annoying kids and the petty high school drama. Mr. Falcone always made me feel good here. And yeah, he's a young teacher and cute...but something in my gut tells me he shouldn't have just done that.

But he wouldn't be a creeper like that. He's never done anything like that before.

He was just being nice.

Mr. Falcone moves away, dragging his touch over my skin. "I have to head to a meeting." He rises. "I won't tell anyone I saw you as long as you don't tell anyone you were with me."

"The secret's safe with me."

He nods and goes to his desk to grab his notebook. "See you later, kid."

My stomach tumbles with a mixture of contradicting emotions as I watch him leave the room. Once he's gone, I reach for my phone to text Cara so she can tell me I'm just being stupid and there's nothing to worry about.

As soon as I go to type a message, my phone lights up with an incoming text from her.

Cara
OMG GUESS WHAT?!?!

Me
what?

Cara
TONIGHTS PARTY HAS BEEN MOVED TO MILES'S HOUSE!!!!!

For the love of God, this girl either needs to hook up

with him and get it out of her system or find someone new.

> **Me**
> that's cool

Cara
please come? pleaseeeee

> **Me**
> hang out with your friends and fill me in after. I don't want to kill your vibe.

Cara
YOU are my best friend. There's no one else I'd rather hang out with

(minus Miles)

I lightly chuckle at my phone. As ridiculous as she is, I love every bit of her.

As I start to reply, Mr. Falcone pops his head back into the room.

"Forgot something," he says, riffling through his desk drawers. "Oh, by the way, some of the teachers are talking about the end-of-the-year dance. Do you have any interest in working on some of the decorations with me?"

"Yeah, that'd be cool."

"Good." He smiles, then places whatever it was he grabbed from his drawer into his pocket. "Maybe you can stay after school today and we can talk about it. Just me and you."

"Um...yeah. Okay."

"Sounds good." Mr. Falcone gives me a wink before leaving once again.

Okay. That was kinda weird.

My stomach stirs once more, so I go back to my phone to text Cara.

> **Me**
> do you have a min to talk in between classes?

> **Cara**
> yeah, what's up? Everything okay?

> **Me**
> Everything's fine, something weird just happened and I need your opinion

> **Cara**
> whose ass do I need to kick?

> **Me**
> Cara, I love you, but you could never kick anyone's ass.

> **Cara**
> I'd at least try for you

> **Me**
> much appreciated

> **Cara**
> meet me in front of room 102 before third period?

> **Me**
> thank you

Sighing a breath of relief, I place my phone down and go back to my drawing. Getting lost in the world of colors and ignoring the chaos in my mind.

At least when I'm alone, I can feel safe here.

CHAPTER FIFTEEN
Miles

PRESENT

I'M FUCKING CONFUSED.

What happened with Rae has been the only thing I can think about over the past week. We had an incredible time in the ocean, and the kiss we shared was the best thing I've ever experienced in my entire life. It's like fireworks exploded in my core the second our lips made contact. As if I was born to kiss *only* her.

However, when we went to her condo and I saw those pictures of me, my gut twisted. It definitely was unsettling, but more than that, it piqued my curiosity. Most people would run the other way the moment the red flags shoot up, but something tells me she's not some stalker who's planning to kidnap me and chop me up.

More than anything, I just want to know what the hell those images are all about.

She's been drawing pictures of me? For how long? When did she start? Why?

These are the questions that roll around in my head over and over again as my feet hit the boardwalk pavement. It's not even six in the morning, and I'm already finishing up my morning run.

I've lapped the entire length twice, passing Rae's condo like I normally would before I knew she lived there.

I might've glanced up at her balcony to see if there was any sign of her.

There wasn't.

And there hasn't been for the past seven days.

Neither of us is reaching out to the other—although I have a myriad of questions to ask her. I have no idea how to even start up the undoubtedly awkward conversation of why she has a shit ton of sketches of me all over her room.

And why they are of me from when I was younger.

Out of all the papers and canvases I was able to see, they were almost all of my mouth, and all of them, except one, were me without a beard.

They were all of me in high school.

Sweat drips down my face, and I pull the hem of my shirt up to swipe it off my cheeks. The longer I stay here and think about Rae, the less time I'll have to get ready. My day's already packed with work calls, and if I start late, then it'll push my entire day back, and Sam asked me to meet him at the storefront he's the proud new owner of at five this evening.

So, instead of driving myself insane with thoughts of Rae, I head back to my house to shower and get my day started.

I get to the storefront at five o'clock on the dot, exhausted, but on time. I've been racing around all day between people's houses and places of business. I'm not complaining, it's my only source of income, and I enjoy the work. I just wish I could do it on more sleep. My insomnia is giving me hell. I've barely been sleeping three hours a night this past week.

"You look like shit," Sam says as I enter his new store.

I chuckle. "Same to you."

"I won't keep you long, I promise."

"Don't worry about it, Sam. I'm here to help." I smile at him and place my toolbox down on a fold-up table that Sam must've recently acquired. The lines in his forehead crinkle as he assesses me, but I brush it off. "So, what's up? What do you need me to do?"

"You haven't been to an AA meeting in a while."

"Oh my god, Sam, I'm not relapsing. My drinking days are long gone, never to return."

"Good. How's your sleep?"

"Fucking awful."

"And how's—"

"All right, old man, enough," I tease. "I'm fine. I swear." I look him dead in the eye when I speak, so he knows I'm not lying.

He nods when he realizes I'm being honest and moves on to work.

"Flooring," he states. "I want to get all new floors. Something durable for foot traffic but looks classy."

I snort. "Classy?"

"Gloria's words, not mine," Sam states about his wife. "We've been thinking about doing something different with this place. Not the same type of crap you see all down the boardwalk."

"So, you want to rent it out to someone who's looking for classy flooring?" I joke.

"Hey, don't knock it. This beach town turns into a zoo during tourist season, and all types of people are down here—even some classy ones."

"I guess you're right." Of course, I wouldn't call any of the women I've hooked up with classy. If anything, they're all the same. Vanilla. Temporary beach bums looking for a fun time.

Scouring through my toolbox, I find my measuring tape and get to work, determining the dimensions of the space. Crouching down, I hold a pencil between my teeth, assessing, then write down the measurements on a piece of paper.

I do this for several minutes in silence until Sam speaks. "How are things with Rae?"

Just hearing her name said out loud sends warmth across my body. "I wish I had something good to report, but I haven't spoken to her in a week."

"Why not?"

Still focused on working, I don't look up at him. "It's complicated."

"Seems like your entire history together is complicated."

"Yeah, we didn't have the greatest start." A small chuckle escapes from my mouth, even though it's a fucked-up reaction. "I was just hoping in this lifetime that things would go smoother for us."

"You like her?"

My stomach flutters. I raise my gaze to meet Sam's, who is smiling at me knowingly. "More than any woman I've ever met."

CHAPTER SIXTEEN

Rae

I VOMIT into my toilet for the eighth morning in a row. Technically, eight afternoons since I've been sleeping well past lunchtime. This started ever since Miles found my artwork of him. A week and a day of constant nausea, mostly caused by guilt and memories.

Leaning my head against the ledge of the shower, I wipe my mouth with the back of my hand. The last time I threw up this much was when I first went to rehab and was having excruciating withdrawals. Just another time in my life when I wished I was dead, much like now.

After sitting on the tiled floor for what feels like an eternity, I regain some strength and manage to stand up. My legs tremble as I hobble over to my vanity to brush my teeth and splash cold water on my face.

Days like this make it hard to do much of anything, let alone breathe.

It would be so fucking easy to make all the thoughts and feelings go away. A simple text to an old number I have memorized. I'd send my dealer my new address, offer him extra to take the long drive out here, and get high as fuck, washing away all of this.

Or maybe I could just knock on the college boys' door down the hall and smoke myself out for the time being. It'll help with the stomachache and racing thoughts.

At least that's what I tell myself as I get dressed and walk out of my condo and into the hallway in search of their door.

My fingernails run up and down my arms, scratching. Needing something to take the edge off.

If this doesn't work, I'm texting my dealer. I don't give a shit.

I have no clue which condo is theirs, but the second I hear guys cheering and laughing, I know I'm in the right spot.

"Hey!" A squeaky voice comes from my left before I can knock on the door.

Startled, I snap my head to the side and see Emma grinning at me from down the hall. She stands near the elevator, holding a box in her hand. "Christ, you scared the shit out of me," I say, placing my hand over my heart.

Emma giggles. "Sorry, didn't mean to." Her gaze travels to the door I'm standing in front of, and her smile immediately turns into a frown.

Oh crap, she probably thinks I'm going to hook up with one of them. Which is the one she likes? Troy? Tray?

"I'm not...I wasn't going to sleep with the one you like—or any of them, for that matter."

With wide eyes, she brings her index finger to her lips to politely tell me to shut the fuck up. Then she waves me over.

Leaving my spot to go over to her, she starts speaking in hushed tones. "I'm not into Travis anymore."

Travis—that's his name.

"He's been bringing different girls back here all week and completely ignoring me when he walks by."

"What a piece of shit."

"Yeah. So, I'm over him."

"You can cut off your feelings that quickly, huh? Impressive."

"Well, no, not really. But that's what I'm telling myself so I can move on and maybe have a future with someone who actually cares about me."

"Good plan." I pat her arm and start to walk off to my condo.

"What were you doing outside their place anyway?" she asks, stopping me from getting too far.

Another round of nausea crashes into my stomach, knotting it even tighter. "Oh, they were being loud, so I was going to tell them to be quiet."

Emma rolls her eyes. "They're so obnoxious."

"Tell me about it," I lie and try to get away once more.

"Wait, before you go—this package is for you." She holds out the box in her hand. "I figured I'd drop it off. It's been sitting behind the desk for the past few days, but I haven't seen you walk by."

That's because I haven't left my condo since the Miles fiasco.

"Oh, thanks." I take it from her and say a quick goodbye, darting back into my room.

Plopping the box on my island counter, I take a

deep breath, realizing what I would've done if Emma wasn't there to be my saving grace in that moment.

I know full well that I wouldn't have just smoked some weed and called it a day.

My hands shake, and tears threaten to make an appearance.

As a way to distract myself, I open up the package, tearing the strip of tape with a serrated knife. Prying the cardboard open, my eyes continue to burn from holding in my tears when I notice the box is packed with all my favorite things: mac and cheese, fluffy socks, bath bombs, and tubes of paint. Plus, a letter from Mom.

It's a care package.

As if I were away at school and needed a reminder that my family still thinks about me.

Mom hasn't been able to do this with any of her kids. Cara and I obviously didn't go away to college, and my little brother Grayson—who's actually not that little—lives at home.

My chin quivers, but I hold everything in. I open the letter and read about how Mom "wanted to send a little surprise to brighten your day."

Pinching the bridge of my nose, I swallow around the lump in my throat, shoving down the rest of my remorse. I draw a sharp, cold pull of air into my mouth to stop myself from losing it.

Once I gather myself, I send her a thank-you text.

Then, killing my pride and being real with myself, I check the time of the next NA meeting and haul my ass over there a few minutes later.

When I approach the community center, it's quiet. I pad my way down the staircase to the basement, where society likes to keep its local addicts hidden.

I first spot the fully stocked snack table, then look over to a circle of empty chairs except for one person who's sitting with his hands folded in his lap, smiling at me.

Sam.

My footsteps freeze. "I thought you only ran AA," I say.

"I run both," Sam answers.

"Oh." I look around the room to see if there are any people standing in the corners, waiting to sit. But no one else is here.

"There are lulls in meetings," Sam says as if he were reading my mind. "Dinnertime is usually a slower time of day."

"Then why hold meetings at that time?"

"People still stop by every so often, so we decided to keep the time slot open."

I nod but still don't move toward the circle of chairs. "You know you can't tell him I'm here, right?" I state, referring to Miles.

Sam smirks. "I know what the A stands for in NA."

"Good."

"Why don't you sit down?" He gestures to the circle.

As if my feet were made of lead, I struggle to lift them. Hesitantly, I move closer and sit on the chair farthest away from Sam.

"Rough day?" he asks.

I nod again.

"Want to talk about it?"

I shake my head.

We sit in silence, the clock in the room ticking as the minutes go by. I know the whole point of my being here is to share my struggles and get support. But I'm not good with words. Art is my way of communicating. Every time I try to speak my story of how I wound up here—the words root to the back of my throat, never escaping. I don't *want* to speak the words. The sentences of pain and trauma all strung together for people to hear but not to understand. No one else would remotely comprehend what my path in life has looked like, except for Miles. I know he understands on some level because he was there for the turning point. When hell became a reality and we somehow managed to escape.

Some days I wish I didn't.

Most days.

Miles was the one who made sure I escaped. And throughout the years, I tried so hard to hate him for that.

"What's your substance of choice?" Sam asks, breaking the silence.

My jaw pops as I unclench it to answer. "Heroin."

"And if you can't get your hands on that?"

"Fucking anything." I snort.

"How long have you been sober?"

"Over three months."

"Must've been a long three months."

I lean back in my chair. "You're telling me."

"How's your sobriety going?" Sam keeps going with the questions.

"Challenging, but I'm doing it." My eyes drift off of him. "Moving here is my chance to start fresh, and I want that for myself. I don't want to keep living in the same torture I have been for ten years."

"Ten years?"

"Yeah. That's when all of this sort of started. Not heroin, but the nightmares and the gut-wrenching sorrow that I wish would've just killed me. So, I tried everything to get out of my head. It took a few years, but I finally fucking found it," I admit. "Nothing worked better to numb my brain and heart than heroin."

My eyes burn.

My throat closes up as if there's a vise clamping down.

"I think I'm done talking about it," I state.

Sam nods.

We're quiet for even longer, but it doesn't feel awkward.

It feels relieving.

"Cookies or coffee before you go?" Sam asks when the time is up.

My eyebrow arches. "Did you make the coffee?"

"I sure did."

"Then I'll grab a to-go cup," I say, walking over to the table. "And thanks for hanging out tonight. I know it probably sucked that you didn't get to hear a more exciting story."

"That's not what this is about. My door's always open for you, Rae."

I give him a tight-lipped smile, and within seconds, I'm trailing up the steps and outside of the building. With my coffee in one hand, my other searches my tote for a stray cigarette and lighter.

My gaze is trained on the inside of my bag, fumbling to find my relief. Not paying attention as I turn the corner, I walk straight into something, causing me to spill hot coffee everywhere.

"Fuck!" I shout, peeling my shirt away from my skin so it doesn't burn.

The something in front of me—which is a human—hisses and I assume I splashed them with burning liquid as well.

"I'm so sorry—" I start to say as my attention drifts upward to look at them. My insides twist when I realize who it is.

"It's okay," Miles answers, doing the same thing with his shirt. "You all right?" he asks.

"Yep, just a fucking idiot."

His eyes soften. "Hardly."

We take a beat, staring at each other. My heart thumps harder the longer I look at his features. I know I owe him an explanation about why it seems like I'm a psycho drawing pictures of him in my lair.

"I know what you saw must've creeped you out, but I swear I can explain everything."

"Okay."

There's a long stretch of quietness. Miles rocks on his heels, waiting for me to speak.

But I choke. The words don't flow from my brain to my mouth like I had hoped.

"Are you going to AA?" I ask, glancing over my shoulder to the building I just came out of.

"I was planning on it, but if you want to talk—"

"No. Go to AA and we can meet up after—if you want."

Miles nods. "All right, meet you on the boardwalk in front of your place in an hour."

Nerves dance around in my belly. "I'll be there."

CHAPTER SEVENTEEN

Miles

AN HOUR LATER, I'm standing on the pavement outside of SeaScape Condos.

Anxiety juts through my bloodstream as I wait for Rae to make an appearance.

A warm breeze rolls through just as she walks onto the boardwalk, an unlit cigarette already between her teeth. Her eyeliner is lighter than usual, but her blue eyes are just as striking, and her frosty hair is tied up in a knot on the top of her head, looking like it hasn't been brushed in a couple of days. Still, she looks exquisite. Like a beautiful mosaic, all her broken pieces fusing together to make her a flawless masterpiece.

"Hey." My words strain against my vocal cords as apprehension takes over.

Rae whips out a lighter from her bag, lights her smoke, and then after she blows out a puff, she says, "Hi." With that, she walks forward, her feet moving quickly.

I immediately match her pace, striding along next to her.

The sky darkens as we walk at least half the length of the boardwalk in silence while Rae chain-smokes. The feeling tumbling in my stomach has shifted from unease to impatience.

Clearing my throat, I begin to speak. "So, the drawings..."

"Yeah" is Rae's only response. She shifts her line of sight so she can avoid making eye contact.

"They were all of me when I was younger."

"Minus one."

"Minus one," I repeat, remembering seeing the canvas of my full face with a beard. "And most of them are of—"

"Your lips."

"Yeah."

"It's going to sound weird. Probably not as weird as you walking into a roomful of pictures of yourself—but still," she says.

"I can deal with weird. What I can't deal with is not knowing what that's all about."

We continue to stroll and pass the amusement park with a handful of kids and teens laughing and shrieking from the rides. I get a whiff of fried Oreos as we walk by a food stand. A group of middle schoolers darts in front of us, cheering that they won a giant bear from one of the games.

Rae takes a long drag, then stomps out her cigarette and flicks it into a nearby neon-yellow garbage can. "Do you ever have flashbacks from that day?" she asks, her brows drawn in tight.

"Yeah. They're not as reoccurring as they used to be, but sometimes I get them."

She nods. "Well, I get them. A lot. And when I feel

trapped—like I'm living the moment all over again—the only thing that gives me a sliver of relief is when I can remember—" She stops herself and fidgets with her choker necklace. "I'm a visual person. I can't remember the exact words people say, and numbers don't make sense to me. The way I process the world is through images. And I have a distinct image—*memory*—of your lips that day."

The dots begin to connect for me, and I sense a lightness in my chest.

"Ever since the day it happened, the only thing that has helped me with the flashbacks is when I can get a hold of something tangible to ground me. So, I draw the one thing that helped me in that moment." Her gaze travels up to meet me, the lights from the rides colorfully flashing across her face when she says, "You."

My heart swells as a sense of belonging radiates throughout my entire body. Up and down my spine, shooting out to my limbs and strengthening my core.

She's held on to me for ten years. Just like I have with her.

However, one of the things she said to me when I was at her condo doesn't add up to what she just admitted. "Then why did you kick me out and tell me I'm not supposed to be a part of your life?"

Rae turns her head, looking away. She doesn't answer.

We keep quietly walking, and my brain processes this new information she just gave me. That's when the answer to my question hits me.

"Is it because of Cara?" I ask in a whisper, and I can see her muscles tense.

Rae nods.

Gently placing my hand on her dainty shoulder, I stop her from moving forward. I shift, placing myself in front of her to make sure her attention is on me. "You're not backstabbing her by letting me into your life, Rae."

A glassiness coats her eyes, and she rolls her lips in an effort not to let her true emotions be seen. With my hand still on her arm, I lightly brush my thumb back and forth to help comfort her.

After a long moment of standing like this, our gazes locked, Rae pulls in a stuttered breath. "I'll feel like a bad sister if I let you into my life," she confesses, her voice laced with sadness.

Her admittance twists a knife in my stomach. I can't even grasp the guilt she must be feeling, but it's unnecessary. "You're not—I swear you're not," I state and the second I do, I know her walls are going back up.

She takes a step back, breaking our contact. Glancing down at her shoes, she tries to hide her face.

"Listen, I don't know what type of war is going on in your head—but I know it's happening," I say, the sound of my desperation to connect with her hanging between us. "And I understand why it is. But don't you think Cara's the one orchestrating all this?"

She vehemently shakes her head as her expression contorts into irritation. "I already told you I don't believe that everything happens for a reason," she says. "I don't buy into 'the stars are aligning, it must be fate' bullshit."

She takes yet another step back, and the urgency to not let her slip through my fingers builds inside me.

"Well, pretend you do for half a second, Rae," I say, the muscles in my shoulders straining with the need to prove her wrong. "Can you play make-believe with me for a moment?"

She rolls her eyes. "No."

"Because you're scared."

"Excuse me?"

"You're scared that if you do, you'll have to admit that you actually have feelings for me."

Rae goes silent once again.

My pulse revs up, needing to get her to stop self-sabotaging herself for a minute. Bubbling over with the intense desire to jump on the opportunity, I lose my filter. "Fine. I'll go first. Rae, you have crossed my mind every day for a decade, and ever since we ran into each other at Sam's diner a few weeks ago, I have not been able to stop thinking about you. You're the only thing in my brain on constant repeat. And although some of the images in my head involve you bent over naked, my feelings for you are more than that."

Her lips twitch.

"Aha!" I point to her mouth. "There it is—you almost smiled."

She immediately schools her features into a frown. "No, I didn't."

"Yes, you did." I clasp her hand and half expect her to either pull away or slap me. She does neither, so I continue. "Rae, you're allowed to smile. Don't stifle it. Let yourself be happy. Let yourself *feel*."

Once more, her icy-blue eyes brim with tears, but she doesn't let them spill over. She's silent again for the umpteenth time.

There's a hammering in my chest, spurring me on, not wanting to let her go.

I give her hand a squeeze. "If you can tell me that

you don't sense the slightest fraction of a connection between us, then I'll leave. I won't bother you again—if we pass each other somewhere in the future, I'll turn the other way. I'll be completely cut out of your life as long as you can look at me right now and tell me you don't feel anything."

Rae's stoic.

Unmoving.

Her jaw is clenched so tight, I don't know if she'll be able to crack it open even if she did want to respond.

"Give me *something* here, Rae," I plead.

Nothing.

She doesn't even flinch as the lights dance over her face once more.

Defeated, I drop her hand, assuming the answer. I turn and walk the other way, my feet unable to keep up with my racing thoughts. My shoulders slump as I hurry past a group of teens as they giggle in excitement about going on a roller coaster. A trail of popcorn crunches beneath my feet, but I quickly move over it and away from the amusement park.

"Miles?" Rae calls out.

Coming to a halt at the sound of her voice, I spin to look over my shoulder and spot her rooted in the same spot. But the second our eyes lock, she begins to move.

My body heats up with every step she takes, getting closer and closer. Her pace gets quicker until she's directly in front of me. The sound of my heartbeat pounds in my ears as I wait for her to say something.

Anything.

Rae takes a deep breath. "Do you want to see the rest of the drawings I have of you?"

My being lights up. "I'd love to," I rasp.

"Miles, I don't know how to do this—I don't know if I *can* do this."

"That's okay, we'll take things at your speed, and if it's too much for either of us, we'll call it off. Besides, you just made it through the biggest hurdle."

Her eyebrows crinkle. "Which was?"

"The first step is admitting you have feelings. Didn't they teach you anything in that rehab of yours?" I make a joke, and I know it lands because the smallest smile appears on her face.

"I believe it's 'the first step is admitting you have a problem.'"

"Not when it comes to being addicted to me."

"Smooth. Real smooth."

"There's a lot more where that came from."

"Fantastic." She adjusts the choker around her neck. "So, what's step two?"

"We ride off into the sunset together."

Rae scoffs. "I don't believe in fairy tales. Only horror stories."

"Maybe you just haven't met your Prince Charming yet." I try to make light.

"I don't believe in him either."

I smirk.

Challenge accepted, Rae.

CHAPTER EIGHTEEN

I CAN'T BELIEVE that just happened.

We both admitted to each other that we have feelings for one another. Now what? What's the next part of this—because I've never gotten up to this point with anyone before.

"This is where my shit goes when I feel like cleaning up," I say to Miles, opening up the walk-in closet in my bedroom. I promised him I'd show him the rest of the sketches I have of him, so I'm keeping my word. While also trying to figure out where the hell we go from here.

"Whoa." Miles's eyes widen when I swing the doors open.

"Yep. Most girls would use this space for clothes, I opted for art supplies."

"There's so much," he states, as his gaze travels around the endless materials. "This is awesome."

"Yeah, my parents hooked me up with all of it. I'll pay them back soon, I just need a job first."

"No luck finding any work?"

"I haven't looked yet. My parents want me to focus on my sobriety, getting my head screwed on straight, finding my footing—blah, blah, blah."

"They sound like great parents."

I lean my head against one of the closet doors. "They are. They definitely don't deserve a daughter like me, they deserve a daughter like Cara." Miles focuses his attention on me, and his features soften. Way too much for my liking. So, I flip the conversation onto him. "You haven't told me about your parents. What's their deal?"

He shrugs. "I haven't spoken to them since I dropped out of college."

My body shoots up straight. "What? Why?"

"I was their ticket to fame and fortune—well, more fortune than they already have. When I started slipping in baseball and school, the dream of being in the major leagues was gone. That was the one goal they allowed me to have, and it vanished."

My brows knit together, dumbfounded. "So, they stopped talking to you because you didn't play baseball?"

"You know how the families are where we grew up in Northview, it's all about status. I tarnished the family name."

"There's got to be more to it than you not fulfilling their dreams of you being a big-shot baseball player." It doesn't make sense if there isn't.

"You're not one for reading the newspapers or watching the news, I assume?" Miles asks, a hint of hesitation growing around his words.

I shake my head. "I have a general disinterest in the news but avoided it like the plague after everything happened. The habit stuck—I don't even remember the last time I glanced at a newspaper article."

"That's good." Miles's attention drifts off me. He clears his throat, noticeably going tense around the topic as he prepares to tell me more. "My dad was a lawyer, and my mom's a leech drawn to his recognition and nothing else. When I was in my sophomore year at Northview High, my dad was elected as town councilman, and his plan has always been to work his way up to governor. Even though my parents hate each other, my mom stood by his side because she would get the perks, and it would look good for him in the public eye whenever he decided to run." His gaze returns to mine, a defeated look blanketing his face. "Both of them used me to enhance their image. Not only did I fail at my sole purpose, but I couldn't even graduate college. I was an embarrassment to them."

My jaw hangs open in disbelief as I process the information he just dropped. "Even after everything that happened in high school, they still treated you like that?" I ask, the sound of my voice rising as my face becomes hot with anger.

"Yep."

"What pieces of shit!"

"Exactly. Try living with them for the majority of your life." Miles chuckles.

There's an aching in my chest as I stare at him. A strong urge to hug him comes over me, but I glue my arms to my side, resisting the impulse.

Miles continues, "I lived at home for a bit after I dropped out of the University of Florida, but things got worse with my parents once my dad got elected as mayor. It got to the point where they made me feel like crap on a daily basis and wanted to hide my existence from their social circle. So, one day, I packed my car, took out all the money my parents had in a savings account for me and drove off."

"To here?" I ask, sucked into his story. His life is fucked up like mine but in different ways.

He shakes his head. "No, I couch surfed, partied a lot—it was fun at first. But then the drinking became a problem, and I got pretty lonely. I lived the nomad life for a while, living in my car or in hotels. Until one day, I ended up here. My drunk ass stumbled into AA one day, where I met Sam, and the rest is history."

"Wow." I stare at him as a million more questions ping-pong around in my brain. Before my mouth can settle on one, Miles speaks again.

"The drawings?" He nods his chin toward the open closet.

"Right." I step in and grab multiple portfolios. I cleaned up since the last time Miles was in my bedroom, and now all the sketches of him are tucked away.

Dropping a bunch of my artwork onto my bed, I plop down with it and begin shifting through my drawings. Miles quietly sits down on the foot of the bed, watching me.

My fingers sift through the different-sized papers, and anytime I land on one of his lips, I take it out and place it on my comforter.

"You can pick them up," I say, still focused on searching through my artwork.

His hand cautiously slides across my bed, picking up the one closest to him.

I open up another portfolio, still skimming through. Miles is silent, taking forever to study the one drawing.

"There's a million more, don't get stuck on just one," I tell him, taking him out of his trance.

"Do you have any of my face? Aside from the recent one?" he asks.

"Um..." I thumb through some more. "I have this one." I pull out a picture of him that has a little more detail than just his mouth, but most of his face is shaded. "This is probably the only other one."

Miles carefully takes it from me, his fingers floating over the sketch. "Wow," he whispers.

"Since it was dark where we were, I can't really remember what your full face looked like. Mostly just your lips. Hence, all this." I motion around my bed to the drawings.

He swallows. "It feels like it was a lifetime ago but also like it was just yesterday, at the same time."

"I know what you mean."

"We can pinpoint the exact date and time we stopped being kids."

There's a deep throbbing in my bones. What I wouldn't do to go back in time and be an angsty kid whose biggest problem was feeling out of place. At the time, it seemed like the worst issue in the world, and now, I would welcome that pain over the one I'm stuck with for the rest of my life. But I guess that's how life works, what you're currently dealing with is the most prominent thing until something bigger takes its place.

"Fuck." Miles puts the drawing down. "I'd love a drink right about now."

"Yeah, I could definitely go for a nice high."

I watch as his hands roam over the pictures.

"These are remarkable, Rae. I don't know how, but you captured my emotions just from a drawing of my lips." He lifts his gaze to lock with mine. "It's incredible."

My insides sizzle with warmth. There's a strum of adoration beating through me the longer he fixates on me.

However, the fleeting, pleasant sensation is challenged by the unease creeping up my neck.

"I can show you other stuff if you want," I say, testing him. Waiting for him to say it's too much for one night, or we should slow down, or maybe he'll see the rest another day.

"Please," he answers.

My brow arches in surprise. Going back to the portfolio next to me, I riffle through what's in there and grab the most fucked-up, stomach-churning one I can find.

"Here." I show an image of a person stabbed in the heart. It's graphic, not shying away from the gruesome details of the pain expressed on the person's face and their body being drenched in blood as a giant sword pierces them through the chest.

Miles's jaw opens, and I can sense the smug look that's appearing on my face.

I knew he'd be disturbed by it.

"I love this," he states.

"What?"

Miles shifts his attention to me with a quizzical expression etched into his features. "I said I love this." He holds up the picture.

"No, you don't—look how fucking horrifying this is."

"Yeah, that's why I love it. Your artwork doesn't shy

away from anything you're thinking or feeling. It's you, completely exposed."

Annoyance tightens around my muscles, and I grind my teeth together. He wasn't supposed to get *that* from my art.

I snatch it out of his hands, pissed that he thinks he can strip me down to my soul just by looking at a stupid picture of one of my nightmares.

"Were you..." He cocks his head to the side, assessing me. "Were you trying to scare me away?"

"No," I lie.

"Good, because you should know no matter what you do or say, you're not going to."

I scoff. "We'll see about that."

"We sure will." Miles's eyes twinkle, and my belly jumps.

Scurrying to pick up everything on my bed and shoving them back into the portfolios, I say, "Well, you get the gist of the type of shit I draw. I think that's enough for now."

"Thanks for sharing it with me. I'm sure it's not easy."

"It's not."

It's extremely personal. It's the inner workings of my mind. I make sense of the world through art.

And I just showed Miles a little bit of what life looks like through my eyes.

That's the highest shit I've ever done, and I'm one hundred percent sober.

"You eat dinner yet?" I ask, pushing off my bed.

He follows my lead and rises. "No."

"We can order something."

"What do you have here? We can cook."

My face scrunches. "I don't cook."

"Well, I do." He takes it upon himself to walk into my kitchen and begin scouring the fridge. "Wow, you don't have much of anything."

"Yeah. I don't cook," I repeat.

"Or eat in general?" Miles teases, checking my pantry. "Here we go." Miles pulls out a box of pasta. "Spaghetti and..." He checks around for sauce with no luck, then goes back to the refrigerator. "Butter."

Not absolutely opposed to the idea, I grab a cooking pot and head to the sink to begin filling it with water.

"I got it," Miles says, standing next to me.

"I know how to cook pasta, Miles. I'm not *that* helpless."

"I want to cook for you."

"It's fine—"

"Rae." Miles softly places his hand on my waist, and I almost drop the half-empty pot of water into the sink. He brings his lips to my ear and begins to speak, his pitch dropping. "Sit your ass down on the couch and let me make you dinner."

Heat instantly crashes into my veins, coloring my cheeks. I nibble on my bottom lip, needing to tame my wildly beating heart. Nodding, I hand over the pot and grab a diet soda before walking into the living room without looking back at Miles.

Taking a long swig of my drink, I let the cold liquid cool down my insides. I can't believe the sound of his command about motherfucking spaghetti just made me have that kind of reaction.

My mind drifts off, thinking about how my body would respond if I'd let him command me in other ways.

I'd fall apart in his arms in a matter of minutes. There's no doubt about that.

Sitting down on my couch, I clench my thighs together, getting lost in the thought of allowing him to take over. Giving him complete control over me.

The condensation from my soda drips down onto the leg of my jeans, and I watch it soak into the denim.

"You only have diet?" Miles asks.

"What?" I twist my head up to look at him.

"You don't have any regular soda?"

I shake my head. "Too sweet."

He squints his eyes. "How do you function?"

"How do *you* function? The only thing I've ever seen you ingest is unhealthy amounts of sugar. I'm surprised it doesn't keep you up at night."

"It doesn't. Insomnia does."

"Maybe if you cut back on your sugar, then your insomnia wouldn't be as bad."

"Thanks, doc."

I take a sip of my drink. "No problem."

Miles spins back around to stir the pasta. With his back facing me, I allow myself to take several seconds to study him. His strong shoulders tug at his shirt, and the muscles in his arms flex every time he moves.

After spending way too much time fixated on Miles's back, I blink myself back into the room once he starts straining the spaghetti.

Without giving him any guidance, I watch as he moves around my kitchen, searching for bowls and utensils. When he finally finds them, he preps both bowls for us—each with some butter—and carries them over to where I'm sitting.

Steam is rising from the pasta as I take it from him

before he joins me on the couch. "We're not having a fancy dinner at my table?" I tease.

"You don't strike me as the type of girl who'd want that."

"I'm not."

"But if you'd like me to pull out all the stops, I could—"

"No. This is good."

This is more than good. This is the best treatment a guy has ever given me. Making me dinner and cozying up on the couch? That's fucking unheard of.

My chest burns with the yearning to experience more moments like this with him. But my brain is quick to throw a bucket of ice on any vulnerable feelings that are popping up.

It's like my insides are being torn apart—ripped at the seams as my mind has conflicting thoughts.

"What are we watching?" Miles scoops up the remote on the coffee table as if he's done this a million times before.

He's comfortable here. He's comfortable here... with me.

After chewing a sizable forkful, I answer, "The only thing I ever watch is true crime documentaries, but I don't care, you can put on whatever. I don't really pay attention anyway."

"Here we go," he says, landing on a TV show.

When my focus goes to the screen, I immediately grimace. "*Friends*? You want me to watch *Friends*?"

"I sure fucking do."

"A '90s sitcom?" I stare at him as he has a tight-lipped grin on his face. "Learn who your audience is, Miles. This isn't exactly my vibe."

His smile gets wider. "I know."

"Oh great, so you're torturing me."

"I'm letting you experience something different. Watching *Friends* is harmless."

"I'd like to do some pretty harm*ful* things to you right now," I mutter under my breath before taking another bite.

"You can bitch and complain about this all you want, but I guarantee in fifteen minutes you'll be laughing."

"Doubt it."

With that, the both of us stop talking and focus on eating our dinner and watching this incredibly corny show. Miles chuckles a couple of times as the TV plays.

My eyes drift over at him every now and again to gauge how he's feeling being here. Each time I spy on him, his features are lax. He's totally stress-free and at ease.

"This is a good part." Miles nods his chin to the TV without looking at me—meaning he knows I'm staring at him. Great.

I focus my attention back to *Friends* and watch as they struggle to get a couch up the stairs. One of the characters screams "pivot" a bunch of times, and even though it's ridiculous, I sense my cheeks rising.

Goddammit. Miles did it again. He made me fucking smile.

"Told you," he says, now completely focused on me, with his eyes brightly shining.

"Shut up. I'm not laughing, I'm smiling—there's a difference. So, don't sit there on your high horse thinking you won and got me to like this show."

He leans back with a smug look on his face. The

way he's staring at me sends a tizzy of emotions through my bloodstream, making me light-headed.

"You finished?" He points to the empty bowl on my lap. Once I nod, he takes it from me and heads to the kitchen sink.

"You can leave them, I'll put them in the dishwasher later," I state.

"I got it, Rae." Miles looks over his shoulder as he says that to me before putting them in the dishwasher with the strainer and pot. "Where did you learn to draw?" he asks, coming back to sit down next to me.

I shrug. "Self-taught."

"Oh. I didn't know if you had any of the art teachers at school help get you started."

"Like who, Mr. Falcone?"

"I guess, yeah." He takes a sip of his soda.

"No. He didn't help me with much of anything. Although I did lose my virginity to him, so I guess you could say he 'got me started' in something."

Miles's eyes bulge as he struggles not to spit out his drink. When he finally swallows, he responds, "For the love of God, please tell me you were eighteen."

"Nope. Sixteen. Fucked me right on the wooden table after class my junior year and never looked me in the eye after that."

Miles stays frozen, his cheeks turning a shade of scarlet red that I've never seen on him before. His jaw is clenching so tight he might crack his skull. "Christ."

"It's okay." I pat his shoulder. "He just saw a sad girl and wanted to make her happy, like all great men do," I say, placing my free hand on my heart in mock sincerity.

"How the fuck could he do that? Especially after

everything happened. Especially what you had to go through—"

I sit back and focus on the opposite end of the room. "Guys take advantage of the weak. It's nothing new, Miles."

"Look at me." He softly places two fingers under my chin to tilt my gaze up to meet his. "You are not weak, Rae."

"My track record says otherwise."

"Your track record says you survived it all, despite the trauma."

"Well, I don't think I'm doing a very good job at surviving."

"Why are you here right now? Living in Golden Bay Beach?" he asks, not letting go of my face.

"To start over."

"And why did you allow me to come over and be here with you?"

"To cook me dinner." I smirk.

"What's another reason, smart-ass?"

There's a loud thumping in my ears as my pulse speeds up. My mouth becomes dry, so much so that my throat gets scratchy. I part my lips slightly, wetting them to try to speak. Miles's gaze follows the movement of my tongue, and sparks shoot off inside my body.

"What was the question?" I ask, my voice sounding breathy. *Why the fuck do I sound like that?*

"Why am I here right now, Rae?" He drops his pitch like he did earlier in the evening, only this time, we're face-to-face. Goose bumps scatter across my skin and I watch his pupils dilate.

"Because I want you to be a part of my new start," I

answer. My brain spins with unease as those words come out of my mouth.

Miles must sense it because he pulls away and sits back.

The spot on my face where he was holding it instantly feels cold the second his fingers are gone.

"I think starting over is a pretty ballsy move. It's a big deal. And for someone to do that, they definitely have to be doing a decent enough job at surviving, otherwise, they wouldn't be able to withstand the change," he says, going back to the original topic. "Starting over is not easy."

"You'd know better than anyone else," I state.

Miles nods in agreement.

For a brief moment, my mind travels back to earlier on the boardwalk when he asked if I thought Cara was the one who was orchestrating all of this. Although I don't believe in that type of stuff, it does seem like a strange coincidence that both my and Miles's long road to "starting over" landed us here.

In the same spot.

A small beach town, hours away from a place we once called home. Neither of us was linked to this destination for any other reason than convenience. Our painful journey over the years both pointed us to the same place as if there was some otherworldly roadmap that had been planned out for a solid decade, leading us to get to this exact point.

A softness reaches my chest as my muscles noticeably relax.

Maybe I'm not a terrible sister if I choose to spend my time with Miles. Maybe it's okay if I do, just for a little while. Maybe, in a weird cosmic way, I'm meant to.

CHAPTER NINETEEN
Miles

THE SOUND of Rachel's whiny voice on *Friends* wakes me up. My heavy eyelids slowly peel open. With the sudden awareness that I'm not in my own home, I spring awake.

Sitting upright, my mind begins to settle when I realize where I am.

Rae's curled up on the opposite end of the couch, passed out. Her living room is dark, aside from the glowing light from the TV.

I swipe my hand over my face, trying to get oriented.

The last thing I remember was us talking about which *Friends* character is her least favorite—which is Ross—and then I must've knocked out.

I can't believe I fell asleep. I haven't fallen asleep without some type of sleeping aid in...God knows when —I can't even remember.

Checking the time on my phone, my eyes widen when I realize it's four in the morning.

Wow, I slept for a long time.

About an hour from now is when I usually start my day. I might as well go back home now and get an even earlier kick start to my morning routine.

Looking at Rae, warmth radiates through my chest. She looks like a tiny puppy coiled into herself.

It took me sleeping on the couch next to her to get almost an entire night's rest.

"Rae," I whisper, trying to get her awake enough so she can finish sleeping in her bed. Something tells me if I carry her to her room, she'd bite my head off, so I figure this is the safest bet. "Rae." I give her calf a little nudge.

Nothing. She's out cold.

"Hey, Rae, do you want to go sleep in your room?" I ask. She doesn't budge. There are only so many times I can call her name, so I try another approach. Getting closer to her and speaking a little louder, I say, "Oh darling...sweet pea...buttercup..."

"Fuck off," she mutters, which instantly has me cracking a smile.

"It's four a.m., why don't you go sleep in your bed?"

Rae grumbles something, eyes still screwed shut.

"Okay...well...I'm gonna head out." I begin to rise.

That seems to wake her up. She pops open one eye and lifts her head off the couch ever so slightly. "It's the middle of the night, where the hell are you going, Miles?"

"Back home."

She huffs and puffs, getting herself into a seated position. Her hair is in a loose bun, with stray pieces sticking out. Her mascara and eyeliner are smudged under her eyes. And even though she's scowling at me right now, I still find her breathtaking.

"Don't be stupid." Rae glares, then stands up and starts walking past me. "Just stay over."

"It's fine, Rae, I can just—"

She spins on her heels to look in my direction. "You woke my ass up so I could sleep in my bed. The least you could do is join me, so I have something nice to look at in the morning."

My brows rise in surprise.

"Don't give me that look," Rae snaps. "My brain's foggy." She rubs her temples. "I'm fucking sleep talking right now."

I draw in my bottom lip, struggling so damn hard not to say something.

"Whatever." Her arms drop to her sides. "Are you staying over or not?"

Well shit, I'm not gonna miss the opportunity to hold her in my arms while she sleeps. "Lead the way."

Turning back around, she trails into her bedroom, with me directly behind. When she reaches her side of the mattress, she unbuttons her jeans and lets them drop to the floor.

Forcing myself to look anywhere else aside from the black scrap of fabric that's being held up by her hips, I move to the window next to her bed and slightly open the curtain a tiny bit.

"What are you doing?" Rae asks, getting under the covers.

"I'm looking at the night sky," I reply, getting into bed with her. I opt for leaving my pants on, not wanting her to get the wrong idea of why I chose to stay here.

Squinting at me, she speaks, "You like looking at the night sky?"

"Yeah."

"Why?"

I shrug. "I don't know. It's calming to look at when I can't sleep. Makes me feel less alone."

"Huh."

Shifting my head on the pillow to see her better, my heart beats a bit faster when our gazes connect. Her focus is so intense as she studies me, neither of us can pull away. If this was any other girl, we'd be kissing, and in seconds our clothes would be off and I'd be on top of her.

But there's something about Rae that makes me enjoy these silent conversations. There's no need to distract myself with talk or touch because I'm too busy reveling in her enigmatic energy.

"Why do the stars make you feel less alone?" she whispers, her breath skating across my skin.

I turn completely onto my side, and she mirrors me. There's very little space between us, and it'd be easy to press my lips against hers and move on from this conversation. But I choose not to shy away from it because I think she'll understand where I'm coming from even if she doesn't believe it. "If you think about it, the sun and moon affect everything: seasons, land, sea, animals—even us. But the stars? They don't serve a purpose. They're just witnesses to what's happening in the world, and sometimes I feel like some of them are watching over me."

She stares at me quietly, letting my admission sink in. Blinking a few times, she parts her lips. "That's a really poetic way to say you think stars are the souls of dead people."

I smirk. "Thanks."

Then Rae does something uncharacteristic, making

my head spin from the sudden whiplash. She props herself up and innocently brushes her lips against my cheek. "Night, Miles." She's quick to flop over onto her stomach, her face turned away, obviously to avoid me.

"Good night, Rae."

I'm going fucking insane. It's eight in the morning, and I haven't slept a wink since coming into Rae's bedroom. Normally, I've already done my workout, showered, tidied my house, and eaten breakfast by now. Honestly, I would've left at least an hour ago, but Rae decided to use me as her human body pillow, and I don't have it in me to be the one who breaks the connection. I'm almost certain that as soon as she realizes her leg is hooked around my hips and her head is on my chest, she'll jump to the other side of the room. Hell, she'd probably jump to the other side of the state if she could.

My hand settles around her waist. My thumb grazes over her exposed skin from where her T-shirt rises.

I guess I can stay here a little bit longer. Not doing my full workout regimen isn't going to kill me.

Suddenly, her legs squeeze me a little tighter, and a small moan comes from behind her closed lips.

Yeah, I can definitely stay here longer.

She does a small movement with her hips, and even though it's the tiniest action ever, a flooding of heat bursts through my core, and my cock is now just as awake as I am.

Her thigh grazes over the zipper of my jeans, and I let out a shaky breath.

Trying to not focus on the aching bulge in my pants, I take the time to admire her—which doesn't really help my current situation, but at least I have the opportunity to study some of her tattoos.

The leg that's currently wrapped around me is adorned with a distorted human, peeling off its skin and exposing its skeleton. It might come across as creepy and unsettling to some, but for me, it furthers my curiosity.

The desire to know what the rest of her body looks like builds inside me, but I push it away so that I don't prolong my current dilemma any further.

The jarring noise of my phone going off startles the both of us. As I search for where I put it last night, Rae shoots up wide-eyed and promptly untangles herself from me.

Once I find my phone, I silence it, noting to myself to call back one of the town shop owners later.

Rae mumbles something under her breath as she scoots over to her side.

"Sorry to wake you," I say softly.

She yawns. "What time is it?"

"Eight."

"Oh my god. Good night."

I chuckle at her dramatic response. "I'm gonna head out so I can catch up on some things."

Rae frowns. "Oh."

"Is that okay?"

"Yeah, it's fine, it's just...I feel kinda weird right now. It's like you're doing the walk of shame, but we didn't fuck. I've rarely stayed the night long enough to wake up next to a guy, and if I did, it was definitely because we slept together the night before."

"Yeah, I know the feeling. It's weird for me, too."

"So...what do we do now?"

"There only seems to be one solution." I give her a sly grin, and she whacks my arm. Laughing, I continue, "I'm joking. We're taking things at your speed, so why don't we each go about our day, and when you're ready to see me again, you can shove another knife down your garbage disposal?"

"It was a fork."

"My apologies. When you're ready to see me again, shove a *fork* down your garbage disposal and text me."

Rae bites down on her lip, fighting back a smile. "You're annoying."

"Does that mean you're agreeing to the plan?"

"I guess."

Leaning over, I do the same thing she did to me last night and place a chaste kiss on her cheek. "Go back to sleep. I'll see you later."

She pulls the comforter up over her mouth, hiding the little grin she's wearing. "Bye, Miles," she says, her voice muffled.

Before leaving her room, I give her a wink, and she continues to shield her face. There's a lightness in my steps as I exit her condo and move on with my day.

As I walk forward, there's a pull to go back to her stronger than there ever was before. Although absolutely nothing physical happened between us last night, I feel even more connected to her. It's an unshakable feeling, like maybe our past happened so that our present could align.

However the cards may land, I know I'm leaving it up to Rae.

It's all in her hands.

CHAPTER TWENTY

"HI, I'm Regina, and I'm an addict," the woman across from me says.

"Hi Regina," everyone in the room says in unison.

It's been twenty-four hours since I've seen Miles, and in that time, I've done nothing but sleep and paint. I figured I might as well go to another NA meeting just to ground myself before diving headfirst into the next phase of our super-snail-speed relationship. I want to be clearheaded and make decisions that aren't entwined in anxiety, impulsivity, or guilt.

Sam isn't leading today's meeting. It's the same woman from the first time I was here, who I learned is named Tonya. She has her dark hair pulled back in a slick ponytail, and she encourages Regina to speak.

"I've been off heroin for a long time now, but I've struggled for months with Suboxone," Regina continues.

Yep, heard that story about a million times in rehab. Suboxone or methadone is supposed to help wean people off the drugs, but people just end up buying them to get high. I've been warned plenty of times by doctors and social workers. I was on it and taking it as prescribed in rehab and eventually got to a point where I didn't need it anymore—which feels really fucking good.

Regina shares about her bumpy road, speaking about how she initially got hooked and how hard it is for her to stay clean.

Pulling some air into my lungs, I silently plead to whatever spiritual entity is out there to let me stay clean. I can't fathom what my life will look like if I end up struggling as much as Regina has in order to stay sober.

"Thank you for sharing," Tonya says to Regina once she's finished telling her story. Tonya's gaze drifts over to mine. "Would you like to share anything today?" she asks me.

I shake my head.

As we move on to the next person and they begin to speak, my stomach knots.

I don't know if I'll ever be ready to tell my story because if I share everything, I'll have to relive that catalyst of my addiction.

My eyes prick with tears that are begging to be released. But I continue to force them to stay inside, just like I do with the story. I've never spoken a word of that day to anyone after it happened. I wonder if Miles ever did, if he ever had the courage to relive the worst moment of our lives and actually tell someone.

With that, I'm taking my phone out of my pocket to send him a text.

> **Me**
> did you ever tell anyone about that day?

A few minutes go by, and I tune in and out to a man named Davis speaking about his recovery.

> **Miles**
> I have. Only one person

> **Me**
> was it hard?

> **Miles**
> extremely.

Slipping my phone back into my pocket, I focus on the others in the circle with me. All different types of people and all different backstories. What I've learned over the years is that addiction doesn't discriminate. It'll eat any person alive, no matter who they are. Addiction doesn't care if you're a teacher, priest, stripper, or parent—it'll find you. In the beginning, it's a better option than to remember the trauma, but eventually the addiction becomes a part of the trauma and fucks you over tenfold.

When the meeting wraps up, I grab a cup of coffee and make my way out of the basement. A sense of gratitude swims through my veins as I walk outside. Oddly, I'm thankful that Miles and I have gone through similar issues stemming from the past incident we experienced together. Because I know I'm not alone.

Reaching back into my pocket, I send him another text.

> **Me**
> where are you right now?

> **Miles**
> working on flooring in a new store Sam
> bought

> **Me**
> oh, okay.

> **Miles**
> come swing by if you're free

He drops me his location, and I see that he's only several minutes away on the boardwalk, near the amusement park.

> **Me**
> I guess there are worse things I could
> be doing than coming to visit you

> **Miles**
> I'm taking that as a compliment

Smirking, I make the decision to turn left toward the shop Miles is at instead of the opposite direction on the boardwalk, where my condo is.

When I approach the store, it's sandwiched between other shops, only this one has glass windows from ceiling to ground. Popping my head in from the door that's propped open, my heart stutters when I spot Miles.

He's at the far end of the store, kneeling as he uses a mallet to bang a piece of laminate flooring into place. He's shirtless, and sweat drips down his hard muscles, accentuating each one as his body glistens. His snug jeans hang low on his hips, letting the band of his boxers peek out. And to top it all off, he's wearing a backward baseball cap—making him look like a damn whore.

"Hey." My voice comes out a lot higher than it ever has before, and I immediately clear my throat to fix my pitch.

Miles's attention springs forward, his face lighting up the moment we connect gazes. "Couldn't find anything better to do than to come see me?" He rises, tossing the mallet next to him, then uses his arm to wipe the sweat off his forehead.

I'm suddenly aware of how hot it is in this space. There's only one small box fan blowing by the front door, but it's becoming increasingly boiling with each passing millisecond I'm in here with him.

"It was either this or let Emma convince me to get my nails done with her," I joke.

"Glad I beat out Emma."

"Oh, you didn't. You just beat out getting my nails done," I tease him once more, and he chuckles. My eyes drift around the room. There's not much in it aside from us and a table with his tools on it. "So, what is this place?"

"I'm not really sure yet. Sam bought it and wants to rent it out eventually, but he wants it to be something different than all the other shops around here. I'm just helping him make the place look nice for potential renters," Miles explains.

"Oh." Checking under my feet, I realize I'm not standing on any laminate flooring yet. "Need help?"

His brow arches. "You want to help?"

"I'm not doing much else."

"All right." His cheeks rise with amusement. "Get on your knees, Rae."

My stomach flutters, and a flushed feeling travels up my neck to my face.

I slowly sink to the floor, my eyes trained on Miles the entire way down. He wets his lips as his gaze drops, studying me. Blinking a few times, he snaps himself back into the present and joins me on the floor.

Miles comes to my side and reaches for his mallet. "Give the wood a little tap like this." He demonstrates. "And then I'll work behind you and use the nail gun."

After he hands me the mallet, I tap on the wood as instructed.

"A little harder," he states. "Here, I'll help you."

Miles then inches closer, and his hand connects with mine. My body can't help but burn up under his touch as we bang against the piece of laminate together. There's a tingling sensation on the tip of my tongue, anxious to taste him again—only this time, I want to taste *all* of him.

His breath brushes against my shoulder, and a droplet of sweat rolls down his arm and crashes right against my skin.

Turning my head to face him, I see his eyes are already fixated on my mouth.

My nerve endings catch fire under his lingering gaze. The sound of my pulse accelerates in my ears.

At the same time, both of us lean forward until our lips are planted on one another's. Bursting with passion, our tongues dance around as our hands do the same.

In one swift motion, as if rehearsed, he scoops me up and carries me to the table, where he seats me and spreads my thighs apart so that his body is up against mine.

Our breathing is hurried as we stare at each other. Opposite from our rushed action, Miles tenderly caresses my cheek, then swipes his thumb over my bottom lip.

My heart pounds faster with every slow movement he takes.

Miles glances down to my neck and swallows. "Can I ask you something?" he rasps as if his words were tumbling over gravel.

"Sure," I answer, my voice unsteady.

"Do you always wear this choker necklace?"

"Yeah. Why?"

There's hesitation in his eyes, as if he's debating whether or not to respond honestly. His fingertips dance around my throat, skimming over the black, thick fabric that's wrapped around my neck. "I've been thinking about what it would look like if my hand was there instead."

"Fuck," I breathe out.

That was the sexiest thing anyone has ever said to me. If I weren't already melting from the heat in this room, now I definitely am.

Before he can say another word, I wrap my arms around him, tugging him into me.

We continue to kiss, the tips of my fingers running over his slick muscles. Desire pools in my core as I ache for more of him.

He latches on to my hips, gripping tight. I snake my hands down his body to the button of his jeans, and he mutters curses under his breath.

Miles brings his mouth to my ear, licking and sucking. Shivers race through me as I struggle to concentrate on getting his pants off of him.

"You ever going to tell me what you like in bed, Rae?" he whispers against me.

My heart rattles in my chest. "It's not so much what I like...it's what I *think* I'll like," I answer truthfully.

He pulls back to look at me. A wild expression flashes on his face. "So, a fantasy?"

"I guess you can call it that."

Once again, he brings his hand to my neck, exploring my soft skin. Needing to drink him in again, I kiss him, unable to stop.

A fire for Miles, and only Miles, ignites within me.

We're so needy for each other, neither of us can stop and finish the conversation without some type of contact.

"What's your fantasy, Rae?" Miles asks into my mouth, my tongue devouring his words.

All of my reserves fall to the wayside. My barriers drop to the floor as I dissolve against him, ready and willing to let him in to what I want. Because if there's anyone I feel could deliver—it's him. "I want..." I struggle to get the full sentence out because my lips are tangled up with his. "I want you to control me—all of me. Everything." My hips have a mind of their own as they grind up against him, needing friction. Miles clutches me tighter, and I try to get more words out. "I want you to talk to me—I want you to tear me down and build me back up again." My thoughts come out staccato, out of breath. "I want to come apart in your arms, only to feel whole."

Miles stops kissing me and inches back. Flames

burst in his eyes, and I get the gut feeling he knows exactly what I want.

"I don't want to think," I pant. "I want to—I *need* to get out of my head."

Slanting forward, he plants his hands on either side of me on the table, his breath blowing against my face. "What's your safe word?"

"I don't need a safe word."

"You absolutely fucking do. What's your safe word, Rae?"

My eyes drift up and land on his backward hat. "Baseball?"

He nods. "Works for me."

Then, he leans forward so that my back is against the table. My legs wrap around his hips the moment his mouth tugs on my earlobe.

"Hey, Miles, I found—" Sam's voice comes from the doorway.

Miles and I instantly snap apart like shrapnel.

"I'm sorry, I can come back—" Sam starts to speak again, but Miles stops him.

"No, it's okay." Miles adjusts his jeans. "We were just..." He looks over to me to help him out, but I got nothing.

"Making out," I state the obvious. No point in trying to hide it.

Miles chuckles, taking his hat off and smoothing over his hair before placing it back on.

"Well, I don't mean to interrupt," Sam states, his cheeks turning red. "I just came over to ask if you would be able to install some new light fixtures. I found some unique ones online. But I can show you another time."

"No, go ahead." I jump down from the table. "I

have to head back to my place anyway." My eyes lock with Miles, and I give him a look that says *you better get your ass to my condo to finish what you started as soon as you're done with this*.

He wets his lips. "I'll catch up with you later."

With that, I'm out of the store and hightailing it to my condo.

My pulse is thrumming in my ears the faster I move. I buzz with a craving for Miles—longing for him to take me and do whatever the fuck he wants with me.

The more I walk, the more the image of him in my bed grows. My body feels like it's about to burst into a million pieces at any second.

"Rae!" Miles calls out from behind me.

Pivoting, I spot him running toward me. Still shirtless and sweaty.

My mouth dries up with the urge to have my thirst quenched by him.

"That was quick," I say as he jogs up to me.

"You won't be saying that again once I'm through with you." His hand links around my waist, and he spins me back around so that we're speed walking toward my condo.

In the blink of an eye, we're about to walk inside, and he only lets go of me for a brief second to take out his T-shirt that's tucked into his back pocket. As soon as he tosses it on, his hand is around me again, practically pushing me through the door.

"Hey Emma." Miles gives her a nod, ushering me toward the elevator.

Emma looks up from her computer, and her face brightens. "Oh! Hey you two."

The corners of my mouth turn upward as I give her

a wave, not having enough time to even say hello because Miles is barreling us forward.

When we make it to the elevator, there's an elderly couple also waiting. Miles quietly lets out a frustrated sigh, but it's enough for me to hear, and I chuckle to myself.

I feel the same, Miles.

Fishing for my keys, not wanting to stall us any longer once we get to my door, Miles guides me into the elevator behind the couple. His hands find the space between where my shirt and pants part, and he rubs his calloused fingertips over my skin.

It's a small, simple action, but it's enough to wind me up even more.

The second we hear the ding and the metal doors peel open, we're racing toward my condo.

Once we're inside, we're on top of each other like wild animals that can't be tamed. Growing hungrier and hungrier with each touch and taste.

Miles clutches my back as he walks forward and I backward until we land in my bathroom.

"I need to shower," he states, pulling away from me.

"Okay," I answer, my chest heaving. "Go ahead, and I'll meet you in my bedroom after—"

"I didn't say for you to go anywhere." Miles pushes the bathroom door, and as soon as the knob clicks closed, his eyes darken with lust, as if a switch has just gone off.

I thought he was hot before, but *this*? The way he's looking at me right now is otherworldly. Like he's going to devour me, but not before savoring every bite.

He pins me in place with his stare. "You sure you want to do it this way?" he asks, letting me know that if

I want tender lovemaking, *now* would be the appropriate time to tell him before he takes over.

My tongue grazes my bottom lip as my body begins to vibrate with excitement. I don't want soft and gentle. I want him to make it hurt, then soothe the ache. "I'm sure," I rasp.

"Take everything off," Miles commands, his voice dropping an octave. Flames burst inside me at the sound. Gone is Golden Bay's sweetheart, as this sexy, authoritative man takes over, corrupting his image.

My breath stutters. With trembling hands, I fumble out of my clothes, watching Miles turn on the shower, getting it ready for us.

Spinning around, he looks at me, drinking in my naked body slowly and carefully. His throat bobs as he swallows, restraining himself not to pounce on me.

The pounding of my heartbeat gets louder the longer he stares at me, not saying a word. I've never been one to feel the need to hide my body or feel uncomfortable being naked around a guy. But the way his gaze is raking over me is making my cheeks burn. It's as if he's looking beneath my skin, all the way through to my very essence.

Miles stalks over to me, and I sense myself backing up against the wall.

I'm not scared of what he's going to do to me. He can fuck me any way he likes, as hard as he wants, and do whatever the hell he pleases. But the emotions that are starting to simmer in my chest, the ones I think might have something to do with being so vulnerable together—*those* I'm terrified of.

Miles tucks a stray hair around my ear and trails his finger down my neck, around my collarbone, and continues until he pinches my hard nipple. "You're absolutely gorgeous, Rae."

I wet my lips, prepping for another kiss. But it doesn't happen. Instead, he lines his cheek up with mine and whispers in a rough voice, "Now, get your ass in the shower so I can give you what you deserve."

Nodding, I do as he says, tensing for a moment when the water sprays against my skin. Glancing over my shoulder, I watch as Miles loses his shirt and hat and unfastens his jeans, pulling them down with his boxers. My pussy clenches on command when I see how ready he is for me.

Joining me in the shower, he steps into my space. Steam wraps around our bodies. Wet skin touching wet skin. Chests heaving against one another. Our breaths mix, the water dripping down our bodies.

My pulse moves quicker and quicker.

He bends down only to pick me up and pin me against the cool tile. I sharply breathe in as my legs naturally wrap around him like they've done before. He lifts me higher than usual, so he's in line with my breasts.

I shudder against his mouth as he draws my nipple in, sucking hard.

Miles gives the same attention to my other nipple, and this time, I moan behind my tightly closed lips. He bites down, and I squeeze his arms as I shamelessly grind against his muscles.

A low chuckle rumbles in his throat. "Someone's fucking needy."

"Miles," I whine, clamping my eyes shut.

He lowers me only slightly, sliding my back against the wet wall. "You want me to give you what you want?" He sucks on my neck so strongly that I yelp instead of answering. But my hips do the talking for me as I continue to search for relief against his skin.

My throat stings from where his mouth just was, and he continues to explore the rest of my neck and chest, giving them the same burning sensation.

My body shakes, not wanting to wait any longer. "Please," I whimper.

His mouth turns upward against my tender flesh. And suddenly, he lets go of me, my eyes flinging open as my feet land on the tub.

With unsteady breaths, Miles takes his long fingers and lets them dance around my thighs. Inching closer and closer.

"You're pretty when you beg," he says, smirking.

Water slides down his statuesque body, and his hand nudges my legs apart. Widening my stance for him, I allow him access—so fucking ready for him to do whatever he's planning on.

Miles plays with my slit, causing me to tremble. His fingertips hover over my clit with a featherlight touch. But he doesn't move them. "You want to come?" he asks, his voice thick with desire.

I nod, breathless from anticipation.

"Then work for it."

I nearly collapse, my body buzzing from the heat. Feeling stripped of my defenses, completely and utterly, I obey his command. Holding on to his fore-arms, I move my hips, working my clit against his barely there touch.

I move faster and faster, trying to rub up against him as much as possible.

He gives me nothing. He doesn't move, doesn't

smirk, doesn't talk. He just watches me trying to get off on him.

Feeling so desperate for him does something to me. Sparks ignite in my bloodstream as my need escalates.

My nails dig into him, and I pick up my pace, chasing my pleasure.

So close. I'm getting so close to finding some relief.

With trembling legs, my moans get louder. My shoulders rapidly lift and drop, and my muscles begin to seize up.

On the edge, just needing to work a little bit harder, I quicken my pace.

Almost there.

So. Fucking. Close.

Miles immediately rips his hand away.

Shocked, I stare at him for a beat. "I-I didn't—"

"I know. You're not allowed to finish yet," Miles states. "On your fucking knees, Rae." Tingles run up and down my limbs. Slowly, I kneel for him, my eyes locked on his the whole way down. "Good girl."

A small moan comes from behind my lips.

"You like when I call you that, Rae?"

I nod, panting.

"What else do you like being called?" he rasps as he begins to stroke himself in front of my face.

"You can call me anything you want," I say before replacing his hand with my own.

Miles smirks at my comment just before I take him into my mouth. My gaze still focused on him, I watch the cords in his neck strain.

"Every inch, princess."

I clench my thighs tighter, hating myself for how much I love him calling me that.

I take as much of him as I can until his cock hits the back of my throat. Pulling back slightly, I begin to hollow out my cheeks and suck.

"Holy shit," Miles grits. His hand latches on to my wet strands of hair as he fiercely moves my head back and forth for me.

I hold on to the back of his muscular legs to steady myself as he fucks my mouth relentlessly. He continues to hit the back of my throat, and my eyes water. But that doesn't stop me from watching him.

Miles clamps his lips shut, his muscles tensing with each stinging yank of my hair. His intense gaze connects with mine, lighting more of a fire in me.

I want more.

More of him acting like this. More of him taking control. More of him making it hurt so good.

"You're such a good slut for me, Rae."

I moan, the sound vibrating against his cock and he jerks.

"You like that? You like when I tell you what a good little whore you are?" he asks as he struggles to keep his voice even.

I nod, my clit throbbing with lust as I continue to get him off. Needing to cure the ache, I drop one of my hands from him and slip it between my legs.

The second he realizes what I'm doing, he pulls himself out of my mouth. "Stop," he demands. "Don't fucking touch yourself."

I freeze, my heart colliding with my bones, sending zaps of desire throughout my entire being. "Please," I beg for the second time tonight.

"Absolutely not. *I'm* going to be the one that makes you come. Understand?" Miles still grips my hair but loosens up enough for me to nod once more. "Good." He drops his hand and tenderly slides it over my jawline and to my chin, where he holds it in place. "Open your mouth and stick out your tongue."

Pressing my thighs closer together, I do as he says, the corners of my mouth tipping up. Miles pumps himself in one hand while keeping his other on me. His abs flex over and over again as he reaches his edge.

Water from the showerhead is heavy on my lashes, but I flutter them open to watch Miles come apart. His legs tense, and my body trembles.

"You're so fucking sexy on your knees, Rae."

Sticking my tongue out farther, he loses his composure and comes all over me. My lips, tongue, cheeks, nose, and chin are covered in his warm, salty cum that he continues to release. Until finally, he lets out one groan and lets go of himself and me.

Even though he's still in a daze, catching his breath, he reaches for a nearby towel. Extending his arm to the towel rack, when he finally grabs it, he bends down and wipes my face.

Once I'm clean, he tosses the towel and helps me to stand. Grabbing my loofah and soap, he silently washes the rest of me. Bringing his lips to brush over my forehead, my breath stops.

After everything that we just did, *that* feels like the most intimate.

Once the both of us are rinsed down, Miles whispers in the shell of my ear, "Your turn."

CHAPTER TWENTY-ONE

MILES LAYS my slick body on my bed, dampening the sheets beneath me. The yearning, building demand to have him make me orgasm, becomes overwhelming.

He stands at the foot of the bed. "Spread your legs for me."

Pushing up on my forearms, I part my legs so that he can get between them. Lust pours out of him as he becomes fixated on my body.

He toys with me, running a finger over my opening. "You got this fucking wet from sucking my cock?"

"Yes." I bite down on one side of my lower lip.

"Such a dirty fucking girl," Miles says right before slipping his finger inside me.

With that, I collapse onto the bed, letting the sensations take over. My hands fist the blankets as he rubs his thumb over my clit. Faster and faster with each swipe.

Euphoria coils around my muscles as my legs begin to shake like they were in the shower. Gasping for air, I cry out his name over and over again.

Miles places his other hand a few inches below my belly button and adds pressure.

"Oh fuck!" I scream, reaching the height of ecstasy.

"Feels good, princess?"

My back arches off the bed the rougher he gets with my pussy. "So. Good." I moan even louder.

The tips of my toes feel like they're on fire, and the burning sensation barrels all the way through my legs and up to my core. Drawing in a sharp inhale, my entire body tenses.

"That's it, Rae. Come for me," Miles says as my insides twist.

One last swipe of his thumb and I practically fly off the bed, writhing and screaming in pleasure. My legs slam shut, but he keeps working me with his fingers.

A round of aftershocks shudders through me, and I tremble, my heart rate skyrocketing.

When I finally regain hold of myself, my body turns limp, resting against the mattress. Catching my breath, I watch Miles draw his hands away from me and stroke his now hard cock.

"Get on all fours," he says, eyes blazing. My brows furrow in confusion because I thought we were all done. "All fours. Now. Don't make me repeat myself."

Excitement prickles under my skin as I reposition myself on my bed. The mattress dips slightly when he kneels behind me.

A pounding in my chest riots against my rib cage as I wait.

And wait.

And wait.

Curling the sheet between my fingertips, I brace

myself, my patience wearing thin. My breath shakes, anxious for him to start.

Then I realize what *he's* waiting for. What he wants.

"Miles," I plead, pressing my ass up against his warm skin. "Fuck me." I hear his uneven breath, but he still doesn't move. "Please?" I whine, begging.

Miles pulls away, and without any further warning, he slams into me. I scream, lunging forward.

My body stings with pleasure.

He grips my hips and thrusts in and out of me, harder and harder each time. Our sounds fill up space as I let him consume me. Making my body his.

Taking one of his hands, he grabs a fistful of my hair and pounds stronger than before.

"Are you on the pill?" he asks, panting.

"IUD."

"Thank God."

With each movement, I sense myself giving in to him even more. Feeling alive in a way I've never felt before.

Feeling alive with Miles. Allowing him to own every inch of my skin.

My muscles tense with each harsh thrust, and I love it. I love the pain that fuses with the pleasure. I love the fireworks exploding in my veins as I shriek from desire.

Miles's cock pulses inside me. "Fuck," he moans as he starts to still.

Slowly, he pulls out, his cum dripping out of my pussy and down my thigh. Lowering myself, I relax my body against the blankets, panting.

My eyes shut as I become completely sated.

As my heart rate goes back to normal, I sense myself becoming so calm I might fall asleep.

Suddenly, there's a heavy arm wrapping around my naked frame.

Popping my eyes open, I sit up, letting Miles's arm slink down my torso as I twist to look at him. He's nestled on his side, looking as cozy as ever.

"What the hell are you doing?" My gaze drifts down to his arm that's still settled around me.

"Cuddling you," he states, dropping his role as Miles the sex god and slipping back into his endearing self.

"Why?"

"Because I just banged the fuck out of you, and now I want to hold you." His brows draw in as he angles his head to get a better look at me.

"I'm not the 'snuggle after sex' type."

"Didn't you say the other day that you've slept over at guys' houses before?"

"Yeah, but we'd either get high or pass out after sex —not lie there and *cuddle* each other," I say as if it's a foreign concept.

Miles narrows his eyes, attempting to figure me out. "Are you freaking out because we just had sex or—"

"No."

"Or what we did during it? Because if you didn't like it, that's what the safe word's there for. We don't have to do any of that again if you didn't like—"

"No, I liked it. I *really* liked it."

"But cuddling is where you draw the line?" he asks, sincerely wanting to know what my boundaries are.

"I..." My belly tumbles over itself as I get fixated on his beautifully painted irises. "I'm willing to try."

"I don't want to push you if you're not comfortable—"

"You're not. I'm pushing myself," I reply, slipping under the covers.

Miles joins me, and our bare bodies connect. "You know, you technically cuddled me the other night."

"I was sleeping, I had no idea what I was doing." I situate myself, tensing, waiting for him to squeeze me into him.

There's silence and stillness as I continue to freeze next to him.

"Would you feel more comfortable if you rested against me instead of me holding you?" he asks.

"Maybe."

I watch as Miles rolls onto his back, waiting for me to perch myself next to him. Scooting closer, I very slowly put my head on his chest and lay one of my arms near his stomach. The strum of his heart bellows in my ear, and I'm happy to find out that it's going just as fast as mine.

Delicately, Miles begins to play with the ends of my hair.

My trembling breath skates across his skin as my nerves try to convince me to pull away and run from any type of couple-y shit.

"Baseball?" Miles asks, checking in by using our safe word.

I shake my head even though it's resting on him. "No."

For a while, the only sound in the room is our breathing. My muscles begin to find some ease as my body starts to mold to his.

Miles runs his fingers up and down my back, goose

bumps forming in their wake. The more they swipe over my skin, the more trancelike I become, sedated by him.

"Rae?" Miles interrupts my daze with his warm and tender voice.

"Yeah?"

"Out of all the men you've been with...how many treated you like Mr. Falcone did?"

My face scrunches, puzzled. "You mean, how many older men did I sleep with?"

"No." He clears his throat. "How many of them took advantage of your pain?"

My throat dries up. I swallow the hard truth. "All of them."

Miles's hand stills on my body. "That's what I figured."

The realization makes my heart sink, and I think he can tell because that's when he fully wraps his strong arm around me.

"You know I'm not doing that, right?" Miles asks.

"Yeah," I whisper. "I know."

CHAPTER TWENTY-TWO
Miles

A WARM WAFT of air from an open window brushes over my bare chest, waking me up. I blink a few times, waiting for things to come into focus. Noticing I fell asleep in Rae's room, I perk up.

There's an empty spot in the bed where she had lain cuddling me just a little while ago. Looking around, I don't see her anywhere, so I make my way into the hallway.

Stopping at the bathroom, I gather my clothes and quickly get dressed. My head is still spinning from how mind-blowing our sex was. It wasn't out of the ordinary for me to play out that kind of dynamic with a woman, but it's never been as incredible as it was with Rae.

My body is aching for more of her, wanting to savor every last drop and then do it all over again.

The way she let herself go under my touch was magnificent to watch. And there's a burning desire in my core to watch her like that a billion times over.

Zipping up my pants, I stroll down the rest of the hallway and spot Rae in her natural state, her icy hair up in a bun, a stained, oversized white T-shirt on, and a paintbrush in hand. Her legs are bare, aside from the artwork that's already inked onto them.

Earlier, I got to see the rest of her tattoos. Every single one. I tried to take my time to ingrain them into my brain, but my throbbing need to fuck her won.

Still, I noticed them. The shattered glass around her heart and rib cage, the monster on her back. But the words that are scribed directly under her collarbones, across the entire length of her chest, are what got to me the most. "Product Of The Problem."

I tried not to let it shake me in the moment, to not let it take me out of our first time of being together. But for a brief second, it did.

A knot in my stomach forms thinking about the phrase. I understand it. And sometimes I feel like that too, but what I wouldn't give to show her she's more than just that.

Rae stands there with a sour look on her face, staring at her back living room wall, completely unaware that I'm right here. There are a few strokes of paint on the plain, cream-colored wall, but nothing else. Nothing like the giant skull mural that's directly opposite it, which I made a comment about the first time I was here.

"Hey," I say, making my presence known.

Rae turns her head. "What's up, Sleeping Beauty?"

I chuckle. "I can't believe I passed out. You should've woken me up."

"Not when you have insomnia. My home must have magical powers since this is the second time you've fallen asleep." *I don't think it's so much the home as it is the company*. "Don't worry, you didn't sleep that long—maybe like three hours?"

"Three hours! Shit, I wasted half the evening."

"Or maybe you were utilizing your time to catch up on some much-needed rest. Not everything's about productivity, Miles."

"Says the girl who's working right now."

"I'm not working. I'm creating."

I stroll over to her. "You're right."

"I know." Rae proudly lifts her chin and faces the wall, her little attitude making my heart dance.

"So, what are you painting this time?"

She dips her brush in black paint and starts smearing it on the wall in a messy cross-stroke. "While you suffer from insomnia, I suffer with the ability to sleep, only to be woken up by my nightmares."

"Seriously? You should've gotten me up—I don't want you to have a nightmare next to me and—"

"It's okay, Miles," she says, her voice getting gentle. "I've been dealing with them for years. I'm sure you have too, which is part of the reason why you don't sleep. But I know how to handle them. The only way to get them out of my head is if I free them." She points to the beginning of her artwork. "I'm not going to hit up my dealer or take a long walk off a short pier—instead, I'm going to paint." She forces the fakest smile I've ever seen in my entire life, and I can't help but tilt my head back with laughter.

"How many times did they have to hammer that kind of stuff into your head at rehab?"

"More times than I can count." Rae goes back to focusing on the wall.

"Does painting it out help, though?" I ask.

"Oh, definitely, I can't even deny that. It's just that the other two options seem a lot more tempting at times."

"I know the feeling," I state, watching her add more black. It's mesmerizing, staring at the tiny flicks of her wrist as more color whips across the large wall.

Without looking at me, she says, "Grab a brush."

"What?" I snap out of my daze.

"Quit staring and come paint with me."

"I'm not an artist—"

"I don't care. Pick up a goddamn brush, Miles."

My face splits into a grin as I saunter over to her coffee table and grab a random brush. "I thought I was the one who was supposed to be giving the orders around here."

"Only when we're fucking. Any other time, I'm the one who's in control."

"I can live with that." The irony is that even in the bedroom, she's the one in control. I might be the one who's playing out the power dynamic, but the moment she says the safe word, the act is dropped.

Rae glances down to my hand. "Why are you holding the brush like that?"

"Like what?"

"Like you're about to stab someone. It's a paint-brush, not a fucking murder weapon."

I look at my tight-fisted grasp around the brush, and yeah, it kinda looks like I'm about to shank someone.

"Here," she says, adjusting my fingers, sending mini shock waves to my chest. Once I have a gentler grip, she goes to her palette and pours a glob of white paint on it. "Start with this."

"What am I doing?" I ask, dipping into the liquid.

Rae goes back to the wall. "Anything."

"I don't want to screw up your art—"

"You won't."

Glancing down at the paint on the tip of my brush, that's when it clicks. "Is that why you're having me use white? So you can cover it up with a dark color after?"

Her lips curl up into a smirk. "Possibly."

Chuckling, I say, "Good call."

Rae's focus remains in front of her, and I study each swift movement she makes. Her talent is striking as she creates a masterpiece out of nothing.

"Can you tell me the image in your head so I have something to run with at least?" I ask.

"I bet you have a pretty clear image of my nightmare already," she states.

I do, but I've pushed it away, and I'm not willing to bring it back to the forefront of my mind. It's kind of nice to have someone who knows what those memories look like without needing to go into detail. She was there. I was there. We both know the mental pictures that are flipping through our heads.

White is the last color I'd use to capture that moment, but I'll stick with it for the sake of her new mural.

"Don't overthink it," Rae says. "It's not about the product, it's about the process. There's something liberating about momentarily letting it out."

"I don't know what I'm doing."

She sighs and stops to look at me. "Did you ever get into a zone in baseball? Where you just let it take over and you forgot everything else around you?"

"Yeah."

"So, just put your brush to the wall and get in the zone. Don't think, just let your arm move."

Rae goes back to painting, and I follow her lead, starting to move the paintbrush back and forth.

It's nothing. Thick lines as if I were getting paid to paint the wall for real.

Suddenly, Rae shoves my arm, streaking the white in a jagged line.

"It's too perfect," she states. "Art isn't supposed to be perfect. It's supposed to be real."

Then she gives me a tiny smile that makes my stomach jump. "Show me what you got, Miles."

And with that challenge, I'm making squiggly lines, adding dots and random shapes like a fucking child. At the very least, I can say it's fun, even though it looks horrendous.

As I get sucked into my own painting, I lose track of what Rae's doing.

Until I hear faint laughter coming from next to me. "That looks...really good." Rae fights back more laughter as she studies my section of the wall.

My jaw drops open, mocking offense. "Didn't you just say it wasn't about the product?"

"It's not." She tilts her head to the side, examining the shitty artwork. "But I actually like it. It's very...you."

I narrow my eyes at her. "Care to explain?"

"No."

Of course not.

She goes back to what she was doing, leaving me hanging on what she meant by that.

On impulse, I dab her cheek with my paintbrush, and she gasps at the sudden action.

"What was that for?" Rae asks, surprised.

Honestly, no clue.

I shrug. "You look cute when you're dirty."

"If you call me cute one more time, I swear to God," she says, struggling not to smile as she speaks. She might be fighting back the urge to allow the corners of her mouth to lift, but the look in her eyes is a giveaway. There's a flicker of joy that melts the icy-blue hue for a split second.

"What if I call you my little lamb instead?" I tease.

"Ew. No."

"Bunny?"

"Never."

"Kitten?"

"You're literally just naming animals."

"Firefly?"

"Ah, I see we've moved on to insects," Rae states.

"Damn, you're making this real tough," I continue to joke. "Guess I'll have to think of something more creative for our date."

"*Our date?*" Her body tenses.

In an instant, I sense her guard come slamming down, shutting me out. I should've predicted this. I can only get so close to Rae before she pulls back. It's a little dance she does, but I'm more than willing to learn the moves.

"Yes," I reply.

"You're not taking me out on a date." She marches over to her art supplies on the coffee table, avoiding me.

I assume being blunt is the best option with Rae, so I decided to state it as it is. "So, let me get this straight. I can come all over your face, but I can't take you out?"

"Exactly."

"That seems a tad ridiculous."

"No, dates are ridiculous. They're boring and an archaic practice. We're hooking up—no need to get food beforehand."

My eyebrows rise. "Wow. Sounds like you've had some horrible dates."

With her back turned to me, she says, "I've never been on one."

"*What?*" I stare in disbelief.

She spins around with fresh paint on her palette, nodding in response.

There's a pit in my stomach, growing for her and what she's missed out on—and what it was probably replaced with.

It's strange how Rae's so worldly yet has experienced the bare minimum in life.

"So, your knowledge of dating is based on assumption?"

"It's based on observation." Rae goes back to working on the wall, but I still her hand with mine.

"You know," I say, my voice becoming tender, even though I know it might get her to close up even more. "Most dates aren't boring. They can be really fun."

Her gaze goes to where our hands touch, and she swallows. The pulse in her delicate veins flutters under my fingers. It speeds up the longer she debates on how to respond.

"What makes your dates so fun?" There's a snide tone to her question.

"Well, for starters, you'll be with me." I grin, purposefully trying to rouse her.

"Cocky asshole," Rae mutters.

I slide my hand off of hers. "Is that a 'you'll think about it'?"

"It's an 'if I'm doing this, then you better not make it suck.'"

A chuckle rolls through me. "All right."

"I'm serious. I'm already going in with the mindset that it's going to be horrible, so you better make it worth my time."

"I'm going to woo the fuck out of you, Rae."

Her lips purse together, holding in a laugh. "Oh god. I'm already regretting this."

"I promise you won't."

There's a flash of something hopeful in her eyes, but she's quick to mask it, turning back to her painting. "Get back to work," she says, gesturing with her chin toward my paintbrush.

"As you wish, princess."

"*That* name is only for the bedroom."

"Noted."

I whirl around the white paint and pretend to doodle, but really, I'm watching her. Captivated by everything she does and all of who she is. There's a stirring in my chest as I make a promise to myself to make our first date one she'll never forget.

Making it so good that, hopefully, it'll take up more space than some of the bad memories.

CHAPTER TWENTY-THREE

Miles

FOLLOWING my art lesson at Rae's, I decided to give her some space and head back to my place.

After making chicken cutlets for one, I place the leftovers in the fridge and sit down at my handmade kitchen table with a cold soda, staring into the abyss.

Usually during the quiet nights, the past starts creeping in, trying to shake up my inner world that I worked so hard to build.

Rae had a point when she said life isn't about productivity.

It's about moments. Little things.

I'm aware of that, but I feel useless when I'm not working toward something. And when I'm not working, or with someone, or watching TV—that's when I'm alone with my thoughts.

It's when I feel lonely.

A reminder that I have no family, and frankly, I never did. I was seen as a prop and a ticket to my parents' dreams. Not a son, let alone a human.

You'd think after having a near-death experience,

my parents would've gotten closer to me. Hell, I would've thought they'd cling to me.

They did at first, but what started as concern for their child turned into them using my experience for clout. Once the interviews stopped and the news stations had other stories to cover, my parents pushed me away even further.

I think a part of that was because they didn't want to feel all the emotions that would come with getting close. Loving a son and realizing he was almost taken away—my parents could never have the emotional depth to experience that. So, it was easier to push me away than it was for them to feel.

Sometimes, when I lie in bed, staring up at the stars for endless hours, I wonder what they're doing. If they regret the way they treated me. Or maybe they regret having me to begin with.

It's thoughts like those that would replay on an endless loop in my brain, which would make my drinking worse. Needing to stop the thoughts with something. Getting them to shut up for a few hours until I was inevitably alone again and feeling even worse. During that time, it was as if my addiction swallowed me whole. Those were the darkest years of my life. If I didn't have the string of hope that I gripped onto, I don't think I would've made it through.

I've always had more of an optimistic outlook on life, and frankly, I have no idea where I got it from. Perhaps the need to be the complete opposite of my parents. I know how evil the world can get, I don't want to add to it. I want to be the one that brings the light into someone's dark world, not continue to blanket their life with wickedness. That little spark inside me was what got me sober.

Sighing, I lean back in my chair, allowing the feeling of pride to swirl around my bloodstream.

I've worked hard for the life I have now. To get back to me—the real me. Feeling positive and cheerful again. Helping others. Creating moments of happiness despite the past.

Living in this bungalow isn't a life of luxury, but it's mine. My home that I can honor as my new beginning.

The next morning, I drive over to Sam and Gloria's house. It's a two-story Tudor with a large stone patio and lush garden in the back. Gloria spends most of her time planting and making both the inside and outside of their house look pristine.

Walking inside, I call out a hello as I make my way to their kitchen like I have hundreds of times before. Sam's getting a jug of orange juice out of the fridge, and Gloria's setting the table.

"Morning, Miles," Gloria beams. "How are you?"

"I'm good, but I bet I'll be even better once I eat your delicious food." I rub my hand over my stomach before sitting down.

I would help him, but I've been yelled at for doing that by both him and Gloria more times than I can count.

When I first got to Golden Bay, they saw a lost, broken kid, and one of the ways they helped me was by being overgenerous with the number of meals they fed me. We used to have weekly dinners, then it turned to monthly as I started working more. Now, they're at random.

We had originally planned for me to come over for dinner tonight, but since I'm taking Rae out, we changed it to breakfast.

"Sam told me that you're dating someone?" Gloria asks with excitement on the tip of her tongue, placing a tray of french toast and bacon onto the table.

The delicious scents whirl together, and my mouth automatically waters at the same time a growling comes from my belly.

"I am," I say, staring at the food, not wanting to start eating before they do. "Her name's Rae."

"You knew her in high school? Is that right?" Gloria looks over to Sam for confirmation on if she got the information correct.

"Sort of. We had one interaction and never saw each other again after that."

"Wow, and you two somehow found each other after all these years," she states with a twinkle in her hazel eyes. She's around the same age as Sam, and it's obvious she's a hopeless romantic just by the way she gazes at him on a daily basis, so it's no surprise that she's soaking up the story of me and Rae.

The two of them finally sit down and start eating, so I join in, piling up my plate.

"Yeah," I say to Gloria in between my bites. "Weird how that kind of played out."

"They mesh well together," Sam states to Gloria.

I snort. "How would you know? You've barely spoken to Rae."

"I know her a little more than you might think."

That's when it registers. Sam must've talked to her at an NA meeting. He won't tell me either way, so I leave it alone and nod at the unspoken words.

"Have you found anyone to rent the new store-front?" I ask, shifting gears.

"A few interests. Nothing that we'd like in there, though." He squeezes Gloria's free hand, and she smiles. It's nice to have a couple like them as role models. It doesn't seem as far-fetched to be in a happy partnership as it once did.

"What kind of store are you looking for?" I ask her.

"I haven't put my finger on it yet, but I'll know it when the right person comes," she states.

I can't for the life of me understand why she's being so selective on who rents out the space and what type of store it is. But it's not my place to pry, so I'll let it be.

"So, tell me about Rae," Gloria circles back.

"I'm taking her out on our first real date tonight."

Her face lights up. "Oh my goodness! Where are you going?"

"Haven't figured out all the details yet."

"Did you get her flowers?"

"She's not a bouquet of flowers type of girl."

Gloria stands up, her chair squeaking. "Miles, you're not showing up to your first date without flowers. Follow me." With that, she walks out of the room and toward the side door to her house.

"Better listen to what she says," Sam mumbles before eating a forkful of french toast.

Nodding, I walk out to the backyard, where I spot Gloria in her extravagant garden. Her clippers are in her hand, ready to make a bouquet for Rae.

"What about roses? Does she like roses?"

"I don't think so," I state, glancing around the array of colorful flowers. Rae would probably only like roses if they were wilted and already dead.

"Daisies?" Gloria asks.

I shrug.

"Peonies?"

"Maybe?" I don't know anything about flowers.

Gloria continues to wander around her vast greenery while my eyes trail along with her. Spotting some small, dainty flowers sprouting from the dirt, I point to them. "What about those?"

She twists around to see what I'm talking about. "Oh, those are just wildflowers. You don't want those, you want something special."

"Those are special. They're the only ones that remind me of her."

Gloria grins. "All right, then. Go ahead and pick as many as you'd like. I'll string them together for you and make a nice bouquet."

Crouching down, I dig through the dirt, pulling up a variety of tiny flowers. They're a mixture of types and colors. Each one is unique.

"Here you go." I hand them over to Gloria. "Thank you for letting me have some."

"Of course, anything for you, Miles." She smiles, patting my arm.

And just like that, I have step one of my date planned.

Now, I just need to figure out the rest.

CHAPTER TWENTY-FOUR

Miles

SEVERAL HOURS LATER, I'm getting out of my car holding a handpicked bouquet for Rae. Gloria fancied the wildflowers up, adding some leaf-looking things and wrapping them in burlap string and lace. It's not too over the top, so I don't think they'll make Rae entirely nauseated by the cliché gesture.

There's a simmering of nervousness in my chest, but more than anything, I'm excited. I can't wait to show Rae what a real date consists of and sweep her off her feet while no doubt annoying her at the same time.

Whistling, I enter SeaScape Condos and spot Emma tapping her pen on the front desk counter.

"Hey, Emma." I flash her a smile.

She perks up, noticing the flowers. "Where are you going with those?"

"About to go out on a date with a certain someone."

Emma gasps. "This is so exciting! Tell Rae to come find me tomorrow—I want to hear about everything."

I chuckle as I move past her and toward the elevator. "Will do."

My heart pumps a little quicker as I make my way to the second floor and down the hallway. Knocking on Rae's door, I rock back and forth on my heels, waiting for her to answer.

When she finally does, my breath gets stuck in my throat at the sight of her. My gaze washes over her, paying attention to every single detail.

Her glacial-blue eyes pop out even more under her thick, mascaraed lashes and precisely lined eyeliner. She wears a black-and-white headband, while her loose wavy hair kisses the top of her collarbones. She wears a tight black tank top, which dips down, showcasing more of her tattoos. Dropping my attention a little lower, my eyebrow quirks when I notice the rest of her.

"A skirt?" I ask, smirking as I admire the denim cutoff skirt she has wrapped around her thighs.

"I'm behind on laundry. Don't read into it," Rae states.

Of course, Rae. I will definitely not read into the fact that you dressed up for our date.

"All right. Let's do this thing," she states with bare minimum enthusiasm.

Ignoring her lackluster standpoint, I hold up the bouquet that's been tucked next to my leg. "These are for you."

There's a slight curl of her lips. "You got me flowers?"

"I sure did."

Extending my hand toward her, she takes them from me and begins to admire them. Her gaze flutters over each one as her fingers thumb through the delicate petals.

"These are cool," she says, and relief settles around

me. I knew she wouldn't call off the date because of them, but I wasn't sure if she'd be pleased. *Good call, Gloria.*

Rae trails into her kitchen, and I lean my weight against the doorframe, watching her. "I don't own a vase," she says, opening up cabinets. "At least, I don't think so. My parents might've stocked me with one, but I doubt it." Taking out a tall drinking glass, she fills it halfway with water and places the flowers inside, centering it on her kitchen island. "This will have to do. Looks nice, right?"

Making sure to make direct eye contact with her and not the flowers, I say, "Looks beautiful."

Her cheeks turn pink, and she clears her throat. "So, where are we going?"

"It's a surprise."

"I hate surprises."

"I figured."

When we pull into the parking lot of our first stop, Rae's face drops.

"Are you serious?" she asks.

"As a heart attack." I get out of the car and dash around to the passenger side to open the door for her. She glares at me as she gets out.

"Okay, I know I'm not an expert on dating—but is this supposed to be romantic? Because I think I missed the memo."

"Trust me, you're gonna love it."

Looping my hand around her waist, I guide us to

the front of Golden Bay's Batting Cages, paying for our equipment and getting us safely into our own cage. The metal chain-linked fence rattles as I close it behind us.

"I thought you didn't play baseball anymore," Rae states.

"I don't. Baseball and going to the batting cages are two different things," I say, slipping batting gloves onto both of her hands. "It's like saying your artwork and getting paid to paint someone's bedroom an ugly eggshell color are the same. Similar in theory, very different process."

Her eyes narrow. "Is that why we're here? You're getting back at me for making you paint?"

"There's nothing to get back at you for. I enjoyed painting with you, even though I was horrible. You showed me something that you love to do, now it's time for me to do the same."

That silences her.

Putting the helmet on, her head wobbles around as it's almost swallowed whole. I chuckle at how charming she looks. Little sparks shoot off in my heart.

"Have you ever played baseball?" I ask, assuming the answer.

"Hell no. I cut gym most of my entire high school career."

"Then I'll show you what to do." Passing her a bat, I show her how to hold it using mine as an example. "Your dominant hand goes on top like this." Rae does as I say, and I walk her over to where she's supposed to stand. "Widen your stance and anchor into your left foot."

"This good?" she asks, following my instructions.

"Almost. Bend your knees slightly." Dropping my

bat, I come behind her, adjusting her stance. "Lean your torso forward a bit." Gripping onto her hips, I pull them back just a little while the rest of her goes forward. She lets out a small gasp, and blood instantly rushes to my cock. "This okay?" I check before going any further.

"Yeah." Rae has a breathy response, and she sweeps her hair over to one side, exposing her shoulder.

Very carefully, I trail my hands over both her arms, reaching all the way down until I hold hers that are wrapped around the bat. "I'm going to show you how to swing."

"Okay."

"You're going to start with the bat up here," I say, moving the bat as I speak, getting her muscles used to the action. "Then as you swing, you twist but stay grounded on your left foot." We practice together a few times, going over the motions. "Got it?"

"Maybe."

"All right, I'm going to step out of the cage and hit the button. They'll be slow at first but will get gradually faster."

"I think I can handle balls flying at my face," Rae jokes.

"Of course you can."

Laughing, I step out, and the gate rattles once again as I shut it behind me. I give her a nod as a heads-up, and she gets into the stance I showed her. Seeing her with baseball gear on, in her skirt, as she stands there pushing her ass out, makes me dizzy with lust.

As soon as I hit the button, a ball is released, and she squeals in an unexpected, girlish manner.

"That was fucking fast!" she yells at me.

"Pay attention!" I point to the next ball that's coming for her. Rae jumps back, startled. "Get back into position," I instruct and she's immediately back to where she should be.

Another ball comes, and this time she actually tries swinging but misses.

"Good job," I tell her. "This time, ignore everything else. Just focus on the ball."

She nods and once again swings and misses. Instead of encouraging her, I keep quiet, letting her get into a zone. Allowing her to feel *my* version of art, where everything melts away and the only thing there is to keep you occupied is what's directly in front of you. Truthfully, I used to love baseball before it became a chore, and at times I miss it. But I wouldn't trade making it to the major leagues for this moment with Rae at all.

The action of hitting and missing repeats several times until the last swing, when she taps the ball with the tip of her bat, making it fly to the side.

"I hit it!" She spins to me with a look of amazement lighting up her beautiful face.

"You sure did!" I say, entering the cage. Rae takes off the helmet, adjusting her headband and smoothing over her hair. Once her hands fall away, I place a kiss on the top of her head, proud of her for giving this a try.

"Now it's your turn to show me up," she states, gesturing toward the bat.

I smirk and get myself geared up as she steps out.

I get into my zone, ignoring the fact that the reason why my heart is beating faster is that she's standing right there. With each delivery, I swing, making the ball speed across to the opposite side of the cage.

I might not play baseball anymore, but I love coming to the batting cages. Not only does it take my mind off things and make me feel better, but it also helps me get some pent-up aggression out. Each hit lets me release my emotions.

By the end of the round, my forehead begins to sweat from exerting myself. I take off my helmet and shake out my hair as Rae steps in.

"Holy shit," she says, blinking. "How do you do that?"

I shrug. "How do you make art?"

She shrugs back, not knowing how to answer, and neither do I. "Watching you was...it was..." She struggles to find the right wording.

"It was that good, huh?" I tease.

Her tongue peeks out, wetting her plush lips. "Honestly, yeah."

"I thought you looked sexy, too." I wink and notice the rosy color brush over her fair skin.

"Even though this isn't what comes to mind when I think of the word date—it didn't completely blow," Rae admits.

I chuckle. "Just wait until you see what else I have in store for us."

I took Rae to one of the nicest restaurants on the water, complete with an oceanside view—not that she doesn't see it every day from her condo, but still, it's nice to have dinner surrounded by beautiful scenery.

Since it's getting warmer, more people are trickling

into town, so we got to see several sailboats and Jet Skis from our table.

Now that we've finished eating, we're strolling along the boardwalk, headed to our next stop. Rae walks beside me, her attention flitting back and forth from the stores to the beach. With a gentle touch, I graze my pinkie finger over her hand, seeing if she'll let me hold on to it for real.

Her head snaps to me, and I sense the tension in her body, but she doesn't stop me from intertwining our fingers into a full grasp.

"Baseball?" I mutter our safe word, assessing if this is too much for her.

Rae shakes her head as she wears a hint of a smile. Her palm is smooth and delicate against my rough skin, and a jolt of excitement seeps through me when she holds on to me a little tighter.

"Where are we going next?" Rae asks, her voice becoming softer.

"Right there." I point to the pier with the amusement park.

She snorts. "Seriously?"

"Yep. We're gonna go on a bunch of rides that make us dizzy and eat a bunch of shitty, sugary food for dessert."

"I thought you'd want something else for dessert," she toys with me, her mouth widening into a playful grin.

My eyebrows rise. "Damn, Rae."

She starts giggling. *Actually* giggling. The sound is so enchanting I can't stop staring at her as her face brightens with delight. It's like another wall has dropped as she radiates an element of joy.

"You should see the look on your face right now." Rae points, still laughing.

"I mean, listen, if you'd rather *that* kind of dessert, then I'll take you back to my place right now."

"Not yet. I want to finish our date. I'm having a... moderately okay time."

"I'm not fully fluent in Rae yet—does that mean you're enjoying yourself?"

"Something like that," she says. "But—the date isn't over yet, so technically there's still time for it to suck and for me to be right."

I smirk. "Whatever you say."

I guide us toward the park, the flashing lights drawing us in. The smell of fried foods swirls around us as a roller coaster with screaming people whizzes past. It must be date night for all the couples in town, judging by the number of people holding hands and flirtatiously laughing with one another.

I steer Rae away from the loud couple play fighting at a shooting arcade game and stop short in front of a food kiosk. "We're starting off with this," I say.

Rae's eyes drift upward to look at the glowing sign, and her face automatically twists. "Cotton candy?"

"Yep."

"It's literally food coloring, sugar, and air."

"Exactly."

Eagerly, I purchase a giant heap of a hot-pink cloud on a cardboard stick. I pluck a piece off and shove it into my mouth, the sweetness instantly hitting my tongue. Rae watches me, her nose scrunching in pure disgust.

As I lick the stickiness off my fingers, her focus goes to my lips, and suddenly the expression on her face switches to something else.

"Your turn," I say, pushing the cotton candy toward her and ignoring the fact that I might've just turned her on a little.

Rae stares at it for a beat and very carefully pulls off a tiny piece. Locking eyes with me, she sticks out her tongue and places the pink fluff on it. She winces as she closes her mouth.

"Oh my god." Her features draw in tight. "This is awful."

I can't help but laugh at her reaction. "You want some more?" I tease.

"Hell no." Rae coughs as if she's choking on the sugar.

I take another gigantic bite, preparing myself for a rush of energy that's sure to come, seeing that I'm the only one who's going to be eating this. "Did I lose points on the date by making you try this?"

"No. But you're lucky I'm open to trying new things." Rae's eyebrow arches.

"I sure fucking am." I wink and watch as it affects her, making her pupils dilate.

Her lashes flutter a times, and she composes herself. "Since you made me eat that crap, I get to pick our first ride."

"That's fair."

She mulls over all her options: roller coasters, a fun house, Tilt-A-Whirl, and the Ferris wheel. "That one." She points.

I follow the invisible line she makes with her finger, and when I see the ride she's suggesting, my head tips to the side. "The carousel?" *I didn't see that coming.*

"Yeah. I used to go on that when I was a kid." Her expression softens as if she's reliving the nice memory.

There's no longer a question on my part—that's what we're doing first.

"Sounds good to me. I'll grab us tickets." I gesture to the ticket booth a few feet away. "Be back in a sec."

Taking the cotton candy with me, I make sure to finish as much as I can before going on rides. I purchase a bunch of tickets, unsure of how long we'll be here, but I'd rather have extra.

By the time I tuck them into my pocket and toss the leftover cotton candy, I spin around to see Rae surrounded by three guys.

I know all of them, they're in college, and their apartment burned down a few months ago. Travis, Evan, and Brad.

They're close to her, like a moth to a flame. But who could blame them? Rae's the kind of person who instantly intrigues someone. She has a paradoxical air about her: tough but delicate, closed off but dripping with sex appeal. There are layers upon layers to her, and I'm sure it's most straight guys' dream to hand-shred them until she's left bare.

I watch as they joke with her while subtly checking her out. She seems half-amused by what they're saying, as a small smile is on her face.

There's a rousing protectiveness in my gut, but I know Rae's the type of person to handle things on her own if there is an issue. I have no doubt in my mind that she'd do much worse than tell them off if they were pissing her off right now.

Strutting over to her, I place my hand on her lower back. A slight power move which all three of the boys seem to notice as they casually create distance from Rae. "Hey guys," I say to them with a genuine smile.

They can flirt with Rae all they want. Doesn't bother me. I know she's hot as fuck. I also know that I'm the one she's going home with tonight.

They all say hey, and give a tip of their chin as a greeting.

"We were just catching up with Rae. Haven't seen her much lately, so we were just checking in," says Travis.

"They were trying to convince me to have a funnel cake," Rae states. "To which I informed them that I'd rather not puke my brains out tonight."

Travis chuckles. "I swear they're delicious."

"I just got her to take a bite of cotton candy. I'll work on the funnel cake on our second date." I make light, but they all get what I'm saying.

"Oh, sorry. We didn't mean to interrupt." With that, they start backing away. "We'll see you guys later. Bye, Rae." Travis flashes her a grin, and she gives him a wave.

When they're out of earshot, Rae cranes her neck to look up at me. "You weren't getting jealous there for a second, were you, Miles?"

I bend down, whispering close to her, "I don't have to worry about college boys, princess." I press a kiss to her temple, noticing as she smirks. "Come on, let's go on the carousel."

Dropping my hand from her back, we meander past people and rides until we reach the one she wants to go on. She picks a dark-gray horse with a red-and-white saddle, and I pick the brown one next to her.

There's a bright glimmer in her eyes as she holds on to the golden spiral rod with one hand. Her skirt hikes up, exposing more of her thighs, and for a quick moment, I wish I could trade places with a plastic horse.

The loud carnival-like music starts playing, and old-fashioned bulb lights flash overhead. The carousel begins turning, and our horses move up and down, opposite from each other.

"You used to come here when you were a kid?" I yell over the music, finishing our conversation from a few minutes ago.

"Yeah, until middle school. My parents used to make me and Cara take Grayson here, and we'd pretend that we hated going on a little kids' ride, but we secretly loved it," Rae states with a sense of joy tickling her words. Her horse moves up as I move down, and she continues, "What about you? Did you ever come here with your parents?"

"No. We didn't take many family trips—and if we did, it was for my dad's work. I usually stayed in the hotel room with a babysitter until I was old enough to be alone. Then I'd sneak out of the room and find a cute girl to keep me occupied."

"Got it."

Before getting lost in thought about my pseudo-family, I shut up and bring my attention back to Rae. She tilts her head back, letting the breeze push her hair back. If she didn't have her headband in, it would probably look wilder, but it's tame for now. Her shoulders relax, and there's a lightness about her energy, as if she's getting sucked back into a time when the chains from her trauma didn't weigh her down.

She lets herself go for the length of the ride until it begins to slow down, and I watch the slight high exit her body.

"Have fun?" I ask.

Rae nods, nibbling on her bottom lip.

Getting off the ride, my hand finds hers, and she slips her fingers between mine. "What's next?" she asks.

I point at the far end of the pier at the massive ride. "Ferris wheel."

Rae stops dead in her tracks, yanking me back with her. "Uh. No."

"Why not?" My face contorts, confused by her abrupt change of heart.

"I'm scared of heights," she blurts out.

"Your condo is on the second floor."

"Exactly. Any higher than that, I'd have a panic attack. That's as high as I go."

"I thought you used to get a lot higher than that," I joke.

Rae chuckles, loosening back up. "You know what I mean," she says. "Look at that thing." Her wide eyes drift up to look at how tall the ride is. "What if our bucket comes loose and we plummet to our deaths?"

"Then, it'll be a really nostalgic moment—the two of us clinging to life as we cling to each other. I'll even give you a kiss goodbye to seal the memory."

She gapes at me, blinking. But not a second later, she bursts into laughter. Louder than I've ever heard her laugh before as her shoulders shake along with her. "Your humor is way more fucked up than you let on," she states.

"Dark humor to cope with trauma—I can't be the only one."

"God no. I'm just glad I finally met someone who's on my same level."

"Me too," I state. There's a slight pause as Rae continues to stare upward. "So...what do you think?"

Her mouth scrunches to one side as she bites down on the inside of her cheek, debating. "I'd think we already survived round one of potential death together. Might as well see if we make it through this round."

"Works for me."

Our hands join once again as we make our way down the pier. When it's our turn to get into the bucket, I can feel her fingers start to tremble as her grip grows tighter. She freezes before stepping on first. Her hesitation makes me have an immediate change of heart.

"Maybe we should do this later," I suggest, sensing her fear building.

"No. It's fine."

"We don't have to do this, Rae. There are plenty of other rides—"

"I said it's fine," she snaps. "Just help me get in." She holds on to the edge of the bucket with one hand while still holding on to me. Walking behind her, I help her step in. The bucket rocks, which causes her to fall into her seat.

This isn't a normal Ferris wheel that you'd find at a carnival. This is Adventureland's biggest attraction. It's just under two hundred feet tall, overlooking the boardwalk and the beach. Each bucket is big enough to hold six people, and there's Plexiglas on every side with a climate-control fan overhead.

The ride attendant closes the door behind us, and Rae lets out a long gust of air.

"Are you—"

"I'm fine," she cuts me off.

The moment we start moving, her hand clamps

onto my thigh. Gently, I run my thumb over her silky skin, trying to ease her.

Rae's eyes dart all around, taking everything in. Her shoulders noticeably rise and drop quickly.

The ride pauses, and we slowly swing back and forth.

"Oh my god—Miles, why are we stopping?" Her words come out rushed as her voice gets higher.

"To let the next people on," I inform her.

"I don't want to stop—I just want to go!" Her entire body begins to shake with nervousness. "I want to get this over with!" She starts taking sharper breaths.

My stomach drops with guilt, realizing she's about to have a panic attack. "Look at me." I try to avert her attention off of how high we are right now. She keeps her focus trained on our surroundings, getting more and more worked up. Changing my tone, this time I command her, "Rae. Look at me."

She immediately does as I say, and our eyes lock. I can feel the fear pouring out of her—something I never wanted to experience with her again and certainly not be the cause of.

Her gaze goes to my lips, and that's when it clicks.

Without any hesitation, I kiss her, trying to take away every last drop of worry. Rae's grip on me moves up to my chest as she clings to my shirt. She pulls me in even closer, begging me to erase her state of panic.

Just as our tongues meld together and her body begins to relax, we start moving again. She flinches, accidentally biting my bottom lip. There's a small shriek of fear as she pulls back, watching us get higher.

"Holy fuck—"

"Keep your eyes closed," I instruct.

"I can't!" Rae's voice gets shrill, and her body becomes tense once more. "Distract me, Miles—please!" Her gaze bounces back and forth between the people under us on the pier, getting smaller, and the ocean on the other side, growing wider. "Please, do *something*, Miles!"

Thinking on my feet, I do the one thing that comes to mind.

Tugging her headband down, I turn it into a makeshift blindfold, covering her eyes. She's thrown off by what I'm doing as her breathing changes.

Bringing my mouth to the shell of her ear, I darken my pitch. "Keep your eyes closed. Listen to the sound of my voice. And do everything I say."

CHAPTER TWENTY-FIVE

MY HEART CRASHES against my ribs as my brain begins to get hazy. No longer able to see anything, all of my other senses become heightened. My ears tune in to the sound of my breath shaking out of my lips, the little fan whirling above us, and the deep resonance of Miles's voice.

I shouldn't have tried to go beyond my limits and go on this stupid ride, but everything else up until now has been better than I could imagine, so I figured going on the Ferris wheel wouldn't be *so* bad.

I was wrong. So fucking wrong. And now I'm panicking like an imbecile, making a complete fool out of myself.

"Still with me?" Miles asks, whispering. I nod, thankful that my headband is thick enough that all I can see is blackness. "I'm going to reposition myself. The bucket is going to move slightly." He takes my hands and curls them around the edge of the bench on either side of my legs. "Hold on if it makes you feel better. I promise you're okay."

"Okay," I whisper back.

"Ready?" he asks. When I nod once more, we begin to swing as he moves somewhere else. My fingers grip onto the bench so tight, my knuckles start hurting.

"Miles?" I stupidly call out, knowing he couldn't have gone too far.

There's a soft touch on both of my knees, and I gasp.

"I'm right here." His words vibrate through my body right before he presses a kiss to my leg.

My breath moves in and out of me so quickly I have to wet my lips before they become chapped.

"Relax, Rae," Miles says, slowly parting my legs. He drags his mouth along my inner thigh.

"W-what are you doing?" Another stupid moment on my part—but my head can't comprehend that he's about to do *that* here.

"Calming you down," he speaks against my skin. "Sit back." A hand comes to my stomach, encouraging my back to rest against the bench.

A switch goes off inside me, hyperfocused on Miles. No longer able to see my surroundings, all of my attention goes on him—his rough fingertips inching closer to my denim skirt, the way his breath rides up my leg, the sound of his need dancing on the tip of his tongue as he speaks.

My fears become diminished as desire takes the wheel.

Miles opens my thighs even wider. My pulse quickens as my body heats up. He slides his hands up my skirt, and I can feel the goose bumps prickling beneath his touch.

His calloused palms run against my skin, taking an achingly long time to do anything else.

Continuing to grip the edge of the bench, I impatiently wait for his next move.

I'm not sure how long we stay like this, but not being able to see what he's doing makes it feel like hours.

The second Miles trails his fingers along my panties, my entire being shudders. I'm already so close to finishing, and I've barely been touched.

He pulls the thin fabric to the side, and I gasp when he blows cool air onto my clit. I try to clench my legs together to get some relief. Ripping his hand out of my panties, he forces my thighs apart even farther.

"No fucking way, princess," he snaps at me, sending a shiver down my spine. Thrusting his hand back under my skirt, the moment he gets to my hips, he yanks me forward. I yelp from surprise as my body becomes slanted. My ass hangs off the seat, and my head now rests against the back of the bench.

I tremble with a flurry of excitement as he pulls my thong down. He adjusts my legs so that my panties are fully off of me. God knows where it landed.

Tension wraps around me as Miles rakes his fingers up my right calf in a calculated manner. My uneven breath escapes my lips at a faster rate as he gets closer to where I want him to be.

Continuing up my leg, his mouth follows behind his hand, kissing my knee and inner thigh. His warmth tickles my skin, and I scoot myself closer to him.

Miles chuckles. "Eager much?"

I don't respond because he knows the answer.

He flips my skirt up, and the cold air hits my bare

body. "God, you're gorgeous," Miles says before circling the pad of his finger around my clit.

My back arches as he continues to send sparks through my veins.

"Another couple could be watching us right now," he states, sliding his finger through my wetness.

"So?" I try to maintain my composure, but it's slipping away from me the more he touches me.

"They could watch you come apart on my fingers." He kisses the innermost part of my thigh. "Or maybe I'll have them watch you come on my tongue instead." Another kiss. "You like that idea, princess? Of having people watch you come for me?"

My legs begin to quake from his words as flames ignite in my core. "Yes," I answer, but it comes out more like a moan.

I'd bet anything that Miles is smirking at me right now.

"I knew my dirty whore would want that." He takes his hand away and blows cool air along my pussy once more, eliciting another gasp from me.

I have no clue if people are watching or if they even could with how we're set up, but the idea of it has me squirming closer to his face.

"Tell me how bad you want it, Rae."

"S-so bad."

"Be a good girl and beg for me."

My heart thumps rapidly in its cage. "Please—please, Miles."

"More." He licks my other thigh, torturing me.

"Fuck," I cry out with frustration that I love. "I want —I need you to make me come."

He shakes his head. "More."

"Dickhead," I mutter, pretending I hate this. But he knows I'm straight up lying because he laughs, enjoying making me writhe with desire.

"Keep going," Miles hums and begins to massage the inside of my legs.

I naturally move my hips along to the tiny rhythm he creates, wishing something other than air was hitting my clit. Heat spirals down my spine as I begin to throb. Unwilling to draw this out any longer, I use the truth to lure him in. "I want you to be the first guy to make me come this way."

Miles freezes. "What?"

I sense my cheeks reddening. "You heard me."

"Has anyone ever tried to—"

"Once, my dealer Ben. It was horrible, and I faked it." My words come out rushed, not wanting this conversation to last any longer.

There's a long beat of silence, then I feel his warm breath lining up with my center.

"On behalf of men everywhere, I deeply apologize that no one has worshipped your pussy like you deserve."

With that, he flattens his tongue against me, and my back nearly flies off the seat. I clamp my mouth shut to dampen the feral sounds coming from my throat.

Miles hooks my right leg around his shoulder and rapidly licks my clit, picking up the pace. Wriggling under his hold, there's an explosion of passion pulsating through me.

He becomes beast-like, the strength of his hold around my thigh becoming bruising as he forces my left leg even wider. His teeth graze over my sensitive skin, causing me to take in a sharp inhale.

Slowly sweeping his tongue over my entire pussy, he lets out a deep moan. "You taste so fucking sweet."

Something about his comment makes me smile. "Don't stop," I say through my ragged breaths.

He brings his mouth to my clit, sucking and licking at the same time. An electric shock scorches through my body. Reaching out, my hands immediately find his hair, and I latch on, pulling him closer to me. I grind myself up against his mouth as he continues to bring me to the edge.

He gets rougher. I get closer.

My head dizzies, intoxicated by Miles.

High off of him.

A beautiful, euphoric feeling swirls around my veins as my legs violently shake.

And with one last harsh suck on my clit, I shatter under his tongue, becoming completely unhinged. Moaning and screaming. Trembling over and over again as he continues to lap me up, not stopping.

Miles keeps his tongue going as my orgasm tears through me longer than ever before. My pulse soars as my body twists and turns from a fiery amount of lust.

Finally, he eases up, and I go limp, turning into a bag of bones.

He kisses my leg and rights my skirt as I lie there lifeless. Pulling my headband back up, he smiles, then stands in front of me. I'm suddenly reoriented to where we are and can feel the sway of the bucket. Before I can fully screw my head back on to realize that we're still on the Ferris wheel, it stops.

"Ride's over," Miles says, extending his hand for me to take.

My legs wobble as I hold on to him, exiting the ride,

feeling an overwhelming sensation of relief for multiple reasons.

We take a few steps away from the ride, and then I gasp, awareness striking me.

"What?" he asks.

"My underwear."

We both turn around to look at the bucket we just came out of, and the ride attendant is just closing the door on another couple. As they ascend, there's a look of disgust on both of their faces.

Miles and I look at each other at the same time, wide-eyed, then burst into laughter.

After a few more rides, Miles and I found ourselves strolling on the beach along the shoreline. We both hold our shoes in our hands. The sand's damp and squishy beneath my toes, but the water comes up to add a refreshing touch every so often. The stars shine brightly, and the lights from the amusement park dance behind us, flashing obnoxious colors onto the sea.

A plume of smoke exits my mouth because after the Ferris wheel and what happened on it—I'm in need of some nicotine. My muscles relax as we continue carrying on, talking about stupid shit that makes my heart bounce around.

Suddenly, my heel hits a cool, hard piece of some-thing. Stopping, I look down to see what my foot just hit. A jade-colored stone catches my attention. Putting my cigarette out on the sole of my shoe that's in my hand, I stuff the rest of it into my pocket, knowing that

Miles would freak if I flicked it into the ocean. Then I bend down to pick up the stone, feeling the smoothness in my palm.

"Sea glass," Miles states. I tilt my head at him, and he continues, "It's a weathered piece of glass. Over time, the ocean smooths out the rough edges."

"It's beautiful," I say, trying to see through the opaque stone. The wheels in my head start turning, thinking of all types of things I can create out of these if I have enough. Slipping the piece into my back pocket, I make a mental note to come back here to scour for more.

Miles grins when he sees me keep the sea glass, and the two of us keep our eyes peeled for any more along our walk.

"On a scale of one to ten, how was your first date?" Miles asks.

"It wasn't the worst thing that ever happened to me," I deadpan, causing Miles to roll with laughter.

"Does that mean you'll consider going out with me again?"

I wiggle my head back and forth as if I'm debating the pros and cons. "I guess."

"It was the orgasm on the Ferris wheel that won you over, wasn't it?"

A smirk plays on my lips. And as if the universe has a sense of humor, there's a strong wind that blows past us, riding right up my skirt, reminding me that I'm going commando and Miles is the reason why.

"It definitely worked in your favor," I answer.

We spend the rest of our time walking, talking, and occasionally picking up sea glass if we happen to spot any.

By the end of the night, he's standing in front of my door, waiting for me to unlock it.

"I'll text you tomorrow," Miles says.

I immediately sense my stomach dropping. "You're not coming inside?"

"No." He shakes his head. "I think a proper first date should end with a kiss good night in front of your door."

My stomach moves back to its original place. "Okay."

Miles moves in closer, cupping my cheek in his hand. My lashes flutter shut, and he brushes his lips against mine in the sweetest, most innocent way.

"Good night, Rae." He pulls away slowly, and I watch as he trails down the hallway and gets onto the elevator.

Finally opening my door, the moment I walk inside, a giddy sensation blossoms in my chest. My cheeks rise into a wide smile as I let myself revel in my very first date.

Crossing to my kitchen island, I admire the flowers Miles got me while taking the pieces of sea glass out of my pocket and placing them around the vase.

I get a burst of energy, wanting to tell someone about the date as if I were a fourteen-year-old girl again. Emma wasn't working downstairs, otherwise, I'd be racing there to tell her the details.

The only other person I'd talk to about this kind of stuff would be Cara.

When the realization slams into me, my eyes well up.

I don't know how, but in this moment, I feel my heart breaking and mending at the same time.

I'm not sure which emotion is brewing behind my eyes, but I blink the tears away before shedding them. A shaky breath flows out from my lips as I head for my paints.

For the rest of the night, my mind jumps around a myriad of feelings, and I let them all out onto the canvas.

CHAPTER TWENTY-SIX

I WAKE UP WELL RESTED, with a sense of transformation floating over me. A feeling of being renewed. I'm not weighed down with guilt like I had expected to be. In fact, I feel the best I have in a very long time.

Stretching, I leisurely get out of bed and start my day. My plans are very simple: search for more sea glass and go to NA.

And so, I move about my afternoon doing just that, with texts from Miles here and there, which stir up the same giddiness from last night.

The bottom of my tote bag becomes filled with green, blue, white, and black stones, varying in the intensity of the shade of color. I've spent at least an hour sweeping through the sand, trailing along until I found enough glass to make something.

As I sift through the sand, my thoughts, along with my sense of time, drift out to sea. A calmness coats me as I begin to welcome a new and unfamiliar sense of peace.

Before I know it, it's time to head to my meeting, so I walk the few blocks to reach the community center. As I hop down the staircase and enter the basement, a few stragglers from the last meeting hang out by the food table. One of them being Miles.

I knew he'd be here since we'd been texting, and when I told him I was planning on going to NA, he liked the idea and decided to go to AA himself.

Biting into a chocolate chip cookie, Miles gives me a wink from across the room.

Warmness trails up my neck, coloring my face. I don't know how someone could make eating a cookie look sexy—but Miles just did.

I pad toward him, giving a wave to some of the other people who are hanging around eating and drinking.

With a slight tilt of his head, Miles motions me to move away from the table. I follow him, and he leads me with his hand on my lower back while using the other to finish his cookie.

He shuffles me faster, nearly making me trip over my feet. "Where are we going?" I whisper.

"This way." He hurries me into a narrow hallway and scurries us into a bathroom.

I'm suddenly pushed up against the wall, his mouth finding mine in an instant. Flustered but instantly turned on, I smile into his kiss, already pushing my body up against his. There's a hint of chocolate on his tongue, making him taste delicious.

Miles squeezes my hips and then roams downward to cup my ass. As I let out a slight moan, he pulls away.

"You look really sexy," he says, catching his breath.

"I'm wearing a Nirvana T-shirt," I reply, glancing down at my less-than-stellar outfit.

"Yeah, well, it looks hot on you." Miles gives me another squeeze, this time harder than before. "How are you feeling after last night's date? Did you freak out after I left?"

I gaze into his eyes and shake my head. "No."

"Good." He moves one of his hands up to my face and gently grazes over my cheekbone with his thumb. "That means I get to do more of this."

Once more, his mouth presses against mine. Rough and tender at the same time as his lips mold to mine, claiming me. My fingers thread through the ends of his hair as my desire sparks.

I'm about three seconds away from doing it in a dirty basement bathroom before my NA meeting. Can't get classier than that.

I drag my hands down his body, and when I find Miles's belt buckle, he freezes. "I'm not fucking you in this gross bathroom," he states while his mouth still hovers over mine.

"Okay, so where?" I say against his lips.

Miles smirks, taking a step back. "Did my skills from last night leave a lasting impression on you?"

"Shut up." I swat at his chest, and he laughs.

"Don't worry, princess, there's plenty more where that came from." My body heats up at his promise. "But right now, you have a meeting to attend." He points to the closed door behind me. "I just wanted to check in after yesterday. And maybe steal a kiss or two."

"When will I see you next?"

"My work schedule is packed for the next few days," he says with an apologetic tone.

"That's okay." My schedule *should* be packed with work, like a normal adult's. The thought of me living off my parents' money makes my stomach churn. Maybe I can get a part-time job and ease my way back into society.

"But I can see you this weekend," Miles adds.

I nod. "Sounds good."

There's chatter coming from the room next to us as more people filter in for the meeting. I turn to leave the bathroom, but Miles stops me.

"Wait," he says before I can turn the knob.

"Wh—"

Before I can get the word out, he thrusts his body against mine, and we crash against the frail door. His hand clasps around my neck, and my stomach flutters as he gives me a bruising kiss.

With his hand still in place, he moves his mouth along my jawline and sucks on my ear. Shivers roll through me, and the thought of not going to this meeting is becoming more enticing. "I wanted to leave you with one more kiss before you go," he whispers against me.

I clutch his shirt, eager for more, but he adds distance between us. Steadying my breathing, I look up at his perfectly sculpted face. "Thanks," I say, bringing my fingertips to touch my tingling lips.

Miles chuckles. "Any time."

He motions to the door, and the both of us cautiously exit so as not to get caught by anyone. However, the second Miles sneaks out of the bathroom, directly behind me, Sam enters the hallway.

A look of surprise flickers over Sam's face, but he's quick to compose himself, giving us a curt nod and walking past us to get to one of the bathrooms.

Pressing my lips together to keep from laughing, I gaze up at Miles, who's doing the same.

We casually reenter the room, and more people are trickling in. I'm starting to recognize a few of them, like Regina and Davis.

"Have a good meeting," Miles whispers, then kisses the top of my head. "I'll see you later."

After saying goodbye, I find a seat next to a stranger. Within seconds, Sam's walking over to his chair and starting the meeting with his normal spiel.

"Who would like to talk first?" he asks the group, but his eyes land on me. An abrupt ache forms in my skull, and I'm quick to avert my gaze, sinking into my chair.

The stranger next to me begins speaking—his name is Walter, and my thoughts dip in and out of my past, my recovery journey, and of course, Miles.

The hour goes by quickly, and all the while, I remain silent. I doubt I'll ever end up speaking in these meetings, but it helps to listen.

"Rae?" Sam calls before I can make it to the staircase. Spinning around, I notice he has a coffee cup in his hand, extending it to me. "Not sticking around for some refreshments?"

I eye him suspiciously. He's never been one to make me feel pressured to talk, but something about this gesture makes me feel like he's going to bring up the bathroom incident. Shrugging the feeling aside, I answer, "I guess another cup won't hurt." I walk over to him and take a sip. "Thanks," I say and try to make a fast exit.

"Hold on," Sam stops me from darting away.

When I pause, I notice a few lingerers scatter away

from us, and my guard goes up, my shoulders tensing. "What's wrong?" I ask.

"Nothing, I just wanted to check in with you." Sam gives me an easy smile, and I begin to relax...sort of. "Just wanted to see how you're adjusting to living in Golden Bay and see if there's anything I can do to help with the transition."

"Oh. I'm good. But thanks."

"Okay, well, if you ever need anything, my wife Gloria and I do a lot around the community and are always willing to assist a newcomer."

I nod and start to back away. But before I can fully escape, my tongue has the impulse to speak. "How do you do it?"

Sam's forehead crinkles. "Do what?"

"Help out with the community, run meetings, own businesses?"

"Just trying to do my part in my little corner of the world." He shrugs. "I employ a lot of people in recovery to help them bounce back."

A light bulb goes off in my head. "You do?"

"Yeah. I know what it's like to hit rock bottom." He pours himself a cup of coffee. "Gloria was there to pull me up, and once I got sober, I made it my mission to give back to as many people as I can."

The bulb shines brighter, encouraging me to ask the question that's bouncing around inside my head. Maybe getting a job would make me feel better about myself. I can start slow and not feel stressed about a heavy work schedule. Sam knows the state I'm in—or can at least assume since I don't say much about myself. I'd feel like less of a freeloader, and I'm sure it would make my parents proud or some shit like that.

"Do you have any positions open?" The words tumble out before I can stop them.

Surprised, his brows lift. "In fact, I do. It's almost the busy season and I could use some extra hands at the diner. Would that interest you?"

"Uh. Sure." I glance down at the floor. "I've never waitressed before, though."

"That's all right, we can train you. What's your schedule like?"

"I'm pretty much free whenever."

"How does tomorrow at seven sound?" Sam asks before drinking some coffee.

"Okay, I'll see you tomorrow night."

"I meant in the morning," he clarifies. My eyes nearly pop out of my head, and he chuckles in response. "Not a morning person, I see. We'll start you on the afternoon shift, does noon sound more manageable?"

"Definitely." I breathe a sigh of relief, grateful he's giving me this type of leeway.

Sam gives a tip of his cup. "I'll see you then."

"See you tomorrow." With my coffee, I make my way toward the staircase but stop before I hit the first step. "Sam?" I turn around to look at him.

"Yeah?"

"Thanks."

CHAPTER TWENTY-SEVEN

Rae

THREE DAYS of waitressing and my feet are burning with pain. Sitting on my couch, I massage them while I relax, watching a true crime documentary. Luckily, I have the day off, so I can do a whole lot of nothing.

I didn't work many hours over the past few days, but holy hell, am I tired. No one told me how exhausting waitressing is. Maybe if I were better at it, it wouldn't be so bad—but, frankly, I suck at the job. I'm not one for hospitality, and apparently, I'm not graceful either, as I ended up spilling almost every single drink yesterday.

At the very least, I have a little bit of cash flow. Hopefully soon, I won't have to depend on my parents to be my financial lifeline. I can actually afford to buy my own art supplies and food.

Placing my foot down on the floor, I wince when I'm met with shooting pain.

Maybe I can also buy some new shoes so I won't have to be sore for the rest of my life.

The thought of going shoe shopping makes me groan. There's nothing more boring than trying on thirty different pairs of shoes to see which ones will hurt less.

It's little moments like these when I wish I had Cara to make the annoying task more enjoyable. She'd probably parade around the store, piling her arms with shoeboxes for me, and I'd act like I was bothered by it, but in reality, I'd love that she helped me.

Sighing, my body deflates, unwillingly accepting that those types of moments will never exist. I stare at the TV, no longer paying attention to what's flashing before me as my mind drifts elsewhere.

After zoning out for God knows how long, the image of Emma flickers into my head, and then the sound of Mom's voice encourages me to make new friends. I already dragged Emma out once, I'm sure she'd be down if I asked her to go shoe shopping—or, at the very least, point me in the direction of a cheap store.

No longer wanting to sit in my lingering emptiness, I push off the couch and head to the lobby to see if Emma's working the reception desk.

When I get there, she's talking on the phone, dealing with a complaint from one of the residents.

"I'm so sorry, Mr. Campbell, one of my maintenance workers is finishing up a job, and when he's done, I'll have him come to your condo and take a look at your refrigerator," Emma says into the phone while typing a note into the computer. She goes silent as the person on the other end speaks. As she listens, her gaze wanders around the room and lands on me. Her eyes light up, and she gives me a wave.

"Hey," I whisper. As I wait for her to hang up, I

casually peruse the lobby, but there's not much to look at aside from pictures of the beach.

Why anyone would choose to hang up pictures of the ocean when you can literally see the real thing from the opposite window is beyond me. They should've fired the interior designer of this place. No one needs a clichéd nautical theme when they live on the fucking water.

"Hey!" Emma says, interrupting my thoughts. I didn't even hear her end the phone call.

"What's up?" I ask, strolling over to the desk.

"You know, just dealing with the same nonsense drama from residents," she says with an eye roll and then immediately schools her features, realizing what she said. "Oh my goodness—I didn't mean to make it seem like I hate all the residents—I don't, and I definitely don't hate you."

I chuckle. "That makes one of us because I'm pretty sure I hate all the residents here, myself included."

"I didn't mean to offend you—"

"There's very little in this world that can offend me. Trust me."

"Okay, good." Her shoulders drop in relief. "So, what's going on with you? I haven't seen you in a while."

"I got a job."

"No way! Where?"

"Sam's," I say, leaning my elbows on the desk.

Emma smiles. "You like it there?"

"Well, I've only worked a few days and I'm a horrible server, but other than that, it's not so bad."

"I'm sure you'll get the hang of it."

I shrug. "I was actually wondering if you'd know of any places where I can get some shoes for work. My feet are killing me, and I don't really know of any good places around here."

She perks up. "Do you want to go shopping tomorrow before my shift starts? I can take you to all the best stores."

A sense of awkwardness makes me clam up for a split second, but I realize it's because I've never had anyone like this in my life aside from Cara. Inhaling, I shove the feeling aside. This is literally the whole reason why I came downstairs to talk to her. "Yeah, that'd be helpful."

"Amazing! I can't wait to show you all my favorite places!" She bounces on her toes. "And when we're out, you *have* to fill me in on what's going on between you and Miles."

My stomach fills with butterflies at the slight mention of his name. "There's not much to tell."

"Not much to tell!? He's been here multiple times to see you."

"We're just having fun." I pick at my cuticles. "The reality is, we're enjoying each other's company, but I know it's not going to last forever."

Emma frowns. "Why do you say that?"

"Have you seen him? He can have any woman on the planet. Any day now, some gorgeous, sexy beach model is going to go after him and catch his attention. I'm not beautiful or charming like any of them. I'm trash—an ex-junkie with a shit ton of baggage. Who would want to spend their time with someone like that? I'll be old news in a matter of weeks."

Metal slams down on the opposite end of the counter, causing both of us to gasp. I snap my head in the direction of the sound and spot a very tense Miles staring me down. His hand's tightly wrapped around the handle of his toolbox, which is what he crashed down, while his cool-colored eyes have me pinned in place as a wild and thunderous storm brews behind them.

A weight drops in my gut as if I were caught doing something bad. But I wasn't. I wasn't shit talking him, I was just saying it like it is. We all know he's going to find someone better any day now.

Miles's jaw tics, and he turns his attention to Emma. "I finished working on the installment in room 304. Anything else for today?"

"Um..." Emma nervously smooths over her hair. "Mr. Campbell's having issues with his fridge. I told him someone would be up there soon."

"Okay. He's going to need to wait a little bit longer." Miles then shifts his gaze to me. "Rae, can I see you upstairs, please?"

The tone of his voice makes the tiny hairs on my arms rise. Any playfulness that I've known about him has completely vanished. I've never seen him so stoic and...*pissed*.

I swallow, coating my now dry throat. "Sure," I say, ignoring my pulse picking up speed. "See you tomorrow, Emma."

"Bye," she whispers.

Miles and I make our way to the elevator in silence.

When the door shuts, I wait for him to start asking me questions, but he faces forward, not letting any emotion show.

Unease juts through my veins. "Miles, I—"

"Not here," he's quick to reply, still not looking at me.

A switch is flipped, and I automatically get annoyed. Men can be such motherfucking babies.

Rolling my eyes, I get off the elevator and march to my condo, aggravated that we're going to need to have some bullshit conversation about this.

With him right behind me, he tosses his toolbox onto my kitchen island and stalks down my hallway— still not acknowledging me.

"Um? Hello?" I call after him.

Miles doesn't respond, he just walks into my room like he owns the place.

"What the fuck do you think you're doing?" I chase after him, only to find him sitting at the foot of my bed. "Are you really gonna act so dramatic over this—"

"Strip."

My mind spins, and it takes me a second to process. "What?"

"No one talks about my woman that way—not even you." Miles leans back, pressing his palms into my mattress as he eyes me up and down. "Now strip."

My jaw hangs open as it begins to click for me.

Holy shit. He's punishing me.

The room somehow darkens as all my focus goes to Miles. His expression is still apathetic but somehow also lustful as he sits, waiting for a show.

My body instantly heats up as his eyes burn a hole into my chest.

Keeping my attention trained on him, my heart races as I slip out of my shoes. Acting as if I'm as unfazed as he is, my fingers find the hem of my joggers, and I push them down, exposing a scrap of lace.

Miles's attention goes to my hips, and I feel goose bumps rise under his gaze. There's a flicker of his tongue as he wets his lips. Desire pools between my thighs.

He forces his focus to meet my face. Silently, he encourages me to continue under the heat of his stare.

Unwavering to the pressure, I tug my shirt over my head and let it drop to the floor.

My chest rapidly rises and falls as I stand there in my black bra and panties. His eyes roam all over me, studying every inch from head to toe. Tingles flood my insides, and I let him drink me in for a few more moments so I can relish in the feeling.

I start to wrap my hand around my back to unclasp my bra.

"Stop." Miles's deep voice echoes in my bedroom as he makes his demand. I freeze, breathing harder, waiting for my next instruction. He continues to wash his gaze all over me. "Come here."

Tiptoeing over to the foot of my bed, I listen to his command.

When I'm directly in front of Miles, he takes his fingertips and softly touches my stomach as if he were painting a picture on a blank canvas. I sharply suck in a breath under his feather-like touch.

His mouth hovers over my body, his breath hitting my skin.

"I heard what you said about yourself," Miles says, glancing up at me.

"I figured."

"I didn't like it." His eyes darken, and my hands begin to tremble with excitement.

I *like* that he's not happy with me. I *like* that he's about to punish me. My twisted brain gets intoxicated from the anticipation as lust bursts through me.

"You think you can talk shit about yourself and get away with it?" he asks.

A smirk threatens my lips. "Maybe."

Miles immediately grips my wrist, pulling me parallel to the bed, and pushes me down so I'm bent over his knees with my ass in the air.

My heart gallops in my chest and I race to catch up with my breath.

"You're not gonna get away with saying any of that, Rae," Miles states right before his palm smacks against my skin, making it sting. A pain that feels so fucking good.

"You think I want to find someone else?" he asks, as genuine resentment coats his words. When I don't answer, he holds my hair in his fist and lifts my head up. My scalp prickles as he pulls, turning me on so much I have to squeeze my legs tighter. "Answer me."

"Yes," I croak.

He drops my hair. "You're wrong." Another spank, only this time it's harder than the first. Pressing my lips together, I moan behind them. "Tell me you believe me when I say I don't want anyone else but you."

"I believe you," I say, my voice straining.

"Tell me how beautiful you are."

My throat starts to close as the words get stuck, unable to come out.

Miles slaps my ass cheek again, causing a loud sound to escape me. "Say it," he demands.

"I'm beautiful," I softly breathe out.

His hand finds me once more. "Louder."

"I'm beautiful."

Again. "More."

"I'm beautiful," I cry out, writhing against his lap.

"Tell me how amazing of a person you are."

My chest tenses as my cheeks burn with anger. He knows I hate myself. He fucking knows it, and he's going to make me say some positive crap about myself. *This* is the worst form of punishment.

My hands ball into fists. "I'm. Amazing," I mutter through my gritted teeth.

Miles chuckles, knowing that he got me. "Like you mean it, princess." With that, his hand crashes down, spiking another round of lust through me.

"I'm amazing," I say slightly louder.

"Can't hear you." Miles spanks me again.

I grind up against his jeans, desperate for relief as the wildfire inside me grows, becoming untamed. "I'm amazing."

"Close. But not good enough." He strikes once more.

Tugging at the roots of my hair and rocking back and forth over him, my pulse thrashes in my ears. "I'm fucking amazing!" I shout, unable to control myself.

Miles smacks me as hard as he can, and I scream in delight. "That's my girl." He thumbs over the lace band of my thong, admiring the artwork of his handprint against my flesh. Then, he brings his lips to my body, delicately kissing the marks, soothing the burn.

My eyelids flutter closed as he drags his warm mouth all over me.

Slowly pulling away, he snaps my panties against my hips. "Get over by the headboard."

Shifting off of him, I crawl over to where he wants me and spin to face him. Only when I turn around, he's walking into my art supplies closet. "What are you doing?"

"Looking for something."

CHAPTER TWENTY-EIGHT
Miles

SCANNING over Rae's art supplies, my brain spins with ideas—but I only have one goal in mind. My heart speeds up as the need to touch her again intensifies. The bottom of my hand still stings from spanking her, and my cock is aching to be inside her.

But not before I find what I'm looking for.

My gaze flickers over paints, pencils, glue, and a whole bunch of other materials.

Excitement zips through me when my eyes land on what I was searching for: ribbon.

Finding scissors nearby, I cut two long strips of the thick, shiny fabric.

"Um, hello?" Rae calls out from the bed.

Turning around, I spot her in the center of the mattress, giving me a dirty look. "Did I tell you to move?" I ask, stalking toward her.

She's quick to snap back into the moment and scoots herself up the bed.

"Take your bra off," I demand.

She listens, then lies down. My mouth waters

looking at the sight before me; Rae splayed out, wearing only her panties, a flushed color creeping up her neck.

The ache in my jeans grows stronger, thinking of just a couple of minutes ago when I had her bent over my knee. Did I have fun with her, pushing her buttons? Of fucking course. But I knew she'd use the safe word if it was too much. And judging by the damp spot I can see on her panties, she'd much rather have me finish the job than stop because I had her call herself beautiful and amazing.

Rae's line of sight travels to my hand, where I'm clutching the ribbon.

Without a word, I get on the mattress, kneeling over her torso. I watch as her breathing picks up, the air flowing out of her at a quicker pace as it stammers against her red lips.

Picking up her right wrist, I lift her arm up overhead and carefully tie the ribbon around it, securing her to the bedpost.

When Rae realizes what I'm doing, she lets out a small whine and raises her hips up so her body pushes against my crotch.

"Not yet, princess." Taking her other arm, I tie her up to the opposite bedpost, then check both wrists to make sure I didn't wrap her up too tight.

Slinking off her body, I hop off the bed and move toward the door.

Rae's head shoots up. "Where are you going?"

"Be right back."

"Are you fucking kidding me?"

Looking over my shoulder, I give her a smirk, ignoring the throb in my pants as I glance at her almost naked body tied up, waiting for me.

I can hear her muttering curses at me as I tread down the hallway and into the kitchen. Opening up her freezer, I grab an ice cube, delicately holding it between my fingers so it doesn't melt from the heat of my hands.

When I reenter Rae's bedroom, she has an adorable scowl in place as she remains in the same position I left her.

"What are you doing?" she snaps, tired of me dragging this out.

Little does she know, I'm just beginning.

Joining her on the bed, I settle next to her legs. "Having some fun," I answer, picking up one of her legs and placing a kiss on her knee.

Without warning, I leisurely drag the ice cube up the inside of her thigh, and Rae gasps. My mouth trails behind, licking up the coldness and running my tongue over her raised skin.

Her hips jut upward as I move to the other thigh, doing the same thing.

"Miles," Rae whines, making my heart leap. The sound of her begging makes me want to forget about teasing her and rip my clothes off and fuck her without any type of foreplay.

But, despite my dick screaming at me and my pulse raging, I keep my composure and continue making her squirm.

Skipping over her panties, I bring the ice to her stomach and watch as the muscles contract under my touch.

Rae pants as I inch upward, following the dark linework on her ribs. She tugs at the ribbon the second the ice touches her nipple.

"Holy shit." She clamps her eyes shut as I make tiny

circles. She looks absolutely stunning as she writhes beneath me, allowing me to control her pleasure.

She tugs again, making the bedpost creak when I focus on the other nipple. The ice begins to melt, dripping cold water all over her and onto the sheet.

I blow cool air on her, and she shudders. "How's this feel, Rae?" I rasp.

"Incredible," she whimpers, her eyes still shut.

"Almost as incredible as you are?"

"Shut up." Her heels dig into the mattress, and she pushes up to me.

I make a *tsk-tsk* sound with my mouth. "I thought you learned your lesson about saying how wonderful you are."

Her lids open, lust pouring from her light-blue eyes. "I don't think I did," she says, her voice daring me to go further with her.

"Then let me teach you again."

Dragging the half-melted cube from her chest down to the top of her panties, I hover over the lace, making her wait for it.

After a few moments, I scoot myself down and carefully dispose of her thong while holding the remainder of the ice in my hand.

Lying between her open legs, our gaze connects as I slowly bring the ice to her clit, making her flinch. She hisses and curses under her breath as she fights to keep her eyes open to watch me.

Adding and taking away pressure, the freezing moisture mixes with the heat of her wetness, sliding down her pussy. Her legs tremble as I change rhythm and motions. "You're not allowed to come until I say so," I tell her.

That revs her up more, and her back bows off the bed.

"Eyes on me," I command, and her focus goes back to me as I quicken my pace, making her tremble harder. "I think you're fucking fantastic, Rae." I add more pressure, and she sucks in a breath. "You're witty, sexy, and snarky as hell." I slip the sliver of ice inside her, and she gasps. "I want to be with *only* you. Understood?"

Rae's body buzzes, teetering on the edge. She furiously nods in response.

"Tell me."

"I understand," she pants.

Yanking the last bit of ice out of her, I suck on it, freezing my mouth, then finally flick my tongue over her clit.

Rae cries out, the headboard rattling from her hands fisting and yanking on the ribbon. She's seconds away from losing all control and I'm seconds away from making a mess in my boxers if I don't get inside her soon.

With only a few lashes of my tongue, her thighs crash against my head as her pussy spasms. She screams and shakes, her body twisting.

I revel in her orgasm as she continues to ride it out.

When her breathing begins to steady and her muscles relax into the mattress, I lift my head to look at her.

My heart soars at the sight. Glowing with a sheen of sweat, hair in a knotted halo, and a smile gracing her face.

If my cock wasn't running the show right now, I could stare at her all day. But before I can get another glimpse, I'm tugging at my clothes, racing to get them off of me as if they're on fire.

The next moment, I'm on top of her. Her smile grows wider as I bend down to kiss the corners of her mouth. "You good?" I whisper.

"More than good," Rae says into my lips.

With that confirmation, I press my palm into the bed, pushing up so I can slide into her. The second I make contact with her tight pussy, I moan.

"Fuck." I toss my head back. "I'm never gonna get over how amazing you feel." Rae excitedly locks her legs around my hips, urging me to move. "How hard do you want it?" I ask, already gasping for air.

There's a flare of desire in her eyes. "*Hard.*"

I smirk. "I knew my dirty girl would."

Positioning myself to hit the perfect angle, I have one hand gripping her hip and the other wrapped around her neck. I rub my thumb over the choker necklace that's always around her and slowly bring my gaze up to meet hers.

There's a silent communication going on between us, and with a small quirk of her eyebrow, she spurs me on.

I thrust into her.

She screeches, yanking on the ribbons. They hang on by a thread—literally, as she continues to tug at them every time I pound into her.

My hold on her neck gets stronger as heat explodes in my veins, singeing my entire being.

I drive into her harder and harder.

Rae wails, screaming out my name, getting me drunk off the sound.

I have a bruising hold on her hip as I use it as

leverage to get even deeper, slamming against her walls, making her clench around me.

My muscles tense with each movement. Sweat drips off my body and onto hers as our breathing accelerates.

With my next thrust, my orgasm rips through me, coiling around my spine and shooting off flames of ecstasy.

My pace slows down as I spill into her, filling her up.

When my body finally relaxes, I drop down on top of her. Our chests touch as we try to pull more air into our lungs.

Before I get too comfortable, I lift up and rip the last of the ribbons off the bedposts and roll onto my back next to her.

"Goddamn," I manage to get out.

"Yeah." Rae stares up at the ceiling, eyes glazed over. "Same."

We lie there, basking in the moment, catching our breath. Ideally, I'd pull Rae into me and pepper her with kisses, but she's just warming up to the concept of cuddling, so instead, I interlace our fingers.

Rae doesn't yank her hand away or make a comment. Instead, she closes her fingers around mine, letting us hold each other this way.

My lids grow heavy as a wave of calmness floats around me.

I could lie here all day.

Until I realize that I can't. "Shit."

"What?" Rae turns her head to look at me.

"I have to get back to work." The mood is instantly ruined as the real world interrupts my post-sex daze.

On cue, my stomach growls, urging me to eat something before getting back to dealing with Mr. Campbell.

Clearly hearing how hungry I am, Rae sits up. "I'll see if I have anything for you to refuel," she says, poking my belly.

We both get off the bed, put our clothes back on, and head to the kitchen.

She opens her fridge and pantry, naming the rather bland food she has, and lets me choose whatever I'd like.

While I make myself a sandwich with some of her cold cuts, Rae gets a phone call.

"Hey," she says to whoever's on the other line. "Pretty good, how are you guys?" She swipes a piece of American cheese from me and eats it, continuing her conversation. "Tomorrow?" There's hesitancy in her voice. "Um, yeah, sure. That's fine."

There are a lot more *okays* and *uh-huhs,* and I sit down on one of her kitchen stools. As I go to take another bite of my lunch, she hangs up.

"So." She eats another piece of cheese. "Wanna meet my family tomorrow?"

The sandwich gets lodged in my throat, and I cough a few times. "What?" I ask, surprised as all hell.

"I'll take that as a no."

"No, take that as I need a little bit more information."

Rae sighs. "My parents and brother are coming to visit me tomorrow night and want to have dinner. Do you want to join?"

Warmth fills my chest. "You want me to meet your parents?"

She nonchalantly shrugs, ignoring how big of a deal

this is. "Only if you want to. I'm sure they'd be ecstatic to know that my first real boyfriend is someone who has their life together." Her cheeks immediately flush as her eyes bulge, realizing what she just said. "I mean, the guy I'm dating—or whatever." She pivots on her heels, cleaning up some of the cold cuts that we left out.

Standing up, I tread over to her, placing my hand on her waist as I press my chest against her back. "Rae," I say, bending down next to her ear. "I think I made it pretty clear about ten minutes ago that I'm your boyfriend. Or do I have to remind you again about where I stand on that topic?" I can't see her face, but I can feel her cheek rise as she smiles. "And yes, I'd love to meet your family."

Rae spins around, and I step back a bit, giving her some room. She stares at me, lost in thought, as the realization of our relationship and my meeting her family sinks in. I can only imagine what's going through her mind as several different emotions flicker across her face in a matter of seconds. Then I see it. Her armor coming back up as she starts to shut down.

This is how it is with Rae: three steps forward, two steps back.

"What's going through your head right now?" I ask.

She flinches but puts her mask back in place. "Nothing."

"Liar."

"Fine." Rae rolls her eyes. "Everything."

"Such as?"

There's a struggle going on inside her as she frowns, her features pulling in tight. Her cold eyes drift off me, and I watch as they turn glassy. My heart cracks as I witness her war with the pain of the past. My arms burn with the need to hold her, but before I can move, she speaks.

"Tell me I'm not a horrible sister for doing this," she whispers, and the rest of my heart shatters. "I feel like I'm living out Cara's dream—like I stole you from her."

"There was nothing to steal," I say softly, not wanting to upset her any further. "Cara had a crush on me, and I didn't even know her." Stepping in, I do what my gut is telling me to and wrap my hands around Rae's body. She's rigid, not willing to give in to my embrace. "You're not a horrible sister by any means," I say into her hair. Her small hands come around my body as she finally begins to hug me back.

We stay like this for a while. I kiss the top of her head over and over again, giving her as much affection as she's willing to take. She bottles up her tears, not letting herself cry. But, at the very least, she's letting me take care of her in this moment.

Rae draws in a long breath, her ribs expanding under my arms. I pull my head away to look at her, and she tilts her chin up to glance at me. "If you tell my family that you got me to eat cotton candy, I'll break up with you," she says out of nowhere, completely serious.

"Does that mean we're moving forward with me coming to dinner?"

She breaks apart only slightly so we can see each other better. "This is my new life and you're a part of it, so..." She lifts up her shoulder. "It is what it is."

I smirk. *It is what it is* pretty much equals *I really like you, so I'm going to try this out and let myself be vulnerable for the first time ever* in Rae's language.

"It is what it is," I repeat, right before planting a tender kiss on her lips.

CHAPTER TWENTY-NINE

EMMA PLACES another shoebox next to me. "Try these," she says, her red hair whipping around in her ponytail as she surveys the store for even more shoes.

"I'm cool with the first pair," I say.

"You said they rubbed the back of your heels."

"Yeah, but I'll get used to it."

"Or you'll get blisters."

Emma does have a point. So, with her encouragement, I try on the latest pair of shoes she picked out, walking around a bit to get a good feel for them. After agreeing with her that these are the best option, I pay for my new work shoes, and we head out.

I assume we're done for the afternoon, but Emma has other plans.

"I have to take you to this new place, it's called Hayden's Boutique, and the clothes are to die for!" she says as we head toward another store. "I can barely afford the socks that they sell—but I like going in there and trying things on."

I snort. "So, you play dress-up and don't buy anything?"

"Pretty much." She links her arm around mine. "This way, come on!"

My shopping bag bangs against my leg as we make our way into the clothing store. The smell of fresh linen and lavender encompasses us the moment we step inside. Emma zooms toward the racks of colorful, chic clothing. My eyes nearly burst out of my skull when I see the price tag on one of the shirts.

"This shit is so expensive," I whisper.

"I know. Too bad I'll never be able to buy anything from here because I'm in love with everything," Emma says.

Glancing around the room, it makes sense that she'd love everything in here, it's her style. Crisp, clean, bright.

"Oh, this would look *so* good on you!" Emma pulls a dress off the rack. It's a shimmery black cocktail dress.

"And where exactly would I be wearing that?"

"I'm sure Miles could think of a good place to take you," she teases. "What happened yesterday after he overheard us talking, by the way?"

"We ironed everything out." I bite the inside of my cheek to suppress my growing smile.

"He's not mad?"

"Not in the slightest." I join her in flitting through clothes, essentially hands-on window-shopping. "He's going to meet my family later today." My stomach flops at the thought. Half-nervous and half battling my stupid guilt.

Emma gapes. "What! Oh my gosh! How did that move so quickly?"

"I'm not entirely sure, if I'm being honest. Things are just starting to click into place."

She lets out a dreamy sigh, clinging to a random shirt. "That sounds lovely. I wish that would happen to me one day. I'm not sure with who, though. Thankfully, I'm over Travis. Any feelings I had for him vanished into thin air—I even start to cringe when I look at him."

"Yeah, he kind of seems like a douche. Now that he's out of your mind, you can focus on someone else. Hopefully a decent person who doesn't think that they walk on water."

"There aren't many of those." She gives a pathetic laugh.

"Trust me, I know."

"You're one of the lucky ones."

Her words are like an atomic bomb going off inside me as it takes every amount of effort not to let any tears surface. An anchor drops in my stomach and might as well sink me down to the bottom of the ocean.

"Miles seems so romantic," Emma continues. "Is he?"

I clear my throat, wiping away any sign of distress, and focus on the clothes in front of me. "Yeah. He'd probably be even more romantic if I gave him the chance, but...that's not really my thing."

"God, I'd love a romantic man."

"Sounds like *you* should wear that dress." I point to the dress she picked out for me earlier. "And then we can go out and find you a good guy."

She gives a weak smile. "I don't really go out much. Just occasionally to hang out with friends between work and school, but even that's a battle."

"A battle with who?" My curiosity piques at the

same time gratitude falls over me, thankful we're done talking about me.

Emma shifts, going to another rack. "My dad. He's really strict."

"But, you're twenty—you're a whole-ass adult."

"Not while I'm living under his roof, I'm not. Which is why I'm saving every penny I can to go toward a place to live the second I graduate."

"Damn. I thought I had it rough with my parents."

"They're strict, too?" She turns to look at me. The both of us are no longer interested in this boutique but rather in getting to bond over something.

"Honestly, they didn't really know how to parent me, not that I blame them. Something awful happened when I was younger, and I kind of went off the rails. They tried to help me by either being super lax or super controlling—neither of which worked."

Emma's face drops. "What happened?" she asks, her voice becoming low so others in the store can't hear.

I shake my head. "I don't want to get into it."

"Okay, well, if you ever want to talk—"

"Thanks." Desperate to change the subject, I grab the first item of clothing within reach. "Here, try this on." Emma tilts her head to the side, giving me a quizzical look. "You said you wanted to play dress-up, right?"

"Sure, but only if you try on the black dress."

I playfully glare at her. "Fine."

"Is there anything I should know about your family before they get here?" Miles asks as we sit at a table in a seafood restaurant that he picked out.

We've barely had time to talk to each other until now. After I went shopping with Emma, I did a quick cleaning of my condo in case my parents want to see it, got ready, then met Miles here.

"Um..." I take a sip of my ice water. The thought of what Miles did to me the other day floats through my brain, and I get distracted.

"Rae?" Miles pulls my attention away from the dirty picture of him between my legs that's replaying in my mind.

"My parents will be fine. More than fine—they'll be shitting their pants that I've been sober for this long and have *you* as a boyfriend."

"And a job," Miles proudly adds.

"Yeah, that too. My brother, Grayson, he's shy. He probably won't talk. Too much trauma early on, he's practically scared to speak to anyone. Including me."

Our table is seated outside, a slight ocean wind hitting us every now and again. My leg bounces up and down as I keep my focus trained on the front door of the restaurant, waiting for my family to walk through.

I bite my nails, tugging at my cuticles with my teeth.

"You remember our safe word?" Miles lowers his voice.

My attention flies to him, my brows drawn in. "Um, yeah, why?"

"Well, if you need to use it tonight—do. If my being here is too much or you want me to take you away from them, just say baseball."

"What happens if we actually talk about baseball?"

"I'll know the difference. Trust me." He picks up my hand and brushes his lips over my knuckles.

And just like that, a sense of ease flows through me.

Not a moment later, the people walking through the door catch my gaze, and I spot my family of three entering. Mom looks overjoyed to see me, and when her eyes fall to Miles sitting next to me, her entire face lights up.

I didn't tell them that Miles would be with me, or who Miles even is, for that matter.

"Hi, honey." Mom rushes over to me, and I get up so she can give me a hug.

"Hey guys," I say as a general greeting.

Once Mom lets go, Dad moves in, giving me a one-armed embrace. "You look great, Rae."

"Thanks." I awkwardly glance down, hating the compliment. I basically no longer look like I'm starving, living on the streets. *Great* is a huge leap.

Glancing over Dad's shoulder, I spot my brother in the back. He's wearing a dark hoodie, blending into the background. He gives me a nod of his chin as a form of hello.

"Hey, Grayson." I give him a weak smile, and he gives one back.

"Who's this?" Mom asks, looking at the giant standing next to me. I didn't even realize Miles got out of his seat.

"Oh, everyone, this is Miles, he's my...boyfriend." The words coming out of my mouth sound funny, and Miles chuckles.

Miles starts to speak, extending his hand, but Mom

beats him to the punch. Gasping with excitement, she reels him in for an embrace.

"I'm Felicia," she says with overenthusiasm. "This is my husband, John, and our son, Grayson."

"It's nice to meet all of you," Miles says after Mom gives him room to breathe. He shakes Dad's hand, then goes to give Grayson one, but Grayson gives him the same type of head nod he gave me.

"I didn't know you had a boyfriend!" Mom beams while Miles and Dad start chatting.

"It's new."

I step back toward my chair, and all of them follow, sitting at the table with me.

"How did you two meet?" Dad asks, jumping right into things before even glancing at the menu.

My eyes dart to Miles's, and he's wearing the same look of unease that I am. My organs constrict as the memory of the first time Miles and I met weaves its way into my mind.

Miles clutches my hand under the table, giving it a light squeeze. "We actually went to high school together," he states. "But I was a senior when Rae was a freshman, so we didn't really know each other. As luck would have it, we both ended up in Golden Bay and reconnected."

"Oh," Mom gently says, and I watch the puzzle pieces in her head glue together as she studies Miles.

Yes, Mom, this is the Miles. The one Cara used to yammer on about.

I drop my gaze to the white linen cloth in front of me, no longer wanting to watch the realization on her face. A wave of nausea swims around my belly.

"What brought you to Golden Bay?" Mom asks

Miles, perking up, eager to get to know him and move on from any topic of the past.

"Fate." Miles chuckles, and I pull my attention to him. He gives me a wink, letting me know he's got this, and my lips slowly curve. "I traveled around a bit after high school, but once I ended up here, I stayed. It's where I got my life together and got everything back on track."

"He's the town's repairman. He can fix anything," I tell my family.

"Maybe you can teach Grayson here a few things," Dad says, patting my brother on the back. "He's going to be starting trade school."

"You are?" I ask in shock.

Grayson nods, eyes averted from me.

Shame rips my heart at the seams. My own brother can barely stand to look at me because of what I turned our lives into because of my addiction.

An awful, sour taste coats my tongue, and I reach for some more ice water to hopefully wash this feeling down.

The waiter comes to the table, and we quickly breeze through the menu options, ordering our drinks and dinner. As we wait, the conversation changes from getting to know Miles to Dad's car trouble to Mom's new carrot cake recipe.

"So, how are you liking it here, Rae?" Mom asks.

My gaze drifts over to the man sitting next to me. "I like it."

Miles smiles. "She even recently got a job." With that comment, my face drops, then my expression turns into a glower as he continues to grin wider.

"Oh, that's wonderful!" Mom bursts with giddiness. "Where at?"

"A diner," I state.

"Are they paying you cash?" Dad casually asks, but I know why he's asking.

"Stop, John, we're out to dinner," Mom whisper-yells at him.

Dad pays no mind to her as his eyes are fixated on mine. He's not trying to intimidate me, but I know the seriousness of that look. "You remember the agreement, Rae?"

"John, please, her boyfriend is right there," Mom tries to whisper once more, but everyone hears.

"It's fine, Miles knows," I state. "And yes, Dad, I remember our agreement. If I end up using drugs again, you're kicking me out of the condo and not paying for a single thing after that. It's carved into my skull."

He adjusts in his chair. "Sorry to bring it up, but I just want what's best for you."

"I know." I take another sip of the water, cooling down my cheeks. "And for the record, I do get paid cash, and no, I haven't spent it on anything to shoot up, snort, or smoke. I spend it on work shoes because my feet hurt like hell from standing my whole shift."

Dad's lips twitch. "Waitressing is tough work."

"You're telling me."

"We're all very proud of you, Rae," Mom states. Dad nods in agreement, and Grayson zones out on something in the distance.

"We sure are," Miles chimes in, running his hand over my back.

Feeling like the spotlight has been on me for too

long, I wiggle in my seat with discomfort. "Can we talk about literally anything else?"

"Of course." Mom clears her throat. "Any new art you've been working on?"

I shrug. "I have a mural on one of my living room walls and started on the other one, but it's nothing great."

"Nothing great?" Miles nearly spits out his soda. "They're incredible!"

"You only think so because you doodled on the one," I tease, and he starts laughing.

"Hey, my doodling belongs in the Louvre."

I snort. "Yeah, sure."

"Right next to yours." He lifts up my hand and kisses the back of it.

For a moment, the two of us forget that anyone else is here, but we're suddenly brought back by the heat of the others' stares.

Turning my head, I see my parents and brother watching my interaction with Miles. There's a glimmer of happiness in their faces—well, at least there is in my parents, my brother's face never gives away any emotion.

Miles rubs his thumb over my skin, unfazed by the attention.

"It's nice seeing you like this," Mom says, getting teary-eyed.

"We'd love to see the murals, and your place, of course, if you're up to it after dinner," Dad states.

I nod. "Yeah, I figured. That's why I cleaned."

My parents chuckle at my comment.

Before long, our dinner is getting placed in front of

us. As we scarf down our food, nervousness pricks my fingertips, and I mentally prepare for my family to reenter my new home.

CHAPTER THIRTY
Miles

WHEN WE ENTER the lobby of SeaScape Condos, Emma's front and center at the front desk. Her face glows as she spots me and Rae, with Rae's family tailing behind us.

"Emma, I know you sort of already met them when they moved my crap in, but these are my parents, Felicia and John," Rae says, doing a formal introduction.

"It's nice to meet you again," Emma says.

"And that's my little brother, Grayson, back there." Rae pokes her head behind her dad.

"Hey," Grayson says, making all of us spin to look at him. That's the first time this kid has said a word all night. I watch as he scans Emma up and down.

Rae's face twists in disgust as she witnesses her brother undress Emma with his eyes, and I have to bite my tongue so I don't burst into laughter.

"H-hi," Emma stammers, coiling a strand of her red hair around her index finger.

"Christ," Rae mutters. "All right, let's move it

upstairs, people." She shuffles everyone toward the elevator, noting the way Grayson and Emma pass glances as he walks by.

Rae keeps the look of repulsion on her face as we make our way upstairs and to her condo. But it starts to fade when we all enter, and her attention gets pulled to her parents, staring in awe at her mural.

"This is fascinating!" Felicia states, tiptoeing over to the finished mural on the wall, taking it in as if she were in a museum.

"That's one way of putting it," Rae comments about her painting.

"Never one to censor your art, that's for sure," John says with a sense of pride.

Rae glances over to the uncompromising image, and I come up behind her, placing my hand around her waist. "It wouldn't be art if there was censorship."

We all stare at the painting, drinking in Rae's talent and pain. It's the image of a skull with a portion of its head broken, bugs, dead flowers, and blood pouring out of it. Everyone seems to be enamored by it, aside from Grayson, who's hanging back, standing by the front door.

"There's also that one." Rae points to the other living room wall that has an unfinished mural. "If you look real close, you can see Miles's white blobs before I cover them up."

I chuckle. "Art was never my forte."

"It's not ours either," Felicia states. "I don't know where Rae got the art gene from."

"Baseball is more Miles's speed, but I can appreciate him trying to paint," Rae says. My eyebrows rise slightly, confirming with her that she's *not* using the safe word. She gives me a soft smile, letting me know all is well.

"You play baseball?" John inquires.

"I used to, in high school. Now I just hang around the batting cages from time to time."

John's head tilts to the side as he stares at me, the light bulb going off in his head. "That's why you look so familiar." He snaps his fingers. "I can't believe it took me this long to put it all together—you're Mayor Dennis Kingston's son. Miles Kingston. You were the all-star baseball player of Northview High."

I suck in a breath. "Yep. That was me."

"I used to watch your plays—man, they treated you like a pro athlete back then, having to do interviews and press conferences."

An iron fist jabs me in my stomach, and I nervously rub the back of my neck. "Yeah, a lot of the press stuff was my parents' doing. They have quite a love for the limelight, so much so they pushed me to be in it."

"Why don't I show you guys the balcony?" Rae swiftly changes subjects, sensing the uncomfortable topic. "It's a nice view during sunset." She guides them to the glass doors and shoots me an apologetic look before stepping outside.

I give her a wink to let her know it's fine. "I'm gonna grab a drink, and I'll be right out."

Rae nods, and as I make my way into the kitchen, Grayson's shadow startles me. I forgot he's been hiding by the door the whole time.

"Can I get you anything?" I ask, opening up the fridge.

He doesn't answer, instead, he stoically makes his way closer.

After grabbing a water, I spin around to meet Grayson face-to-face. His jaw is set tight, pain swirling around his dark irises. "What are you on?" he snaps.

My brows draw in. "What?"

"Drugs. What type of drugs do you use?"

Shaking my head, I reply, "I'm not on anything—"

"Bullshit."

"Grayson, I promise I'm not using anything. In fact, I'm in recovery. Three years sober."

His eyes narrow, assessing me. Glancing behind him, I check to make sure Rae and her parents are still out on the balcony as Grayson and I have this impromptu meeting.

"I swear to God, if I find out you're lying, I will hunt you down and fuck you up."

I can't help the look of pure shock that pops up on my face. After Grayson's silence the entire night, *this* interaction was the least expected.

Grayson continues, "I already have one dead sister, and Rae would've been dead too if I had found her a minute later. If you're one of those asshole lowlifes who's gonna drag Rae back into that shit, mark my words—I *will* find you."

My lips curve up as I nod in agreement. "I appreciate where you're coming from. On my honor, I have every intention of keeping myself and Rae sober." I pat his shoulder. "You're a good brother, Grayson. You should come hang out with her more often."

His muscles seem to loosen, only a slight amount, as the others come back inside from the balcony.

"Well, we don't want to take up all your time tonight," Felicia says to Rae. "Just wanted to pop over to see how you've been doing."

"Better than I thought I would." Rae's line of sight drifts over to mine, and warmth stirs around in my heart. A growing connection for her that I can't seem to get enough of.

"You're doing great, Rae." John gives her a small hug, and Felicia comes over to me.

"It was wonderful getting to know you," she says.

"Likewise, I hope to see all of you again soon."

She clutches my hand. "I hope so, too."

We all say our goodbyes, Grayson giving me one of his signature wordless nods. As the door shuts behind them, Rae blows out a puff of air.

"Your family seems awesome," I say.

"They are." She sits down on the stool at the kitchen island while I lean against it. "I can't fuck it up this time. For them."

"For you first, them second."

Rae rolls her eyes. "Yeah, yeah." She swipes my water bottle from me and takes a sip, then wipes her mouth with the back of her hand. "Did you see the way Grayson was eyeing up Emma—gross! The guy has his mute button on all night but manages to say one word, and it's to her."

"I don't think your brother is as introverted as you assume he is. I think he's very selective on who he speaks to and what he says."

"What makes you say that?"

"Because he threatened to kill me if I got you hooked on drugs."

"*What!?*" Her jaw drops.

"Honestly, it shocked me too, but it's commendable as fuck."

"Holy shit." Rae blinks in disbelief. "Who would've

thought my little brother would try to be a badass?" She starts chuckling.

"I could take him."

"Oh, for sure."

"But still, the sentiment was nice."

Rae's mouth begins to drop into a frown as the light-heartedness exits her body. "Kinda sad that we're virtually strangers," she says, her tone echoing the melancholy statement.

"There's still plenty of time for the two of you to have a relationship, Rae," I tell her, and she looks up at me, her eyes wide. "Even after everything," I assure her.

Rae's shoulders drop. "Yeah. Maybe." She pushes away from the counter and hops down off the stool. "Feel like doing a little painting?" she asks, changing up the mood once more.

"Only if it's the kind where we can draw all over each other's bodies and lick it off."

That has her laughing again. "That's not a thing."

"It *has* to be a thing."

"Fine, you look it up while I get my stuff so we can add to my mural."

Digging my phone out of my pocket, ready to Google edible paint, I reply, "Already on it."

Rae drifts into the hallway, and instead of scrolling through random links, I stare at her. Watching her move forward as excitement in me unfolds, thinking about what type of path for us lies ahead and what else we'll create together.

CHAPTER THIRTY-ONE
Miles

THE NEXT DAY, after finishing an easy job at a local bookstore, I decide to head to Sam's Dinette so I can see Rae in action.

When I enter, the bell chimes above my head, and I get a whiff of french fries and apple pie. It sounds like a strange combo to enjoy, but the two scents work off each other. Instantly, my stomach growls as I make my way toward the counter where Sam's pouring a tourist coffee.

"How's it going?" Sam says to me after taking care of the customer.

"Just came in for caffeine," I state.

Sam gives me a knowing smile. "And to check in on someone?" he asks, pouring me a to-go cup.

"Possibly." My gaze drifts around the room until it lands on Rae in the back, coming out of the kitchen, struggling to hold a trayful of drinks. "How's she doing?" I ask Sam.

He follows my line of sight and also begins to watch her have a difficult time balancing the glasses. "Miles," he says. "She's the worst employee I've had in a long time. Drops things constantly, curses up a storm, and can't do small talk with the patrons to save her life." His grin widens. "But I think this is a great opportunity for her, so I'm keeping her."

Can always count on Sam to put others before his business, even if that means losing a few customers because my girlfriend swears like a sailor.

"Motherfucker." Rae's words travel throughout the diner as she spills a glass of soda just as she reaches the table.

Sam and I let out a low chuckle. "There's your girl," he says, grabbing a towel, ready to help her.

I take it from him and go over to Rae, bending down to wipe up the sticky drink from the linoleum floor. She talks to herself under her breath, unaware that I'm here, helping her clean.

"Hey," I say, grabbing her attention.

Her gaze flicks over to me, and she blows a stray hair out of her face, trying to magically get it up there with the rest of her hair that's pulled into a bun. "What are you doing here?"

"Visiting you at work."

"To watch me make an ass out of myself?"

"You're not doing a bad job, you just started."

Rae rolls her eyes, and together, we quickly clean up the remains of the spill, then stand up. She apologizes to the table and promises to get their drinks as soon as possible. Making her way into the kitchen through the swinging doors, I follow her.

"You're not supposed to be in here, employees only," she states, not even bothering to look behind her, knowing that I'm here anyway.

"Technically, Sam employs me to do maintenance."

Rae lazily turns her head to look at me, a scowl perfectly put in place. But I can tell she's at least somewhat amused, judging by the glimmer of delight that flashes across her features. "If you're going to stalk me and pretend you're allowed in the kitchen, the least you can do is help me carry out those people's drinks," she says, struggling to maintain a frown.

"Deal."

Rae fills up the cups with ice and soda, carefully placing them on two trays—one for her to carry and one for me. The cooks give me a wave, and I make small talk with them while I wait for Rae to finish.

"You carry this one," Rae instructs, pulling my attention away from the others. She pushes the tray with four drinks on it toward me. Before she picks up hers, she stares at me, putting her hand on her hip. "Did you really come here just to visit me?"

"Of course I did. I feel bad I haven't been able to stop by here any earlier than today. I've been swamped —otherwise, I would've been here on your first day," I say, and she blinks a few times. "Why?" I ask.

"That's really...sweet."

My insides melt when I hear her say that. A phrase I'm not sure she's ever uttered to a man, let alone another person. The simplest, smallest gestures mean a lot to her, which fills me with mixed emotions. Glad I can be the one to make her feel this way, but also so upset that she's impressed by the bare minimum.

"Maybe you have less of an aversion to sweet things than you originally thought." I give her a wink.

Rae snorts. "God, you're so annoying," she says

through a smile. "Help me with the drinks." She picks up her tray and heads toward the swinging door.

"Wait."

"Yeah?" She turns back around.

"What time are you done with work?"

"Seven. Why?"

"I want to have you over to my place tonight. I can pick you up when you finish your shift."

"Okay." There's a little twinkle in her eyes. "But—pick me up at my place at eight. I need to shower first. I'm pretty sure I smell like bacon grease." She lifts up her arm to smell her shirt and, in doing so, accidentally knocks over one of the cups of soda on her tray. I smash my lips down, pressing them into each other to keep from laughing, but it's a poor attempt. Rae flings her head back, and on a sigh, she says, "Fuck my life."

"And that's pretty much it," I say, ending the tour of my small home.

"This place is so cool," Rae responds, examining every inch of the cozy bungalow. Her fingers run over the refurbished hardwood kitchen table. "I can't believe you made this—well, all of it really. You flipped this entire house yourself?"

I shrug. "There's still a lot of work left to be done. But yeah, I fixed it up."

Rae drifts over to my sofa and plops down, making herself comfortable. "So, I know how you ended up in Golden Bay, but how did you end up *here*, with this as your home?"

"Sam," I simply state, making my way to her. I sit down next to her, and she adjusts herself, draping her legs over my lap. My hands massage her calves as she urges me to continue talking with her eyes. "If you haven't caught on by now, he owns a lot of places around here."

"Yeah, they might as well name the town after him."

"My thoughts exactly." I chuckle. "On top of a few businesses he owns, he also rents a few houses out. This being one of them."

"So, it's technically Sam's?"

"For now. We're doing a rent-to-own deal. When I first got here a few years back, he didn't realize I was living in my car. Once he found out, he had me stay in this vacant bungalow. I gave him whatever I had in my bank account each month until I had a steady enough income to afford a regular monthly rent. Then, he drummed up this idea of me doing rent-to-own. So, one day, this place will officially be mine."

Rae smiles, her gaze floating around my living room. There's not too much in the way of decorating because that's not really my thing, but the room's not barren. A bookshelf, a small plant on the end table, and a massive TV make the room seem less lonely.

Of course, now that Rae's in here with me, all the loneliness that once lingered in the air has dissipated.

"You need something there." She points behind the couch. "On that wall."

"Like what?"

"I don't know. But it's too empty," she states. I watch as she continues to assess my home, taking everything in. "This really is the perfect bachelor pad."

"I'm hoping it won't be just me living here for the rest of my life, but yeah, it does the trick for now."

Rae's gaze lands back on mine. "You want to live with someone else?"

"I'd eventually like to settle down with someone." My heart rate begins to pick up as my hands roam over her smooth legs. "What about you?"

She shrugs. "I never thought about it before."

It blows my mind that she's never had any dreams or goals to aspire to. She just lives every day like it's her own blank canvas, making it whatever she wants with no foresight of what might lie ahead of her. It is terrifying and thrilling at the same time.

"You never thought about getting married someday?" I inquire.

She lets out a sarcastic laugh. "Oh, I thought about that plenty. Marriage is a big no for me."

"I had a feeling that would be your answer."

"I don't believe a piece of paper is what binds people together for the rest of their lives. If people want to be together, they don't need to sign a contract and spend thousands of dollars just to prove to the rest of the world that they love each other."

"Weddings *are* a giant waste of money," I say in agreement.

"Exactly. What about you? Do you need to get married?"

"No. I'd like to settle down with my person, but I don't need to do the whole marriage part if the person doesn't want to."

Rae nods, and I catch her cheeks turning that beautiful shade of pink that I've come to admire.

"You want kids?" I ask.

Her eyes become wide, and she shakes her head. "I could never bring something so pure and innocent into such an ugly and hateful world."

My hands stop moving. "Same," I state. But I already knew we'd be on the same page about that.

"Certain people shouldn't be parents, and with how fucked up I am, I'm one of those people who shouldn't procreate."

I smile. "You'd make a wonderful mom if you wanted to be. But I know what you mean. Sometimes, I really wish my parents would've decided to use a condom the night I was conceived."

"They sound like assholes from the one time you mentioned them."

"They are."

Silence fills the room as my mind floats somewhere else, lost in a different time. A younger me who only wanted the love and approval of his parents, but the goalpost kept moving.

"What was it like growing up?" Rae asks, sinking farther into my sofa, her legs still on top of me.

Taking a deep breath, I run my hand over the back of my neck, figuring out how best to answer her question.

"Hostile? Detached? Fake?" I search for the right words. "My parents had an image to uphold for the community. In secret, they had affairs and barely spoke to each other. To everyone else, they were a happy couple." I shift around on the cushions. "You know how we're addicted to substances?" I ask and she nods. "Well, they're addicted to money and power."

"Is that why they pressured you into having a baseball career?"

"Yep. Once they realized how talented I was, that was it. The plan was for me to go to the major leagues and they'd get the glory of saying that they were the ones who got me there. That's what would make them good parents: my image and my career. And if people thought they were good parents, they were more likely to vote for my dad and he'd keep climbing the ranks with my mom riding his coattails."

"What's your mom like?"

"She's just as bad, if not worse. She was really only home for public appearances or if she was in between boyfriends."

"Jesus." Rae stares at me in disbelief. "How the fuck did you end up so normal?"

I let out a loud chuckle. "I'm a raging alcoholic."

"Okay, aside from that." She props herself up, her legs folded under her so that she's kneeling next to me. Her face getting closer to mine. "You don't seem jaded or pessimistic. If anything, you're obnoxiously cheery."

I laugh again, only this time, Rae joins me. "I don't know." I shrug. "This is just who I am at heart, I guess. I got lost for a while but found myself. And I'm thankful for that. I know how horrible life can be, so I try my very best to make my life one that I enjoy, and I try to make others feel that way, too."

Rae's quiet, her gaze intent as she studies me. A rush of heat consumes my chest the longer she stares at me, her attention fixated on my face. Softly, her hand comes up to meet my cheek, and her thumb strokes the short hairs of my beard. Leaning in, she presses her lips against mine, and in an instant, we're melting into each other's embrace.

She crawls into my lap, and my greedy hands

explore her body. "I'm glad you didn't end up like them," she whispers into my mouth.

"Me too," I reply just as quietly, my lips rubbing against hers.

Rae's fingers trail down my chest, past my belt buckle, and land right over my crotch. Immediately, I'm hard for her as she begins to palm me through my jeans. Her hips slowly sway over me, washing away any haunting thoughts of the past, landing me right into the present.

I sneak my thumbs under her shirt, connecting with her skin. My mind is already turning wild, thinking of all the places in my home where I want to make her mine.

"And," Rae starts to say but kisses my neck first. "I'm really glad your parents skipped the condom that night."

My eyes squeeze shut, cringing. "Don't talk about my parents right now."

She chuckles. "Sorry." Then she removes her hand and lowers her hips, grinding herself over my cock. I shudder at the sensation. My grip on her goes from gentle to harsh.

Our mouths collide once again as our kisses become deep and untamed. The fuse in my brain has officially been lit by her once more as lust pounds into my veins.

Knowing exactly where this is headed, Rae breaks away to peel off her shirt.

"Fuck," I sigh, my mouth watering when I see her gorgeous body on display. She hops off me and wiggles out of her shorts, letting them drop at her ankles before she steps out of them.

"Talking about my shitty family makes you hot?" I tease, even though I just told her not to mention them.

"Does talking about them hurt?" she asks, her voice so kind and gentle. My head gets fuzzy, feeling confused between discussing my past and being turned on by Rae at the same time. She stands there half-naked, waiting for an answer.

"It does," I admit.

"Then I want to make you feel better." The thick sultriness in her words sends the blood rushing to the lower half of my body. My nerve endings catch fire when she says, "Use me to make yourself feel better, Miles."

The last of my composure snapping, I hook my fingers around the fabric of the middle of her bra and yank her toward me. The wind nearly gets knocked out of her as I pull her on top of my lap.

Her eyes warm up with desire as a sly grin appears on her lips. "Where do you want me first?" She innocently bats her eyelashes.

About fifty images of me screwing her in different areas of my house pop into my brain. They all look so enticing, I can't pick just one.

Rae rocks back and forth on my lap, and my thoughts spin. Glancing behind her, I suddenly know where our first spot will be.

She lets out a little squeal when I scoop her up and hurry us over to my kitchen table. Lying her down, I adjust her to where I want her. Taking two fingers, I press them up to her lips, and she closes her eyes as she sucks on them. Her tongue dances around, coating them.

When they're nice and wet, I take them from her

mouth and slide her panties to the side, pushing my fingers inside her.

Rae moans, her back arching off the table as I pick up the intensity. My free hand reaches for her neck and applies pressure on the sides.

She writhes under me as she gives me complete control over her. "You want to make me feel better, Rae?" I begin to taunt her, continuing to get her off. "That's the kind of whore you are? You want me to use you so I feel good about myself?"

"Yes," she cries out.

"You better keep your fucking word because I'm just getting started." I press my thumb over her clit, and her body shakes as she gasps for air. "I'm going to make you mine all over this house, understand?"

Too busy moaning, the only thing she can do to respond is nod her head.

I work her faster and harder until she's clenching around my hands, twisting and turning as she shouts loud enough for the next-door neighbors to hear.

I keep going after she's finished, letting her ride out the aftershocks. Coming down from her high, her muscles relax against the wooden table, and I slide my fingers out of her. Licking them clean, savoring her taste.

A lazy smile appears on Rae's face. "I'm ready for more," she says, her voice breathy and eyes hooded. A flushed red blossoms on her chest, partly hidden by her tattoos.

My thoughts get lost in my lust for her. And for the rest of the night, she allows me to feel better. *A lot* better.

CHAPTER THIRTY-TWO

Rae

THE PAST WEEK has flown by and I think I'm starting to get into the groove of work, Miles and meetings. Today, Tonya ran the NA meeting. I didn't speak, as usual, but even if I don't share my story, I'm starting to feel a stronger sense of community just from listening and surrounding myself with others.

Once the meeting's over, I walk over to the diner with Joe. He's one of the cooks and has been sober for fourteen years. In our meeting, he ended up sharing about how he recently lost his grandmother and he's struggling with his grief, which has been making it more tempting for him to start using again. So, I've been trying to distract him and shoot the shit while we head closer to work.

"How's working in food service treating you?" he asks before stomping on his cigarette.

I take one last drag and do the same thing before walking into work. "It sucks."

Joe laughs. "Sounds about right. You're doing a good job, though."

"Yeah, Sam keeps lying to me too and saying the same thing," I joke.

"You'll get the hang of it."

"That's the rumor I keep hearing."

We move inside, the bell chiming overhead and get right to work.

Since the weather's getting warmer, we're getting busier as more tourists pop out of the woodwork. I still struggle on the slow shifts, so thankfully, I haven't moved to the more hectic ones yet.

The day moves fast as I take care of my tables. Miraculously, I haven't spilled anything or gotten any orders wrong.

With my shift ending, Miles appears and sits down at the counter, ordering a soda from Sam.

"Hey." I press up on my toes to kiss his cheek.

"Hey, beautiful," Miles beams. "How much longer you have?"

"I'm free to go once that table finishes." I gesture with my chin toward the couple in the back. "What are we doing tonight?" I rest my elbow on the counter, getting closer to him, hoping he'll tell me our plans. He told me he'd meet me at the end of my shift, and then we'd go back to my condo so I could get ready before he took me out—but he won't tell me *where* he's taking me.

"Wouldn't you like to know?" he responds with a smug look. The bells over the door chime, signaling another customer entering, but I'm too busy trying to get Miles to ruin his surprise for me than to pay attention to the person who entered.

"Tell me." I shake Miles's arm, only to make him grin wider.

"No way. A surprise is a surprise, Rae."

"But—"

"Excuse me," the man who just walked in says from behind us.

I peek over Miles's shoulder. "You can have a seat at any empty table, I'll be right with you."

"I was hoping you could help me with something. I'm looking for someone," the man says.

I watch as Miles's body becomes rigid, his face paling as he recognizes the voice coming from behind him. My eyes bounce from Miles to the man with greenish-blue eyes and dark-brown hair.

The second it registers, my stomach drops.

"Uh, who are you looking for?" I ask, already knowing the answer.

"Miles Kingston. I believe he's been living near here."

On cue, Miles slowly turns around, every muscle in his body tense as his expression hardens with a frown.

I notice the man's face light up when he realizes Miles is right here next to me.

"Hi, Son," Miles's father says with a breath of relief.

"Dad." Miles remains cold.

"It's great to see you, it's been two years—"

"Three." He spins back around and sips on his soda.

His father, who, if I remember correctly, is named Dennis, looks over to me. His eyes plead, asking for some type of assistance in getting Miles to give him the time of day.

Fuck that. If I were in Miles's position, I'd be doing the same thing.

Mr. Kingston clears his throat, but both of us ignore him. "Miles." He takes a step closer. "I was hoping we could spend some time together and catch up."

There's a gnawing feeling in my gut, telling me this isn't a good idea, but when I glance over at Miles, I can already see him tempering. The lines on his forehead smooth over as he considers his dad's proposal.

"We were heading out soon," I say before Miles can respond. "But you can sit down and talk for a bit while he waits for my shift to be over." This way, if things go south, we can bust out of here as soon as possible.

Miles looks over to me, silently thanking me. I give him a slight dip of my chin, then move out of the way so that his dad can sit on the stool next to him.

Trying not to seem like I'm eavesdropping—even though I one hundred percent am—I grab the salt-shakers off empty tables and fill them up at the opposite end of the counter.

Miles won't look directly at his dad as he tries to awkwardly make small talk. I catch every few words, and as of right now, it doesn't seem awful.

As I pour the tiny white crystals into the glass shakers, Sam walks out of the kitchen, noting Miles speaking to someone. Sam's expression evolves from indifference to a shocked realization when he notices the resemblance between the two.

"Is that?" Sam whispers next to me.

"Yep," I say, focusing on the salt, still trying to hear the conversation.

"Huh."

Sam hangs around the front of the restaurant, even though he's not needed as I continue to make myself busy.

There's a thumping in my chest, anticipating the worst. Anxiety prickles at my fingers as they nervously tinker with the tops of the saltshakers.

"Excuse me." Dennis Kingston flags me over.

"Yeah?"

"Can I get a coffee?"

I nod. "Coming right up."

As I pour his drink and walk it over to him, I catch the tail end of their conversation.

"Things are looking up for next year's election," Mr. Kingston informs Miles.

"Finally going for governor?" Miles asks.

"No, skipping right over that and going for senator." He gives a shit-eating grin, and I shove the cup of coffee in front of him. "Thank you, sweetie."

"Don't call me that," I snap.

Dennis's brows rise, and I watch as his gaze drifts over me. It's not in a sleazy, horny old man type of way, it's more of a judgmental assessment. The look in his eyes tells me he thinks I'm trash or some ridiculous nonsense. It's a look that used to get under my skin, but now it pleases me. It lets me know that, on some level, I intimidate the person. This is exactly why I don't back down or walk away when Dennis's attention falls back on my face.

"Is there a problem?" I ask.

He gives me a fake smile. "I would like some sugar," he says, lifting up the mug.

"Of course, you would." My focus then goes to Miles, who's fighting back a chuckle.

I swear to God that better be the only quality Miles inherited from this man.

Going to grab the sugar, Dennis continues his conversation with Miles. "Your mother's already acting the part of a senator's wife, telling all her friends to support me and getting ready to go out on the political campaigns with me."

"I bet the two of you are basking in all the attention," Miles says.

I slide the sugar over to Dennis, and he barely looks my way. "You know, son, it'd be nice to have you with us on the campaign. After I get elected as senator, who knows what'll be next for us—heck, you might be looking at the future president!"

I inadvertently chortle, then immediately try to cover it with a coughing fit. Miles glances over at me, smiling, and I know he sees right through my act.

"So, what do you think?" Dennis says to Miles, not realizing my reaction. "Want to head back home and do some campaigning for your old man?" He places his hand on Miles's shoulder.

"My home is here now," Miles says, smoothly readjusting himself so his dad's hand is no longer on him. "But good luck with the campaign." He stands up and looks at me. "Rae, you ready?"

"Um..." I glance at my last table, which is still eating, then over to Sam, who's wiping down an already clean table.

"You can go," Sam says. "I'll take care of the back table for you."

"Thank you." I walk out from around the counter.

"You're going to leave that quickly?" Dennis says to Miles before we can step away from him.

"Yeah. There's nothing left to talk about."

"Actually, there is something else I'd like to tell you about." He runs his hand over his scruff as if he's debating telling Miles more. "A television network reached out to me."

"Okay?" Miles snaps, his patience wearing thin.

"Looking for you."

Miles cocks his head to the side. "Me?"

"It's been ten years since the *event*," Dennis informs Miles as if he didn't already know that it's been a decade since the worst day of his life.

Knots form in my stomach, sending a sharp cramp into my abdomen.

It's strange how everyone I know who was impacted by that day can never utter the words. We all call it something similar to "the event," "that day," or "when *it* happened."

"I'm aware," Miles says, his jaw tensing.

"There are producers who are looking to make a documentary and want you to be a part of it since you were a big name at the time."

A flash of anger explodes through my bloodstream, my body heating up with rage.

"A documentary!?" I spit out, my blood boiling before Miles can get a word in edgewise.

Dennis looks over to me, blinking as if he didn't notice I was standing next to his son. "Excuse me, but this is a conversation between me and Miles. You don't know what it pertains to—"

"Yes, I fucking do! I was alone with Miles that day!"

Dennis silences, examining me, then flicks his gaze to Miles, then back to me. Realization washes over his features. "You're the girl from the newspapers," he says.

My brain gets whiplash, and my brows pull in tight, puzzled. "The girl from the newspapers?" There's no doubt that my sister was on the news, but *me*? Dennis must be mistaken.

Miles lets out a sigh, his head dropping in disappointment as he shakes it. "Dad."

"What newspapers?" I ask Miles, who's not glancing at me.

Confused as all hell, there's a pit in my core, making me feel sick. I don't know whether to puke or cry. I'm not sure if I even want to know what Dennis is referring to.

"Well," Dennis carries on, taking out his wallet and placing a ten-dollar bill on the counter. He then extends a business card to Miles. "They're offering you a pretty penny, you might as well call them. We can set it up so that it airs before Election Day, and we can have you talk about it the entire campaign. Of course, we'd have to prep you for interviews so you don't swing the votes the opposite way." He heartlessly chuckles, and my fists ball up, ready to punch this man square in the face. "Our voters don't like being told what to do, but if we keep to a wholesome story about our family sticking together during that time, I think I'll have a good turnout on Election Day." Dennis shifts his gaze to me. "You might be able to weasel your way into the documentary," he says. "I'm sure they'll offer you a better stipend than working here."

I slap the business card out of his hand. "Suck my—"

"Rae—" Sam says from behind me, obviously having been paying attention to this entire exchange.

"Dick!"

With that, I grab Miles's shirt and yank him out of the diner.

My thoughts race, and my feet move with them,

speed walking toward my condo. My pulse pounds against my eardrums as my mind becomes jumbled.

Flashes and flickers of memories.

So many questions burning my tongue, but I want to make sure we're far away from that man before I speak.

As we quickly move forward, sweat forms on the back of my neck.

My breathing becomes labored.

Sharp inhales are making my lungs ache.

My hands tremble.

"Slow down," Miles says, carefully touching my arm.

He stops me from continuing forward. I spin to look at him, his eyes displaying pain—probably from his interaction with his self-absorbed father. But my head is too murky to ask him if he's okay.

My heart pounds.

Louder.

And louder.

"What did your dad mean about me being the girl from the newspapers?" I ask, out of breath. More words continue to tumble out of my mouth before Miles can answer. "I'm really fucking confused. How does your dad know me? What newspapers?"

Miles draws in a deep, unsteady breath, and my chest twists in unsettling anticipation. "You know how I'd have to do interviews for baseball?" I nod, and he continues. "I did one immediately after that day, and what I said got blown out of proportion."

"What did you say?"

"You didn't see any of the articles? Nothing on the news?"

"No," I snap. "My family and I stayed away from the media—especially because reporters kept harassing us. We didn't turn the TV on for weeks—months! Do you really think the four of us sat at our kitchen table, flipping through the motherfucking newspapers or scrolling through articles online? I had a dead sister to mourn and didn't want to see her face everywhere I looked!"

"That makes sense." Miles gazes down, avoiding eye contact as he tells me, "I was interviewed, and the reporter asked me what happened." He pauses, and a round of nausea hits me. "I didn't mean for it to come out that way, but I said that I found a girl and protected her while everything went down, and I stopped her from going out—which ultimately saved her." He slowly pulls his attention from the pavement and up to meet my face. "I was crowned a hero. It was everywhere—my face next to all the people who died, saying that if it wasn't for me, more would've been dead. They quoted me, and '*I saved her*' was in big black letters in the headlines."

Those words press up against my skull, making my nose run and my eyes burn. I stay silent as Miles keeps speaking.

"That's another reason why I dropped out of college. I got there, and not only did I feel the pressure of gearing up toward the major leagues, but I also was deemed a survivor *and* a hero. I hated it. I hated people looking up to me and treating me like I was an idol. And I hated that I even brought you up in the interview to begin with when I didn't even know your name. It was like I patted myself on the back and the rest of the world did the same—but no one knew how horrifying that day was." I watch as his ocean eyes become watery, forming their own waves. "How awful it must've been for you. I've been feeling guilty about it ever since."

Bile rises in my throat. I swallow, allowing the reality of what he just said to settle in. "So, were you just dating me to clear your conscience? Treat me nice for a while and it'll even out you feeling guilty for getting your fifteen minutes of fame for saving my life?"

"No!" Miles clutches both my hands in a tight grip, scared that he might let me slip away if he holds too loosely. "God, no—not at all."

I nod, the tears in my eyes getting dangerously close to being released. My throat gets thick, making it more difficult for the air to slide through. Even though we're outside, it feels as if I'm getting closed in on.

Everything feels close.

Too close.

As if the sea breeze is wrapping around my neck, strangling me.

"I think I need to be alone right now," I say, backing away and out of his grasp.

"Please believe me, Rae. I'm not with you out of guilt or pity or—"

"I know. I just—" My head dizzies. "I just need space. My thoughts, they're too much."

"What are you going to do while you're alone?" he asks, concern splashed across his face. It's enough to make my vision blur with more tears because he's scared I'm going to relapse.

Which means he cares.

More weight piles down on me, but I shake off the look of distress. "I'm going to do some art. I need to let everything out." I separate myself further from him.

Miles nods. "Call me if you need anything. Please."

"Uh-huh."

Spinning around, I dash to my building. Running past Emma and leaping up the steps, I make it to my home, gasping for air.

Memories bombard my brain, clouding my ability to distinguish the present from the past.

A horrible ache strikes my body as I hear the noises as if they were yesterday.

Loud. Blaring.

I squeeze my eyes shut, but every time I do, all I can see is red.

Crimson.

Staining the bottom of my shoes.

"Get it off! Get it off!" I scream at the top of my lungs.

My eyelids fling open, and even though my current shoes are clean, I rip them off and toss them on the other side of the room. A loud thud echoes as each shoe strikes my floor.

Every fiber of my being trembles, sweat soaking through my clothes as I pant.

The visions of the past keep invading my brain, and I slam my palm against my head to get them out. Hitting myself harder, wishing the thoughts would fall right out of my ears.

Wishing I could shatter my skull to rid them.

My very soul is getting eaten away by the trauma.

The yearning desire to quiet the memories—destroy the past—sparking inside me. A thirst that I knew would always linger.

A thirst for numbness.

Fighting with my inner demons, begging me to get

high to get rid of this terrible feeling, I stumble into my bedroom and head for my art supplies.

Reaching my paints, I grab whatever I can and go back to my living room to finish the partially completed mural.

With nausea rolling around in my stomach, I paint.

Every flick of my wrist, each color I concentrate on, helps me to get in a zone.

Slowly, I gain control of my world by getting lost in my art.

Solely focusing on the brush in my hand, I expel the ugliness living inside me without giving it a second thought.

Letting whatever needs to come out flow onto the wall.

My hands are covered in red, and I smear the paint across the length, wiping the color off of me and swiping over what I had just drawn.

The red blends into the picture, droplets sliding down, making it look more realistic.

More like blood.

Taking a long breath of relief, I step back, examining my artwork.

A choppy, gigantic monster looms over panicking children as they run away from it. It grins with fangs, and its razor-sharp claws reach out for the kids, piercing some of them. No one else is in sight to save them. They'll either end up dead or wishing they were.

Staring at it for a beat more, I shudder.

I hate it.

But it was living in my head, so I'm glad I got it out. At least now that it's out of my head, I feel like it has less power over me.

My adrenaline crashes, and I begin to settle down and back into reality.

Letting my body deflate, I step away from the wall, even though I can still sense my creative energy swimming through my veins.

Taking some much-needed time away from my painting, I walk into my kitchen and run my hands under the water, letting the flakes of paint fall off my skin and into the sink. Taking in a steady breath, I settle myself, my heart rate going back to normal.

Grabbing myself a drink, my eyes float over to my kitchen counter, where I have a pile of sea glass waiting for me to do something with it.

Maybe I'll create something peaceful. That'll be a change of pace for me.

CHAPTER THIRTY-THREE

Miles

TEN YEARS AGO

IT'S NEARING the end of second period when I get called into Coach Carson's office. Not that I mind, I'd do anything to bail out of history class early. Walking under the balloon archway that's celebrating tonight's starting game, I stride down the long hallway.

"What's up, Coach?" I say, walking into his small office that's connected to the boys' locker room. I don't know how the poor guy doesn't pass out from the smell, having to sit in here all day.

"Hey, Kingston." He peers up from his glasses and gestures for me to sit in the chair across from his desk.

Before sitting, I grab a stray ball on the floor, then lean back in the chair, playing catch with myself.

"How are you feeling about tonight's first game?" Coach Carson asks.

It's my senior year, and I have multiple universities hounding me to join their team—most of which will have a scout in the stands tonight, along with the press and news reporters. But I'm not the slightest bit fazed.

"Just peachy," I respond, the ball flying up above my head, then dropping back down into my hands.

"There's going to be a lot of big names out there ready to see Miles Kingston."

"Then I'll make sure to put on a good show." I flash him a smile, and he chuckles.

"Listen, I didn't have you come down here to give you a pep talk, I know you don't need one."

I stop playing catch and focus on him. "What'd you call me into your office for?"

"I caught wind of something." Coach takes his glasses off and places them on his desk.

"Oh?"

"Rumor has it your parents are out of town, and there's going to be a big party at your house."

I laugh, blowing off any concern he might have. "To be fair, they're not out of town *yet*. After I win the game, they'll leave."

"And once they're gone, the entire student body is invited to your house?"

"I can neither confirm nor deny that information."

But he knows the answer. This party's gonna be epic. Word spread as soon as I texted it this morning in the group chat.

Coach rests his arms on the desk and leans in closer. "Kingston, you have a lot riding right now, and you don't want to lose all of it on some stupid house party."

"Hate to break it to you, Coach, but I've been to parties before—everyone on the team has."

"Yes, but have any been at your house with your

parents' names on the line? And was the entire school invited?"

Shutting up, I sink down in my chair, knowing he's right.

"Don't do anything idiotic," he says, his gaze pressing into me.

"I won't." Worse comes to worst and it gets out of hand, I'll just kick everyone out, and my teammates and I will drink all the liquor I scored.

"Good." Coach straightens his posture and reaches for his key ring. "What's your next class?"

"Science," I groan.

"Do you mind being late so you can help me out with something?"

"Is that even a question?"

"I was hoping you'd say that." He twists a key off of the ring and slides it across his desk. "I need you to go to the supply closet and grab a bunch of the mats and bring them into the gym."

"Which supply closet? The one next to the bathroom or the one next to the weight room?"

"Next to the weight room, across from room 102."

The bell rings, signaling the end of second period.

Standing up, I take the key and start heading out of his office. "You got it, Coach."

CHAPTER THIRTY-FOUR

Miles

PRESENT

IT'S BEEN twenty-four hours since Dad casually strolled into Sam's pretending he missed me, all to try to use me like a pawn.

I didn't get a wink of sleep last night. No matter how long I was stargazing, no matter how much melatonin I took—my mind wouldn't shut off.

Since I couldn't do anything but lie in bed and think about the sucker punch to the gut Dad gave me when I realized he only wanted me for his campaign— and then had the nerve to bring up doing a documentary to boost his votes—I decided to start my day earlier than normal.

My morning run was at four a.m., where I sped up and down the boardwalk, passing Rae's condo, hoping her light would be turned on.

Anxiety consumed me all night, worried that bringing up the past might cause Rae to spiral. I hope and pray that if she were really going to relapse that she'd call me or someone or go to NA. Something.

I don't want to bother her. She wants to be alone, some space from me and everything I represent.

As I work on my fifth job for the day, installing light fixtures at Sam's new storefront, my mind goes back and forth between worry for Rae and resentment toward my parents. There's a searing pain in my chest, pouring salt in the wound as I think about my interaction with Dad. How little he cares about me, not even knowing it had been three years since we last saw each other.

It's a pain I had once thought I moved on from, but seeing him again reopened the stitches, making it sting my whole body.

While Rae might've been struggling with her past last night—I was also dealing with mine. It was the first time in a very long time that I craved alcohol. The urge to take the edge off was strong, but I pushed through and went to AA.

Trying to ignore the thoughts in my head, I grab four screws from my toolbox and step up on a ladder to drill in the industrial-looking fixture.

Working on the third screw, I stick the last one between my lips as the taste of nickel fills my mouth.

I can hear the sound of the front door opening the moment I let go of the power button on my drill. Glancing over my shoulder, Rae stands off to the side with a timid smile, holding something wooden in her hands.

Relief seeps into my bones when I have confirmation she's okay.

Stepping off the ladder, I place the drill down and remove the screw from my lips, dropping it into my pocket. Warmth fans through me when I take Rae in. There's a soft glow of the sun setting behind her, making the wisps of stray hairs stand out. Her light eyes are wide and vulnerable, letting her armor slip.

She doesn't look distraught like she did yesterday. Instead, she seems settled.

"Hey," Rae says, her volume low.

"I'm glad you're okay," I tell her, skipping right over pleasantries.

"I'm fine. I had a tough night, but I went to NA today and am feeling better."

Taking a step closer, I speak gently. "I'm sorry—"

"No, I am."

My forehead wrinkles. "For what?"

"Not being there for you yesterday. I freaked out about my own thing, and I realized I left you to fend for yourself when you were probably hurting." She shifts her gaze off me. "It was a shitty girlfriend move."

Smiling, I meet her toe-to-toe. With my fingers, I tilt her chin to get her to look at me. "I'm okay, too," I assure her.

"Are you upset about your dad? Because I am, and I don't even know the guy."

"Yeah. But I'm working through it."

"You know you could've just told him to fuck off and you didn't have to endure a conversation with him? You don't have to be nice to everyone, Miles."

"I know. I'm not really sure why I stayed as long as I did in the first place, even if it only was for a few minutes."

"Maybe you were secretly hoping this time would be different." Rae's voice becomes quieter. "Probably has something to do with that decent heart of yours that likes to give people the benefit of the doubt." Her words tug at something deep inside me, making me feel something I've never experienced before. I go to thank her, but she starts talking before I can. "That, plus a hearty dose of people-pleasing." She playfully takes a dig at me.

My face scrunches at the comment. "I am not a people pleaser."

"Says the guy who will go running to anyone in town if they so much as need their garbage disposal fixed."

I chuckle at the memory of me and her from several weeks back, and I run my fingers through her silky hair. "I would've fixed anything you needed just to be with you." There's a beat of silence as I let the truth behind her statement sink in. "You might have a point, though. However, I've been trying not to jump the second someone needs me to do something. I think turning down the documentary my dad wants me to do is a good start."

"It's the perfect start. Fuck him."

We tenderly smile at each other, allowing ourselves to be supported by one another. My attention goes to her hands, where she's still clutching a piece of driftwood roughly the length of my forearm. "What's that?" I ask.

"I wanted to make you something."

"You made me something?" My brows shoot up as a lightness fills my once-aching chest. "How come?"

"Partly because you have an ugly blank wall in your living room...and partly because I wanted to make you feel better."

I smirk. "We both know you have other means to make me feel better."

Rae chuckles. "That's also included in tonight's events."

"Tonight's events? You planned something for us?"

"Yeah. I figured we'd watch *Friends*, you can eat an unhealthy amount of sugar, and we could end the evening with you doing whatever you want with me."

I should be focusing on the last part of that sentence, but my brain picks up on something else. "*You* want to watch *Friends*?"

"No. I'd rather gouge my eyes out. But it's your show, so I want to watch it with you."

Tingles shoot through my veins at the same time my stomach does backflips. My attention goes back down to the object in her hand. "Can I see what you made me?"

Rae flips over the piece of wood, and I almost lose my breath at the sight. It's a mosaic of the beach and night sky, made completely out of sea glass.

"It's superglued down, and I shook it a bunch of times to make sure there are no loose pieces," she says, running her fingers over the colorful chunks of glass. "I've been collecting sea glass since our first date and didn't know what to do with it until last night. I made sure to make the sky dark, and I even added some smaller white pieces for stars—you know, so during the daytime, you can still be reminded that dead people are watching us."

If I wasn't so captivated by the gesture, I'd laugh at her comment. But I can't because there's a prickling behind my eyes as my heart swells. This overwhelming sensation cascades down my body, through my limbs, and radiates out of me.

I bite down on my lip to keep my emotions in check.

No one's ever done something like this for me before. No woman has even listened to me speak to the extent of picking up on what makes me happy and calm. I've never even given them a chance to get to know me on that level because I knew none of them would get it. But Rae, she's the only one who gets me. Who knows me.

"I went for a walk on the beach last night and found the driftwood," Rae continues. "Then I had to smash some of the glass to get the pieces to fit together. I probably should've worn goggles or some shit, but luckily the only war wound I got was a couple of cuts on my hand." She shrugs it off and brings her focus back to the mosaic. "You like it?"

"Rae, I love it," I whisper, but the second the words fall from my lips, I know with complete certainty that it's not just the artwork in her hands I love.

It's Rae.

All of her.

The bruised and damaged, rough edges of her, and the heartfelt, tender glimmers of her soul.

"Good," she replies, taking a step back. "We can hang it on your wall when we go back to your place after you're done working."

I take my gift from her and admire it up close. "I don't know how you do it, Rae."

"Do what?"

"Have the ability to turn anything into art."

She loops her hair behind her ears and shrugs. "It's nothing, really. Just a project to keep me busy."

"Thank you. This means a lot to me."

"Of course."

CHAPTER THIRTY-FIVE

MILES'S LIPS trail along my bare shoulder, waking me up. "Morning, princess," he whispers against my skin.

The corners of my mouth tip up, and I pop one eye open to look at him. He's sitting on the edge of his bed, shirtless and sweaty.

"Did you already go for your run?" I mumble against the pillow.

"Yep." He pushes off the bed. "I'm going to shower, then make us breakfast."

"Or you could go back to sleep."

"I'm wide awake," Miles states.

"You're a psycho."

"I'm a morning person."

"Exactly my point."

He chuckles, dropping his gym shorts. A little more awake at the sight before me, I open my other eye, clearly checking him out—as if I didn't get my fill of him last night.

After I gave him the mosaic, we went back to his

home, hung it up, watched approximately twelve minutes of *Friends,* and then got each other off all night long.

I know I can't take away any of his pain from his family, but at the very least, I can let him indulge in me to help him get his mind off things. I'm not the type of person who will hold someone for hours as they cry. It's not me, it's unnatural. However, using my body to aid someone has never been me either—but right now, that's the best I can give him. And I hope he's okay with that.

Although, little by little, Miles is chipping away at me, letting my vulnerability peek through. So, who knows, maybe a few months from now, I'll be coddling others and offering them a shoulder to cry on.

Fat chance, though.

"Go back to sleep, I'll wake you up when the food's ready," Miles says, stripping out of his boxers.

I stare at him a beat longer, taking a mental picture so that when I shut my eyes, I'll have something sexy to look at.

With the both of us off from work, we decide to spend our day together doing nothing and everything at the same time. It's wild how meaningless, mundane tasks like cooking and going for a walk suddenly have a weighted significance with Miles. His presence somehow makes trivial things important. The weirdest part of it all...I'm actually enjoying it.

"Okay, I got one," Miles says as we stroll along the

beach, my toes sinking into the warm sand. "Joey, Ross, Chandler."

"That's easy," I state. "Fuck Joey, marry Chandler, and kill Ross."

"Damn, you didn't even flinch before killing off Ross."

I laugh, tipping my head back. "His character sucks."

"Heads up!" someone shouts from afar. A moment later, a volleyball is soaring through the cloudless blue sky, aimed right at my chest. I leap back, and at the same time, Miles sticks out his hand, catching the ball right before it strikes me.

Letting out a loud breath, I take a moment to study how Miles flawlessly stopped the ball from knocking me on my ass with one hand. One large, veiny hand with long, thick fingers.

"Sorry, guys!" the person who threw the volleyball calls out as he and two of his teammates jog up to us.

Squinting through the sunlight, I get a better look at who the people are as they get closer. Travis, Evan, and Brad.

"Here you go." Miles tosses Travis the volleyball back.

"Thanks, Miles," he says. "Evan's still working on his aim."

"Yeah, sorry about that," Evan says.

"No problem, just glad I caught it in time before it hit Rae," Miles states.

All of their attention swings to me, and they offer another apology with flirty smiles and wandering eyes.

"You want to join us?" Travis asks me, gesturing

toward the volleyball net. "Both of you," he adds, glancing over to a grinning Miles.

"I don't think anyone wants me on their team, I'm lacking in any athletic ability," I state.

"We'll pass this time, but thanks," Miles says.

They nod but don't go very far, not wanting the conversation to end. "I heard you're working at Sam's Dinette," Brad speaks up.

"Yeah, still getting used to it," I reply.

"That place seems fitting for someone like you," Travis states.

My head tilts to the side. "Someone like me?"

"Yeah, you know."

I narrow my eyes, sensing a flame igniting inside me. "No. I don't know."

"Well, you—I mean," he stumbles over his words. "I'm studying business, so we're two different types of people in two different industries."

Miles opens his mouth to say something, but before he can, I say, "And someone like me wouldn't be fitted for the business industry?"

"No, that's not what I meant. It's just I can't picture you in a suit." Travis and his buddies try to laugh it off like a joke, but it's not. It's far from it.

Once again, Miles tries to interject, but I put a hand out to stop him because I got this. "Oh? What do you picture me wearing when you're envisioning me, Travis?"

His face flushes, and his gaze darts to Miles. "I-I don't—I just meant that because I've never seen you in a suit that I can't picture you in one."

"So, because I don't wear suits, that means I'd do a poor job as a businesswoman?"

"No—"

"If the career is dependent on outfits, then why are you bothering getting a degree?"

"You're more alternative. That's all I meant."

"You don't like my tattoos, Travis?" I keep pushing him with my words. The joy of watching him fumble over himself makes my heart sing, but I keep my scowl in place, not letting him know I'm getting an inkling of pleasure from this.

"Your tattoos are awesome," Travis says.

"And your hair," Evan adds.

"My hair?"

"Yeah, it's really nice."

"But not suitable for the business world, right, Travis?"

He lets out a desperate chuckle. "I'm gonna need to backtrack on this entire conversation. I think you'd be great at anything you want to do, Rae." He tries to save himself as he swipes away sweat from his forehead.

Smirking, I end the little game I was playing. "I'm so thankful to have your approval," I say with obvious sarcasm.

"Uh, we gotta head back," Brad chimes in from behind Travis and Evan, and he starts taking steps backward.

"We'll see you guys around," Travis says, and we all give a short goodbye.

Once they're stationed back at the volleyball net, Miles bursts into laughter. His hand lands on the small of my back and he guides me forward so we can continue on our stroll.

"You loved making them squirm, didn't you?" he asks.

"Sure fucking did," I state with pride, and Miles continues to chuckle at my enjoyment. "People like them need to squirm every once in a while."

"For the record, you'd look sexy in a suit and make a badass businesswoman."

"Thank you, but that role is far from what I'd ever desire. I would hate the corporate world, and I have a feeling it wouldn't take a liking to me either. I'm not exactly designed to fit in that box."

"You're not. And I think that's one of the reasons I enjoy being around you so much," Miles admits, making my stomach flutter.

"Because I'm weird?"

"Because you're not afraid to be you. Unapologetically you, whether people take to you or not."

I nod in agreement and begin talking more freely about the thoughts that have been pent up in my head for years on end. "Why should I shrink myself to make others feel more comfortable? So that it's easier for them to look away?" I rhetorically ask as Miles attentively listens to me ramble. "I don't want people to look away. I *want* to make people uncomfortable. I'm not conforming to what society wants me to be, and that's unsettling for some people. Well, good—some people *should* be unsettled. They need to start understanding that people outside of their circle are also walking this planet. They need to be reminded that people like me exist and we're only fucked up like this because the system failed us. Society failed us. They need to stop living in a goddamn bubble and explore all the shit that makes them feel unnerved because that's the only way they'll grow." I let out a loud sigh of relief.

"Wow, been holding on to that for quite some time, huh?" Miles says, his face sparking with intrigue.

I should be used to him being open to what I have to say, but it's still surprising to me that none of my thoughts scare him away. He's willing to go along for the ride.

"There's a lot more where that came from. That's only the tip of the iceberg."

"Vent away, I'm all ears."

Looking up at him, I smile, admiring how the sun brightens the jade flecks in his eyes and paints his cheeks a rosy-bronze color. His offering me the space to let my feelings out lets me breathe easier, as if a cinder block has been lifted off my rib cage. "I'm good," I say. "But I might take you up on that offer later."

"Any time you're ready." Miles threads his fingers between mine. "I'm here."

My grin widens as we continue onward, enjoying the warm weather.

There's a spot around my heart that's beginning to soften. A place that I've kept protected for years on end for a multitude of reasons, but with Miles, I'm becoming more okay with letting my guard down.

I could get used to this...maybe.

CHAPTER THIRTY-SIX
Miles

RAE STILL HASN'T GOTTEN sick of me yet, after we spent the entire day together. In fact, it was her idea for me to spend the night. So, here we are, sitting on her balcony, stargazing and staring out at the sea. We talk for hours as if we didn't already talk all day.

When silence finally falls between us, I lounge back in her oversized chair and stretch out my legs.

"I'm gonna put on some pj's," Rae says, standing up. "Need anything?"

I shake my head. "I'm good."

She slinks away behind the glass door and back inside her condo.

As she changes her clothes, I continue staring out into the distance. It's a strange experience to feel so small compared to our vast world, yet also feel connected to everything and everyone around me, as if I'm intertwined with some cosmic story that's being brought to life right before my eyes.

The loneliness that I've felt for most of my life doesn't hurt as bad as it once had. It's barely even there most nights. I know it has everything to do with Rae and our relationship. Not only how she sees me and listens to me but also because she understands. And what she doesn't understand, she tries to.

The glass door clicks open behind me, and a few seconds later, Rae appears. She's wearing cotton shorts and a worn cami with no bra underneath. She tosses a pack of cigarettes and a lighter onto the small round side table.

"Don't smoke those yet," I say, smiling.

Rae's brow arches, and a sly look appears on her face. "How come?"

Extending my arm out, I reach for her hand, tugging her toward me. I place her on my lap and press my lips against the space right under her ear. "Because I want to do this first." Sliding my hand against her cheek so I'm firmly cupping it, I draw her in for a deep kiss.

Rae shifts herself, arms wrapping around my body as her tongue excitedly enters my mouth. Giving me more and more of what I want, she presses into me, bringing my cock to life.

Our breaths are already ragged as I pull away slightly so I can see her face. The admiration in her eyes fills me with an overwhelming sense of joy.

"You're the only person I like spending all day with," she says. If it wasn't so dark out, I'd bet her cheeks are turning pink at the admission.

"Same here."

"And..." Her fingertips trail down my chest and stomach, stopping right before my jeans. "All night." A smirk grows on her face as a flash of mischief ignites in her eyes.

"You just can't get enough of me, can you?" I tease

even though my gaze drops down to her low-cut shirt, where I have the perfect view of her cleavage—letting her know that it's *me* who can't get enough of her.

"What can I say? I like a man who knows what he's doing."

I chuckle. "Is that the only reason you're with me? So I can pleasure you until you pass out?"

"Duh," she sarcastically answers. Her fingers toy with the button of my pants. "I've been thinking about what it'd be like to have you take me on the beach," she says, popping the button open.

My hands run up and down her back, heat stirring in my veins. "You'd love it if I fucked you out in the open in broad daylight, wouldn't you?"

Biting into her bottom lip, Rae nods, slowly tugging down my zipper.

With a growing desire burning me up inside, I decide to give her what she wants. It might not be daylight, and we might not be rolling around in the sand, but night sex on her balcony seems like the next best option.

Mustering up my best authoritative voice, the kind I know she gets off on, I bring my mouth to her ear and say, "On your fucking knees, princess."

As if my words sent zaps of lightning bolts through her body, she's off of me in an instant, grinning at my command.

I don't think I'll ever get tired of seeing her kneeling before me, her body ready and eager to listen to every demand I make.

My heart beats faster as I shuffle out of my jeans. Rae's attentive and helps me to step out of them, then pushes them over to the side.

Her focus goes straight to the middle of my boxers, which are becoming extremely tight. Licking her lips, her lashes flutter as she looks up at me. "Can I?" she asks permission to take me out, and my body immediately tenses from her soft plea.

I nod and watch as she takes my cock out of my boxers and starts stroking. Groaning, I toss my head back, resting it against the chair. She takes me in her mouth and begins sucking.

Letting out a low moan, I force myself to keep my eyes open so I can watch her.

My body buzzes with intensity the longer she continues and the more I stare at her. She's fucking gorgeous. Perfect.

She picks up her pace, and I know that if she doesn't stop soon, I'll be finishing inside her mouth—which isn't what I want right now.

"Stop," I command.

Rae pulls back, making sure to suck every last inch of me as she backs away. Her lips are swollen as she pants, waiting for her next order.

"Take everything off," I tell her.

She nods, rising. Keeping eye contact with me, she strips bare. Anyone walking the boardwalk can see her sexy, naked body if they were to look up. A part of me wishes they would just so they know what they're missing out on.

The idea of others wanting her but not being able to have her makes me go wild. A fire blazes in my chest as all of my reserves go out the window.

Precum drips down my length the longer I gaze at her out in the open like this. So free from any of her past restraints. It's beautiful to see her hair move against the wind and know it's caressing her skin, too.

I want to tell her that she's stunning—breathtaking. I want to wrap her in my arms and make love to her right here, out in the open, all night long. I want to kiss her endlessly. But most of all, I want to tell her I love her.

"How do you want me?" Rae rasps, reminding me of our dynamic when we have sex. It's not all fluff and tender moments because she doesn't need that as much as she craves to be dominated. To be out of her thoughts, even if for a few minutes.

She lets me control her. It's more than just a good fuck. It's trust.

And right now, I'm going to act on everything that's stirring inside me. All the feral, hungry, depraved thoughts that bounce around my mind. I'm going to show her just how much I love her by owning her in this moment.

Leaning back in the chair, I take one long look at her. "Sit." I point to my hard cock.

Glowing with lust, Rae tiptoes closer. Very carefully, she straddles me, then lowers herself down. Her wetness envelops me, and the both of us moan at the same time.

She rides me, grinding her hips into mine over and over again. My hands roam all over her sexy curves as little whimpers escape her mouth.

"Miles," she moans my name—my favorite fucking sound.

"That's my good girl. Riding my cock like the dirty slut you are."

She shudders and picks up her pace, chasing the high. Bringing my mouth to her throat, I devour the thin skin with my lips. Sucking and licking every inch of her that's in reach.

As I continue to mark up her body, the sound of a door shutting pulls my attention from Rae. She doesn't notice, as she keeps fucking me like it's her goddamn job.

My gaze flashes forward, two balconies down, to one of the college kids staring at us like a deer in headlights. There's murmuring going on, but I can't hear what's being said over Rae's moaning.

Not even a second later, the other two appear, and now all three of them, Travis, Evan, and Brad, are staring at Rae getting off on my cock. They stand there in shock but with grins on their faces.

"We have an audience," I whisper into Rae's ear.

She slows down and looks at me with her brows furrowing, confused. I gesture with my chin toward the balcony behind her, and she follows my line of sight. When she sees who I'm referring to, she scoffs.

"I don't care," Rae says and goes back to her original pace.

I had a feeling she wouldn't be bothered by them, and the fact that they're watching this ethereal woman bring herself to the point of ecstasy by the use of my dick doesn't make me jealous. It makes me incredibly turned on.

"Stop," I demand, and her lashes fling open, once again puzzled. "Turn around. I want them to see your face when you come on my cock."

Smiling, Rae gives a nod and then swiftly changes

her position. Her back is to my front as she plants her feet on the ground. She holds on to my thighs for balance, and when she's ready, she rocks back and forth.

My hands tightly grip her hips, and I move her faster. The quicker I move, the louder her moans. My attention is glued to the guys standing on their balcony, making sure none of them are taking out their phones because if that happens, then this shit is over.

I watch as they stare at Rae, enamored by her.

"You like this, don't you?" My words grow husky as she keeps moving. "You like those guys knowing how much of a whore you can be, don't you?"

"Yes," Rae cries out.

"You like them watching, knowing they can't touch you."

"Only you—" She stops speaking and moans loudly the moment I thrust up.

"Only I what, Rae?" I thrust harder.

Her grip on my thighs strengthens.

I go harder.

Her walls tighten around me.

Harder.

"Fucking say it, Rae," I say behind clenched teeth, trying not to come.

"Only you," she pants. "Can touch me."

The moment she utters those words, I become unhinged. Unruly. I take over, forcing her delicate body up and down. She's sure to have bruises on her hips from how tight I'm holding her.

The three guys gawk at the sight.

"Fuck!" Rae screams as her pussy spasms around me.

"That's my fucking girl," I growl out as my body

tenses. Squeezing my eyes shut, I keep slamming her down onto me as my orgasm thrashes through my bones.

Sweat coats my skin as my heart pounds against my ribs.

My cum fills her and she continues to cry out.

Rae suddenly collapses against me, and my body goes lax with hers. I sit back on the chair and let Rae use me as hers as we catch our breath.

Travis, Evan, and Brad have their jaws on the floor and watch as Rae slides her fingers over her slit, getting covered in my cum.

"That was fucking amazing," she says, dazed.

"You like their eyes on you?" I ask softly, my beard brushing up against the side of her face. Rae nods, unashamed of what turns her on. "Then keep going," I command.

"What?"

"Spread your legs for them and touch yourself. Let them see my cum drip out of your gorgeous pussy while you soak your fingers in it."

Without hesitation, she adjusts herself so that she's comfortable sitting on my lap, then widens her legs, draping them over mine. She leans back, resting on me, and she begins to circle her clit.

It's hard to draw my attention away from her to check on what's happening on the balcony across from us, but I do, just to keep tabs on them.

So, while she moans and arches her back off me, I find the three guys in front of us, leaning over the banister as if wanting to get a better look. One grins, the other looks stunned, and the last one looks like he's about to come in his pants.

"They're going to be thinking about this for the rest of their lives," I whisper to Rae. Her stomach muscles contract and release as she sinks her fingers into herself. "They're going to get off to this show you're putting on years from now when they're in bed with their wives." Her breathing becomes sharper, and I know she's getting closer. My fingers twist her nipple, and she gasps.

Rae's legs begin to shake, and she clamps them together.

"Stop," I snap.

She automatically freezes. "What's wrong?"

"Did I tell you to close your legs?" I ask, and she shakes her head. "Keep them open." Rae does as I say and exposes herself once again. "I want them to see how beautiful your pussy is when you come."

"Okay." She starts to finger herself again.

"Did I tell you to continue?"

Rae stops, and I can see her bite back a smile as she shakes her head again.

"Do I have to punish you?"

"Maybe," she says in the most seductive voice.

"You want me to punish you in front of them?"

Her body relaxes against mine. "Please."

With that, I lean forward and take my palm, slapping it hard against her wet pussy.

"Oh!" one of the college guys exclaims.

Rae moans and bucks her hips up. "More?" I ask.

"More," she confirms, pleading.

"You're such a fucking slut, Rae." I slap her again. "Wanting me to make it hurt so you can get off." Another slap. "Having these guys watch you take this." Slap.

"So. Good." Rae writhes against me.

I draw my hand away and move hers in place. "Continue."

Going back to getting herself off, I hold one of her legs in place—wide and open. Letting her embrace this kink of hers. This is Rae, unashamed, nonconforming, in-your-face, and unafraid.

My eyes drift over her perfect body as it trembles. A sheen of sweat covers her while sinful sounds fall from her plush lips.

As I watch her get closer and closer to the edge, I fall more in love with this woman. The one who doesn't cower away for the sake of making others comfortable. She's here to challenge people on all fronts, and I admire every part of her for that.

Warm cum hits my thighs as it leaks from her pussy. She takes in a sharp inhale, and I know we're there. "That's my good girl," I praise. "Come for them. Let them see how amazing you look when you fuck yourself."

She violently shakes against me as she struggles to keep her legs spread apart. Her moans grow louder from the back of her throat. Her nails dig into me, no doubt breaking the skin. She falls apart in my arms, only for her to willingly let me put her back together again once she's settled.

With one last cry, she crashes back against me, her body boneless. Her hair is a mess, and mascara is smudged under her eyes. Before she can fully relax, she sits up and places an innocent kiss on my lips. Then, she glances over to the other balcony and gives a small wave with a grin on her perfect face.

Picking up our clothes, Rae scurries inside as if she

doesn't want to get caught in the nude, which makes me laugh.

Going to follow her, I turn to look at Travis, Evan, and Brad on their balcony. "Have a good night," I say before going inside.

CHAPTER THIRTY-SEVEN

Miles

I PASSED out on Rae's couch shortly after our balcony rendezvous. Typically, I'd be a little embarrassed by how often I fall asleep afterward, but not with Rae. It's because I feel so relaxed with her that my body can finally rest.

Glancing around the room, I find Rae painting. She sits on the living room floor with a blanket wrapped around her naked body. Clearly, she didn't want to get dressed after we fucked.

Pushing myself up, I cross over to her to get a better look at what she's creating. I sit down next to her, kissing her bare shoulder.

I notice her cheeks rise as she continues to work. My eyes drift forward to the painting on the easel. She's working on a thick piece of paper, not a canvas. There's an outline sketched in pencil of two naked bodies joining together.

Taking a thin paintbrush, she traces over her outline using watercolor.

"That's beautiful," I whisper.

"I just started, how can you think it's beautiful already?" Rae quips.

"Because with just a few brushstrokes, you've already captured us."

"Who says this is us?"

"It's not?" I ask, genuinely curious.

Rae turns her head to look at me. "No. It is. I was just messing with you." She turns back to the image.

I can't help but notice this and the mosaic are wildly different from the type of art she usually creates, and my mind begins to wonder what might've changed that.

"I like watching you create," I say.

"Want me to walk you through what I'm doing?"

"Please."

Rae swirls her brush in water, then chooses a color. "First, I'm going to outline your body with black," she says, giving me a step by step.

"Why'd you pick black?" I ask, watching her every move.

"To signify your difficult past."

My heart thuds, feeling exposed and cared for in the same breath.

"Then," Rae continues, cleaning off her brush and dipping it in fresh water before going in for another color on her palette. "Midnight blue for the night sky." She fills in my head with the dark color but doesn't let it go too far as she changes it up for something else. "Next, some turquoise and seafoam for the ocean living inside you—expansive, refreshing, and mesmerizing all at once."

My stomach jumps around at her compliments, and I continue to stare, enthralled by the various greens and blues she fills my body with. She leaves an empty space where our bodies connect, and excitement flutters through me at what she has planned for the rest of the painting.

Dipping her brush in bright-yellow paint, she colors on the opposite side of the black outline, away from my body, coloring the rest of my side of the page.

"What's that for?" I ask.

"Your aura." Rae twists once more to glance at me. "Like a big ball of light."

A warm, fuzzy feeling glides its way into my chest. Just when I thought I couldn't be more in love with this woman, she goes ahead and turns us into art.

"Do you want to do me?" she asks but automatically corrects herself when she realizes how that sounded. "Not like that." She chuckles. "Although you're more than welcome to do *that* again." She lifts the paintbrush toward me. "I mean, paint my side of the picture."

I nod, feeling up for the challenge. She instructs me on which cup of water to use, and once I have a clean brush, I pick my first color.

"Black to honor your difficult past," I say, outlining her figure.

"Copycat," Rae mutters.

I go in for my next choice. "Pink—"

"*Pink?* Out of all the colors, you choose that?"

"I'm the artist. I get to pick what colors I want."

"Why pink?"

I dab the brush on the paper over the inside of her face. "Because your cheeks get all rosy when you blush."

Her jaw drops open. "I do *not* blush."

"Yes, you do, and it's adorable." I give her cheek a peck, and when I pull away, I immediately see a scowl.

Laughing, I move on to the next color, painting the rest of her body. "Red, for that fiery passion you have." I catch her smiling out of the corner of my eye. "And dark purple." I fill in the blank spaces but make sure to leave the space toward her lower half empty like she did for mine. "For your creativity and mystery."

I'm almost finished, but now I need to choose a color for the opposite side. Not exactly her aura—as she puts it—but more of what she presents to the world. Spotting the exact color I need, I add the finishing touch.

"Why gray?" she asks, her voice becoming soft.

"That's your armor."

Rae nods in understanding.

Once I'm done, I place the brush down and wait for her to add her magic. Saturating the brush in water, Rae aims for where our bodies are joined and whirls the colors around. Both hers and mine mix together, creating a perfect blend of each of us. The light and the dark effortlessly combine as if they belong together.

Rae leans back, tilting her head to the side to examine our art. "I like it," she states.

I smile. "Me too."

CHAPTER THIRTY-EIGHT

I'M GETTING USED to the sting at the bottom of my feet and the small burn in my calves. If anything, it's a nice reminder that I'm doing more with my life than just sitting around trying to dissociate by getting high out of my mind.

"Table seven!" Joe shouts to me in the kitchen.

"Thank you!" I take the plates from him and pile them on the tray, then exit to take care of my table. I've gotten better at the balancing act—though I almost had a spill yesterday.

Now that we're in mid-May and college kids are done with school, we've officially started the busy season. Rumor has it this is just the beginning, and within a couple of weeks, Golden Bay will be packed with tourists.

Dropping off the food at table seven, I spin around to my next batch of customers. Spotting a few familiar faces, I give them a smile.

"Hey guys," I say to Tonya, one of the NA leaders, and Regina and Davis, who attend meetings with me.

"Long time no see, Rae," Tonya makes a joke, as I just saw all of them last night.

"We were talking about getting a bunch of people together to go bowling this Saturday. You in?" Davis asks.

I must not have a very good poker face because they all start laughing. Here I was thinking I did a good job at keeping my cringe internalized.

"Oh, come on," Regina says. "It won't be that horrible. Besides, it'll be nice to interact outside of meetings and feel like regular people."

Chuckling, I nod my head, knowing what he means by that. As much as I hate bowling, I think it'll be good for me to have contained fun.

I can get my fill of wild fun with Miles like I did a few nights ago on my balcony. Ever since then, my body has been begging me to have a repeat occurrence.

"So what do you say?" Tonya asks.

I sigh, knowing that the old me would probably slap me for saying, "I guess I'll join."

"Nice! You think Miles will come?" Davis asks.

"Oh, he doesn't have a choice."

He smirks, and all of us continue to chat for a bit. When I first rolled into town, I had zero desire to befriend anyone, yet here I am, shooting the shit and making plans to do something lame. I'm mildly impressed with myself for being able to start and maintain real friendships and relationships.

"Are you going to tonight's meeting?" Regina inquires.

"Yep, I'll be there."

"Sam's running it," Tonya tells us.

"Great. More time with the old geezer," I joke, knowing he just passed by behind me.

"I heard that!" Sam says on his way to the kitchen.

We all laugh, and I go on to take their lunch order before drifting away, moving on to my next table.

My shift moves quickly, and before I know it, I'm clocking out, saying goodbye to the rest of the staff. Before leaving, I let Sam know I'll see him later, and he teases me about my comment from before.

When I get back to my place, I head for the shower and change into fresh clothes that don't smell like fried food.

As planned, Miles knocks on my door with our dinner before I head out to NA.

"How was work?" he asks, placing our sushi on my island.

"Good," I say, fishing through the brown paper bag. "You're coming bowling with me and a bunch of people from NA on Saturday."

Miles shrugs. "Okay."

We each pull up a stool and dig in, sharing about our time at work.

"I was thinking we could have a movie night when you come back from your meeting," Miles suggests. We had already agreed that he'd come here for dinner and hang out while I went to NA, and then we'd spend the rest of the night together.

"Sure—but no fluffy rom-com shit."

He chuckles into his napkin as he wipes his mouth. "Deal. How does action sound?"

"Perfect."

Checking the time on the microwave clock, I still have several minutes until I have to leave, but I decide to start cleaning up anyway. Miles is quick to help, cleaning off the granite.

As I'm tossing the brown bag into the trash, there's a knock at my door.

"It's open," I shout to whoever is on the other side.

Emma appears with a box in her hand. "Delivery," she says with a grin, gesturing to the package in her hand.

Going over to her, I take the box from her. "You should've just texted me, I would've come down and gotten it so you didn't have to come up." Glancing down, I see my parents' address on the label and already know it's another care package from Mom.

I gesture for Emma to come in, and she and Miles say their hellos as I place the package on the island.

"If I'm being completely honest, I didn't come up here just to drop that off," Emma says, twirling a strand of her red hair around her finger.

"What's up?" I ask, opening the box.

"Well, I wanted to ask about Grayson."

I pause before I can look inside to see what Mom sent me. "My brother?" I exchange looks with Miles, and he holds in a bout of laughter.

"Um...yeah." Emma nervously looks around the room, avoiding eye contact. "Is he...is he single?" Her voice comes out mousy when she finally gets the courage to ask.

"I have no idea."

"Oh, okay. I was just wondering."

"But...I could find out?" I offer.

Emma's eyes finally land on me, her face glowing. "Would you? I know I barely said two words to him, but still, he was just so—" She stops herself from saying a word I'd wince at and then continues rambling. "Anyway, I figured he must be nice because he's your brother, and you told me to go after a good guy, so I thought, why not?"

"Rae told you to go after a good guy?" Miles says, pleased, as he wraps his arms around my shoulder.

"Yeah, we were having a girls' day, and you know what type of conversations come up during those. Well, I guess you don't." Emma chuckles. "But I'm sure you can imagine."

"I sure can," Miles gloats, knowing that I spoke about him to Emma.

Not hiding my smile, I wiggle out of Miles's hold and turn my attention to my package.

"My mom likes to send me care packages as if I'm at a sleepaway camp." I switch up the topic, checking what's inside.

"What'd you get?" Miles asks.

"Some bags of chips and boxes of pasta." I take out the food, and Miles puts it away for me. Rummaging around, I see what else is inside. "Lots of paint, fine-tip markers, and..." I pull out the last thing, which is all the way at the bottom.

My pulse slows down when I realize what it is. *"The Outsiders."*

There's a prickle behind my eyes as I delicately hold the book in my hands as if it's an antique. Opening the cover, I immediately spot Cara's name in hot-pink writing with a heart next to it. "It's Cara's copy," I say. Within seconds, I can feel Miles's presence next to me.

"Who's Cara?" Emma asks.

"My sister."

"I didn't know you have a sister."

"Had."

She lets out a small gasp. "Oh my gosh, I'm so sorry! I didn't know—"

I shake my head, not wanting to get into it. I hate when people tell me they're sorry for my loss—even though there's not much else to say. But I like Emma, so I want to avoid biting her head off by ending this conversation before it begins.

Miles's firm hand runs up and down my back, soothing me as I thumb through the pages. Out of all the words and all the sentences, there's only one thing that's highlighted.

"Stay gold, Ponyboy. Stay gold."

A lump forms in my throat, but despite it, I smile, relishing in the memory of her and us. Staring at the highlighted letters, I swallow down the emotions that are threatening to surface. "When we had to read this in school, I used to tease her and call her Ponyboy because she was so innocent and naive." My fingertips skim down the page. "And then I'd say if she were Ponyboy, that meant I was his best friend, Johnny—the 'lost puppy that had been kicked down too many times.' She hated when I'd say that though, because Johnny dies in the end." My breath shakes as I slowly close the book. "I guess the universe didn't get the memo or got our roles reversed or something," I try to joke.

Looking up at Emma, her eyes are pouring with empathy and curiosity to know more of the story. Miles presses his lips to my head, giving me a tender kiss. My body trembles as I struggle to keep it together. Taking in a deep inhale, I bottle everything up and place the book back in the box.

"I should put all of this in my room," I say.

"I'll do it." Miles grabs the box, and I watch as he pads down the hall.

"Rae, I—" Emma starts to speak, but there's another knock at my door.

My brows furrow because the only two people who've ever knocked on my door are currently standing inside my home. "Come in?"

The door slowly opens, and a strange man in his mid-thirties, wearing glasses, stands in my doorway with a spark of excitement in his features. "Are you Rae Hansley?" he asks.

Emma and I glance at each other in suspicion. "Uh...yeah," I answer to the man, noting that Miles is just down the hall. "Who are you?"

"Jake Alberts." With a wide grin, he extends his hand for me to shake, and I stare at it for a second before I give him a limp hand. He doesn't seem to notice my lack of enthusiasm, though, because he instantly begins talking as even more eagerness bubbles out of him. "I'm sorry for coming to your condo unan-nounced, but no one was at the front desk, and I happened to cross paths with a few young men who said I could find you in room 214."

"Sorry, I'm supposed to be downstairs," Emma interjects. "Can I help you with something?" she asks, stepping closer to me in unspoken girl code, letting me know she's got my back if this dude decides to go rogue and attack me. Not that he'd be very successful since Miles is now walking out of my room and over to us.

"Nope," Jake says to Emma. "I found the exact person I was looking for."

Narrowing my eyes, my muscles tighten. "Why are you looking for me?"

Miles appears on my other side, shoulders tense as worry shadows his face. Jake looks up at him, and pure bliss beams out of his pores.

"You're Miles Kingston!" Jake says, ecstatic.

Miles's jaw tics. "I am," he responds slowly, unsure of who this person is and why they're here. "Is there anything I can do for you?"

"Actually, yes! I'm with IntraFilms—we're an upcoming streaming service going up against platforms like Netflix and Hulu."

"Okay?" There's an edge to Miles's tone, one that I'm not familiar with. A tone that tells me he's teetering on snapping.

Jake continues, "We're creating several original movies and miniseries to introduce ourselves to the world."

A sense of unease coils around my bones. The strum of my heart grows louder.

"I've been working on this passion project of mine for quite some time, and I've been doing a lot of research," Jake explains, pushing up his glasses. "I'm in the middle of creating a documentary for the ten-year anniversary of—"

"Who fucking sent you here?" Miles's voice bellows. The veins in his arms push up against his skin as he balls his hands into fists. His face turns beet red with fury as he stalks over to Jake, towering over him.

Heat blasts through me, causing moisture on the back of my neck.

My legs tremble.

Jake nervously swallows, craning his neck to look up at Miles. "Um, your father reached out to me, letting me know you live in Golden Bay." He glances over to me. "He said that I could also find the girl Miles was with that day in Golden Bay. He only knew your first name, but after I did some digging, I found your full name: Rachel Hansley. You're one of the victim's sisters."

My stomach drops. The weight is so heavy, it's enough to push me to the ground.

But I don't fall. I don't move.

I'm stuck, frozen. Barely even blinking as I hear him refer to me as *the victim's sister*.

A phrase I haven't heard in years, but fuck, does it puncture my heart just the same. Tearing the erratically beating organ to shreds. Making me feel every single paper cut as it burns with pain.

"Are you fucking kidding me!" Miles screams—rage bursting through him, losing every bit of cool he once had. His fists shake as his muscles flex with anger. He looks like he's seconds away from strangling Jake, but instead, he makes a sharp turn, pacing around my kitchen.

Miles tugs at the roots of his short hair as he furiously stomps back and forth.

I still can't move.

I'm locked in place.

My lips sewn shut, my jaw bolted.

"You're telling me it was my piece of shit father? He's fucking dead to me!" Miles points to Jake. "Better yet—I will!" Miles digs his phone out of his pocket and, in an instant, is screaming obscenities into it, racing down the hall and into my bedroom as if we can't hear him if he's in there.

Jake blinks, taken aback. "I'm so sorry. I think I started off on the wrong foot here. I'm not affiliated with

Mayor Kingston at all," Jake explains to me. "The mayor reached out to *me*, saying you two would be interested in my project."

I slowly blink as if stuck in slow motion.

Emma gently touches my arm, trying to snap me out of my trance.

But it doesn't work.

I know it's coming.

The flashbacks.

My body shudders.

Miles continues yelling on the phone while Jake continues to apologize to me.

But I'm getting sucked in.

My vision goes spotty as flickers of the past invade my mind.

"I'm very sorry, Rae," Jake says once again. "I didn't mean to cause any more distress. I honestly just wanted to bring light to an important issue and have you two share whatever part of your story you wanted to." There's a look of pity on his face, and it strikes me right in the chest. As he pivots to leave, something catches his eye. I watch as his attention floats over to my mural. The one with the horrific creature chasing after children. "Wow." His voice softens in awe. "Did you paint this?"

I nod, sensing myself getting drawn into the image and not being able to claw myself out.

Jake continues as he admires the gruesome image before him. "You know, a lot of people are drawn to escapism when it comes to art. But this...this is..."

"It's me." The dry words croak from the back of my throat. I stare at the morphed figures, the bloody stains, and the screaming and crying kids. "My art isn't escapism—it's the truth. It's my reality." There's a strong tremble rocking my core as my heart speeds up, water pricking behind my eyes. "It's activism!"

My voice cracks, but my sense of agony and fear converts into anger.

Wrath.

Pure, heated madness that *this* has to be my reality. And that there are people out there who still don't fucking get it and still don't fucking care.

Steam pours out of my ears as I continue to express my words to the wall. "My art is in your motherfucking face so that people *can't* turn away. I *want* to make people uncomfortable. I *want* people to feel all the terrible, horrifying emotions that we have to live with on a daily basis—because maybe if people start feeling and empathizing more, they'll start acting more!"

"Rae?" Miles appears out of nowhere, his voice now calm as he tries to soothe me.

But it's no use.

My head pounds, spiraling with emotions and pain.

There's a pinching in my lungs, and I can sense them shriveling up inside me. Memories flood my brain, and I suddenly feel like I'm sinking.

Everything's suddenly piling up. The images of that day are becoming more intense. The weight of them crushing my body, snapping my bones into pieces—destroying my rib cage that is now no longer a protective shield.

My heart races.

Blood.

Bright-red blood is all I can see every time I blink.

The walls are closing in. Squeezing me in tight.

I can't escape.

Sucking in more air, I try to calm the storm brewing inside me, but I can't.

If only I could get out of my head for just a few minutes. A few seconds. Just to stop the memories. Just to stop the pain.

A burning, monstrous craving juts through my veins. An appetite for venom.

I pace as if my feet were on fire as I try to push down the urge.

It's no use because, in seconds, it feels like bugs erupt under my skin, skittering all over my body as the memories continue.

It's too much.

Holding Cara's book. Telling Emma that she's dead. Talking about my mural.

It's all too fucking much.

"I need to go to my meeting."

CHAPTER THIRTY-NINE

I JOG to the community center, trying to outrun my thoughts, hoping I'll lose them along the way. Miles keeps up the pace next to me, not saying a word but knowing everything I'm thinking.

My chest heaves as I run faster.

I keep seeing the blood.

Each time I touch the pavement, I feel like I'm stepping in it. As if it's sticking to the bottom of my shoes all over again.

As the building gets closer, I try to focus on something else. Forcing my brain to switch modes and think about the only thing that calmed me that day.

Miles.

His lips.

The scar.

Our kiss.

"I got the door," Miles says, running ahead of me to open it for me.

I sprint down the stairs. My body trembles so fast I

nearly trip and fall down the steps, but Miles catches me.

The moment I'm able to, I continue down to the basement.

Everyone's eyes land on me as I bolt in, looking distraught and disheveled.

Gasping for air, my attention lands on Sam, who's offering me a gentle smile. The smallest gesture has my eyes watering.

"We were just about to start," he says. "Would you like to go first, Rae?"

I glance at Miles, who nods his head, encouraging me to talk.

Just the thought of sharing anything that's on my mind has my stomach in knots. But my tongue burns with the need to let the words out. Let someone hear my tale.

"Yeah." I pinch the bridge of my nose, shoving the tears back in.

Miles sits down on a chair, and I glance around the room at the familiar faces. Joe, who I work with. Regina and Davis, who visited the diner earlier. And Walter, who regularly attends meetings. All waiting for me to speak.

My cheeks get hot. "I'm Rae, and I'm an addict."

"Hi Rae."

Staring at my shoes, I sniffle. "I started using in high school. It wasn't any of the hard stuff at first—you know, just like weed and stuff. But then—" I stop myself. My lips get dry as my tongue puffs up in my mouth, making it harder to talk. I raise my gaze up to look at Miles and can feel his unwavering support pouring out of every part of him. His presence alone is enough to hold me up in this moment.

"But then," I continue. "Something bad happened at the end of my freshman year, and that's when my addiction really started."

"Do you want to share what happened?" Sam asks gently, as if not to push me too much.

Miles and I lock gazes. "Yeah," I say. "But I'll need Miles's help to tell the whole story."

CHAPTER FORTY

TEN YEARS AGO

> **Me**
> do you have a min to talk in between classes?

> **Cara**
> yeah, what's up? Everything okay?

> **Me**
> Everything's fine, something weird just happened and I need your opinion

> **Cara**
> whose ass do I need to kick?

> **Me**
> Cara, I love you, but you could never kick anyone's ass.

> **Cara**
> I'd at least try for you

> **Me**
> much appreciated

> **Cara**
> meet me in front of room 102 before
> third period?

> **Me**
> thank you

I spend the rest of second period painting, but can't seem to get the icky feeling of Mr. Falcone passively hitting on me out of my head. He complimented me— not weird for a teacher. Saying he wants to meet with me alone after school, and then he winks at me...could that be crossing a line? I'm probably reading way too much into this and Cara will set my head straight.

Shaking off any remnants of worry, I go back to my artwork. The bell rings, and I rush to put away the paints and brushes. "Shit," I mutter to myself. "I'm gonna be late for my next class."

Cleaning up as quickly as I can, I grab my bag and run out to the hallway.

Of course, Cara had to pick room 102, which is on the opposite end of the school. But I pick up my pace so I can hopefully catch her just in time.

Room 102 is down a secluded hallway, with only that classroom, the weight room, and, I think, some closets. As I get closer to meeting Cara, a group of rowdy upperclassmen runs through the hallway, laughing and making crude jokes while barreling into others. Someone knocks into me, and my phone flies out of my hand. It slides across the floor, and I watch as several people stomp on it as they rush to class. It's completely shattered. It gets kicked around and I struggle to find it.

I try to chase after what's left of my phone—but my heart suddenly drops.

A booming noise stops me dead in my tracks.

MILES

Coach straightens his posture and reaches for his key ring. "What's your next class?"

"Science," I groan.

"Do you mind being late so you can help me out with something?"

"Is that even a question?"

"I was hoping you'd say that." He twists a key off of the ring and slides it across his desk. "I need you to go to the supply closet and grab a bunch of the mats and bring them into the gym."

"Which supply closet? The one next to the bathroom or the one next to the weight room?"

"Next to the weight room, across from room 102."

The bell rings, signaling the end of second period.

Standing up, I take the key and start heading out of his office. "You got it, Coach."

Whistling, I enter the hallway and make my trek toward the supply closet. I give a few fist bumps and head nods to people as they pass by, calling my name.

Within a blink of an eye, the halls go vacant, with seconds to spare before the bell for third period rings.

There are a few stragglers bullshitting in front of the doors and underclassmen shoving things into their lockers.

Just as I'm about to round the corner, a bloodcurdling sound echoes off the walls.

The blood in my veins freezes over.

A sound that I never thought I'd hear resonates throughout the school, bouncing off the windows and sending a shiver straight down my spine.

Gunshots.

My heart rate catapults, but my feet cement to the floor.

Screaming.

The thudding in my ears makes it hard to hear anything else—but I can hear the screaming and the shots being fired.

I can't move.

Why can't I fucking move!

Doors slam. Shades are down.

It's just me in the hall. I'm all alone.

Terror explodes in my bloodstream, and a gust of paranoia gets me to move.

I run to the nearest classroom and try to open it, but it's locked.

I jiggle the handle. "It's Miles!" I whisper-yell. "It's Miles Kingston, let me in!" I rattle the knob, but no one opens it.

Darting to another door, I try the same thing, but no one will unlock it for me.

My throat closes, and I struggle to squeeze air in and out of my passageway.

"Open the door! It's Miles!" I try a third classroom.

The pit in my stomach grows.

Quiet footsteps pad across the floor from far away.

My teeth chatter with fear and my fingers tremble.

Just as I'm about to try another classroom, I feel the metal key in my other hand. In my one moment of clarity, I run to the supply closet and open it as fast as I can, praying no one sees me.

Panting, I try to remain as quiet as possible.

The footsteps get louder.

The person gets closer.

I clamp my eyes shut, every muscle in my body hardening with fear.

The tiptoeing gets closer.

The person is right here.

Right outside the supply closet.

Holding my breath, I pray I'm not heard as my veins twist with horror.

"Cara? Cara!?" some girl whispers.

My eyelids fling open.

I'm heaving, my chest constricting so tight around my heart as I try to gasp for air. But even through my deep breaths, I can hear this girl calling out for her friend.

Aside from her, the hallway is quiet.

Dead quiet.

Until suddenly, it's not, and a burst of screams comes from somewhere in the building. Anxiety explodes in my bloodstream, and my heart rattles in my chest, hard enough to break the bones around it. Salty moisture hits my lips as I shake in the dark closet, not knowing what the fuck to do.

"Cara!" the girl shrieks, hysteria barreling through her voice.

For the love of God, this girl needs to shut the fuck up!

I take a peek through the shuttered slots toward the top part of the door. A blonde girl is looking back and forth, searching for whoever Cara is, with tears streaming down her face.

She looks just as terrified as I feel.

Struggling to inhale, I only watch her for a moment longer before she screams out the name again. "Cara!"

She's going to get herself murdered if she keeps going. And I won't let that happen.

In a split-second choice, my need to save her overtakes the need to hide myself. I swing the supply closet door open, yank her by the wrist, and drag her in here with me.

My hand goes straight to her mouth as muffled screams come from behind it while she fights against me.

"Shh! You're safe—you're safe!" I assure her as I close the closet door as quietly as possible. She cries into my hand that's still covering her. "You have to be quiet," I whisper. "It's fine—you're fine—just be fucking quiet. Can you do that for me?"

She slowly nods. Her rapid breaths slow down, but she still quivers against me.

Very carefully, I release my hand, and the two of us stand here in the dark, living out our worst nightmare.

RAE

Someone grabs my wrist, dragging me into a closet. Terror bursts into every cell of my body as a hand clamps over my mouth. Uncontrollably shaking, I scream and try to fight against whoever this is.

"Shh! You're safe—you're safe!" he says. I know that voice—the person who makes the morning announcements. Miles Kingston. But the familiarity doesn't ease my panic. I cry into his hand, still unsure if he's the one that's going to hurt me or not. "You have to be quiet," he whispers. "It's fine—you're fine—just be fucking quiet. Can you do that for me?"

I instantly recognize the fear laced in his words.

He's petrified, just like me.

I slowly nod, trying to not have a full-blown panic attack and make noise by hyperventilating. He releases his hand, and the two of us stand here in the dark, staring at each other.

I think Miles might've just saved my life.

"I'm scared," I whisper so quietly I'm not sure he can even hear me.

But he does because he says, "Me too."

The room is small. The walls are closing in.

My vision is spotty.

I feel his warm breath against my body as he pants.

My head gets dizzy. I'm not sure if I'm going to pass out or have a heart attack, but it's getting harder to stand as my wobbly knees begin to buckle.

His arms lock around my sides, keeping me steady.

Needing to focus on something, I look up at Miles's face.

The light from the hallway is peeking through the

slots on the top of the door, only lighting a portion of his face.

My eyes zone in on his lips.

The scar on the left upper side.

For a moment, I get lost in how they look. And I choose to mentally stay here because it's the only thing that's giving me the smallest dose of ease.

Tears run down my cheeks, and I can't stop them from falling.

My heart hammers in my chest, hurting my insides with each thud it makes.

"I don't want to die," I whisper.

"We won't," Miles assures me.

But neither of us knows if that's true.

In a moment of blind fear, not knowing if we're making it out of this closet alive, our lips crash together.

A goodbye kiss.

His salty tears mix with mine, and the only thing I can think of is if I do make it out of here, then Cara's going to be the one who kills me.

It seems to last forever but is over in an instant, the moment another round of shots is fired.

We both jump out of our skin, horrified.

Glass shatters. More screams fill our ears, making them ring.

Miles's strong arms wrap around me, and I hold on to him. Our chests shake together, trying to keep quiet and not whimper through our tears.

The sound of someone creeping closer makes me squeeze him tighter.

He does the same as we brace ourselves.

"Where are you?" I hear a whisper from the hall-way. My stomach drops at the sound of the voice.

It's Cara.

Holy shit, she's looking for me just like I was looking for her.

Immediately, I break free from Miles and reach for the knob. But the second I do, he quickly pulls my hand away, not letting me open the door.

As I attempt to wrench free from his hold, I hear Cara gasp.

A gunshot goes off, piercing my eardrums.

Everything goes black.

Someone's screaming.

My lungs burn.

My shoes are wet.

The first thing I see when my vision returns is my sneakers. They're saturated.

They're red.

My shoes are red.

The cloud gets lifted, and I realize I'm standing in blood.

My sister's blood.

The screams are louder.

My throat burns.

There's more screaming. More and more screaming.

MILES

The girl in the closet with me wails—shrieks—as the both of us stand in someone's blood that's pouring in from the bottom of the door.

The cops are here.

More gunshots go off.

I can't tell what's happening. All I can hear is her screaming.

It lasts an eternity.

She collapses to the floor, and I hold her.

"It's okay," I whisper into her hair, lying through my fucking teeth. "It's okay." We both know we're far from okay, but it's the only thing my brain can think to say right now.

Minutes feel like hours. Hours feel like seconds. It's all a blur, fast and slow at the same time.

She gasps—short, sharp inhales. Her body sinks farther onto the floor, becoming covered in blood.

I hold her up as much as I can as she goes limp, only moments away from passing out.

The sound of police radios sends a wave of relief through me. They shout through the halls that they're here and they're instructing us on what to do, but my mind can't process anything right now.

As long as I know it's safe to get out of here, I want to get the both of us out of this fucking school as quickly as possible.

The sound of students running out of classrooms, hysterical, as the officers try to speak and calm them down fills my ears. Over the screaming and sobbing, I can hear the police officers tell them to go out the main doors and not this hallway.

But the only thing I care about is getting me and this girl out of this godforsaken closet.

Reaching up, I twist the doorknob, creaking it open.

I try to lift the girl up and open the door all the way

at the same time. But when I do, she cries out even louder.

My gaze darts over to what she's looking at, and my stomach plummets.

My face turns as white as a ghost as I stare at a bloody, lifeless body in the hallway.

"No!" the girl screams. "No!" she repeats over and over again, hysterically crying.

Bile rises to my throat, and I sense myself getting woozy.

I push through it, picking up the screaming girl in my arms.

"Cara!" she shouts, thrashing against me. Her voice goes shrill, laced with deep agony, forever imprinting the gut-wrenching sound of pure pain into my soul.

She claws at me, trying to get to the body lying in the middle of the floor. She's covered in blood as she tries to get out of my arms. Shoes, clothes, hands.

My heart drops, knowing that I probably am too.

The louder she gets, the faster I move.

I can't be in here a moment longer.

Students are filing out of classrooms, crying and throwing up.

Cops are checking all the rooms, EMTs are stationed at every corner, and families and news reporters are lining up outside.

I push through the emergency exit, still carrying the girl as my body sways.

Spotting the first EMT nearby, I pass the girl to them. "Take care of her."

They start asking me questions, but I can't hear them. I stumble backward but right my footing. I think they tell me to stay so they can examine me, but I don't.

My blurry vision drifts over the thousands of people that are around the perimeter of the school. I move past all of them, needing to find the two familiar faces.

"Miles!" someone calls out.

Turning around, I see Mom with puffy eyes and makeup running down her cheeks. Dad's not too far behind, his face flustered. They both embrace me, but I'm in such a daze, I can't feel their arms around me. "We're so glad you're okay," Mom says through tears.

They're moving me away from the crowd and toward the car.

I can barely walk straight.

"Son, Channel Seven wants to ask you what happened," Dad says, guiding me toward a news reporter. The mic is being shoved in my face, the camera too close for comfort. Mom's still crying next to me while Dad holds on to my shoulder for support.

They ask me questions, but all I can hear are the remnant sounds of the girl in the closet screaming.

RAE

They check my body for gunshots.

They check my eyes and head for a concussion.

They check my skin for cuts.

They check me all over for any wounds. But the wound I have isn't physical.

People move around me. Things are happening. But I don't feel like I'm really here.

I'm watching all of this play out.

This isn't my life.

This is a movie.

Water rolls down my face and onto my neck.

I don't realize that it's tears until I taste the salt hitting my lips.

They lay me down, saying I'm going to pass out.

I watch as a needle goes into my arm, but I don't feel the slightest bit of a pinch.

They hook me up to an IV so I don't get dehydrated.

I lie down, feeling nothing and seeing nothing.

But hearing everything.

"At least ten are in critical condition."

"The gunman is in police custody."

"The names of the deceased have not been released yet."

"Where's my child!"

"Did you know the shooter?"

"Let me in the building!"

"He's losing oxygen."

"Two dead on the second floor."

News reporters, parents, cops, and students.

They all speak at the same time, and I can pinpoint every word.

"We have a third confirmed deceased."

"Name?"

"Cara Hansley."

CHAPTER FORTY-ONE

PRESENT

THE TEARS WON'T STOP. I try to look at everyone in the room, but every time I do, my eyes well up. I draw in short breaths as I try to calm myself down so I can continue my story.

"I started using drugs to cope," I tell the room, everyone in NA giving me all the space I need to speak. "I used it as a way to get out of my head. Get away from everything for a little bit." I look over at Miles and notice his own tears staining his face. "And truthfully, sometimes I don't know which lifestyle is worse. Being an addict or being sober. Because being sober means I have to live with the memory of the school shooting and the pain of losing my sister. My best friend."

My voice cracks as I keep talking. "I don't want to live in a world where I have to pick the lesser of two evils. I don't want to exist in a place where what we went through is common. I don't want anyone else to feel what I feel on a daily basis." I take a few deep breaths in an attempt to compose myself.

"I don't want to live in a world where no one cares." My gaze drifts around, looking at everyone here. "We've all been through shit—all of us have been through trauma. We survive life-threatening, brain-altering experiences, and then what? We're supposed to get nine-to-fives like regular people? We're supposed to have thriving, functional families when we ourselves are barely hanging on?"

The room is silent as everyone soaks in what I'm saying.

"Sometimes." My voice comes out shaky. "I feel like I'm in the middle of the ocean, screaming for help as water floods my lungs, making it harder to breathe. But the only people who can hear me are the ones drowning alongside me."

Those words instantly bring me back to the supply closet and my screams as I listen to my sister being murdered. And sit in her blood.

As if I'm reliving it all over again, a sob breaks out from deep within my chest. I burrow my head into my arms, hiding my face.

"Rae, I'm right here," Miles says, running his hand along my back.

My body rocks back and forth as he holds me.

I can't stop crying.

I've somehow ended up on the floor.

Everyone joins me, supporting me in this moment, but I can't stop sobbing to thank them.

I cling to Miles's shirt, feeling light-headed.

"Let's get you home," he whispers.

And with that, I'm being carried outside.

CHAPTER FORTY-TWO

Miles

I SCOOP Rae off the floor, assuring everyone in the meeting that I'll be taking care of her and we'll both be okay.

"Call if you need anything," Sam says, clasping his hand on my shoulder right before I head out.

Rae continues to sob, clutching me.

I can't help but feel the reminiscent sorrow as I move forward with her in my arms. I don't hold back my own tears, setting them free as they roll down my face and onto Rae.

The memory is too much for us to bear.

The leftover pain punctures our hearts, and the terror of the past snakes around my bones as if trying to make me relive it in the present.

"We're almost back," I say to Rae, for my benefit as well, as I force myself to realize that what happened was ten years ago and I'm not actually carrying her out of the school right now.

When we get to Rae's building, Emma's stationed at the front desk, her face turning pale as she realizes the state we're in. She silently watches as I head toward the elevator and up to Rae's condo.

Once we're inside, I try to place Rae on her couch, but she tightens her grasp around me, not wanting to let go. Instead, I sit down and hold her on my lap as she curls up into a tiny ball.

"Miles," she cries into my chest. Her tears soak through my shirt as I kiss the top of her head.

We stay like this for a long time. Holding on to each other for dear life until she suddenly pulls away.

"Get my shoes off." She kicks her feet, trying to get them off as quickly as possible, and I work with her, letting them drop to the floor. "My clothes." She tugs at her shirt, struggling to get it over her head. "I feel gross —I feel covered." I know what she means by that, and I help her take the rest of her clothing off. "I need to shower. I need to get rid of this feeling."

Rae wipes her wet cheeks even though more tears trickle down. She begins to rise, but the moment she does, she collapses.

Catching her just in time, I haul her into the bath-room, trying to steady her in the shower.

"I can stand now," she says, leaning up against the tiled wall. She trembles as she reaches out to turn the knob and get the water running over her body. I notice her legs begin to wobble, her knees locking and then unlocking.

"Sit down," I instruct.

Rae defiantly shakes her head, but her body gives her no option when she starts to fall. I catch her once more and carefully place her down in the porcelain tub.

Stepping out of my clothes as fast as I can, I join her in the shower, sitting down in front of her.

The warm water rains down on the both of us, attempting to soothe the bottomless ache felt in our souls.

Taking her loofah and a bar of soap, I lather her up, letting the bubbles cover her tattoos. I want her to see that there's nothing on her. She's not marked with blood like the memory that's floating through her brain.

She's clean.

I scrub her arms and chest, then drift down to her torso and legs. She stares at me wordlessly, with black streaks from her makeup all over her face and dark, messy rings around her light eyes. But the expression that dances across her features is one that I can't read. It tugs at my heartstrings but also makes my stomach flutter.

Rae's breathing begins to even out, and I'm pretty sure she stopped crying, but it's difficult to tell with the water from the shower.

Working my way down her calves, I wash her feet, both top and bottom, saturating them in soap.

Once I'm finished, I go to place her loofah back on the hook, but she stops my arm from continuing. Still silent, she takes it from me and begins to wash my body.

I sit back on my heels, kneeling, and watch as she carefully drags the bubbles across my skin. She remains focused on what she's doing, trying to rid me of any last memory that might be sewn into my fibers, even though we both know it won't work.

Rae washes along my forearms, and when she reaches my hands, she flips them over and scrubs my palms. Her gaze flickers up to mine, but instead of remaining locked on my eyes, she stares at my mouth. I notice the slightest movement her gaze makes as she looks at the small curves of my lips. Her shoulders soften the longer she's fixated.

Warmth radiates out of my heart and down the rest of my body.

Taking my free hand, I gently run my fingers along her jawline and inch even closer. Her breath hitches just before I cup her face and bring my lips to hers.

The shower continues to run over us, mixing in between our kisses. Cleansing us, offering a new beginning—one that honors our past but does not dwell in it.

We stay intertwined on the bathtub floor, just like this, long after nightfall.

Hours tick by, and we eventually make our way to her living room.

A more relaxed Rae sits cross-legged on the couch next to me in her pajamas.

"Don't judge me," she says as she draws in her sketchbook.

"I'll only judge you if you put my scar on the wrong side of my mouth," I tease, and she smiles as she focuses on her artwork.

Her pencil scratches against the paper in fast movements, creating an image of my lips in a matter of seconds. She does it over and over again until the page is filled with me.

I rest into the cushions as I witness the stress exit her body with each swipe she makes. I swear, every time I watch her work, I become more hypnotized by her. Falling more in love with her and the vulnerable parts of herself that she captures through her hands.

I study her, from her fingertips down to her toes, noticing every glimmer of who she is. The ink that's on her skin, the scars that tell a story.

Rae is walking art.

The very heart and soul of the definition:

To disturb the comfortable and comfort the disturbed.

And my tortured mind finds solace in her arms.

We stay like this, in our natural habitat, for a while until Rae lets out a cute little yawn.

Smiling, I reach out and give her neck a soft massage. Her eyes flutter closed for a brief moment, and she yawns again. "Why don't you go to bed?" I suggest.

She shakes her head. "I don't want to risk having nightmares."

"Yeah. I get that." My eyelids feel heavy, but I know I won't get a millisecond of sleep tonight either.

A sudden idea strikes, and I decide to act on the impulse. Standing up, I gather her fuzzy throw blankets in my arms.

"What are you doing?" Rae asks, looking at me like I have fifteen heads.

"Taking you to the beach." I extend my hand toward her, and she doesn't hesitate to take it.

Whisking her away, we walk out into the warm air and gradually stroll our way from the boardwalk and toward the ocean.

We end up sitting on one of her blankets on the sand while wrapping the other one around us.

Rae curls into my arms and hums. A sweet sound that I never thought I'd hear from her and never thought my heart would leap when I heard it.

The ocean is calm, with barely any waves, as the water trickles up to the shoreline and gently pulls back in a slow, methodical motion.

The sky above us is still dark, a few stars twinkling

as if they're winking at us. But, looking out over the sea, the sun begins to peek out, bringing in a little color to the quickly fading night sky.

"Watching the sunrise like this makes me hate the world a little less," Rae says, cutting through the quiet.

I smirk. "Me too."

"I don't think I'll ever not hate it. But a moment like this makes it a bit more tolerable." She's silent for a beat as we get lost in the scenery before us. "Sometimes, I get so fucking angry," she whispers, not hinting toward any anger in her tone, but more like profound sadness. "Like, the world spits out 'thoughts and prayers' on social media for a few weeks, goes back into denial, and then does it again for the next tragedy. And nothing changes. No one gave a fuck what would happen to us as adults years later, and now we get treated like shit by society because we're addicts. People really fucking think this is the kind of life we willingly chose for ourselves—meanwhile, every addict I know has been through something traumatic. But our world doesn't care about helping people through the trauma."

I nod in agreement. "The reality is, everyone's there for you when the event happens, but as the months and years fade, the trauma is still there, but the support is gone."

"Yeah, it's as if there's a time stamp on how long you're allowed to process something, and then society snaps its fingers and you have to play the role of worker or family member without batting an eye. So fucked up." She shakes her head in frustration and then goes back to sitting in silence.

There are still a few stars sprinkled above us, but no

matter how many pierce through the sky, they don't capture my attention the same way Rae does.

Her icy hair gently blows in the breeze, skimming across the sharp features on her face.

The fierceness wrapped around her grace is something that'll always intoxicate me.

"Did your parents stop being dickheads for a little bit after the shooting?" Rae suddenly asks.

"For like two weeks." I let out a humorless chuckle. "It's messed up because for that brief time, I felt cared for—like I was their son and not just a stepping-stone to get somewhere else."

Rae scoots her way between my legs and nuzzles into my chest, my heart rapidly beating against her.

"You were supposed to have a party that night," Rae remembers.

A faint smile hits my lips. "Yep. I was pissed at my parents, so I planned to have a giant rager just to spite them."

"I always think about what would've happened if the shooting never occurred and that day went on as planned." She plays with the blanket between her fingers. "If Cara went to your party and you guys hit it off. What would've come of it." The amount of guilt that seeps through her words is so strong I can feel it land straight into the center of my chest.

I rest my chin on the top of her head but stay silent. I know I can't say anything that would make her feel better. Even the words that stain my insides. The one that wants me to tell her that I don't believe I was supposed to meet Cara.

I was supposed to meet the other twin. *Her.*

We gaze forward, the sun making more of an

appearance as the sky lightens. Traces of orange, yellow, and pink brighten our surroundings. The blending of colors reminds me of something that Rae could conjure up in minutes, only hers would somehow look better than the inspiration that evoked it.

An abrupt jolt of my own inspiration flourishes in my mind. An unexpected idea of a surprise for Rae comes out of nowhere as if the universe struck me with electricity, letting the light bulb in my head go off.

Needing to somehow put all the pieces together for this idea, I keep it to myself, wanting to do something nice for her that'll blow her out of the water.

My mind drifts, thinking about how quickly I can pull this off as I squeeze her a bit tighter.

After a long silence fills up the beach, she clears her throat. "I'm sorry your parents suck."

"I'm sorry—" I stop myself.

Rae adjusts herself, allowing herself to melt further against my body. I watch as her eyes look up, spotting one star above us.

"I don't think Cara's a star," she states.

"No? What do you think she is?"

Rae's attention shifts, her gaze landing on the rising sun.

"I think she's gold."

CHAPTER FORTY-THREE

Rae

THE WORST THING about coming down from a high is the empty, shitty feeling that follows it. It's like being drenched with self-hatred and yet hollowness at the same time. It's an awful sensation that usually drives me to get high again, so I don't have to sit with the pain for too long.

However, right now, I feel as if I'm coming down from a high, yet the residual effects are the complete opposite.

I feel whole.

Turning my head to the side, I glance at Miles, who's passed out next to me in my bed. Yesterday was a hell of a day, but we were by each other's side all night and morning until we eventually hiked it back to my condo when tourists started popping up on the beach.

Sadness lingers—truthfully, I don't think it'll ever go away, but I also have a sensation of something unfamiliar swimming through my veins. It's more than happiness, but I can't put my finger on what it is.

Giving Miles a small peck on his cheek, I roll out of bed and let him sleep.

Without a clue as to what time it is or what fucking day it even is, I ignore all my responsibilities and focus on the one thought that woke me up. My mural.

Going to my closet filled with art supplies, I grab as many bottles of black paint as I can hold and walk into the living room.

Blowing out a puff of air, I give the piece of art one last look, briefly acknowledging the monster and children and blood. Not wanting to get lost in those dark memories, I immediately start splattering black over it.

Splashing the color all over, letting it get as saturated as possible, so the original image doesn't peek through.

Taking my big brush, I begin to spread the paint all around.

I don't know what I'll create out of this, but a giant black wall of nothingness is better than my past looming over me.

Maybe I'll turn it into a night sky. I'll even let Miles add his own dead-people stars.

"I leave you alone for five minutes, and you're already painting?" Miles appears in the hallway. One of his hands holds his phone while the other rubs his eye, waking himself up as he walks closer to me. He's wearing only his boxers, which hang low on him.

Shrugging, I respond, "I wanted to do something about this." I gesture to the wall, then continue covering it.

I hear him tapping on his phone, texting someone. His phone vibrates, signaling a message, and he takes a few seconds to respond before talking to me. "I have to go meet up with someone real quick, but I don't want to leave you alone if—"

"I'll be fine." I give him an honest answer.

He pads closer. "Are you sure? It shouldn't take too long."

I stop painting and turn to look up at him. "I promise. Go do whatever it is you have to do, and hopefully, by the time you're done, I'll be finished with this."

Miles presses his lips together as if he's debating saying something.

"What?" I ask.

"How would you feel about meeting me somewhere later?"

"Like, for a date?"

He wobbles his head from side to side. "Sort of."

My brows draw in. "Okay..."

"Text me when you're done painting—no rush—and I'll tell you where to find me."

"All right, weirdo."

Miles chuckles and kisses the top of my head, letting me be while he gets dressed and heads out to wherever he's going.

I'm left alone to process the thoughts in my brain, but I quickly go on autopilot, only paying attention to the black paint and brushstrokes.

I'm unsure of how much time has passed when there's a light tap on my door. Wiping my forehead with the back of my hand, I take a break and answer the front door.

When I open it, I spot Emma wearing track shorts and a tank top—obviously, she's not scheduled to work downstairs and came here on her own accord. Her lips turn up to a small, friendly smile. "I wanted to check on you," she says, getting straight to the point.

Nodding, I move aside so she can come in. "Feel like painting?" I ask, walking over to the small section of the wall that's left to cover.

"I'd love to." Emma's quick to join me, not worried about staining her clothes. After a few minutes of silence, she clears her throat. "I don't know what to say exactly. But I want to be here for you."

There's a tug at my heart. "You don't have to say anything, Emma," I say, speaking low. "You showing up is more than enough."

"I Googled you and Miles," she blurts out, as if she'd been harboring a dirty secret and couldn't hold it in any longer. "I found an article from years ago—I had no idea." Her eyes turn glassy. "I-I..." She struggles to find the words, but in reality—what the fuck *do* you say to someone who's been through that?

"Thanks," I tell her, then finish covering up the very last bit. Emma helps me, streaking the black over the drops of red.

When we're finished, I toss the brushes aside, and we wash off our hands.

"So, you really have a thing for my brother?" I ask, shifting gears off of the heavy topic.

Emma's lips curl up. "He's really hot."

"Ew, okay, I shouldn't have asked."

She lets out a giggle. "And I'm also assuming he's a good person, considering he's related to you."

"I'm not a good person, Emma." I scoff. "I've lied, stolen, fucked random guys for drugs." Not to mention I'm currently dating the only guy my sister was head over heels for—but we'll just sweep that under the rug for now.

"We've all done things we aren't proud of, Rae." Emma dips her head down at the admittance. "But you're a good person at heart."

My throat dries up, creating an irritating itch.

This conversation is a little too much for me.

"I'm supposed to meet Miles in a few minutes," I say, changing the subject. "Maybe we can grab dinner tomorrow?"

Emma enthusiastically nods. "Okay!" She starts backing away toward the door. "Have fun with Miles—and I better get all the details tomorrow!"

I smirk. "You got it." I watch as she starts to leave, but I suddenly stop her. "Emma?"

"Yeah?" She turns around in the doorway.

"Thanks for coming."

"Of course, Rae."

She gives me a wave before shutting the door behind her.

I clean up the rest of my mess, putting the supplies away and changing out of my clothes before I text Miles, letting him know I'm free.

He quickly replies to my message, dropping me his location.

My face scrunches. "The diner?" I say to myself, perplexed.

Without badgering him on why he couldn't just tell me to meet him at Sam's instead of making it out to seem like we're going somewhere special, I head out my door and onto the boardwalk.

A few minutes later, as I approach the red-and-white

awning, I spot Miles waiting outside. He's anxiously rocking back and forth on his heels as his fingers drum against his thigh. When he spots me, he beams.

"You okay?" I ask, a little concerned about the mix of energy that's pouring out of him right now.

"More than okay." Miles flashes me a smile. "I'm taking you somewhere."

"Where?"

"It's a surprise."

I glare at him, but he laughs it off. Not a moment later, he puts his hand over my eyes so I can't see.

"We should really invest in blindfolds if this is going to be a recurring theme," I say, as I'm blindly led by him.

"I'll add it to my Amazon order, along with edible paint," he jokes.

We keep walking forward, and my ears pick up on the conversations of strangers we pass along the way.

"Where are we going?" I ask, feeling like this journey is taking hours.

"It's still a surprise, Rae."

Even though he can't see it, I give him an eye roll underneath his hand.

Finally, our pace slows down until we come to a stop.

"I have to open the door, but swear to me you'll keep your eyes closed until I say so?" Miles asks.

"Yeah."

"I'm serious, Rae. I'll be pissed if you ruin this."

"I swear I'll keep my eyes closed."

With that, he peels his hand off of my face, and there's a sudden cool sensation taking over where his palm once was.

Keeping my eyes clamped, like promised, I stand here, not knowing what's waiting for me. There's a bubbling of excitement in my chest as I continue to wait.

Miles slips his fingers between mine, and I'm being guided forward once more.

We take a few steps, then stop. He pulls away, and I can hear the squeaking of his shoes against the floor as he creates distance between us.

The excitement now twists with nervousness as I realize I'm in some type of room without Miles by my side.

"Open," Miles says, the gentleness in his voice causing goose bumps to rise on my flesh.

Peeling my eyelids open, I'm instantly confused as I stare at a wide-grinned Miles while the two of us stand in Sam's vacant storefront.

My head turns around, waiting for something remarkable to show up or someone to pop out of the back room. But no one's here. Just us.

Our feet touch the planks of laminate flooring I sort of helped install. There's nothing on the walls, the giant windows don't have anything special hanging in them, and there's still a fold-up table in the back. Only, instead of housing Miles's toolbox, it has a few papers on it and a pen.

"Uh..." is the only sound that comes out of my mouth because I don't know what the hell to say. This isn't a surprise. I've been here before. Twice. With him.

"What do you think about this space?" Miles practically bounces on his toes.

Oh fuck. Did I miss something? Did he do some

special home improvement thing and I'm completely missing it?

My stomach sinks as my anxiety builds.

This is what separates the good girlfriends from the shitty ones. I'm supposed to pick up on this type of stuff.

"You did a really great job," I say, not knowing what the fuck I'm even referring to.

Miles chuckles. "So, you like this storefront?"

"Yeah. It's nice and...modern. And it looks like you put a lot of work into it."

He goes to the table and picks up a piece of paper, then walks it over to me. He extends his hand so I can take the paper from him, and I glance at it, unsure of why I'm looking at a lease agreement.

"A one-year lease for Anything Rae Touches?" My gaze drifts up to meet his. There's an abrupt strum of apprehension vibrating against my rib cage.

"It's a little corny, I know. But you can change it to be anything you'd like. I picked that because the acronym is ART."

My mouth begins to dry up as the pounding in my chest gets harder. "Um—I—what?"

Miles's lips tip up. "Rae, I've watched you turn literally everything into art. Everything about you is art. It's destruction and creation—all done by your hands." He tucks a strand of my hair behind my ear, and I swallow, hoping to coat my dry throat. "Everything you touch has your mark on it, Rae. Everything you do is breathtaking."

"I-I don't understand." I lift the lease up higher even though my attention is fixed on the swirling blues and greens in his irises.

"I spoke to Sam earlier, and this place is yours if you want it—and I know you'll probably chop my balls off if I put any money toward it, so consider the first month's rent a loan."

"What—Miles, I'm so fucking confused right now. What's the purpose of renting out this storefront?"

Miles takes a step back and animatedly showcases the room to me. "You said it yourself when you were talking to that documentary guy—your art is activism. Well, Rae, how can it be activism if it just sits behind closed doors?"

Every particle in my body tenses.

My lungs begin to shrink.

"Imagine what it'd be like if you could have this entire space to display your art." He outstretches his arms. "To share a part of yourself and raise awareness for the things that matter most to you."

"No one's going to want to buy my disturbing artwork while they're on a motherfucking beach vacation, Miles," I snap at him.

"I beg to differ. We get all sorts of people that flock here for the summer—and I think they'll be people in the market for your art." He continues floating around the room, and my head spins with him while my body stays in place. "You don't have to display anything about the school shooting or addiction or anything like that if it's too much. I mean, hell, everything about you is a rebellious form of activism. You're here to shake up people's perceptions and challenge the norm—and that's one of the things I admire most about you."

Miles continues circling as my heart hammers. It suddenly becomes difficult to see him through the glassiness that's welling up in my eyes.

"Or, whatever—" Miles continues. "It doesn't have to be any type of activism. You can create hundreds of mosaics out of sea glass. Or carve little figures out of bars of soap—which I noticed you did with the soap in your kitchen the first time I was there." He finally pauses in place, stopping right in front of me. "Whatever you want this space to be—it's yours, Rae. You deserve it."

A decade's worth of guilt smashes down on my body. My chest aches the longer I stare at Miles.

He stands there, perfect.

Being the perfect boyfriend. The perfect partner. The perfect man.

As soon as I realize how real this all is—me and him and the potential of a future together—my body recoils into itself.

Retreating, all the thousands of walls I let down for him all come popping back up in an instant.

Miles continues to look at me, waiting for a response.

But I end up muttering the only thing I can think of. "Baseball." The sound of our safe word barely leaves my chapped lips.

His face drops. "What?"

"Baseball."

CHAPTER FORTY-FOUR

Miles

SHIT.

I should've known this would be too much for Rae.

She hates surprises, and my idiotic self decided to give her a huge surprise just twenty-four hours after she spoke about what happened to us—for the first time ever.

How could I be so fucking stupid?

"Rae." I try to speak in the most soothing voice so it doesn't freak her out any further. "I'm sorry. I didn't think about how you'd respond to this. The idea came to me when we were sitting on the beach last night, and I just rolled with it."

I take a step closer and her muscles stiffen, and once again, I watch as her armor comes flying up. Her vulnerability and emotions become trapped inside as she fights with herself not to cry.

Never in a million years would I think that she'd be using our safe word for something like this.

"All I wanted to do was give you the ability to have

your own art studio so you can make your mark on the world in whatever way you want," I tell her.

Inching closer, she takes a step back. I open my mouth to start saying more, but before I can, a zap of energy shoots down Rae's body. In the blink of an eye, she's darting out of the store.

It takes me a second to realize that she just ran away from me, but once I do, I'm chasing after her.

The heat from the day hits my skin as I weave in and out of groups of people to catch up to Rae. With my focus trained on the white-blond hair ahead of me, I watch as she hangs left and dashes off the boardwalk and onto the beach.

Moving fast, I catch up to her as she barrels toward the water.

Sand kicks up, the small particles stinging my ankles and calves.

"Don't do this," I shout behind her. "Don't run away."

She keeps running forward as if she's headed straight into the ocean and not planning on stopping once she gets there.

"I'll tell Sam to scrap the lease agreement—let's just forget the whole thing ever happened," I say, making my way next to her.

Her pace slows down, and she holds her hand over her chest, catching her breath. Coming to a stop right where the sea meets the land, she turns to look at me. Her eyes are wide with devastation and brokenness.

"I can't forget about it, Miles." Rae's voice cracks.

"Why not?" I ask, letting in a big inhale. "What's the big deal?"

"The gesture..." She looks away from me. "It was too special."

"You're upset because I was too nice?"

Something about my question flips a switch, and anger blossoms across her features. "God, Miles—why couldn't you just let things be like they were? Why did you have to go fucking overboard?"

"I'm not trying to go overboard. I care about you, and I wanted to show you that I—"

"Well, stop!" Her hands fly up as she pins me with a fiery glare. "Stop fucking caring about me—I'm not even supposed to be here right now!"

"What are you talking about?"

"I should be fucking dead!" Rae screams, a toxic blend of rage and guilt ripping through her and landing straight into my heart. "Do you know how much time I've spent over the past ten years trying to hate you for saving me!"

The bones in my body snap, breaking into thousands of pieces just from the intensity of her words.

Tears trickle down her face. "It shouldn't have been me in that closet—it should have been Cara. *She's* made for this world. I'm not." Rae fights back the big sob building inside her body. She wildly paces in the sand, not knowing where to go or who to turn to. Her agony echoes out into the endless ocean. "I've hated myself every single day for going on without her. *I* should be dead—not her."

Her comment renders me mute. I have zero response. Because I know what she's saying wouldn't have been possible—I was there.

"Millions upon millions of times I've played it out in my head," Rae continues, not bothering to wipe the tears or snot from her face. She looks like she's gone mad from her pain. My eyes begin to burn, wanting to cry for her, wanting to lessen some of the heartache she's been carrying with her. "If only Cara had gotten to that closet first, then she would've been in there with you." Her cheeks suddenly burn with frenzy, and she storms closer to me. "Or if only you would've let me open the goddamn door!"

Rae bulldozes toward me, shoving my chest in grief-stricken anger.

"Why didn't you let me open the door, Miles?" she cries, pounding against my chest.

The pain behind my eyes becomes unbearable, and I let my tears escape me. I try to capture her in my arms, but she resists, fighting me. Striking me over and over again. Each hit builds up my own hidden sorrow.

"Why didn't you let me open the motherfucking door!"

"If I did, then both of you would be dead," I blurt.

"You don't know that!" she snaps.

"And you don't know that if things played out differently that she would be alive right now!"

"Fuck you!" Rae spits out like I mean nothing to her.

Like *we* mean nothing.

All the fight exits my body, my shoulder slumping. I step aside and let her go.

She pierces me with her stare one last time before she spins the other way and walks down the beach.

I stand here, letting the ocean reach the soles of my shoes, watching Rae walk away until she's so far gone that she blends in with the rest of the landscape.

My breath rattles inside me as my heart rips into shreds.

Guilt and sorrow twist together, curling around my bloodstream. My body gets heavy from carrying the pain of the past.

Not knowing what to do, I turn back toward the boardwalk, ignoring all the whispers and stares from beachgoers as I pass by.

As if I'm on autopilot, I continue walking until I reach the parking lot behind the stores and restaurants on the boardwalk.

Getting into my car, the familiar sensation of loneliness settles into my muscles.

My fingers wrap around the steering wheel, the strength of my grip hurting my joints as I try to get rid of old memories that are beginning to resurface.

As the houses and streets blur together, I try reliving the moment the way Rae envisions.

My pulse picks up, sweat rolling down my neck.

If I let Rae open the door, would Cara be alive right now? Did I let her sister get murdered because I was too scared? Was it my fault?

My chest crushes from the pressure of the anvil of regret that's dropped inside my body.

My vision becomes consumed by my haunted past as I breeze past my home.

My foot presses harder on the gas pedal.

I quickly move down the road until I reach my destination.

On impulse, I hop out of my car and go into the liquor store. Hanging my head low, I hurry down the narrow aisles and grab the first bottle of whiskey I can find. I can't look the store clerk in the eye as I pay.

There's a gnawing feeling of shame eating away at my soul as I drive to my house with the bottle of alcohol next to me.

When I get inside, I slam the glass bottle onto my wooden table, anxious to twist open the top and let the entire bottle of liquid slide through my insides, burning the whole way down. Allowing me to focus on the physical pain instead of the emotional burden that's ripping me apart.

I sit down on my chair, staring at the bottle.

Yearning so badly to make everything disappear—if only lasting a few hours through blind drunkenness. I salivate the longer I fixate on the amber drink.

My leg bounces up and down because there's a bigger part of me that knows I shouldn't do this.

I shouldn't succumb to my disease even though it's so fucking easy.

It's right in front of me.

Wringing my hands together, my restlessness grows stronger. An internal battle starts inside my head.

Right versus wrong.

Good versus bad.

The "what-ifs" and "I should've done this" play on repeat.

My mind dizzies as I continue to war with myself.

Adrenaline courses through my veins, and my body gets hot.

I reach for the bottle, holding it in my hand. My fingers skim over the black-and-white label as I feel the weight of it tugging my arm down.

My tongue peeks out, wetting my dry lips, anticipating the quench that could hit my mouth.

I get closer and closer to giving in to temptation.

The beat of my heart picks up.

My insides buzz with the need to have one drop.

Suddenly, my phone goes off, signaling a text.

Immediately, I'm snapped out of the haze and make myself aware of my surroundings. Glancing around at my home—the one I've worked so hard to create and make mine—I place the bottle back down on the table.

A shaky breath leaves me as my shoulders round.

Conflicting feelings of disappointment and pride weave their way around my mind.

Pushing my chair back away from the table, I stand up so I can dump the whiskey down the drain. I notice the clock in my kitchen and my eyes bulge as I realize it's almost ten p.m. I spent hours going down a rabbit hole, fighting with myself. At least I won.

My fingers go to twist the cap open, but before I can, there's a knock at my front door.

CHAPTER FORTY-FIVE

I WALKED along the beach until the sun disappeared. Endlessly wandering while my mind spun thousands of overcomplicated webs.

Tangled up in the past, I loop back around toward my condo. I make my way onto the boardwalk and stop at a random shop to pick up a pack of cigarettes.

Lighting up in a matter of seconds, I take a deep inhale and hold the gray smoke in my lungs as long as I can. Still jittery from my thoughts, I decide to sit down on an empty stray bench. It looks out to the beach, but there's not much to see, considering it's nighttime.

I don't have it in me to glance upward at the stars, so I stare at my shoes. I let myself become fixated on my rubber soles scraping against the pavement while I sit and chain-smoke.

Cigarette after cigarette.

The smoke envelops me, a thin coat of toxins sticking to my skin.

My mind bounces from past memories with Cara to

the present, where Miles welcomes me to join him with open arms.

He had the idea to rent out an art studio for me, and he put all the pieces together on his own accord. You don't do that just to be nice to someone. You don't do that kind of shit for your new girlfriend. You don't do that for someone you *like*.

Regret shoots through my heart like a bow and arrow for what I screamed at him earlier. He didn't deserve any of that.

He's the most amazing person I've ever known. He would've made the best partner for Cara. And that's what makes me hurt so much.

She deserved someone like him.

She deserved to live.

The world needs more people like Cara and Miles. Hell, more people like Emma, too.

It doesn't need more broken, distraught scum-of-the-earth people like me. There's already enough of us.

The bench suddenly rattles, and my annoyance switch is instantly flipped on. Snapping my head to look at who the fuck would sit next to me when there are plenty of other open benches, my scowl is suddenly wiped away when I notice who it is.

"Got another one in there?" Sam gestures to the pack of cigarettes placed next to my thigh.

My brow arches. "Are you trying to bum a cigarette off me?"

He chuckles. "No, just curious to know if you smoked them all yet."

"Almost," I say before taking a long drag. After aiming my puff away from Sam's face, I speak. "What are you doing here? The diner's closed."

"Left my wallet in the kitchen, so I had to come back. Tore my whole damn house apart looking for it. I should've listened to Gloria the first time she told me to check the diner."

I smirk. "Smart woman."

"She is." He nods fondly, thinking about his wife. "Did I ever tell you what my life was like before I met Gloria?"

"I know you had a drinking problem, that's about it."

Sam shifts his attention toward the sea. "I was married to someone else before her." His voice softens. "Carol. She was the love of my life." Sam lets a sad smile appear on his face, and there's a tug on my heartstrings because I know where this story is going. "We got married right out of high school. We were eighteen —kids."

"Damn."

"Yep. We knew nothing of what it was like to venture out on our own, let alone how to have a successful marriage. But we did it." There's a glistening under his eye, and he swipes it away. "Carol got cancer when we were in our mid-twenties. We thought she'd make it, but..." His voice trails off as he becomes lost in thought.

"I'm sorry, Sam," I whisper.

"When I lost Carol, I dove into a dark depression. Trying to drink myself to death," he admits. "My father tried to help any way he could—one way was getting me to work at his diner." He glances at me. "I was worse than you when I started."

"Wow—that must mean you were fucking awful."

Sam lets out a soft laugh. "I was. I hated working

there. Until one day, this pretty little lady walked through the door and swept me off my feet without me even realizing it. Gloria eventually helped me with my recovery—she was by my side while I pulled myself up from the nightmare I found myself in." He clears his throat. "I thought Carol was the only love in my life, but it turns out I was lucky enough to get two. I'm a big proponent of giving your life a second chance."

"What if I've already had more than one second chance?" I ask, my tone gentle—desperate for a real answer.

"Then, I think there's a reason why those chances keep landing at your feet, Rae," Sam responds, making my eyes prickle. "What's got you out here late at night, smoking like a chimney?"

I press my lips into a thin line, debating telling him the truth. But hearing his story makes me loosen up my own defenses. "Miles," I say.

"Honeymoon phase over?"

I shake my head. "Quite the opposite. He's perfect. He makes me feel...good." That's the lamest word to describe what Miles makes me feel, but it's the only word I can get out in this moment. I take another drag of my cigarette before I continue. "I don't know if I should feel good—I don't know if I deserve to," I whisper.

My eyes water, and I tilt my head up to stop the tears from falling. The second my gaze is lifted, the stars greet me. And there's no use in holding back crying.

"I don't know why I'm here, Sam," I choke out. "I don't know why I get to live and have a bunch of second chances when my sister didn't even get *one*."

Out of the corner of my eye, I see Sam lift his head

up to look at the night sky with me. "I know what you mean, Rae. However, you're not really getting all these second chances if you're stuck in the past. You're stopping yourself from actually living."

We're silent as I allow his words to sink into my pores while getting lost in the stars.

"Out of everything I've been through, you want to know the two things that have been the hardest for me?" Sam asks, shifting his focus onto me.

"What?" I ask, turning my head to look at him.

"Letting go and acceptance. There's a difference between honoring your past and staying stuck in it. Holding on to your pain as if you're currently living in it does nothing but destroy the present," he states. "And accepting that life did not turn out the way you initially thought it would made it easier to create a new future."

I nod, attentively listening to every word.

"There's something heartbreakingly beautiful about letting go. And something freeing about acceptance," Sam says.

I draw in a breath, knowing he's right.

For a brief moment, I shut my eyes and let myself be. The scent of the ocean air whips around, calming me. My body settles into the wooden bench as my muscles begin to loosen.

The emotion I've been denying myself feeling about Miles is stirring in the center of my chest.

I think back to what he said when I first decided to give a relationship a go—how maybe Cara is the one pulling the strings here and was the one who actually guided us together. I pray he's right and that Cara doesn't hate me for what I'm about to do.

Opening my eyes, I grab my phone and send a text to Miles.

> **Me**
> you home?

I wait all of point three seconds for a response, but before I get a message back, I rise to my feet. "Fuck it. Sam, can you drive me to Miles's house? I want to talk to him."

"Of course."

With that, we walk off the boardwalk and toward Sam's car.

There's a jolt of energy running through my veins as I get more and more eager to talk to Miles.

First, I need to apologize for being an epic bitch. Second, I need to be real with him.

My stomach lurches at the thought of letting certain words fall from my lips. Nausea creates a storm in my gut, and suddenly, I'm not sure if I can go through with this.

At the very least, I'll apologize.

"Here we are," Sam says, pulling up to Miles's bungalow. "Take the second chance, Rae."

I smile. "I'll try."

Jumping out of the car, I dash to Miles's front door and knock. Even though it's ten p.m. I know he won't be sleeping. He probably won't sleep at all after the shit I said to him.

I fidget with my choker, my fingers nervously rubbing the necklace.

The front door peels open, and Miles stands in the

doorway with bloodshot eyes. There's a flash of relief on his face when he realizes it's me.

"Come in."

CHAPTER FORTY-SIX

ENTERING MILES'S HOME, my stomach twists and turns as if I'm riding a roller coaster. I glance around, noting the mosaic I made him hanging on the wall behind his couch.

"I didn't make you anything," I state.

His brows scrunch together. "Make me anything?"

"As an apology," I jog his memory of why I made the mosaic in the first place. "I walked and chain-smoked for hours and eventually ran into Sam, who talked some sense into me, so I didn't have time to make you anything." My thoughts come out fast as my pulse speeds up.

"Rae, I don't need you to make me something."

"No, I know. It's just..." A lump forms in my throat the longer I stare at Miles. So, I begin to pace his living room to avoid gazing at him for too long. "I'm not good with words, and I'm worse with apologies."

My feet move back and forth as I glance at him, then at random objects in his house. Table. TV. Lamp.

"What I said to you earlier was awful—it was

disgusting," I admit, ashamed of myself. "Sometimes, I don't know how to deal with my anger, and it just comes out in the form of vile words." I pick at my cuticles as my pacing becomes wider, now dipping in and out of his kitchen. "I can't believe I blamed you for Cara's death. I've just spent years on end wondering what life would be like if things played out differently— but that was all before I met you, before—"

Something stops me in my tracks.

My thoughts and body come to a screeching halt when I spot something by Miles's kitchen sink.

Blood drains from my head. My stomach wrings tight.

"Did you relapse?" I whisper to the bottle of whiskey, not looking at Miles.

He darts into the kitchen, blocking my view of the liquor. "No. I didn't drink it."

Forcing myself to meet his gaze, I reply, "But you were going to."

"I was tempted, but I had just walked into the kitchen to dump it when you knocked on the door."

"Because of what I said to you." My hands go up to my hair at the same time there's a stinging behind my eyes. "Oh god, I'm such a horrible person." I continue pacing, the nausea becoming stronger. "I'm so, so sorry, Miles."

"It wasn't just because of that." Miles reaches out and gently stops me from making a hole in his floor from all my back and forth. "It was a mix of everything. Telling the story again and telling it with you."

"And then we had a beautiful night together, and you did something spectacular for me, and I fucked it up by selfishly blaming you for losing my sister."

"That didn't help the situation," he admits.

"I'm *so* sorry, Miles," I state, my vision becoming glassy as our gazes connect. "Promise me you won't relapse," I plead.

"I promise."

"We're doing this together. Staying sober, starting over—everything. We're in this together, Miles."

He cups my cheek with his palm, and I lean into his touch. "Sounds good to me."

I let myself linger in his touch for a few more seconds before breaking our contact and marching over to the sink. Lifting up the bottle, I pivot toward him. "Do you want to do the honors or me?"

"I'll do it." Miles strides over to my side. Twisting the cap off, the smell instantly burns my nostrils. He glances at me, and a sense of pride fills my heart as I watch him dump the liquid into the ceramic sink.

We're side by side as the entire bottle empties, disappearing down the drain.

When there's not a drop left, Miles places the bottle on the countertop, the sound resonating in the house.

"I'm proud of you," I tell him. He places his hand on my lower back, then leans over to kiss the top of my head. "And I'm sorry," I add.

"I know," he whispers into my hair.

Taking a deep inhale, I step away from the sink, and the two of us naturally move back into the living room.

My nerves still jump at the reminder that I came here for a second reason.

"Did you really spend the last ten years trying to hate me because I stopped you from opening the door?" Miles asks, sadness threading around his words.

"Honestly? Sometimes." There's a buzzing in my

veins as I prepare myself to be as vulnerable as I've ever been. "But I couldn't, no matter how hard I tried." I wet my lips as the pounding in my chest gets louder. "I don't hate you because you saved me, Miles."

He tilts his head to the side. "You hate me for other reasons?"

Nibbling at my bottom lip, I struggle to hold in the tears welling behind my eyes. Miles takes a step closer, and on instinct, I take one back.

"What is it, Rae?" he asks, his voice wrapped in concern. His colorful eyes lock with mine as he stares into my soul, wanting to know everything. Wanting to know the reason I hate him. His shoulders start to rise and he continues to grow tense, waiting for an answer. Worry etches his glorious face, and I can't bear to see him heartbroken—especially over me.

Swallowing, I tell him the truth. "I hate that you make me feel...*happy*." My breath trembles, and the harder I hold in the tears, the louder my heartbeat gets. "I hate that you make me laugh. I hate that I get excited to see you. I hate that I trust you." A tear slips down my face. "I hate that, aside from my family, you're the only one who cares about me. I hate that you're so different from me—but that somehow seems to work." My voice cracks, and I try to swipe the tears away, but it's no use. "And I hate that I want to be with you."

Miles carefully approaches me, only this time, I don't back away.

"Rae." He smiles. "That doesn't sound like hate. That sounds a lot like love."

"I know." A cry escapes me as all my feelings are set free. "I'm so stupidly in love with you, Miles, and it scares me and makes me feel guilty. But I want to try to believe in what you said—that Cara is the one who put us together. I *need* to believe that because I can't envision living this new life without you."

Miles caresses my face, letting my tears touch his fingertips. "I love you, Rae. And I don't doubt for a second that Cara's the one behind us meeting again." He presses his forehead against mine. "This was fate. *We* are fate."

My arms link around his neck, and I allow myself to be led by fate, kissing him and coming back to life. My new life.

I silently thank Cara for this chance right before I become enmeshed with Miles.

His lips roughly take ownership of mine, and I'm willing to give him every part of me.

I'm willing to live again.

CHAPTER FORTY-SEVEN

A WEEK HAS GONE by since I first uttered the words "I love you" to Miles. I feel lighter and settled all at once. Not much has changed in terms of my routine of work, meetings, and dates—but internally, there's a massive shift going on.

Strolling off the elevator, I head toward the front desk. "Hey." I pop over to Emma.

"Hey!" she replies with her usual chirpiness.

"I have something to tell you." I tap my nails against the counter, trying to get her more eager to know what I'm about to say.

Her eyes widen in excitement. "What!"

Before I can open my mouth, Travis, Evan, and Brad all enter the lobby. When they spot me, their faces become glued to the floor. They mumble a hello to me and Emma as they make a noticeable effort to avert their eyes away from me. Without bothering to wait for the elevator, they dash up the stairs so they don't have to stay a minute longer in my presence.

"That was weird," Emma states to me. "What do you think that was about?"

I shrug. "Probably because they watched me and Miles fuck on the balcony last week."

Her mouth hangs open for a moment, and then she bursts into a fit of giggles. "What!" Her laughter continues, causing me to chuckle along with her. "God, you're a lot braver than me—I could never do that."

"It's nothing about bravery, I'm just into uncommon things. Or, who knows, maybe it is common, but people are just nervous about admitting what they enjoy. Either way, if those boys thought it was for their benefit, they're sorely mistaken."

"You make me feel like a nun—do you have more stories like that?"

"I'm sure Miles and I will add to the list." I smirk, and Emma continues to giggle.

"You'll have to fill me in on some of them so I can live vicariously through you. I'm not exactly the wild type. Plus, I've been stuck in the single life."

"Oh, that's what I wanted to tell you!" Her comment about being single reminds me of what I came here for. "I spoke with my brother—and even though the conversation was awkward as hell because we haven't had a real conversation in God knows how long —I got it out of him that he's single."

Emma gasps. "He is?"

I nod. "I wanted to make sure it was cool if I gave him your number."

"Of course!"

"Okay, I'll message him later and brag about you."

"Oh my goodness! Thank you so much, Rae!"

"No problem—but if you guys do end up getting

together, please spare me the details." I shudder at the thought.

"You got it," she promises.

"All right, I'm off to meet Miles. I'll see you later." I push off the counter and head to leave.

"Rae," Emma calls after me and I spin around. "You seem really happy."

I smile. "I am."

Stepping away, I walk into the sunshine as I make my way down the boardwalk. Miles agreed to meet me at Sam's storefront, and when I open the door, he's already standing in the empty room.

"Want me to give you a few minutes alone to decide?" Miles asks.

I shake my head. "I want you with me."

Standing in the center, I take in the blank walls. The fold-up table with the lease agreement is in its original spot. Neither of us has been in here since he suggested I make this an art studio.

A place where I can share a part of myself.

The raw and uncensored parts of my journey. A road of loss, pain, and addiction, but also community, healing, and love.

The longer I stare at the nothingness that encompasses the room, the more I become struck with ideas for the space. Which of my pieces would go where, what I'd add to the studio, and how I can make this more than just a place for people to peruse my artwork.

"What do you think?" Miles's voice comes from next to me.

"I think this is my next move," I state. "I want this to be my art studio. And I think Cara would, too."

Miles wraps his arms around me, holding me tight,

and I smile. I feel him grinning too, even though my next comment might stop that.

"I think you should consider doing the documentary," I say.

His body goes stiff, and he slowly pulls back. The expression on his face tells me that he thinks I'm crazy. "What?" he asks as if he misheard me.

Tilting my chin up, I reply, "I don't think you should do it for your dad. I think you should do it for you."

"But that documentary guy is working for my dad."

"No. He's not. You were out of the room, but he told me your dad initially reached out to him." Even though Miles's features pull in tight, I continue. "I think this would be a great opportunity for you to tell your story. Tell the truth. Tell people what it's like *after* the shooting. The loss of your career, your loneliness, your addiction, the lack of support from your parents."

"What would be the point of that?"

"Because you've spent most of your life saying and doing what others wanted. Over the past few years, you regained your sense of self, and this is an opportunity to do an interview where you're free to be you."

I watch as his gaze wanders. He nods, considering what I'm saying.

"I don't want to be another person to tell you what to do," I state. "But just think about it from that perspective for a little bit."

"I will."

My hand reaches out, and I interlace our fingers. "I know that you hated being crowned a hero in the past. But you are a hero. You're my hero, Miles."

The words instantly make his eyes glisten. "And you're my hero, Rae."

He bends down, only to scoop me up, and my legs naturally wrap around his torso. My hands frame his face as I lean in.

We kiss, losing track of time and space and everything in between.

The only thing that exists is us. Right here, right now.

Miles's fingertips find their way under my shirt, trailing along my skin, caressing. My body melts against his the longer I'm in his hold.

"I love you, princess," he says between my parted lips.

"I love you too," I whisper back, my lips dancing over his.

We stay locked in each other's embrace, devouring each other. Wanting to taste every last drop as we relish in our affection for one another.

With a spark of vigor lighting up my spine, I speak against his mouth once more while we continue to kiss. "I want to sign the lease agreement," I manage to get out.

Wordlessly, Miles carries me over to the table and sets me down on it. My eyes dart to my side, where the papers and pen rest, but I'm easily distracted by Miles. Not willing to break contact for a millisecond, his lips sear a path down my jaw and neck.

His beard lightly brushes against my delicate flesh, tickling me. "I can't sign papers while you mark up my throat," I say, giggling at the sensation.

"Sure you can."

Mile's tongue swipes over me, and my eyelids go

heavy from the touch as if he's slowly drugging me by way of mouth. As my muscles relax, I let out a calming sigh.

"Sign the papers, Rae." Miles's rough voice brings me back into the room, his lips trailing down to my shoulder.

Smiling while Miles is attached to me, I glance over the paperwork and give the sloppiest signature of my life on the dotted line.

"It's official," I state. "This place is mine."

Miles pulls away, a sly look crossing his face. "I think we need to celebrate."

Reaching out, I run my hand over his shirt. "How should we commemorate the moment?" My voice becomes thick with lust, already anticipating his next move.

"I think you already know the answer to that." He smirks, tracing the outline of my mouth with his thumb.

A spiraling of heat enters my core. "In broad daylight? With giant windows?"

"I know what my dirty girl likes."

Desire races between my thighs as he sticks his thumb inside my mouth. Closing my eyes, I suck his finger, soaking it with my tongue.

"Off the table, princess." His tone drops in pitch, immediately sending flares of passion into my chest.

Without a second thought, I release his thumb and hop off the table. We're standing in the back of the store, and probably no one can see through the windows with the glare from the sun—but still, he spins my body to face the glass panes.

I shudder as Miles stands behind me, his calloused hands grazing my skin as he takes off my shirt.

Anticipation builds inside me, and my mouth begins to water with need.

Sweeping my hair to the side, he latches his mouth to my throat once more as his hands roam free over my figure.

My shorts are the next to go as he unbuttons them and lets them drop to the floor. They pool at my ankles, and I start to step out of them, but he pulls me tight against his hard body.

"Did I say you could move?" his voice strains next to my ear.

Shaking my head, I bite down on my lip to hide my wide smile.

Any time spent with Miles is amazing—but sex with Miles is electrifying. He knows exactly what I want and how to give it to me.

I get my power by giving it over to him, and he pleases by dominating me. It might be unorthodox for some, but it's heavenly for us.

Miles likes to serve. And he serves by controlling me during sex.

I like to escape. And I escape by allowing him to take over.

"You ready to *really* make this place yours?" Miles rasps, his breath skittering over me.

Eagerly, I nod, standing only in my bra and panties.

Miles slowly skates his fingertips over my stomach, heat rippling under his touch. Leisurely, he begins to toy with the hem of my thong, casually brushing the fabric. His other hand pushes up the cup of my bra and starts teasing my nipple.

I purposefully push my ass up against him, and he

lets out a deep groan. The two of us begin teasing each other in slow, calculated movements.

The tension in my body builds, my clit pulsing.

"Can you lower your hand?" My whisper comes out as a whine.

"You're always so needy, Rae."

I hold on to his arm, trying to coax it downward. "For you, I am."

Miles chuckles. "My little slut." He kisses the space between my neck and shoulder, and I shudder. "You keep your eyes open the whole fucking time and watch everyone walk by as they hear you get off from my fingers. Understood?"

Fire spreads out of my chest. "Yes."

The moment I agree, Miles dips his finger into my thong. His punishing touch swipes over my clit, and I immediately cry out as I crash against his body.

His other hand roughly twists and pulls at my nipple, and all the while, he's sucking on my ear.

An overflow of sensations sends me into automatic pleasure. My moans grow louder as my heart continues to soar.

"Eyes on the windows," Miles demands.

I didn't even realize I had closed them, but I force my gaze open, even though I'm not able to fully take in the blur of people passing by.

Miles's fingers move quicker and harsher. He pushes inside me, the sound of my arousal filling up the empty room.

"So fucking wet for me," Miles's voice strains as he gets closer to getting off from getting me off.

My legs tremble, and he lets me rest my weight against him as I chase my high.

"Keep looking out the window, Rae. Look at all those people who can hear you moaning for me right now." He takes his hand out from under my bra and drifts it upward, clutching my neck. My head presses against his chest as ecstasy starts to spiral through my veins.

Circling my clit once again, my body squirms in his embrace.

Crying out in pure desire, the heat of my orgasm incinerates my insides.

Miles holds me the entire time until I go slack in his arms.

"Damn. You didn't even make me work for that one." He innocently kisses my temple.

"Shut up," I say, out of breath.

Miles lets out a small laugh and then snaps back into character. "Take the rest of your clothes off and get on the floor." He releases me, and I sway, still coming down from the high.

My fingers shake as I unhook my bra and pull my panties down. As I go to step out of them, Miles lands a strong smack on my ass cheek, and I smile, knowing it's definitely going to leave a mark.

Listening to his command, I lie on the floor once I'm naked.

Glancing up, I watch as he strips down to nothing. Once he's ready, he practically pounces on me, pushing me against the laminate flooring.

In a raw act of possession, Miles's cock enters me without any warning. He thrusts in and out of me, hungry with passion.

My hips buck up to meet each of his movements.

"You know we're going to do this all the time in

here, right?" he says in between heavy breaths. "I'm going to fuck you and make you mine in every inch of this space." One of his hands grips my thigh, and he tilts me so that he's hitting just the right spot.

My mouth opens, but no sound can come out as I get overtaken by blinding lust.

Miles continues to pound into me and whisper sinful words next to my ear. My body completely surrenders to him, submitting to every touch.

His movements grow wilder, and my nails sink into his back.

With one last unforgiving thrust, his body tenses and he gasps for air, filling me up with his warm cum.

Miles stills on top of me, catching his breath, his chest pushing against mine.

When he's ready, he slowly rolls off of me and lies beside me on the floor. A smile parts my lips as I study him. A dazed look crosses his face as he relaxes, staring up at the ceiling.

"I think that was a decent start to my new art studio," I state.

Miles chuckles. "I'd say so." Without looking at me, his hand wiggles against the floor and reaches out to connect with mine. Our fingers twirl around each other as my stomach lightens with butterflies.

"You should paint the ceiling," Miles says, pointing up to where he's gazing with his other hand. "Go straight-up Michelangelo in this place."

"You want me to paint a bunch of dudes with their dicks out?"

"It would certainly be a wow factor."

"Not exactly the vibe I was going for."

Letting go of my hand, he turns onto his side to face

me. He props himself up on his forearm. "What kind of vibe do you want?"

Turning on my side, I mirror his position. "I don't know. Something more Rae-inspired," I state, drifting my eyesight upward. "Although Michelangelo is a close second."

"Well, if you decide to go with my vision, you can use me as a model." He sweeps his hand over his naked body. "You can paint me like one of your French girls."

I cringe. "Did you just quote *Titanic*?"

"I sure fucking did." Miles leans over to kiss me, gently guiding me onto my back once more. "And you loved it."

I laugh against his lips because he's right. I love every single thing about this man—even his corny lines.

Before getting too caught up in each other, Miles shifts off of me. "We should probably get dressed in case someone walks in, the door's still unlocked." He rises, and the two of us search our surroundings for our clothes.

Once we're dressed, I walk back over to the table and pick up the signed documents.

A wave of excitement hits my bones.

Anything Rae Touches. My fingers drift over the words as a burst of creativity has my mind on overdrive.

Turning to Miles, the amount of pride pouring out of him is evident, and he continues to stare at me in adoration.

With a budding exhilaration flooding my nerve endings, we trail out of the storefront. When we get to the door, Miles shoves his hand into his front pocket and digs out a key.

"Sam told me to give you a copy if you signed," he states.

Grinning, I accept the key to my very own art studio. I press it into my palm, feeling all of its edges. Gazing up, my eyes connect with Miles's. "What do we do now?" I ask.

"We ride off into the sunset together, just like I planned."

Chuckling at his comment, I go to lock the door to my new space. Before I shut it all the way, I take another peek around the room.

There's an energy in here that I can't quite identify, but it's cheerful and peppy and bright. My heart swells with love as if golden rays are swirling all around me.

I close the door and lock it.

"I can't believe I'm doing this," I say to Miles, smiling while showcasing the lease agreement.

Miles beams. "Welcome to your new life, Rae."

Epilogue

RAE

ONE YEAR LATER

MILES POURS purple liquid onto my chest. It drips down, pooling at my belly button, and he watches it spill over until it trickles down the length of my naked body. My bare back wiggles against one of the plush blankets that we laid out on my living room floor.

"Damn. I'm such a good artist," Miles says, admiring his work on my skin.

"Shut up and fuck me already!" I snap.

It's been like this for an hour.

He's been playing with our edible body paint for a motherfucking hour!

If I had known he'd become this enamored with it, I wouldn't have bought it for his birthday. I should've gone with skimpy lingerie that he could tear off me in one second, instead, I'm being spread out on the floor as he tortures me by having me teeter on the edge for an endless amount of time.

Flattening his tongue, Miles licks around my hip bones, causing me to shudder.

Who am I kidding—this is a kind of torture that drives me insane, but I crave it so much.

Miles reaches out for a paintbrush, dips it into the paint, and swirls the butter-soft ends over my body once again. Spending extra time on my nipples, he flicks the brush over my sensitive skin so many times I end up bucking my hips.

"Seriously, Miles, I'm never buying you anything again if you're going to torment me with it."

He lets out a dark chuckle. "I'll take care of you, princess. Don't you worry."

My insides flame, knowing full well that he's going to take care of me. There's not an inkling of doubt that would make me think otherwise—sexual or not. He's taken care of me in every way possible for the past year.

Lowering his mouth once more, he draws my nipple into his mouth. Arching my back off the blanket, I push up against him.

"Can you take care of me now?" I whine, my patience wearing thin. Miles bites down, and the shock causes me to yelp. "*Please*, Miles," I beg.

He lifts his head, smiling right at me. "Since my dirty girl asked me so nicely." With that, he dips his head back down and makes good on his promise.

Over and over again.

Until my body crashes down into a puddle of desire and edible paint.

Later in the day, after we've cleaned up the mess we left in the living room, both of us get ready for tonight's big event and agree to meet at my art studio before the doors open at seven p.m.

Jitters spark at my fingertips as I add the finishing touches to my makeup and head down to the lobby. Emma isn't working the desk because she took off for my event, so I give a polite smile to Armando, who's working up front.

"Best of luck tonight, Rae," he says.

"Thanks. I'll need it," I say before exiting out the door and onto the boardwalk.

The days are getting longer and the temperature is rising the closer we get to the official start of summer. The humidity from the salt air clings to me as my heels clink on the pavement. I can't remember the last time I wore heels, but Emma insisted that I wear them with my new dress.

Glancing down, I take note of the shimmery black fabric wrapped around my body. It doesn't look half-bad on me.

As I continue to stride forward past Sam's Dinette, my hands naturally draw to my neck, adjusting my choker. Spinning it back and forth so that it's in the perfect placement, my mind drifts to Cara.

I feel her energy all around me every day, but tonight her energy seems to be particularly strong.

Approaching ART, I dig in my tote bag for my key, then unlock my studio. I've made quite a drastic change to this place in just twelve months.

On the two side walls, different types of paintings and drawings are hung up, along with various mosaics I've created. There isn't a particular theme that I go for.

Whatever inspires me or hurts me ends up living on these walls. Beautiful, heartbreaking, disturbing, peaceful, gut-wrenching—it's all here. It's all me.

My favorite piece isn't on display for sale. It's straight ahead, the wall that greets me every single day. My mural of the significant parts of Golden Bay.

The backdrop is brought to life with the colors of the ocean: aqua, midnight blue, seafoam, cloudy white, and indigo. Through the various shades, stars emerge. Some vibrant, some dull. And in the center, a gold, radiant sun, giving life to this space. The brilliant energy the sun gives is felt by everyone who enters. I know this because everyone says so.

One of the first things a newcomer says when they step foot inside is usually something along the lines of "look at that sun!"

While I had my doubts that this studio would draw in a crowd, over the past year I was proven wrong. My art sells quick—albeit more of the "feel good" mosaics and landscape paintings of the beach, but every once in a while, a kindred spirit will enter and find their solace in more of my "uncomfortable" artwork.

However, now that people know my backstory, all sorts of my pieces are selling—and fast.

The thudding of my heart gets stronger, thinking of the attention that'll be brought to me after tonight.

"Wow," Miles says, coming out of the back room with a bottle of sparkling grape juice in his hand. His gaze washes over me, making sure to drink in the image of me in a dress and heels.

While he studies me, I do the same to him. A flushed feeling bursts across my chest as I admire him in a black suit and white shirt with a few buttons at the top left undone.

"You look..." he starts.

"...sexy as hell," I finish his sentence, letting my own thoughts come out.

His brow quirks. "Yeah?"

"Usually, I'm repulsed by men in suits, but you..." I circle him, checking him out as he beams. "I'm definitely taking you home tonight."

Miles hooks his arm around my waist, pulling me into him. "Not before I have my way with you here first." He presses his lips against mine, and I slowly grind into his body. As our tongues find their natural rhythm, he wraps his other arm around me, the cold bottle of sparkling juice icing over my skin.

Pulling back, I touch my lips, feeling them tingle. "People will be here soon," I remind him.

"Fine. But once everyone clears out—it's me and you in the back room."

I grin, knowing he'll keep true to his word.

Miles places the bottle down on one of the hors d'oeuvre tables, then begins making a few adjustments to the food placement.

Spinning around, I take a look at the layout: cocktail tables—with nonalcoholic drinks, obviously—some chairs, a laptop for the live stream, and big canvases on easels ready to be purchased.

"This looks great," I tell him.

"Emma did everything earlier. I can't take any of the credit," Miles informs me. "She even bought these fancy tablecloths."

I run my hand over the shiny, inky-blue fabric. Joy swims around my veins as I think about all the people who have helped me and Miles prepare for tonight's event. Emma did the decorating, Sam catered, and my parents helped advertise.

"I can't believe we're doing this," I say to Miles.

He drifts over to me, running his fingertips over the exposed part of my back. "Me neither. It feels surreal."

I turn to look up at him. "Our whole existence together feels surreal."

He smirks. "Yeah, you're right."

Before either of us can settle into the moment, the front door opens. "Hey!" Jake from IntraFilms pokes his head in. "You guys mind if we set up?" He gestures to the video and sound guys behind him.

"Go for it," I say, welcoming them into my space.

"How's it going?" Miles approaches them, helping them with their equipment.

"Excited about tonight," Jake states, with a face to match his statement.

Miles grins. "So are we."

"And nervous as fuck," I chime in.

"It's going to be great," Jake assures me. The video guy unzips his bag, and the large camera, which I've become familiar with, is getting taken out.

"What if this totally bombs?" I ask all of them.

"After all the viewers and supporters we got from the first documentary—I don't think you and Miles have anything to worry about," Jake says.

I nod, realizing the truth in his comment.

Miles ended up doing the documentary that his father wanted him to. Only Miles did it the correct way—telling the story of the school shooting and the pain that he was scarred with afterward. Jake had asked if I wanted to be part of the documentary as well, and after some consideration, I decided to partake in an interview. It ended up becoming a film about much more than just the event. It pushed beyond that moment and started exploring what happened to us after.

There was a giant response from viewers all over the world, reaching out to everyone who was a part of the documentary, but especially me and Miles because of our connection. More people started visiting my studio and buying my art. So much so that I ended up with an influx of cash.

It didn't feel right to keep it all to myself.

Which brings us to tonight's event.

Miles and I came together to create a wellness center in Golden Bay. It'll be specifically for those who've experienced trauma and need extra support. We haven't put all the pieces together yet, but tonight's event is a fundraiser to help us hire specialists.

Sam found the place and is the owner, and we'll be renting it from him. He's also agreed to lead meetings there so people don't feel hidden in a basement but rather welcome and valuable members of society.

Miles will do all the handyman shit and actually get the place up and running, and Emma has already volunteered to do the "cute decorating" as well as be our front office manager.

In addition to having groups and meetings, we'll also have space for people to create and do art.

Miles and I decided to name our center Cara's Haven.

We reached out to Jake about it, wondering if he could do some advertising on his business page, and he decided to go above and beyond, producing a miniseries about our fundraising and starting up the wellness center.

Once we hit our goal, we'll donate the rest to Golden Bay's gun safety organization. We made a promise to ourselves that we'll fight until we can't any longer to make sure that no kid has to go through what we did.

"Rae, anything you'd like to say before your fundraiser starts?" Jake asks with his cameraman next to him.

"Um...buy my shit so we can officially open up the place?" I say. "Please," I add for good measure and hear Miles laugh from the other side of the room.

Jake and his crew join in the chuckling. "That's perfect," he says, then spins to Miles. "Anything you'd like to add?"

Miles looks directly at the camera, his charming personality shining through. "Thank you so much to those who've already generously donated. We're continuing this venture by putting some of Rae's artwork up for sale, going with the highest bidder. We'll be auctioning in person and online. We hope that after tonight, we'll have enough funds to kick start Cara's Haven by the end of the summer."

Hearing the name out loud sends a tizzy of excitement throughout my body.

"Yeah, what he said," I chime in.

Within a few minutes, the clock strikes seven, and there's already a crowd of people parading in. Sam and Gloria are the first ones, greeting both me and Miles.

"I don't think I've ever been prouder of two people," he says, his eyes glistening as he looks between us.

I lean my head against Miles's chest. "Thank you,

Sam," I say, hoping that he knows I mean that for more than just complimenting us in the moment.

Gloria hands me a bouquet of flowers and gushes about how done up my studio looks while someone else grabs Miles's attention.

Throughout the whole night, we're getting pulled in different directions by both strangers and friends.

The live stream has started, and all the while I talk to different people, the bidding on my art begins.

Nerves eat away at my gut, and I don't have it in me to check how much people are kindly offering or if we're even close to our goal.

But the nervousness subsides the more the room becomes filled. It's loud and filled with excitement and laughter. There are so many people I lose track of where the camera is and if I'm even being filmed at this point.

Pivoting to greet another straggler from the board-walk, I spot my parents giving Miles a huge embrace. Watching the three of them interact makes my cheeks hurt from smiling.

I glance around the room and eventually spot Emma admiring one of my paintings. Her long red hair is pinned back on either side, and I notice a large hand claiming its spot around her waist. My gaze drifts up to see Grayson whispering something in her ear, and she bursts into a fit of giggles, making her face almost as bright as her hair.

Even though there's so much action swirling around me, I take a moment to be still and take it all in.

My vision becomes blurry as a mixture of joyful and painful tears well up behind my eyes.

I wish more than anything that Cara could be here, living this moment with me.

But I swear to God, I feel her right now. Her light fills up this entire room, making everyone shine with pure goodness. Pure gold.

This is how my sister would want to be remembered—bringing people together to help others. This is her legacy.

And I promise with everything in me, I will not let her down.

I will let her brilliant presence bring joy and healing to as many people as possible.

A loud clinking of glass brings me out of my thoughts. Glancing over, I spot Miles tapping a fork against a champagne flute filled with sparkling juice.

He clears his throat. "If I can have everyone's attention," he says, getting people to settle down and hush. "I'd like to call up my stunning girlfriend to be by my side before I begin."

My face heats up, sensing people's eyes on me as I walk over to him. I give him a playful glare as I sidle up next to him.

"First." Miles goes back to speaking to everyone. "We'd like to thank all of you for coming out to support us tonight. We can't believe the response and the amount of support we received when we decided to turn Cara's Haven into a reality."

I nibble on my bottom lip, waiting for this part to be over. I knew we'd have to give some type of speech, but I'd love for this to be over sooner rather than later.

"As many of you know," Miles continues. "Rae and I have had a troublesome road—to say the least. But together, we've been able to mend our brokenness, and we hope to give the gift of community and healing to others."

Glancing around the room, I watch the people around us. Mom wipes under her eyes, listening to Miles speak and Jake's in the back, recording the reactions.

Miles pauses, passing his glass to Sam, who's standing nearby. Then he shifts his attention to me. "Rae," he says, taking my hand in his. "There's no one else in this world I'd rather be on this journey with."

Oh no.

"I love you more than anyone," he says.

Oh fuck—this can't be what I think it is.

My stomach sinks, and I watch Miles drop down to one knee and hear a round of excited gasps from the crowd.

Why is he doing this? He knows I don't like the idea of conventional marriage and signing a piece of paper to say it's official. I don't believe in any of that old-fashioned shit.

Panic seizes my chest.

Heating up, I plaster a fake smile on my face. "Get up—get up—get up!" I whisper through clenched teeth.

Miles ignores me, his ocean eyes sparkling with enthusiasm.

Oh god, I'm going to have to embarrass him in front of everyone. On fucking camera.

My palms get clammy at the same time my mouth dries up.

"Rae Hansley," Miles says.

My heart pounds. *Please don't do this, Miles. Please, please, please.*

"Will you do me the honor of never marrying me?

But instead, being my forever person, by my side wherever this crazy life takes us, until we become stars?"

I let out a giant sigh of relief, the hysteria immediately exiting my body. "You motherfucker." I laugh.

"Do I take that as a yes?"

I nod. "Until we become stars."

There's a round of cheering and applause going on around us as Miles takes out a pen from his pocket. Pulling the cap off with his teeth, he takes my left hand and draws a star on my ring finger. When he's done, he tips the pen toward me.

With a beaming grin on my face, I take his left hand and draw a star on his left finger.

"We're getting them tattooed later," he informs me.

"Pretty ballsy of you to make that your first tattoo."

"There's no one else I'd rather be ballsy with than you." Miles winks, and I shake my head, giggling.

Gripping both of his hands, I yank him up, and we instantly meld into a loving kiss. More cheering ensues, but it becomes background noise.

All that's happening is us. Here and now.

I'm captured by all of Miles, loving him for all that he is and knowing that he loves me back just as much.

Happy tears trickle against our lips as we continue to get lost in the moment.

Wrapping my arms around his neck, he lifts me up, spinning me around.

Never in my wildest dreams did I think I'd end up here. I never thought I deserved to feel loved. Or to have Miles.

It's suddenly as if golden sunbeams dance across my skin. Bliss swims around my heart. My excitement continues to flourish, knowing that after our fundraiser and celebratory sex in the back room, we'll be getting each other's art tattooed on ourselves.

Our art is a promise to one another.

A promise to embrace all the ups and downs of life.

There are some moments in life that are agonizingly tragic and some moments that are epically beautiful. And our art to one another is capturing the entire spectrum.

There's an art to everything.

An art of grieving, an art of surviving, an art of starting over—in my case, it's all three.

But with Miles, I also learned that there's an art to living.

An art to loving.

And an art to us.

Resources

Substance Abuse and Mental Health Support: **www.samhsa.gov**

Advocating for Gun Safety: **www.everytown.org**

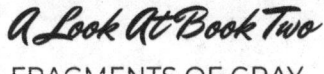

A Look At Book Two

FRAGMENTS OF GRAY

He wasn't looking for love. She wasn't expecting to be seen. But sometimes, the most broken hearts find their way to each other.

Grayson is angry, adrift, and one misstep away from burning every bridge he has left. Sent to spend the summer in Golden Bay Beach with his sister Rae, he has no intention of healing—just surviving.

Then he meets Emma.

She's Rae's best friend. Quiet, kind, and carrying shadows of her own. What starts as a late-night check-in through her bedroom window slowly becomes something deeper—something Grayson never expected to feel again.

But pain has a way of recognizing pain. As their summer unfolds, so does a fragile connection neither of them saw coming. Emma sees past Grayson's walls, and he finds himself wanting to be better—for her, and for himself. Still, the pieces of them are jagged. And some cracks *run too deep*.

Can two broken people put each other back together, or will the weight of their pasts tear them apart before they even begin?

AVAILABLE DECEMBER 2025

Acknowledgments

If you've made it this far—thank you.

Rae and Miles came to me in a dream in 2022. The scene was the two of them in the supply closet. I woke up the next morning knowing I had to tell their story, but I wanted to explore what they were like as adults. I have so much more left to say on the topics that were touched upon, but I don't want to ramble for another couple hundred pages. So, if you'd like to continue this conversation with me, send me a message! There's nothing I love more than hearing from my readers.

Which brings me to the first person I need to thank: you!

Without you reading and supporting my work, my creations would stay locked away on my computer. Your support helps me become more comfortable with sharing my art with the world. In a way, you are the Miles to my Rae.

Second, to my wonderful alpha, beta, and sensitivity readers—you're all amazing! Thank you for taking the time out to read my book in its messy stages and helping me bring it to life.

Thank you to Ellie, Kayla, and the whole Love N. Books Press team for believing in my work! It's so surreal having Rae & Miles's story be my first traditionally published book. I am beyond grateful.

Last, thank you to my husband. I couldn't do any of

this without you. (For someone who has written multiple romance books, I sure do suck at summing up how much you mean to me.)

My final parting words to anyone who is still reading: you're the artist of your own life, enjoy the beauty and the mess.

Until the next book,

Holly

Want to connect?

Follow me on Instagram @hollycaste_author

Holly is a new adult & contemporary romance author. Lover of all things steamy and angsty— you're sure to get your fill of these in her books! She also likes to have an underlying message in all of her stories, bringing awareness to bigger issues that are close to her heart.

When she's not reading or writing, you can find her eating an unhealthy amount of bread and cheese, rocking out to emo music, or cherishing wife/mom life

www.hollycasteauthor.com

More Trigger Info

Hi!

If you're back here, then you either finished the book (thank you, I hope you enjoyed the journey), or you're checking out more details of the death scene before you commit to reading the story. I'd love for people to try to piece things together as they read, however I'm aware that the topic is very sensitive, so I'd like to be mindful of different readers. The death scene depicted is a school shooting, including gunshots and blood. Please note, by knowing this information, you might lose the element of trying to draw your own conclusions as the story progresses.

If you're still planning on reading, I hope you fall for Rae & Miles. And I promise they get a happily ever after!